A House Divided

MICHAEL PHILLIPS • JUDITH PELLA

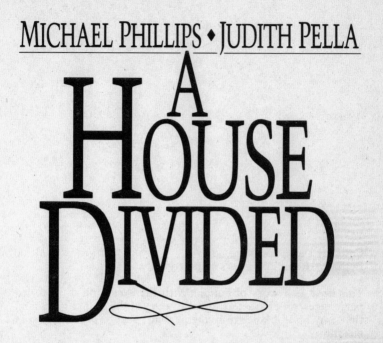

A HOUSE DIVIDED

BETHANY HOUSE PUBLISHERS
MINNEAPOLIS, MINNESOTA 55438

Cover by Dan Thornberg,
Bethany House Publishers staff artist.

Published by Bethany House Publishers
A Ministry of Bethany Fellowship, Inc.
6820 Auto Club Road, Minneapolis, Minnesota 55438

Printed in the United States of America

Library of Congress Cataloging-in-Publication Data

Phillips, Michael R., 1946–
    A house divided / Michael Phillips, Judith Pella.
        p.   cm. — (The Russians)
     1. Soviet Union—History—19th century—Fiction.   I. Pella,
Judith.   II. Title.   III. Series: Phillips, Michael R., 1946–
Russians.
PS3566.H492H68   1992
813'.54—dc20   91-46226
ISBN 1–55661–173–0   CIP

To

Catherine Jean Phillips

The Authors

The PHILLIPS/PELLA writing team had its beginning in the long-standing friendship of Michael and Judy Phillips with Judith Pella. Michael Phillips, with a number of nonfiction books to his credit, had been writing for several years. During a Bible study at Pella's home he chanced upon a half-completed sheet of paper sticking out of a typewriter. His author's instincts aroused, he inspected it more closely and asked their friend, "Do you write?" A discussion followed, common interests were explored, and it was not long before the Phillips invited Pella to their home for dinner to discuss collaboration on a proposed series of novels. Thus, the best-selling "Stonewycke" books were born, which led in turn to "The Highland Collection," and the "Journals of Corrie Belle Hollister."

Judith Pella holds a nursing degree and B.A. in Social Sciences. Her background as a writer stems from her avid reading and researching in historical, adventure, and geographical venues. Pella, with her two sons, resides in Eureka, California. Michael Phillips, who holds a degree from Humboldt State University and continues his post-graduate studies in history, owns and operates Christian bookstores on the West Coast. He is the editor of the best-selling George MacDonald Classic Reprint Series and is also MacDonald's biographer. The Phillips also live in Eureka with their three sons.

CONTENTS

A Cast of Characters ────────────────

The Burenin Family:
Yevno Pavlovich Burenin
Sophia Ilyanovna Burenin
Anna Yevnovna Burenin (Annushka)
Paul Yevnovich Burenin (Pavushka)
Tanya
Vera
Ilya

The Fedorcenko Family:
Prince Viktor Makhailovich Fedorcenko
Princess Natalia Vasilyovna Fedorcenko
Prince Sergei Viktorovich Fedorcenko
Princess Katrina Viktorovna Fedorcenko (Katitchka)

Count Dmitri Gregorovich Remizov—Sergei's best friend, Katrina's love
Basil Pyotrovich Anickin—Katrina's boyfriend, revolutionary son of Dr. Anickin
Lt. Mikhail Igorovich Grigorov (Misha)—Cossack guard, Anna's friend
Count Cyril Vlasenko—Chief of Third Section, the Secret Police
Kazan—Paul's revolutionary friend

Other revolutionaries:
Sophia Perovskaya
Andrei Zhelyabov
Alexander Mikhailov

Fedorcenko Servants:
Mrs. Remington
Polya
Leo Vasilievich Moskalev
Olga Stephanovna
Nina Chomsky

The custom in Russia is to be known by three names—the Christian name, the patronym ("son of . . ." or "daughter of . . ." your father's name), and the surname. The patronym is formed by adding the appropriate suffix to the individual's father's Christian name. The endings are usually *vich* or *ovich* for a male, and *vna* or *ovna* for a female. These patronyms are often used almost interchangeably with the surname. Nicknames or "little" (diminutive) names are also used in intimate conversation between family and close friends—Pavushka, Annushka, Katitchka, Misha, Sasha, etc.

Prologue

A SEASON OF PARTINGS
(March 1878)

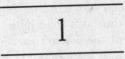

1

The garden was once again still.

Since her first days at the Fedorcenko estate, Anna had often come to this garden to seek solace. Here she had first met the princess . . . and here the prince had spoken to her his first words of love.

Then a war had parted them, and throughout the long months she had carried the secret silently within her breast: A prince of Russia, whose father counseled the tsar, was in love with *her*—a mere peasant girl. The memory of his softly spoken words of love became a quiet treasure Anna would keep forever.

But the war had changed Prince Sergei Fedorcenko. He had made clear that he still loved Anna and still wanted her to be his wife, but he had changed in his attitude toward himself, toward life.

"I have to get away," he said that first day after his return. "I have to think about many things. I have to . . ." He paused, glancing around nervously. "I don't know, Anna," he went on. "I just don't know any longer what is important, what really matters. I feel as if I'm looking down a dark tunnel—at the end, in the only ray of light, I see your face. But the path in between is so dark. I'm not sure I could find my way. And if I did, how could I touch you with so much blood on my hands?"

His words stopped. She looked into his eyes, eyes that spoke of pain, of confusion, of a sad guilt she could not reach. She longed to soothe his tormented soul, yet she felt powerless.

In the few days he was home, Sergei contrived to see Anna several times. He spoke to her of the war, of what he felt, of the pain, and of the horror of taking a life. He wept unashamedly before her, as he was too proud to do before his own family and peers. He spoke of his wound, and the infection that had developed, and about his book.

"I'm almost finished with it, Anna," he said, his eyes brightening with more enthusiasm than he had shown about anything. "I worked on it the whole time, especially after I was laid up. I wrote to Count Tolstoy, and he has agreed to critique it for me. He even extended an invitation for me to visit Yasnaya Polyana! Can you believe it, Anna?"

But Prince Sergei's enthusiasm was short-lived, and he soon relapsed into the morass of dark thoughts and emotions. Anna wondered if the war had destroyed Sergei's love for life. She wondered if his book was as bleak as his countenance and outlook. If so, his words would not find a ready reception in the ears of Russia's leaders, for Sergei made no attempt to hide his bitter views of the stupidity of the war effort.

"This wound in my leg has warranted me an extended leave from my military duties," Sergei said. "Perhaps I shall visit Tolstoy. I shall finish the book there, then perhaps travel in the provinces. Six months . . . a year. After that I shall return for you, Anna."

Anna smiled, but inside she knew how foolish it would be for her to hang on to false hopes. She knew Sergei was not at peace—with himself, with his country, or with the world. There was more to his determination to leave St. Petersburg than merely finishing his book. He was searching for something he had no idea where to find—meaning to life, hope in the midst of the futility he felt, relief from tormenting guilt, an outlet for the anger burning inside him over the unnecessary loss of life.

"I love you, Anna," he said. "I will come back for you. Once my book is published, I shall have the prestige to allow me to quit the military, and you and I shall live in the city. I will write, and—"

Anna quietly silenced him with her finger. "I will still be here when you return" was all she said.

Their final meeting before his departure had been brief.

"I will carry your smile with me until I return," he said,

but his own smile as he spoke the words was sad and tired. The time at home had done nothing to assuage his inner turmoil and conflict, and clashes with his father had not helped. "But there is one last request I have to make of you, Anna," he went on. "Let me depart with the assurance of your love. Let me hear it from your own heart. Please say it, Anna, and may it be the last thing I hear from your sweet lips, until we meet again."

"I do love you, Sergei Viktorovich," said Anna softly.

Supporting himself with one hand on his cane, he reached out with the other and drew Anna toward him, pulling her tightly to his chest. Without looking up, Anna knew there were tears standing in her young prince's eyes.

That was all. He released her, then turned and, still gripping his cane tightly, he limped out of sight.

Anna's eyes clouded over with tears as she watched him go. Even though they had both confessed their love, a pang of loneliness stung her heart. She knew she might never see him again.

By late afternoon he was gone, and a pall of silence hung over the Fedorcenko estate. Father, mother, and sister all knew that Sergei had set his course upon a path that for the present no one else could follow.

Anna Yevnovna Burenin, peasant girl of Katyk, maid to Princess Katrina Fedorcenko, had matured greatly in the year and a half since she had come to St. Petersburg. No one knew how much Sergei's love for her had affected that process of maturity. Perhaps no one would ever know.

2

As Katrina approached her in the garden, Anna remembered their first meeting, when Princess Natalia's dog had run away, bringing the angry young princess across her path. How greatly the princess had changed since that day!

Her mistress walked with an uncharacteristically quiet gait. Anna watched as she came closer; Princess Katrina had been crying! Her eyes were red, but her expression was quite different than the pain that had filled her countenance two weeks ago, on the evening of her brother's and father's return.

Katrina's face was flushed with shock, hurt, and betrayal. "He's not coming home!" she burst out. Anna could not tell whether the princess meant the words for her, or was only venting her pent-up emotions.

"Who, Princess?" asked Anna.

"Dmitri! How could he do this to me!" she half-shouted, seemingly uncertain whether to give grief or anger the upper hand. Her lower lip trembled.

"But why . . . where is he? Have not all the soldiers been sent home?" asked Anna, her own mind still full of her brief meeting with Sergei a short while earlier.

"I don't know! Who cares why? He's not coming home— what does anything else matter?"

In her anger, the princess sounded like the old Katrina, the petulant princess Anna had first met in the garden—impulsive, quick to anger, intent on having her own way, and furious when anything stood in her path.

"But surely, Princess," Anna said, "there must be some reasonable explanation. Did not Prince Sergei give a reason?"

"Oh, yes, he gave a reason, and it didn't help one bit! How dare Dmitri behave so like a barbarous Cossack!"

"What happened?" asked Anna.

After fuming and ranting for another minute or two, Katrina managed to calm herself enough to describe, with barely controlled emotions, the conversation with her brother. The telling, however, did nothing to mitigate Katrina's turbulent state of mind. If she showed anger now, it was only to mask the bitter painfulness of the truth.

Knowing it was her last chance to get at the truth about Dmitri, Katrina had asked her brother with frustrated sharpness, "Why do you avoid telling me about Dmitri?"

"He was wounded at the first attack on Plevna, you know," Sergei said.

"Yes, of course, we heard that."

"But he recovered fully by the end of summer and joined in the rest of the fighting. He was a real hero!"

"But *after* the war—I want to know when he's coming home! I . . . heard some rumors."

"Oh, *that*." Sergei shook his head. "Knowing how rumors go, it probably wasn't as bad as what you heard. But I will have to say, Dmitri will never learn his lesson where women are concerned."

"He had trouble with a *woman*?" Katrina made no attempt to hide her dismay.

"A sordid episode, Katitchka. You are too young to hear about it."

"Tell me!" she all but shrieked, gripping her brother's arm.

"Katrina! What is this all about? You are not in love with Dmitri yourself . . ."

She made an attempt to calm herself, but it was too late. The stern look of concern on Sergei's face made him look more like his father than ever.

"Has Dmitri been—?" he began.

Katrina cut him off, hurrying to Dmitri's defense. "He has done absolutely nothing to hurt me."

"If he has," continued Sergei, his blood rising, "I'll break every bone—"

"Nothing, Sergei," insisted Katrina, then added almost to herself, "and that is exactly the problem! He's never given me so much as a nod."

Sergei eyed his sister cautiously.

"I'm not a little girl anymore!" she said defensively. "You said so yourself. I'm old enough to know what I'm doing."

A silence followed.

"I pray you are right, my dear little sister," said Sergei seriously. "Dmitri is my best friend, but I have never condoned his behavior with women. I fear he would only hurt you, Katrina."

"He would never hurt a woman he truly loved."

Sergei shrugged. "Perhaps," he replied. "But I doubt he has ever really loved before. I even wonder if he knows how."

"You still have not answered my question—when will I see him again?"

"That may not be for some time," he replied, then paused.

"Tell me, Sergei!" insisted Katrina.

"All right, if you will have it. He's probably in Siberia by now."

"He's been banished?" exclaimed Katrina, her faced reddening again.

"*Banished* is a bit too strong a word, Katrina. In the army we call it *re-assigned*." Sergei made no attempt to hide the rancor in his tone.

"What happened?"

Sergei drew in a long breath, seemed to hesitate a moment more wondering whether he should tell his sister the truth, then plunged ahead.

"I was interned at a military hospital in Bucharest for a while after the armistice. That is where I wrote a great deal about what had taken place. Our commander had also been wounded and was staying there too, and his daughter came down from Moscow to be at his side. It was quite an arduous journey for a woman, but she was an independent sort. She and Dmitri became acquainted on the first day Dmitri came to visit me."

He paused, hoping perhaps that Katrina had had enough and would let the rest of the story go unsaid.

"And. . . ?" she said after a moment.

Sergei sighed. "Do you really want it all, Katitchka?"

"Every word," she replied determinedly.

"All right, you asked for it," he said. "Dmitri will never learn his lesson with women—he charms them mercilessly. I don't think he's half aware of his effect on them. Not that he doesn't enjoy it! And most are smart enough not to take him too seriously—at least so far. That is, until the commander's daughter came along. She was duly charmed by Dmitri's winning manner, but not so charmed when she came to realize his intentions were not . . . shall I say, serious. Dmitri did nothing blatantly dishonorable; I will say that in his defense. Nevertheless, she interpreted his actions as a proposal of marriage. Dmitri was backed into a corner, for the girl would have no excuses from him."

"He didn't marry her?"

"It might have come to that, if the girl's father had had his way. How Dmitri could have been foolish enough to toy with our commander's daughter, I will never know! Too long at war, I suppose. The long and the short of it is that the colonel offered Dmitri a very clear-cut choice: marry his daughter, or find himself reassigned to a company in Siberia. When Dmitri chose the reassignment, the man became so incensed he had the orders drawn up, effective immediately, without even the benefit of a leave home. Dmitri was trundled off on the first train. I expect by now the trains and carriages have run out, and that he is aboard a dogsled someplace on his way east."

"That's awful," said Katrina, sinking into a chair, her face now pale.

"Poor Dmitri. No matter what his indiscretions, it was a tough break. To have no visit home after fighting a war—it's a cruel turn. Though perhaps no more cruel than much of the rest of what happened," he added bitterly. Suddenly his mind was once more occupied with the futility of life as he had seen it in recent months.

"But how long will this last?" asked Katrina after a moment.

"Knowing Dmitri, he will find some way to connive his way back to civilization soon enough. But not before he has more than his fill of snow and ice and wilderness. Sometimes such assignments last for years."

Neither brother nor sister had said anything further, each lost in their own dismal thoughts. Katrina rose, and after a distracted farewell to her brother had fled to the garden, where she knew she'd find Anna.

Now they were together, the heart of each girl quietly and painfully filled with private thoughts of the soldiers each had lost.

Katrina's eyes were red but her face stoic. Anna's tears over Sergei's departure had since dried, and she carried the mingled pain from his parting and joy of his words of love deep in her heart where not even her mistress could see them.

Anna made room on the bench, and Katrina joined her. Neither spoke a word. Anna opened her arms, and by common consent the princess and the peasant maid embraced, clinging to each other for comfort.

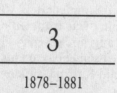

3

1878–1881

Unfortunately, the tender scene of affection between princess and peasant girl, the coming together of two diverse elements within the spectrum of Russian society, was not to be played out widely within the borders of the Holy Motherland.

Instead, contrast and dissension, strife and hardship became its enduring hallmark. Russia was becoming a house divided.

In the 1870s, few Russians had ever heard of Karl Marx. But during this critical time of change, the passionate spirit of the words that would make the German philosopher and socialist immortal began to take root in that huge land:

> Let the ruling classes tremble at a communist revolution. The proletarians have nothing to lose but their chains. They have a world to win!

Immediately following the Russo-Turkish War, Russia became a powder keg of revolutionary activity. Russia's war efforts had drained the country of both manpower and finances, and the nation was ripe for revolution.

The Decembrist Revolt of Russia's military in 1825 came within a decade of the closing of the Napoleonic Wars. The Crimean War of the 1850s saw only simmering unrest within Russia's huge borders, but a major revolt was forestalled as Tsar Alexander II opened his reign in the final days of the war, giving his people hope for the future. In his first declaration he said: "It will be better for our nation if we work to abolish serfdom from above than to wait until the serfs themselves attempt liberation from below."

And abolish serfdom he did, as well as attempt many other areas of reform. But the changes proved insufficient to satisfy the radicals of his society, for all of Europe was in the throes of massive modernization and change, and the free thinkers and students and revolutionaries of Russia expected their nation to keep pace.

The terrorism and rebellion following the Turkish War of 1877 and 1878 proved a preliminary testing ground for the major revolutions to come. In the half decade after 1877, young revolutionaries throughout Russia experimented and became proficient in the use of the seditious printed word, terrorism, even assassination. In that short five-year period, they succeeded in putting the nation of Tsar Alexander II on the run. They had no Lenin—who was but seven years old at the time—to guide their efforts and harness their passions. Trotsky, Kerensky, and Stalin had not even been born yet. But the roots of the movement they would one day lead were burrowing deep into the soil of discontent in Russia, and in a short time a world would be turned upside-down as a result.

Tsar Alexander II was not left unscathed by the upheaval. These years were the darkest of his reign. Having done his best to be a benevolent "Little Father" to his people, he felt personally hurt and betrayed by the rebellion against him. He had shown more compassion than any tsar in history. He had freed the serfs, reformed the army, revamped the legal system, and won a war. What were his crimes that he should be so maligned?

"Am I an animal," he agonized, "that these rebels and assassins must hunt me down?"

Yet his inner distress only resulted in reactionism, further widening the rift between government and revolutionaries. At the prodding of his conservative advisors, Alexander clamped down harder on the already heavily burdened people.

Perhaps the results would have been different had the tsar followed the sensitive and humanitarian instincts that had guided him at the beginning of his reign. But the Romanov tradition of absolute autocracy was too deeply ingrained in Alexander to permit the far-reaching reforms that would please the rabid revolutionaries.

Two hundred and fifty years of Romanov tyranny would never be overthrown without the shedding of Russian blood.

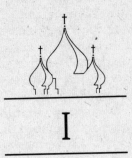

I

SEEDS OF REBELLION

(March 1879)

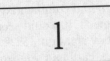

1

St. Petersburg was as magnificent as Paul had imagined it. He wished he were free to enjoy the pleasure of standing at its center and feeling the pulse of its life.

But he could enjoy no such liberty—neither freedom of body, for his was pursued; nor freedom of soul, for his was tormented. The days of youthful joy had been left far behind. Even his own sister, if he knew where to find her in this sprawl of buildings and people and activity, would look upon him as a stranger—and a despised one at that!

The years following the Turkish War were filled with great agitation and discontent in the huge land at the outposts of Europe's eastern frontier. Its cities had become cauldrons of terror. This was no season for the idealistic dreams of youth; and it was certainly no time for a young man whose dreams were steadily being shattered on the shoals of realism to venture into a nation's fomenting turmoil.

But young Paul Yevnovich Burenin had been drawn toward the great Russian capital as one whose destiny could find itself fulfilled in no other place. A short time ago, his hopes had been high. He had been enthusiastic about his studies, and had applied himself diligently and with single-mindedness. He had tried hard to honor his word to his father and put aside ideas of politics and rebellion in exchange for the opportunity he had been given at the Gymnasium in Pskov.

His dedication had even earned him the praise and admiration of his teachers. Yevno had been proud of his son, who had quickly risen to the top of his class. Paul worked with such fervor that he had no time for secret meetings, or any reading matter beyond what his studies required. He appeared in every way the shining example of a reformed young man who had at last put the ideas of his radical friends behind him. Even the constable in Akulin had commented on the fact to Yevno.

"Well, Yevno Pavlovich, it would seem that a night in my jail straightened the boy right out, eh?"

Whatever the cause, Paul had seemed well on the pathway of becoming a useful, perhaps even influential, Russian citizen.

Then his friend's death . . . the attack on the headmaster . . . again the jail . . . and then his flight. Suddenly his hopes faded into obscurity, and his eyes were opened to the true nature of things.

He had been a fool to imagine that attending school could make any difference. Kazan and the others had been right all the time! A glance around him in any direction as he walked along Nevsky Prospect confirmed it. With mingled wonder and chagrin he gazed about at the gaudy display surrounding him—the profusion of carriages filled with dandily outfitted bourgeois, the opulent grandeur of the railway buildings, shop windows crammed with a dazzling assortment of Western wares.

Had he dreamed of coming to St. Petersburg for this? Could a true and loyal Russian possibly survive this great defilement? Could a man of conviction maintain his resolve and passion for change in the midst of such corrupt influences from the West?

In his loneliness in such a strange place, Paul vacillated between hatred of everything he saw, and a longing to return to the warmth and safety of his father's cottage. He wondered if he had done the right thing by leaving Pskov and making this pilgrimage to the capital. He did not know he would end up here—alone, cold, with no place to go. Part of him longed to try to find Anna. But would she turn against him too?

In reality, his decision to flee, to leave forever behind him the scenes of his boyhood, had been no real decision at all. His choice had been thrust upon him unsought by evil circumstances, by the nagging hand of fate that seemed to be dogging him his whole life.

His whole life . . .

Even at seventeen, Paul could not help but feel as if long, gray years had already passed him by. The gulf between his past and future already seemed to yawn widely as he looked forward, then back.

He was no longer a boy. He had relinquished all the securities and comforts of youth the day when shame, and the business with Aleksi Alexandrovich, forced him to turn away from the loving circle of his family. He had fled to the harsh uncertainties of St. Petersburg, rather than to seek solace and hope and shelter in the arms of an understanding and compassionate father.

Whether he had done right or wrong, he could not judge. He was hungry and uncertain; how could he trust what he might think?

He was here. Only that he could say for sure. And he could not go back. For the present, St. Petersburg—and fate—held his future in their hands.

2

Alexandrovich was the son of a poor shopkeeper.

A sensitive, somewhat frail lad, Aleksi was a year younger than Paul, who befriended him almost immediately after his entry into the Gymnasium. The poor boy had desperately needed an ally, for the older bourgeois and gentry boys had cruelly capitalized on his weaknesses and insecurities. As a peasant himself from an even lower social strata than Aleksi, Paul had sympathized, especially in that he too had been bullied and tormented from his first day at school.

Paul had enough inner fortitude to ignore their mistreatment, for most things in his life at the time were subjugated to his studies. Offering poor sport for their malicious designs, he was eventually left to himself. Aleksi, on the other hand, yearned for nothing more than to be accepted by these upperclass rogues. His pleadings, tears, and visible show of distress, however, only fed their merciless prodding.

Try as he might, Paul could not remain aloof indefinitely. The driving force behind his former discontent had always been an abhorrence of the mistreatment of others, and ultimately he found himself in the middle of the fray. Not able to tolerate seeing the sensitive boy made fun of and beaten, Paul finally took a stand, and quickly became the victim of both verbal and physical abuse.

Tensions mounted until the shocking day when poor Aleksi was driven to extremes. Unable to find him one afternoon, Paul had searched the school building high and low. Hearing a dull groan in the basement, he investigated further. There, deep in the darkness behind several tall crates, he found his friend hanging from one of the open beams. In panic he ran for help, found one of the headmaster's assistants, got a knife, then sprinted back, climbed upon one of the nearby boxes, and hastily cut the rope. The limp body of his pathetic friend fell to the ground in a heap.

Fortunately, Paul had come just barely in time to save the boy's life, but he was unable to prevent the sinful act from becoming publicly known. Aleksi was looked upon with more contempt than ever. There was no sympathy for him; suicide was one of the dreadful mortal sins. Far from being shown compassion, Aleksi came under heavy censure from the school authorities and was threatened with expulsion.

Had the entire affair remained in the realm of the students only, even with increased persecution, Paul might have been able to maintain his staunch efforts at keeping his mind away from political channels. But the unsympathetic and heartless response of the school's officials shattered his determination once and for all. These representatives of authority proved once more that there existed no justice in the world for the common man, much less the common *boy*. One's birth in society—that most illogical and absurd measuring stick of worth—was all that mattered!

Just as the school condemned a poor youth for that over which he had no control—his birth, his societal rank, the status of his parents—so too did the government condemn and degrade all who fell outside Peter the Great's Table of Ranks. This hundred-and-fifty-year-old outmoded institution was a relic of the past. Ninety percent of Russia's entire population had no hope of advancement, according to Peter's rigid system!

When the dam of his patience finally broke, some two weeks after the would-be hanging, Paul expressed his outrage to the headmaster with all the passion and eloquence he had learned from his former revolutionary friends.

His words were dismissed with a curious smile and a wave of the headmaster's hand. The self-important man said nothing to the excitable peasant-son from Katyk, but he took serious note, and resolved to keep a watchful eye upon him. It would never do to allow such young rabble-rousers a free rein with their seditious tongues.

One raw, blustery winter afternoon about two months later, a despondent Aleksi left the school alone; whether he had merely a walk in mind or some darker motive, no one ever knew. Paul might have stopped him, if he had known, for the boy was of no constitution to be abroad on such a day. As soon as he realized Aleksi was missing, Paul went out to look for him, and kept frantically searching half the night until his own life was imperiled by the harsh elements.

As soon as the light allowed, Paul went out to resume the search. He stumbled upon his friend's stiff and lifeless body in a snowdrift. He had never seen death before that moment, but the pain was quickly buried by the gathering rage within his bosom. It was a meaningless way to die.

In stupefied grief and anger, he carried the corpse back to the school doorstep, gathering around him a crowd not only of curious onlookers, but many of the boy's former tormentors as well. In a few moments the headmaster appeared, took one look at the sight, and shook his head with an unsympathetic show of distress.

"So, the ungrateful lad has finally succeeded in his sinful designs." The man crossed himself sanctimoniously. "May God have mercy on his poor lost soul," he added, then turned to go back inside.

Suddenly a great fury seized Paul, and he lost all his remaining self-control.

Dropping Aleksi's body, he flew at the headmaster as one possessed, screaming words he could not now remember. When he came to himself he was crouched over the man like a vicious animal, his fingers squeezing tightly into the headmaster's fleshy throat. Several others were attempting to pull him off the man's body. When he came to his senses and realized what he had done, Paul was more horrified by his own behavior than by the coldhearted attitude of the headmaster himself.

3

Pskov's jail proved a wretched, stinking hole that made Akulin seem like a palace. Paul would have willingly put up with the insults of that viper Vlasenko—although he had heard the man had been promoted and was no longer there—to be spared Pskov's dungeon.

He was there three days before hearing a thing. Then a representative from the school came, saw him briefly, and left to talk with the police chief. Paul could hear only parts of the conversation through the corridor. What he heard sounded anything but pleasant, and seemed to have to do with his probable sentencing. In dismay Paul spent the following nights tormented with nightmares of hanging or being shot in front of a firing squad.

On the eighth day Yevno had tried to visit him in his prison cell. Paul heard his father's voice, and the sound sent a stab of remorse and guilt shooting through him. A moment or two later the jailer appeared, saying that he had a visitor. But how could he look into the eyes of his father, who had placed such faith and hope in him, who had sacrificed so much that he might be able to attend school? In the end, Paul had refused to see his father, and then had spent the next hour weeping bitter tears of grief, until at last sleep overcame him.

Paul was in the jail ten days before the headmaster decided not to press the matter further. His seemingly generous act was motivated not by remorse, or by compassion for Paul. The violent young miscreant had already been expelled from the Gymnasium. But the scandal caused by the death of Aleksi Alexandrovich was known all over Pskov, and the school, not to mention the contemptible headmaster, could ill-afford any further stir. A trial could prove devastating to the school's reputation, especially in light of recent public mood by which several radicals throughout the country had been acquitted for crimes far more serious than Paul's.

The day of Paul's release was cold and bitter, like the day of Aleksi's death. And Paul felt alone within his own soul, just as his friend must have felt.

The doors of education, open and inviting with promise just a short time earlier, were now forever barred to him. He could not face his family—not now, after what he had done. How disappointed they would be in him! He could not return to Katyk and drag his father into the disgrace he had brought upon his family. He must bear his shame alone.

What could he do but set out upon the path that destiny appeared to have already mapped out for him? Cut off from family and from ties to his former community and boyhood acquaintances, the one door left open to him was to turn to the only friends he had left—the circle of young radicals with whom he had been involved before his trouble with the constable in Akulin. A number of them had gone to St. Petersburg, Paul had heard. He could follow them and see whom he might locate. Without even a brief farewell to his family, the decision was made, and he turned his footsteps northward.

Paul Yevnovich had been in St. Petersburg for two days, sleeping in back alleys of the seamier parts of the city, pillaging food from the discarded refuse of inns or stealing it from poorly watched kiosks. As bitter cold as it was, this was a mild March; had a blizzard descended upon him during his trek northward, he would have perished like poor Aleksi.

More than once his thoughts turned to Anna in her fine mansion. He knew she lived someplace in the elegant South Side district; he had even ventured in that direction once or twice. But he could not bring himself to continue the search. Even if he were able to locate the house by questioning passersby, he could never approach it. Anyone who saw him would think he was a common beggar.

The more he thought about Anna, the more he realized she would probably not turn him away after all. She might even welcome him warmly, bedraggled though he was—she was too kind to do otherwise, no matter what he had done. Yet for this very reason he continued to avoid her. He deserved no such kindness. And he could not jeopardize her position with her employers, no matter how kind she said they were. They were aristocrats, after all, and he could never let go of his suspicion.

As he walked aimlessly down the broad avenue wondering only where he would be able to beg or steal his next meal, he suddenly heard his name called out from some distance.

"Paul . . . Paul Yevnovich!" cried the voice.

He turned quickly, scanning the street in all directions until he caught sight of a figure hastening toward him. As the figure came nearer, Paul recognized a fellow he had met only some days ago on the road as he walked north—a homeless vagabond himself, just like Paul.

"Some luck!" he exclaimed, slapping Paul jovially on the back. "In a city of a million people, imagine running into you again!"

A certain warm feeling surged through Paul to be greeted in such a friendly fashion, even if by a near total stranger. It lasted but an instant, however, for Paul hadn't cared much for the man at their first meeting. His friendly exuberance had struck Paul as overdone; he seemed to be trying to hide something. He had invited the young son of Yevno to travel along with him, but Paul had led the man to believe he planned to remain where he was a few days, and thus he went on alone. Paul couldn't even remember his name, if he had heard it at all.

"Yes, quite a coincidence."

"Well, perhaps not," said the other, falling in stride with Paul. "You see, I was keeping a lookout for you."

"Oh?" said Paul, raising his eyebrows in question. If nothing else, a week in a Russian prison had taught Paul wariness and suspicion. He had taken on a sharp edge; the once idealistic seventeen-year-old was well on the road to becoming an experienced cynic.

"You mentioned a friend you hoped to see in St. Petersburg," the vagabond said.

Paul nodded. He had regretted speaking so freely about his friend Kazan almost immediately after the words were out of his mouth; even he should have known better. The life of a revolutionary must always be guarded with secrecy. Names could never be bandied recklessly about until one was absolutely certain of his listener. Maybe that was why this fellow hadn't given *his* name.

"Well, you'll be glad to know I have seen your friend."

"You have?" In spite of his cynicism, Paul brightened considerably. "Did you tell him you had seen me?"

The man nodded. "He said he hoped to see you. I expect he's on the watch for you as well."

"Where is he?"

"I'll take you there myself."

As much as Paul would have preferred going alone, he could not pass up the opportunity of again seeing Kazan. As they walked down the street together, Paul thought to himself that perhaps he had misjudged his companion.

Anyway, he was beyond worrying about it. All he wanted was to lay eyes on the familiar face of someone he trusted, someone who could help him get settled and perhaps even find work and a decent place to live.

But more than that, Paul hoped Kazan might help revive the meaning in his life, now that he was cut off from family and home, and now that the hopes he had for an education were shattered.

In any case, he had nowhere else to turn.

4

Paul and his unsought companion walked a mile or two farther until they came to the Admiralty Quay. To their left, in all its lifelike bronze majesty, rose the statue of Peter the Great mounted on his rearing horse.

"Cursed tsar of the barons!" sneered Paul's guide, continuing with several derogatory remarks under his breath.

Paul heard, but continued to gaze in awe as they passed. Here was a symbol of all he had come to despise, of the detestable Romanovs, of the hated tsarist government. Yet Peter also represented the very essence of the Motherland and its history, a history he had acquired a deep fondness for during his year at the Gymnasium.

Would his loyalties always be so torn? Would he ever find peace within himself?

They crossed Isaac's Bridge to Vassily Island. The water below teemed with ships, small steamers, and pleasure barges, all taking advantage of the river now that the winter's ice was at last melting and breaking up.

Paul had to admit he was fascinated and enthralled by this beautiful, odd, interesting, many-faceted city. St. Petersburg was contemptible to many Russians since Peter's time because of its decidedly Western atmosphere, yet its buildings and streets and statues and broad avenues were so picturesque that they could not help but draw admiration—especially from a sheltered country boy. His old friends would no doubt scold him for his romantic notions of a city rife with poverty and corruption, housing all the hated bureaucracy of the tsar. He wished someone could help him put all his confusion into proper perspective.

As if to mock his youthful naivete, the first sight to meet Paul's view as they reached the end of the bridge were the buildings of St. Petersburg University. He should have one day been a student here! He had cherished such a dream. His instructors at the Gymnasium had been hopeful.

But it would never happen now; he was branded as a troublemaker! And even though universities throughout the land were known for their wealth of troublemakers, Paul knew *he* would never have another chance of being accepted. They had told him upon leaving the Pskov jail that his name had been added to the government's list of radicals. Should a purge occur, he was likely to be among the first arrested.

He was a fool to be so bedazzled by the stories and characters of Russia's history. What was history but a whitewashed accounting of the government's atrocities toward the common man? All the history that mattered lay in the books the teachers at the Gymnasium conveniently omitted from their curriculum; accounts of ill-fated boys fallen victim to evil—victims of selfish systems, corrupt *governments*!

Suddenly Paul was more anxious than ever to see his old friend Kazan. There was work to be done, wrongs to right, truths to be proclaimed to the unsuspecting masses.

"How much farther?" he asked.

"Some ways yet . . . do you need a rest?"

Indeed, Paul was quite out of breath. He had attributed his light-headedness to his growing agitation of spirit, but in truth he had eaten very little in the last week, and they had been walking at a brisk pace. And they did not possess enough coppers between them to hire even the poorest *droshky*.

"I'll rest later," he replied, shaking his head.

Except for a few nicer flats on the waterfront, Vassily Island drew its population largely from the working classes, minor civil servants, factory workers, and poverty-stricken students. Off the bridge they turned onto the street called Maly Prospect, to which the lowest of these lower classes had gravitated. Perhaps it was not the worst of slums in St. Petersburg, as it was rivaled by the Tartar district of Grafsky Lane and the shabby fisherman's hovels along the Chernaya River, but the area was bad enough that even policemen were not apt to patrol the deplorably filthy and overcrowded section of the island except in pairs.

Paul had already spent more time than he wanted to in such places. He hoped his acquaintance might be leading him to better appointments. But apparently this was not to be the case.

They paused before a row of dingy tenements. Smudge-faced children with rags of clothing hanging from them played at some game with a faded, lopsided ball. An old woman with bent shoulders and a tattered black shawl wrapped around her shuffled past, giving the two young strangers a sour appraisal before moving on with a scowl.

Paul followed his guide as he ducked into a dark, drab courtyard between two buildings.

The structures towered above them, letting no sunlight reach the ground. The dirt in the narrow passageway was littered about with trash, old newspapers, rotting food, broken bottles, a dilapidated old chair, and discarded bits of clothing. The stale air reeked of filth, urine, and dog droppings. A breeze blew through the stinking corridor, and the odors rose up anew, as if to defend their right to hang putrid over this black hole.

At last Paul's guide stopped in front of a door toward the rear of the narrow courtyard. He gave several sharp raps with his fist.

"Who is it?" came a muffled voice from inside.

"Valiev," replied Paul's companion. "I have brought you a visitor."

"What visitor?" said the voice in guarded tone.

Paul's heart leaped as he recognized his friend. "It is I . . . Pavushka!" he shouted, unable to restrain himself.

The next instant the door opened wide. Paul's face brightened.

"Kazan!" he cried joyfully.

"It *is* you, my little protege!" said Kazan amiably, throwing his arms around Paul in welcome. "So, you've finally come."

"I've been in the city two days."

"Two days! And not come to see me in all that time?"

"I didn't know where to find you," said Paul.

"Well, no matter, my friend. You are here now. I thank you, Valiev, for finding him and bringing him here."

"I will be on my way," said the man known as Valiev. "I have other business to attend to. I am certain I will see you again," he added, looking at Paul.

"How can I ever thank you?" said Paul, embracing the man warmly. "I am in your debt."

"There is no debt among brothers in the cause, eh?" replied Valiev.

Again Paul wondered if he had misjudged this fellow.

"You are right there," added Kazan. "And here is a true brother, you can be sure of that!"

Kazan closed the door firmly. The moment they were alone, he turned to Paul with a look of concern on his animated face.

"You look dreadful, Pavushka! How long has it been since you have eaten?"

Paul shrugged. The truth was easily apparent.

"Come," Kazan went on. "Sit and tell me your story while I fix tea. I am afraid I can offer you no feast, but I do think I may find enough to fill that empty stomach of yours."

5

As Paul sat in Kazan's poor and dirty flat, he felt as though mere days rather than a full year had passed since he had last seen his friend.

Without hesitation or shame, Paul poured out every detail of his past year, surprising even himself with the tears the still-raw memory of Aleksi's death produced from deep within him. For the first time since the ugly incident, he received sympathy and support for his actions. Kazan praised his courage and applauded his righteous wrath that had expressed itself so valiantly.

"They all made me feel like a vile criminal," Paul said at length.

"Nonsense!" cried Kazan. "*They* are the criminals, you the champion of justice!"

"I would like to believe you," faltered Paul, "but—"

"Did I not tell you your time would come?" interrupted Kazan. "You are truly one of us now, Pavushka!"

"One of . . . *us*?"

"Yes! One of the league. We can use you, Paul. Your timing could not be better."

"Then you are still involved in . . . the cause?"

"More than ever. And you will be also!"

"How . . . how will *I*—"

"Wait till you meet the others. We have purpose now. And we possess the leadership to enable us to fulfill our goals."

"Leadership? You, Kazan?"

"As well as others. And, since Vera's acquittal, we even have public sanction for our cause!"

"Public authorization—that is truly incredible!"

"Even the courts of the tsar may work for us in the end!"

"But who is Vera?"

"Come now, even in the provinces you must have heard of Vera Zasulitch."

"Until Aleksi's death, for the past year I concentrated only on my studies," answered Paul in an apologetic tone. "I . . . I found it best to avoid association with political circles."

"That is well. Your studies were important, Paul, and you need not apologize. But I must tell you about Vera. An amazing woman!"

He paused to chuckle.

"I suppose you have not heard of Trepov either?" he added after a moment.

Paul shook his head.

"Well," Kazan began, warming enthusiastically to the prospect of fresh ears to bend to the will of his rhetoric, "Trepov is the chief of police in St. Petersburg. A more malicious, evil man it is not possible to meet. Even the aristocracy despises him. He ordered the brutal beating of a friend of Vera's who was being held in the Fortress. The lad nearly died of the man's abuse. And I understand that now, almost a year later, he is still plagued with a limp."

He paused a moment before going on. "We were all incensed," he said, "but Vera most of all. She wasted no time in laying her hands on a pistol. When Trepov received petitioners, as was his weekly custom, Vera filed in with the queue, drew her pistol from inside her coat, and emptied it at nearly point blank range. The no-good scum survived the attack. Vera was arrested immediately, and there was not the slightest question of her guilt. Dozens of witnesses saw the whole thing."

He let out another hearty laugh. "But at her trial it was Trepov, not Zasulitch, who found himself actually in the dock. The public had no intention of allowing Vera to be convicted for firing on a man everyone hated, and the jury brought down an acquittal. The *not guilty* verdict met with thunderous cheers and applause from the listening crowd."

"I can scarcely believe it!" exclaimed Paul.

"Believe it—I was there!"

"Is it possible apathy can so quickly turn into such support against the tsar's regime?" asked Paul.

"I suppose disenchantment after the war has colored public opinion," said Kazan. "The tsar may have won a technical victory for Russia, but certainly not a moral one. Good Russians sacrifice themselves—and for what? Nothing changes. Corruption grows in government, and the imperial iron fist becomes heavier. Look around you—nothing will ever change! The small minority bask in wealth and opulence, while the vast majority bears the crushing burden of taxes and labor and poverty. It will not change unless we *make* it change, unless we *force* change upon such a cruel system! The time has come for this change, Paul, and we must not let it slip by us! It has already begun, and you are just in time to join."

"How? What can I do?"

"We are taking advantage of this change in the wind," Kazan continued. "Who knows how long it will last? After Vera's trial, the chief of the Secret Police, Mezentsev, was killed—stabbed in broad daylight on the city street. Prince Kropotkin of Kharkov was murdered a few months back, and just weeks ago unsuccessful attempts were made on the new chief, Vlasenko, and—"

"Vlasenko!" interrupted Paul.

"That's right. Why? Do you know him?"

"Indeed I do! He's from Katyk—a monster. I hate him!"

"All the more reason why, I say, it is good you have come. Here you will be able to direct that hatred to useful ends. Besides him, there was even an attack on the tsar himself! Why, there is not a minister in the city who dares leave his house without a Cossack escort. We have them all running scared, Pavushka!"

"But, Kazan," objected Paul, speaking with hesitancy. "You are speaking of violence . . . murder. That is not what we talked about in Katyk."

"Pavushka," replied Kazan in the tender voice of an experienced mentor, although he was only twenty-two years old himself, "our failure in the country regions south of here has only proved, if nothing else, that change will not come to Russia on a gentle breeze, but only by a violent hurricane. Do you seriously think the Romanovs will relinquish their dynasty any other way?"

"I suppose not," replied Paul slowly.

"Of course not! They must be brought down to a violent end, my friend—and why not? Their entire tenure since the early 1600s has been singularly marked by violence and blood—the blood of the people, our own countrymen, the very people whose protectors they are supposed to be. The time has come for the tables to be flipped upside down!"

"I don't know, Kazan." Paul's tone betrayed that at seventeen, he did not feel equipped for the man's business of murder.

"You will know, Pavushka," rejoined Kazan, paying no attention to the other's timid hesitation. "You will know when you see a brother die at their hands!"

Paul glanced up suddenly, his countenance marked more deeply than ever by the pain he suffered in Pskov.

"But I forget," added Kazan more gently, "you *have* seen a brother fall by the hand of injustice. You *do* know what I mean."

"I wanted to kill that day, Kazan," admitted Paul.

"The feeling comes to us all sooner or later."

"Sometimes I still want to kill that man for his cold-hearted, sneering words. But I am afraid that once I start I will not be able to stop. I will become just as unfeeling as the animals I despise."

"Perhaps you are right," said Kazan, moderating his tirade. It was difficult to tell whether he did so momentarily only for the sake of Paul's feelings, or if he genuinely believed the words Paul spoke. "Maybe that is what sacrificing for the cause means. We must sacrifice our very humanity to bring liberty to our beloved Motherland. Some of us must do this, Pavushka. Some of us must kill, even if it *does* make animals of us. There is no other way."

They fell silent a long while.

41

Kazan busied himself preparing tea and slicing off several thick slabs of brown bread from a crusty loaf. Paul leaned back on the wobbly, unpainted chair, his mind reeling with shock and alarm at the frightening words.

Yet why should it surprise him? Perhaps Kazan had never spoken of outright murder before. But more than once he had declared that the Romanovs must be eliminated before lasting change could come to Russia. When the peasants had stubbornly resisted the idealistic messengers, Kazan had hinted that they would have to use more *direct* methods to force the peasants to help themselves. They had talked often of pulling the government down at its foundations.

It had seemed like only so much talk back then—talk to drive passions. The reality and ugliness could be kept at bay by the blindness of boyhood. But Paul was a hundred years older now. And if he felt shock at what he heard on this day, it was only because he could no longer deny the truth of Kazan's words.

Kazan carried steaming glasses of tea to the table, along with a tray of bread.

"It is not much, my friend," he said, "but help yourself." He took one of the glasses, then resumed his own chair.

The poor fare and even poorer furnishings of the one-room flat reminded Paul that he had not heard Kazan's personal account of the time since they had last seen each other. The last Paul had heard, his mentor was bound for Siberia.

"I was there a year," Kazan explained. "I have only been in St. Petersburg about two months."

"Was it terrible for you?"

The young revolutionary chuckled in reply. "You must think me crazy for my humor," he said, "but we laughed there whenever we could. It kept us warm if nothing else. But to answer your question—a year is nothing. I met men who had been there *ten* years and more, their crimes no more heinous than the writing of so-called seditious books. The notion of Siberian exile might well prove the grandest imperial mistake made by the Romanovs. If we ever do succeed in overthrowing them, the seeds will no doubt have been born and nurtured in Siberia.

We called our camp 'the University of Revolution.' Many a long winter's night were spent exchanging ideas, crystallizing our goals, planning for the eventual destruction of those who had sent us there. I met many true heroes of our cause, and I learned more there than I could have learned anywhere else. The cold and ice and deprivation—it only strengthens you!"

He rubbed his hands together vigorously, almost as if he longed for the cold numbness. "But now it's time to put that year of preparation to use," he went on quickly. "Mere words must be turned into action. Ideas must become hard realities— guns, explosives, printing presses, pamphlets . . ."

He paused again thoughtfully. "Do you know what we talked about?" he asked after a moment. "Not comparisons of Herzen and Bakunin, but rather methods of tunneling and setting charges, falsifying travel documents and identity papers, who the best contacts were in Geneva, and what the targets of highest priority would be. All at the expense of His Majesty the Tsar!" Kazan laughed. "It's a sweet irony: He put us together so we could discover the best means to overthrow him."

Another pause followed. Finally Paul spoke.

"I have waited a long time to become part of your circle, Kazan," he said, still overwhelmed by what he had heard. "Yet I never expected any . . . all of this. I don't know if I can . . . if I will be useful to you." The last words fell from his lips almost helplessly, for he could not bring himself to an outright repudiation of Kazan's motives and methods and goals.

"Don't worry, my young friend. You need make no commitments now. Only watch and listen—your heart will guide you."

Paul drank his tea. It was not the best he had ever had, for no one could make it like his mother, but it certainly surpassed any he had tasted in the last month.

"What happened to the others who were in jail with us in Akulin?" Paul asked after he had swallowed the last of another piece of bread.

"All administrative exiles," replied Kazan bitterly.

"What does that mean?" asked Paul, embarrassed that he did not know even the rudiments of this system he so deplored.

"In my case," Kazan began, "since they had me pegged for a leader and wanted to make an example of me, I was given the benefit of a *trial*—if you can call that travesty of justice a trial. I was sentenced to ten years hard labor, to be followed by exile for life."

The look on Paul's face stopped Kazan in his tracks.

"Of course, I escaped," he added, and at his listener's gaping expression of shock at the words, he let out a jovial laugh.

"Yes, Paul," he went on, after recovering himself, "you are in the presence of an escaped prisoner of the Russian state! I did not even make it as far as my assigned labor camp. I got the slip on the guards while we were still on the road. I am living here under a false name with forged papers."

"I can hardly believe it."

"But back to the others you asked about. As *administratives*, they were exiled *without* trial. It's the government's handy way of disposing of someone who is obnoxious in the eyes of the state but who has broken no laws, even by petty imperial standards. They have no right to demand a trial and certainly cannot call friends or family to vouch for their good character, for fear of bringing the same fate upon them. They are usually trundled off to Siberia with no right of redress. They may not end up in the labor camps, although some do. Usually they are just forced to stay put in some village there, and are watched to make sure they do. If they have a bit of money, some are able to make a life for themselves there, but that is rare. And even that does not lessen the injustice of the system. It is vile . . . evil . . . unjust, that a man's whole life can be disrupted and brought to an end at the mere whim of some irritated official, whether the charges be valid or not!"

"That's terrible!" exclaimed Paul.

"Just one of many reasons why we must act without delay! And I'll tell you something else, Paul. Our present dear 'Little Father,' our so-called Tsar *Liberator*"—Kazan spit the word out of his mouth with mocking disdain—"has taken advantage of this despicable allowance of the law more than any other tsar. In the last five years he has sent droves of 'politicals' out of his sight in this manner."

He brought his fist down on the table, which shook precariously on its decrepit legs.

"Is it any wonder I have set upon the path of violence?" he asked, his eyes flaming. "Don't tell me there is any justice apart from it! I have seen too much. I will never believe it!"

"Nevertheless, Kazan," said Paul, speaking softly but with a little more boldness to question than he had yet shown, "it seems to be a sorry end to the high hopes and dreams of better—"

"It is not an end. It is the true beginning!"

Paul thought better of saying more and shrugged noncommittally.

Kazan noticed his hesitation, and then went on in a milder tone, his passion spent for the moment. "Tell me, Pavushka," he said, "did you not once mention that you had a sister in St. Petersburg?"

"She lives as a servant in the house of Prince Viktor Fedorcenko."

"Hmm . . . Fedorcenko, you say?"

Paul nodded.

Kazan rubbed his chin, clearly in deep thought. "Does she share your mind in matters of politics?"

"She has no interest in politics whatever," replied Paul.

"I thought she was going to get you a position with the prince."

"We spoke of it. But that was well over a year ago. Then I began at the Gymnasium, and the subject never came up again."

"Have you seen her since arriving in the city?"

"No. I . . . I'm not even certain how to find her." His voice was hesitant.

"It would be an easy matter to locate—"

Paul interrupted, speaking his mind at last. "I will *not* see her. I will ask for no position. I am dead to my family!" His voice seemed to ring with the timbre of Kazan's own anger, yet underlying the words was the confused pain of a lost young man, crying out in the anguish of loneliness.

Kazan eyed him carefully, weighing his young friend's emotional outburst. "You can see how such a position could be most advantageous," he said after a moment. "Fedorcenko is close to the tsar."

"Is he also targeted . . . ," Paul hesitated, "for . . . justice?"

"Fedorcenko is known for his liberality," replied Kazan. "That does not make him one of us by any means, but at least he is sympathetic with some of our views. On the other hand, he *is* a minister and an adviser to the tsar. And sometimes it is the liberals, the so-called moderates, I despise the most. They straddle the fence. They could do so much if they would exert their influence, but their only concern is to protect their own backside."

Paul was silent a minute. "I will not involve my sister in any of this," he said finally. An invisible shudder went through Paul's body at the mere thought of gentle Anna being drawn into the violent world that was Kazan's life.

"Give it some thought."

"I will do nothing to endanger my sister," said Paul firmly.

Kazan laughed, slapping Paul congenially on the back. "I understand perfectly. I will say no more."

Paul seemed satisfied with his promise.

"In the meantime," Kazan added, "you will need work. I will see what I can do for you. Now . . . finish the last of this bread before it goes stale."

Paul had eaten of his friend's provision because he was too hungry to refuse. He did not know, however, if he would be able to swallow Kazan's new politics of violence. Had the noble movement to which he had idealistically thought to sacrifice his future truly gone so far as to embrace murder as the cornerstone of its policy? Was there really no other way?

With his own eyes he had already witnessed much injustice and misery from the direct hand of the corrupt, evil, self-sustaining government. He could not deny it. He hated the system as did Kazan.

Yet he wondered if he could bring himself to say, *The government must be destroyed, and those who were its tools must perish—from the tsar down to the lowest magistrate!*

What would his father say to such twisted and ugly logic?

Or his sister? Dear, sweet Anna . . . she could never conceive of such depravity, and he would *never* make her an unwitting party to it.

As for himself . . . he must think on it. If Kazan *was* right, perhaps it was for this very reason his life had been uprooted and he had been forced from home and family. Perhaps *this* was his future—being part of a new order that was swiftly coming to the great land of Russia.

6

Cyril Vlasenko gazed out his window at the Secret Police Headquarters onto the wide St. Petersburg avenue.

Ah, St. Petersburg! He could still hardly believe his good fortune. He would not rejoice over another man's death. But if the tsar needed a new chief for the Third Section, the growing secret police force, then it might as well be he. He was as good as any other who could have been selected for the prominent post.

Better! he thought to himself.

He would dedicate himself ruthlessly to rooting out the radical swine who were behind all the unrest. He would also watch himself more closely so that danger could not get close, as it had three weeks ago. He was not about to be such a fool as Mezentsev and get himself killed in the middle of a crowd! Cyril chuckled to himself. Perhaps he did owe something to the rascal who had stabbed the old chief. Otherwise he would not be seated behind Mezentsev's desk at this moment. Yes, he would show his favor all right, by unearthing the miscreant and slipping a tight noose around his neck—and all his filthy compatriots with him!

Cyril Vlasenko, new Third Section chief, was not one to be cowed before those villainous tactics of violence and intimidation. The very might of the tsar's fist was behind him, and no handful of student rabble-rousers was capable of toppling so vast an empire.

Vlasenko breathed deeply, as if he could feel the morning air drift into his lungs through the glass of the window. But his heady exhilaration was clouded slightly, as always, when a nagging thought of his haughty cousin intruded into his ponderings. Vlasenko's spy in the Fedorcenko house had definitely paid off! It had been a chance in a million that he'd uncover such a choice tidbit. Ha! Far more than a mere "tidbit"! He'd had a vague suspicion of it previously, and so had been able to set the servant girl in a specific direction. But obtaining proof positive of the little skeleton in Viktor's closet was a coup indeed.

And what had made this particular item an even more potent weapon was that it did not strike directly at Viktor himself. The high-and-mighty prince might not have bent his so-called honor to save himself. But to save a loved one, no less than his frail and pampered wife? That Viktor could not ignore.

But Vlasenko could not erase from his mind's eye that look of utter disdain Viktor had worn when he had capitulated to Cyril's demand for Viktor to get him a substantial governmental position in exchange for his silence. "High up, Viktor," Cyril had said, "and *in* the Capital. You get me right into the center of power, or your name will become hateful in the tsar's ear!"

"You are a swine, Cyril," Viktor had seethed, "lower than the scum of this earth. You will have your high office, and I dearly hope you rot in it! But if we are lucky, some rebel's bullet will cut you down and save everyone the annoyance of your presence."

Oh, he was proud and arrogant, this aristocrat with the lily-white hands of a woman!

Cyril would prove to him and everyone else what they all should have known long ago—that *Count* Cyril Vlasenko was a man of skill and cunning, not to be taken lightly.

And Cyril could not keep from wondering how much further he might be able to go in government. Maybe he had blackmailed his way this far, but there was no reason why he could not go even further on his own merits. Perhaps to the Winter Palace itself . . . perhaps as a minister one day! If not . . . well, he might yet be able to get more distance out of his information on Natalia.

At that thought, however, Cyril slowly and reluctantly shook his head. Viktor was not a man you could push too far. If Cyril became greedy—and he had to admit this weakness as a primary element of his character—he could well find himself back at the beginning, shuffling papers in some provincial outpost even more isolated than Akulin or Katyk.

No, it was best he remain content for now, and work hard to prove himself worthy of promotion on his own abilities.

As if to punctuate his silent resolve, Cyril returned his attention to the papers on his desk. Several dossiers of insurgents and rebels lay before him. He perused them carefully, for in them lay his ticket to prestige and advancement.

He paid special note to one in particular. It was the file on a young man he had encountered a time or two before in the Akulin district. It would be a sweet irony that a criminal from his old district might catapult him forward now. And the capture of this fellow would indeed be a feather in his cap, for, though he was by no means one of the most notorious rebel leaders, he was apparently close enough to the top to have a ream of information that could bring down the leadership.

The man went by many aliases—Adrianov, Jarnev, Kazan— who knew what his real name was? What did it even matter? Kazan had been his name in Katyk.

Cyril ran a stubby finger across the scraggly beard that barely covered the ample folds of his two chins. The jewels of the rings on his hand caught the morning light, glinting and sparkling in an impressive manner. Only the cunning glint in his eyes matched the display on his fingers. Cyril recalled that Kazan, an obvious outsider and agitator in Katyk, had befriended a few of the local youth, one in particular named Paul

Burenin. He himself had questioned the Burenin boy when he was arrested with Kazan. Back then Cyril was interested in Paul's sister's position in the Fedorcenko household, thinking he might use her as his behind-the-scenes plant. But it was too late, for the girl had already been incorporated into the household staff. Fortunately, Cyril was able to install someone fresh and new.

So even if the brash young son of that insolent peasant Yevno Burenin had not proved helpful then, he might still be of some use. At least it would be worth the effort to send one of his lackeys to Katyk in order to grill the boy regarding his association with this insurrectionist named Kazan. Paul might well know something about the fellow's background, perhaps even his family.

If only I could get my hands on the family of this Kazan, or whoever he really is, I would have him in no time, thought Vlasenko confidently. And once he had him, he'd send the whole lot of them, the Burenins included, to Siberia! That was the only place for troublemakers and sympathizers and those associated with them.

Cyril pushed back his chair, rose, and strode to his office door. Opening it, he addressed one of a handful of men who were working in the anteroom.

"Surkov, come into my office. I have an assignment for you."

Surkov scurried quickly to his feet, and in three strides was in the office of the chief of Russia's secret police. Vlasenko shut the door and, eagerly rubbing his hands together, returned to his desk and picked up the dossier.

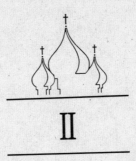

II

TURNING POINTS
(April 1879)

7

An eighteenth birthday symbolized an important turning point for any girl, but especially for a young princess of Russia!

Accordingly, the parents of Katrina Viktorovna Fedorcenko planned a gala party to mark the day of her coming out—the moment of her arrival on the threshold of womanhood. The day coincided with the close of Lent, and after the pious emphasis of the holy season, the whole of St. Petersburg society was quite ready for a festive celebration.

Katrina made still one more appraisal of herself in the dressing table mirror. She had already examined every inch of her face and body a dozen times, but she still couldn't quite satisfy herself.

She wore a dress of fine pale green tarlatan gauze. Its scalloped hemline was trimmed with clusters of diamonds, as was the neckline. A silk ribbon circled her waist, falling at the back in several whimsical streamers. The dress had cost her father two thousand rubles, and were he to lay eyes upon his daughter at this moment, he would be pleased to see his money had been well spent. It was fortunate she was the guest of honor tonight, otherwise she would have stolen the attention from some other unfortunate girl of less lavish means.

"Anna, are you sure the hem is straight?" Katrina asked, twisting around to get a better view.

"It's perfect, Princess," replied Anna, smiling. She was as proud of her mistress's beauty as if she had fashioned it by her own hand. In fact, she had actually done so with Katrina's hair. While the princess wiggled restlessly like a child, Anna had spent hours twisting the ringlets and weaving the colorful ribbon and delicate sprigs of baby's breath through the curls to get the best effect. "You are lovelier than any grand duchess!" Anna added.

What neither young lady voiced was the truth that would be all too apparent before the night was over—that the two young grand dukes who vied for the favor of the young Fedorcenko princess would be most proud to make her a *real* grand duchess.

Katrina's mind was not on such trifles, however. She harbored not the slightest interest in impressing a single member of the royal family. After more than two years, her heart could not be swayed even by the tsar's own sons; it still belonged to a mere count. And if no one else realized it, at least Anna knew that all her efforts on this most special evening had but one purpose in the mind of her mistress: to once and for all win the heart of the only true love she had ever known—her brother's best friend, Count Dmitri Remizov.

True to Sergei's prediction, Dmitri had somehow managed to inveigle his way out of Siberia and back to civilization. A rumor was circulating around Moscow that he had won back his freedom in a card game, wagering his return to his old regiment against *another* five years in the Siberian outpost. It sent shudders up and down Katrina's spine just to think of the awful possibility! Soon after hearing of his return to St. Petersburg, Katrina was halfway out the door on her way to his home, throwing propriety to the wind, when a simple suggestion by her maid caught her fancy instead.

"Why not invite him to your birthday celebration?" Anna had suggested. "If you really want to please him, Princess, why not let him first lay eyes on you as you make a grand entrance like a princess in a fairy story?"

Katrina stopped, thought a moment, then smiled. The idea appealed to her flamboyant nature.

"Why, Anna," she said. "I do believe I am rubbing off on you! That is a very clever idea!"

"I was only trying to help, Princess," replied Anna. "It's just that I was thinking how anyone who had not seen you for two years would be sure to—"

She hesitated.

"Would be sure to what, Anna?"

"To see how you have changed, Princess. You are so much older . . . as beautiful as any woman in Moscow. At least *I* believe so."

"Oh, Anna, how can you always be so kind to me? I don't know whether to believe you half the time—except that you're the most trustworthy person I know."

It had strained every fiber of her tempestuous and impatient nature, but Katrina had managed to wait. At last the moment had come, and her long years of anticipation would be rewarded. Dmitri could not possibly fail to notice her tonight—and see her fully as the enchanting *woman* she had become.

Only moments before, Anna had returned from the ballroom. Katrina had contrived an errand for her to be about, although the only thing she really wanted was a report back whether Count Remizov had yet arrived.

"I am afraid your father is growing quite impatient," Anna had said. "The guests are arriving, Princess, and he was mumbling something about you shirking your duty in not being there to receive them."

"Well, I don't care. I'm not budging until Dmitri arrives. There would hardly be any sense in making a grand entrance at all if the only one I am trying to impress isn't here!"

"But he *is* here, Princess. He stepped through the front doors when I was there. He has only just this minute come!"

"Then let me be on my way at once! Oh, but Anna," she added, feeling a momentary fluttering of nervousness, "are you *certain* the dress is—"

"Perfect, Princess," said Anna. "Everything is perfect."

Had Anna remained in the ballroom only a moment or two longer, she would have observed Dmitri more carefully. But as it was, she missed the one detail that would again smash all Katrina's hopes and dreams to dust.

8

Katrina Viktorovna Fedorcenko descended the marble stairway into the ballroom of her father's mansion with all the grace and aplomb of the grand Russian aristocrat and princess she was.

Mother and father beamed radiantly where they stood to welcome her after the slow and stately descent. To the many pandering compliments directed her way, Princess Natalia nodded and murmured "Thank you" over and over, as if she had had a significant share in the nurturing of the girl. Viktor stood tall and erect, as befitting a man of his stature, nodding his respectful appreciation for the congratulations afforded him by his colleagues. And he did have to admit that Katrina was a beautiful young lady. She nearly made up for an errant son who was off God only knew where trying to find his soul, and then to write about whatever he found, for heaven's sake. At least his daughter wasn't filled with any such nonsense!

Katrina was not oblivious to the admiring stares and praises being heaped upon her as she made her grand entrance. In truth, such flattery was rather commonplace for one in her position, and she would have noticed it more if she hadn't inspired such comment. Even as she returned animated smiles and greetings to her guests, her mind focused on searching among the hundreds of faces present to find the *one* face above all the rest she desperately longed to see.

Anna said she had seen him. *Where was he?* His height . . . the breadth of his rugged shoulders . . . he would stand out in any crowd! Why couldn't she see him? He couldn't have already slipped away somewhere!

No! She dismissed the thought immediately. He would not have come only to leave before personally greeting the guest of honor. Ah, she had it! He had no doubt arrived thirsty and had only at that moment retreated to the refreshment table.

Suddenly her probing eyes found him! Her heart leaped into her throat for a moment, but she swallowed it just as quickly.

Dmitri stood on the fringe of the crowd toward the back of the hall, leaning nonchalantly against one of the walls. He almost seemed to want to remain unobserved. *Surely the years away have not made him shy,* thought Katrina.

But no! He was staring directly toward her when her gaze finally turned in his direction. He *had* been looking for her! A thrill unlike anything she had ever known tingled throughout her entire body.

A year in the frozen wastes of the distant east had not diminished the stunning handsomeness of his face and frame one degree. A year of war followed by a year in exile had, in fact, served to deepen what was most desirable about him. Slightly thinner, the power of his features was more clearly evident. His limbs seemed more muscular, his cheekbones more prominent, his eyes older, his gaze steadier. To the dashing glint of his eye and the sardonic slant of his grin a certain portion of character was added. The new element she perceived could not exactly be termed *maturity*—Dmitri remained still too spirited and careless for that. Nor did his bearing possess the depth of sensitivity of someone like his friend, Katrina's brother Sergei Viktorovich. Yet what she saw somehow added still more mystery to his vast appeal.

Such details of perception, however, passed so rapidly through Katrina's consciousness that she was scarcely aware of them. What she *did* notice, however, in that tiniest of instants when their eyes met was a look—she was sure of it!—be it ever so fleeting, of *mutual* desire.

Could it be that at last he *saw* her . . . with the eyes of a man?

In that moment, had he remembered the touch of her lips

against his? It had been nearly two years ago, but Katrina had never forgotten that instant of ecstasy.

Without hesitation she began to make her way toward him. This was no time for caution or timidity. When she had learned of Dmitri's return from Siberia, this evening had taken on but one single overpowering purpose—and now she bent herself upon its fulfillment.

Two years ago, when she had put so much hope in the tsar's New Year's Ball, she had been but a child. She had grown and matured in many ways, more than merely in the contours of her body.

To be sure, the influence of her gentle peasant maid had wrought much good in Katrina. If Dmitri's gaze had been as insightful as it was keen, he would have seen the changes that maturity had brought about in her. More sensitivity accompanied by a degree or two *less* of self-absorption was plainly evident in the young Fedorcenko princess. Her strength of will had grown, it is true, although it had been somewhat mellowed by other attributes.

Yet she remained a determined young lady, and the passage of time had certainly not dulled her feelings toward Dmitri— nor her will to make him her own. And now here she was, at last face-to-face again with the man she loved.

She smiled with all the grace of her ripened charm and held her hand out to him with apparent confidence that at least this he would never reject.

"Dmitri," she said with as much calm as she could muster, although a trace of girlish cracking escaped into her tone. "I am so glad you could come!" Her voice reflected complete sincerity as well as youthful eagerness. He was, after all, a family friend returned from a long absence.

"I would not have missed my dear Katrina's coming out for all the best wine in the Crimea!" he replied. His tone lacked the patronizing quality she halfway expected. Yet it held some other inexact quality she could not readily define.

"And I know how much you enjoy your wine!" she rejoined playfully. They both laughed.

"You look lovely, Katrina," he went on with unexpected earnestness.

"A little less like my brother's baby sister?"

"Oh, a great deal less!" he answered with a knowing look.

"There you are, Dmitri, *darling*," interrupted a voice into the exchange of surface pleasantries.

Katrina scarcely had time to turn her head before a young woman glided between them, slipping her arm possessively through Dmitri's. He received the girl's attentions with only a slightly disconcerted smile.

"Katrina, you know Alice Nabatov," he said.

Katrina hadn't seen Alice since the day the flirtatious young woman had spoiled her afternoon of skating on the river two winters previously. Alice Nicolayevna's father, though not a hereditary aristocrat, was a wealthy industrialist and had lately been dubbed a count by the tsar, and the two girls ran in different social circles.

"Yes, of course, we have met once or—" faltered Katrina. But before she could finish Alice broke in.

"I hope you don't think me a party-crasher, Katrina dear," she said with a giggle. "But I told Dmitri it would be perfectly acceptable for him to bring his fiancee to your celebration."

At the word *fiancee*, Katrina felt as if she'd been broadsided across the face by the blow of a fist. None of the fantasies she had nurtured concerning this night had included *this*!

Too shocked to utter a sound, she stood staring, a blank smile painted across her face as if etched in stone. She began to feel the color drain from her cheeks, but struggled to stand stoically like a well-disciplined soldier, a trait inherited from her father.

"Fiancee?" she finally managed.

"Yes," Alice tittered on. "Isn't it wonderful? We plan to host a soiree to officially announce the event soon. I do so hope you will be able to come, Katrina dear. I know how close your whole family is to Dmitri."

"Yes ... yes, of course," Katrina mumbled graciously. "Thank you." Her control began to slip. She had to get away! "Please, you will excuse me ... I must greet my other guests."

She slid away, keeping her lips turned upward in the general shape of a smile, and somehow managed to stumble on through the motions of a proper hostess and honored guest. For the next thirty minutes Katrina functioned in a complete fog. As if from a distance she was aware of her legs and hands gesturing and her voice sounding, yet without any feeling of reality. She was amazed afterward to realize that she had apparently managed to keep from making an idiot of herself, for her father came to her side fifteen or twenty minutes later, gave her hand a loving squeeze, and whispered in her ear that it all seemed to be quite a success.

The moment the greeting of guests was over, the orchestra began with a waltz, her favorite piece, which she danced as planned with her father. A second number followed, and with all the guests occupied, Katrina seized the opportunity of no longer being the center of attention. She excused herself politely from her father and slipped away to her room. She *had* to get a moment by herself to vent her pent-up emotions, or she was likely to explode.

Anna could see instantly that something had gone seriously wrong.

"He's engaged!" cried Katrina, wasting no words, the moment the door closed behind her. "Engaged . . ." she repeated. Her anger had spent itself in the single outburst, and wounded hurt came in its wake. Tears of mortification and pain instantly began to flow.

Anna approached her mistress and sat down next to her on the edge of the dressing table bench, laying a comforting arm gently around Katrina's heaving shoulders. This was no time for her to act the reticent part of a maid. The two girls had come far enough in their relationship over the course of two years that Anna knew how desperately Katrina needed a friend in that moment.

Many girls of Katrina's acquaintance came and went around the Fedorcenko household. Katrina went shopping with some, to social gatherings with others. But she was far too independent and strong-willed to develop any deep and lasting relationships of intimacy.

With Anna it had been different. She was neither threat nor rival. For all Katrina's strength of temperament, there was a part of her that was too insecure to open her true self up to anyone else. But she had found safety in Anna. Neither harbored secret expectations from the other. And Anna's innate gentleness had pulled Katrina easily into the kind of relationship that her insensitive, self-centered fellow-aristocratic girl-friends could never have cultivated.

The two girls sat side by side together in silence for well over five minutes. Except for Katrina's continued sobbing, there was no other sound in the room.

At last Katrina spoke, and once the words came, they poured out of her like a rampaging flood. For ten minutes she raged and ranted—against Dmitri, against herself, but mostly against that wanton hussy Alice Nicolayevna Nabatov. In the midst of it, with sobs and sniffles, she berated herself for being such a fool. Then she started up raving angrily all over again.

When most of the words had gushed out and the initial reservoir of tears had nearly emptied, she turned to Anna.

"Oh, Anna," she said despairingly, "what am I to do?" Her voice was drained and hollow. "I've tried absolutely everything with Dmitri. And now it seems as though it's too late!"

"Is the date set yet, Princess?" asked Anna.

"No. But it will be soon. Oh, and it isn't as if Alice Nicolayevna couldn't find another husband. She's attractive enough, I suppose . . . in a brassy sort of way. Why does *she* need to hang on to Dmitri so!"

"Do you think there is any possibility Count Remizov does secretly care for you, Princess?" asked Anna.

"Oh, Anna, how can you ask me something like that? I always thought he did. But after tonight, I'm not sure of anything anymore!"

"Perhaps there is some other reason he has chosen to marry Countess Nabatov," suggested Anna. "Something other than love."

"Hmm . . . there have been rumors that his family's fortune has been declining," said Katrina thoughtfully. "That is an interesting idea. If I were to, say, still be able to do something to *discourage* their plans, I would be doing them both a favor, wouldn't I, Anna? No one wants a husband who cares for someone else. And I'm *sure* he does, even if but a little."

Suddenly Katrina perked up. She stood and faced her maid.

"Thank you for letting me talk to you, Anna. I feel much better now. I think I can face the party again."

She glanced quickly in the dressing table mirror.

"Oh, but I look a sight! My eyes are all red."

"Let me fix it, Princess."

In ten minutes Katrina's appearance was restored to its previous loveliness. A cool washcloth had reduced the puffiness of her eyes. A deft turn of a comb had smoothed her ruffled curls. But Anna could do nothing to remove the hollow emptiness of Katrina's countenance.

Anna crossed herself on her mistress's behalf and prayed for her as she returned to the party.

9

Katrina avoided Dmitri for the remainder of the evening, managing to swallow some of her wounded pride and have some semblance of a good time.

She did not have to look far for a diversion from Dmitri. Dozens of rich, handsome, and titled young men were close at hand to pay her every attention she could possibly wish for. She danced until she was breathless, and soon was laughing and conversing enthusiastically.

During a break in the music, she stood sipping at a glass of punch in the center of six or eight admiring and fawning young men, among them the two cousins of the tsar. As she chanced to glance beyond one of them, a man standing off by himself caught her eye. He was staring straight at her with a most intense and penetrating look. She was far too accustomed to the attentions of the opposite sex to be unnerved by it, yet neither was he unnerved that she had seen him. He did not glance away, and seemed not the least embarrassed at having been caught observing her. He did not smile, but when she smiled at him, he did allow the corners of his lips to twitch ever so slightly upwards.

Katrina pulled her gaze back into the surrounding group of her admirers and went on with the conversation in progress, thinking little more of the incident.

After a rousing quadrille some time later, Katrina and her partner, laughing, half-stumbled off the dance floor to take a break. When Katrina came to herself, panting from the exertion, there was the stranger again, standing only a few paces away, his eyes still upon her as if he had never removed them. The unexpected persistence of his gaze was momentarily disconcerting, even for Katrina, although she could not consider his attention altogether unpleasant, for the young man *was* quite handsome.

In a second or two, the princess took in his appearance with a bit more care than she had earlier. He was a bit taller than Dmitri, but not so stocky in build, with wavy hair, thick and very blonde to match his thick, pale eyebrows. The lightness of hair and complexion was strikingly offset by stunning, dark brown eyes. They were extremely deep-set, rather close together, and filled with as much intensity and seriousness as Dmitri's were with constant amusement. They gave the impression of looking *at, into,* and *through* all at the same time. They drew in their object and did not easily let go. Katrina felt her heart pounding within her, a condition that could not be entirely attributed to the dance just ended.

"Nicholas," she said to her partner, "would you be so kind as to fetch me a glass of punch? I am utterly parched after all that exercise!"

"Most gladly, Princess. Excuse me."

The moment young Nicholas was gone, Katrina made no pretense of trying to be coy or subtle. She walked directly toward the mysterious stranger.

"Good evening," she said simply.

"Good evening, Princess Katrina." He bowed slightly. Still he offered no smile and no attempt at the frivolous flattery in which most of the young men around her had been so thoroughly schooled.

"I feel rather at a disadvantage," she went on. "You know me, but I must admit I am at a complete loss to recognize you."

"We have met," he replied, "but you can be forgiven for not recalling an event which occurred eight or nine years ago."

"Eight or nine years . . . I would have been about ten." Katrina rubbed her chin in thought.

"I am Basil Pyotrovich Anickin."

"You cannot be Dr. Anickin's son!"

"I am afraid so."

"There is nothing in the fact to be apologetic over. Our family greatly admires your father. He has quite a high reputation in St. Petersburg."

"Thank you, Your Highness. You are very kind."

"And did you follow in your father's footsteps? I mean, did you follow him into the medical profession?"

"No. I read for the law."

"So you are a barrister?"

"Yes."

The conversation was stilted, and Katrina was growing flustered at her inability to draw so much as a smile out of the fellow. She could not have misread the distinct impression that the doctor's son had wanted to meet her. But now he acted as if he were being interrogated by the police! She decided to attempt a frontal assault.

"Are you always so serious, Basil Pyotrovich?" she said, finishing off the words with her most bewitching smile.

"I am afraid so."

"Well, this *is* a party, you know," she went on. "And it is *my* party, a celebration of my eighteenth birthday. And I simply won't have any dour guests on my hands. Besides," she added, flashing her eyes at him, "I should feel as if I had failed altogether as a hostess if you did not have a good time."

"But I am having a good time," he replied most earnestly.

"I have greatly enjoyed watching you, Katrina Viktorovna."

A definite flush rose to Katrina's cheeks. The reaction came not just from his actual words, but from the way they were spoken. His tone held a fervency that seemed to go far beyond mere sincerity. She had never heard Dmitri utter a single syllable with such depth of wholeheartedness. She knew young Anickin *meant* what he said. And when he spoke her name, a new kind of thrill coursed through Katrina's whole body.

"I don't know what to say," she replied, attempting to fill the uncomfortable moment with words. "You . . . flatter me. But now, please come," she added, regaining her poise, "dance with me. This is one of my favorite numbers." She took his hand without waiting for a response and tugged him toward the dance floor.

"But your partner . . . he will be back with—"

"Never mind him," laughed Katrina. "I'm sure he can drink my glass of punch and then find another partner!"

The orchestra had struck up with Strauss's lovely "Emperor's Waltz." Katrina led him into the very middle of the crowded floor, then turned to face him. He took her right hand in his left, then slipped his right hand around her waist, holding her with firm assurance. They began to flow in graceful rhythm to the music, and she found herself surprised at what a good dancer Basil Pyotrovich turned out to be, moving with all the grace his lithe figure promised. Feeling the confidence of his movements as he led her this way and that through the crowd, Katrina suddenly realized how limited her experience with men really was. As she considered it, she thought to herself that she had never before had the attention of a *man* at all—not a man like this one! Boys and youths swarmed around her in plenty, just as Dmitri once predicted would happen.

But Basil was no boy. He was likely older even than Dmitri, somewhere in his early twenties, she guessed. Yet more than his age, he carried himself, even if a bit too seriously, with authority and self-assurance, as one who had matured and knew what he was about. Dmitri, on the other hand, had a good-natured frivolity that sometimes made him seem younger than he was. No one would ever accuse Basil of being

65

frivolous! Katrina wondered how the jovial, rotund Doctor Anickin could have a son who was such an antithesis to him.

But the deepest impression upon Katrina came from how
the doctor's son treated her. His hand resting comfortably in
the small of her back seemed alive. From the touch, and the
movement of his fingers and palm in response to the music,
she felt a kind of raw energy, a possessiveness that sent all her
untried youthful emotions into a flutter.

Now she knew why a woman longed to be held by a man.
This was how she was supposed to feel—protected, enveloped
in masculine care and vigor. It was how she had dreamed Dmitri would one day hold her!

Every time Katrina let her eyes stray upward to Basil's face,
he was gazing down upon her. He never took his eyes off her.
And the depth of his gaze, its purposefulness and earnest passion, seemed to increase.

The heady experience gave her almost the same rush of
exhilaration as speeding down Nevsky Prospect in a racing
troika on an icy winter morning. It was easy to overlook the
vague sense of uneasiness she felt.

They danced several waltzes together, one after the other.
When they stopped at last, Katrina was breathless. Basil led
her to a secluded corner of the ballroom.

"Katrina Viktorovna, I thank you for favoring me with your
company this evening," he said with a gallant bow.

She nodded with a smile of acknowledgment.

"I must confess," he went on, "that since seeing you three
nights ago at the ballet, I have wanted . . . to meet you."

"And why did you not introduce yourself then, Basil Pyotrovich? I would have been pleased."

"You are from a great family," he replied. "I am but the son
of a lowly doctor."

"Hardly *lowly*," objected Katrina.

"By the standards that govern our country."

"But your parents are friends of my parents. They come to
our home socially."

"Yes, that is true." Something in the momentary glazed
look in his eye indicated that he was agreeing in word only.

Katrina, however, was so taken at being the object of a man's distant admiration that she scarcely took note of these conflicting details.

"Well, I am glad that we finally had opportunity to meet . . . again," she said.

"I could not be content forever in merely looking at you from afar. You are very lovely. I only wish . . ."

He did not finish the sentence. His eyes narrowed slightly and he was silent.

"You only wish what?"

"I must go now, Princess," he replied, ignoring her question. "I would like to see you again." Though his final words were spoken in the tone of a question, Katrina felt they had not exactly been a *request*. He *would* see her again, that much was plain.

He bowed, took her hand in his, and kissed it lightly. He stepped back, caught her eyes one more time with his intense gaze, then turned and strode quickly away. Katrina expelled a tremulous sigh, hardly noticing that someone had drawn up next to her.

"Now there's an odd one," said a youthful male voice. Katrina turned to see Nicholas Osminkin, the partner she had deserted earlier.

"Oh, Nicki, there you are!" she said, showing little sign of embarrassment. "I am so sorry about leaving you like that. But I ran into Basil Anickin and had the feeling he didn't know a soul here. I felt it my duty as a hostess to entertain him for a while. You don't mind, do you?"

"Of course not, Princess Katrina," he replied, attempting to conceal his displeasure. "I wouldn't feel too sorry for the fellow though. In fact, I was surprised he was even invited tonight."

"Oh . . . why is that?"

"Don't you know *anything* about him?"

"I know he is a perfect gentleman."

"Well, he has been away from St. Petersburg for some time," Nicholas went on, eager for the opportunity to enlighten the princess. "He has been attending Moscow University."

"Oh, dear me! How absolutely mortifying!" exclaimed Katrina with mock horror, taking no pains to hide how insignificant such gossip was to her.

"That is not the half of it," young Osminkin went on. "He was in Moscow because he had been expelled from the University here in St. Petersburg."

"Is that all?" said Katrina. "Since Dmitri Tolstoy has been Minister of Education, students are being expelled for looking cross-eyed."

"Believe me, your Basil Anickin did more than that!"

Katrina desperately wanted to ask just what he had done. But she resisted the urge to give way to the gossip, and instead gave an uninterested flip of her hand. "I refuse to talk critically about a guest, Nicki!"

"Then you wouldn't like to know what he has been doing since he came back to the capital?"

"You'll probably tell me anyway."

"Maybe I won't."

"Oh, don't be difficult, Nicki. What has he been doing?"

"He is a lawyer now, you know. And he has taken to defending seditionists and revolutionaries!" The triumph in the lad's tone was unmasked.

"I don't believe it," replied Katrina rather lamely.

"That is up to you, Princess," he said. "I'm getting a bit hungry, will you excuse me?"

Katrina was glad to be rid of him. Just because she had left him to dance with someone else was no reason to go spreading malicious lies about a friend of her family. She would have to make it up to poor Basil when she saw him again.

Suddenly the young lawyer had become all the more intriguing to her. So what if he defended radicals? Someone had to defend them, didn't they? It was his job.

And even if he had radical ideas himself, who cared? Sergei had some peculiar ideas, too, and he managed to be accepted in society. Although lately, she had to admit that she didn't know what to make of Sergei. He had all but disappeared off the face of the earth. They hardly ever heard from him. *What had driven him away?* she wondered. *Surely nothing to do with*

*his ideas. It must have been something else. An argument with
Father, no doubt.*

Well, Basil Pyotrovich could not be that much different
from her brother, at any rate. And she fully intended to see him
again, no matter what Nicki or anyone else thought. As for
Dmitri Remizov—for once maybe she didn't care what he
thought, either!

10

Anna sat in her room at the desk Katrina had procured for
her. A warm beam of sunlight streamed through the high ceil-
ing window, sending a splinter of light across the sheet of paper
in front of her.

It was now early summer. Several weeks had passed since
Katrina's birthday, and the past few days particularly had been
reflective ones for Anna Yevnovna. Writing a letter home
seemed only to intensify her mood.

She had been in St. Petersburg for two and a half years. In
some respects she could hardly believe it had been so long. Yet
in other ways, it seemed as though a lifetime had passed since
she had last laid eyes on her beautiful little village of Katyk.

So much had happened to her in such a short time! She
remembered so clearly her last day in Katyk, with all its mingled fear and anticipation at the prospect of facing the great
unknowns before her. She had then harbored such a sense of
high expectation, almost of destiny. Now she had fallen to wondering what had come of it all.

Surely she could find no reason for disappointment. She

was privileged to study under a learned and esteemed tutor who had only recently told her she was fully qualified to study in any of the best universities of the land. She was gratified by his comments and hardly bothered by the fact that it was difficult enough for a peasant *boy* to gain admission into a university. For a girl, it was nearly impossible. But she had never planned to take her education even as far as it had already gone, and was thus fully content with what God had been gracious to provide her with here in the Fedorcenko home as maid to the prince's daughter.

She could speak and write French fluently—better than Katrina, in fact. She possessed an adequate grip on English, thanks in large part to the interest Mrs. Remington, the head housekeeper, had taken in her progress. She read English well enough to tackle Charlotte Bronte and, of course, Byron. She had even attempted some Tennyson and Wordsworth. On her birthday last year Katrina had treated her to a most generous and joyful gift. They drove together to Marskaya Street where the English bookshop Watkins was located.

There Katrina had said, "Now, Anna, I want you to select any books you want."

"Oh, Princess," said Anna excitedly, "I couldn't!"

"It's my birthday gift to you, Anna. I insist."

"Anything?" exclaimed Anna.

"There is only one stipulation," Katrina had said. "They *must* be in English."

Anna had chosen four titles, and felt terribly greedy at that. But her mistress had not allowed her to stop before she had at least that many to take home with her. One had been an edition of Byron's works. Then she had chosen Tennyson's *The Princess*, Elizabeth Barret Browning's *Sonnets from the Portuguese*, and Hawthorne's *The House of Seven Gables*. She had read from all of them a great deal since, understanding more than ever what Sergei had meant about a piece of literature being best in its native language. Still, Anna would ever remain partial to the French translations by which, from Sergei's tongue, she had first learned to appreciate the English poets.

She reached up to the bookshelf above her desk and gently

fingered the binding of the copy of *The Best of England's Poets* Sergei had given her. A stab of pain gripped her heart and knotted her stomach momentarily, as if he had left St. Petersburg only yesterday. But whether it had been a year, or a hundred years, she doubted time would ever dull the sense of loss she felt. Their love had developed so quickly; how could it have gone so deeply into her very being?

Yet as quickly as it had come, and as brief as their time together had been, there was no denying that she had been changed forever by Sergei's love.

Never in the past had she imagined that she could be happier than the days back in Katyk, when she sat, book open in her lap, under the leafy shelter of the old willow near the stream. But Sergei had added to that memory, giving her life a richness and meaning of equal depth and value. Did she compare him to the willow trunk at her back—strong and secure? Or to the book in her lap—a gateway to enlightenment and happiness? Or to the gentle spring breeze carrying the fragrance of life and purity?

Since that day a year ago she had often wondered where he was and what he was doing. His parting, so soon after returning home from the war, had been a painful shock for his family, and the princess herself had wept in the telling. He and his father had exchanged angry words. Prince Fedorcenko had, according to what Anna had heard, ranted to his son about duty and responsibility, while poor Sergei sat silently receiving the tongue-lashing. The stoic old soldier had no concept of what the changing times were doing to the young people of the Motherland, nor the nature of the deep and tormenting confusion that would drive a thoughtful and sensitive young man away to the country to try to come to terms with himself and the wartime demons that hounded him. To the controlled soldier from the old school, wedded to his tsar and the ways of the past, it was at best weakness, at worst insanity. He could not respect a son with no more backbone than that! And Sergei did not help his cause with his silence. He made no attempt to explain himself beyond the broad terms of fatigue from the war, and certainly made no mention of Anna.

There had been scant word from him since then. He had mentioned to Katrina his hope to visit Yasnaya Polyana. She had written him there telling him of her birthday celebration. There had been no reply except a note from Count Tolstoy saying Sergei had been there but had already departed his estate some time ago. He had left no hint as to his next destination.

Love was no easy thing to bear silently in one's heart. How much better were the old traditions back in her village at home! The matchmaker never considered *love* in her thoughts of putting a man and a woman together. And her matches were always successful.

Well, there had been *one* case where it had not turned out so well. . . . Matvie Turovec's wife had nearly driven him crazy with her constant nagging and complaining. He finally had all he could take and disappeared one day, never to be seen again. But such an outcome was rare. And even if a husband and wife happened not to get along perfectly, at least they were spared the pain caused by love *before* marriage.

She knew Katrina would disagree vehemently with her if she said such a thing, although she had been one of love's most pathetic victims. How many years had she wasted pining over Count Remizov? How many more years to come?

Of course, for the moment she seemed quite taken with this Basil Anickin. But Anna knew her mistress well enough to suspect that this sudden interest, as gratifying as it probably was to her young feminine ego, was intended primarily to impress Dmitri, his engagement notwithstanding.

Whether or not Katrina was aware of her deeper motives, she had seen the doctor's son frequently since the party. And if Katrina's regard was less than authentic, Anna knew Basil's wasn't. He gazed upon Katrina with such rapture, such possessive affection, such a brooding look of total preoccupation. Perhaps Anna should have been glad that at last someone had come along to distract her mistress from the ill-fated and doomed liaison with the count.

But oddly, whenever she watched Katrina and Basil together, Anna felt disturbed. They seemed so different, the innocent young princess and the grim barrister; the one so full of smiles, the other full of such sobriety. But Anna could pinpoint nothing but a vague sense of disquiet to support her uneasiness.

Anna glanced down once again at the blank sheet before her.

Her mind had wandered far afield—none of her thoughts of the last fifteen minutes would be appropriate to share with her family. She had not written for some time. With Paul away at the Gymnasium in Pskov, she knew it would be difficult for them to have her letters read anyway. Tanya and Vera should have known how to read well enough by now to manage. But as soon as Anna had left home, their interest in studying had flagged considerably. When Anna heard this news, she was deeply saddened.

Anna's thoughts turned to Paul, as they often did. It had been nearly eight months since she had heard from him. The last word to come was that he was doing extremely well with his studies. He said his marks were the highest in his class, and he hoped he might be able to complete the course of study well in advance of the others.

She was so proud of her brother! She would never be able to go to the university, but she was confident that he would. She had even discussed his future with Katrina, who had in turn mentioned Paul to her father. By this time Anna was perceived as such a part of the family that Prince Fedorcenko offered to recommend him for the university and support him financially as well.

Anna had said nothing yet. When he graduated, she planned to tell him this wonderful news, as a present—her gift to him for his hard work at the Gymnasium.

She remembered how he used to express skepticism at her faith in "fairy stories." But some good magic seemed to be working for Paul now, too. She knew *magic* was a poor word for it. Papa would, instead, marvel at the wondrous and mysterious hand of God at work in the lives of all His people, rich and poor, nobles and peasants.

And Papa was right. In His mysterious way, God seemed to

be caring for the simple Burenin clan from Katyk. Perhaps God was giving a special blessing to her own dear papa, whose prayers and simple faith were unwavering.

Inspired with thoughts of Paul and her papa, the accomplishments of the one and the faith of the other, Anna at last set pen to paper. The letter, it turned out an hour later, proved a rather sentimental one, expressing more of her feelings than the events of her life. But it suited her mood on this day to pour out her grateful heart to the family she cared for so deeply.

She was still in tears when Katrina burst into her little room in an excited flush.

"My goodness, Anna!" she exclaimed, not noticing her maid's reddened eyes. "I completely forgot! Mother and I are supposed to be at the Winter Palace today for tea with the Grand Duchess Marie. I have less than an hour to get ready!"

The princess's flurry of activity and frenzied words only verified Anna's earlier thoughts about Katrina's infatuation with Basil Anickin. Tea with the Grand Duchess, the tsarevich's wife, had always been important to Katrina. It was unlikely under normal conditions that she would forget it.

11

Anna negotiated her way around the tsar's Winter Palace now with ease. There were certainly many places in the sprawling edifice where she had not been and where she would never go. But within the limits of her experience as a maid to a princess who was a regular guest there, she had managed to become proficient enough.

While her mistress visited with the Grand Duchess, she walked down the familiar corridor to the small library. In the middle of the hallway, she heard a wide set of double doors open. A second later Lieutenant Grigorov backed out, closing the doors behind him, then turned in the direction from which Anna approached.

"Ah, Anna Yevnovna," he said. In spite of the cheerful words, Anna had seen the dismayed expression he had been wearing as he pulled the doors shut. He tried to mask it quickly the moment he saw her, but his words sounded stilted nonetheless.

"Lieutenant Grigorov," replied Anna, pausing and curtseying slightly.

The two had seen each other around the palace on several occasions since their first meeting, but not since his return from battle.

"It has been some time since I have seen you, Anna Yevnovna," he said briskly, recovering his composure. "I am glad to see you are still in St. Petersburg. And you remain with the Fedorcenkos?"

"Yes, Lieutenant."

"You have not forgotten so soon? It is Misha to you."

"Then yes, I am still with them . . . Misha," replied Anna. "Nothing has changed for me. And you?"

"The work of the Palace Guard is getting no easier with all the trouble and threats that have been brewing lately."

"You mean the violence and discontent in the streets?"

"Yes, and we of the Guard must be much more careful."

"There is hardly a guest who comes to my master's home," said Anna, "without a Cossack escort. But the prince himself refuses to allow a guard near him. He will not give the terrorists the satisfaction, he says."

"That sounds just like the tsar," rejoined Misha, "and he is the prime target. Yet still he insists on going about unescorted."

"Out in the streets?" asked Anna incredulously.

"He refuses to give up his morning constitutional. Oh, he can make my life tense at times!"

"I shall pray for your safety, and the tsar's."

"Thank you, Anna."

"I do not think he deserves such hatred from his subjects. I will not ever forget how gently he smiled at me the evening I saw him here in the palace."

Misha did not reply immediately, but paused in thought.

"Would you care to walk and talk a few moments, Anna?" he went on with resolve after a moment.

"That would be nice," Anna replied. "My mistress will not require me for an hour."

The Cossack lieutenant led her along the corridor, down a flight of stairs, and to one of the garden courtyards outside. It was the very place where Anna and Sergei had walked the night of the New Year's ball. Anna struggled against a shadow of melancholy that tried to rise at the recollection, reminding her how long it had been since she had seen Sergei.

She tried to smile cheerfully. "I have heard some say that winter is the only bearable season in St. Petersburg," she said.

"The summer is dreadfully hot and muggy. It is no secret to me why so many nobles make the mass exodus to the south. Winter probably is preferable to that."

"But the beginning of spring is so fresh and clean. This spring past was my third here, and I still felt a thrill of joy to stand on the English Quay and watch the chunks of ice bigger than buildings floating down the Neva."

" 'The Giant's Dawn,' " said Misha.

"Yes," smiled Anna. "The giant who sleeps under the ice all winter and then wakes up furious to find his home being destroyed."

"You are right—spring is a pleasant enough time. But you cannot like the summer!" laughed Lieutenant Grigorov. "In a few more weeks, you will remember—heat and dust and murky water . . . and cholera. It is enough to weary even a Cossack!"

"The family usually travels to their estate in the Crimea. So I have only spent the one summer here during the war. Princess Natalia wanted to remain close at hand for any reports. Her husband and son were both involved."

"Yes, I know. I fought next to Sergei Viktorovich."

"You did!" exclaimed Anna, an unexpected thrill surging

through her at the sound of Sergei's name.

"Prince Sergei saved my life."

"I had no idea!"

"That is how he received his wound. I am not surprised that he would keep that piece of information to himself. He is a good and brave man, and I am honored to be indebted to him. I owe him a great deal, though how a poor Cossack soldier could ever hope to repay a wealthy prince, I do not know."

Anna grinned with pleasure at hearing Sergei spoken of with such praise.

"I am glad to see you are so pleased my life was spared," laughed Misha. "Or perhaps this look of delight comes because your master's son acquitted himself so honorably on the battlefield."

"Well . . . both of course," replied Anna, flustered that her emotions were so transparent. "That is . . . they have been so very good to me. I am always pleased to hear a good report of the family that employs me."

"Ah yes, of course—I see."

They fell silent, walking and enjoying the fresh leaves and bright new shoots of green on the lime trees overhead. The breeze carried on its breath the tangy fragrance of the rushing river that flowed a stone's throw from where they walked.

"Just a month ago, the blossoms were still on the trees," said Misha at length.

"In our garden, too," replied Anna. "It was beautiful."

Again there was a long silence.

"I have greatly enjoyed this time with you, Anna," Misha said finally. He stopped walking, and as she paused next to him, he turned a keen gaze directly into her face. "Anna," he said, "perhaps the next time we meet it could be intentional, and not merely by chance?"

"I . . . I don't know what—"

"The warmth of early summer does suit you, Anna," he said, reaching up to finger one of her pale yellow curls. "The sunlight makes you glow. And if—"

Suddenly he broke off in mid-sentence and turned sharply away from her.

Bewildered over Misha's sudden amorous turn, Anna said nothing.

"It's no good!" he blurted out in a distressed tone. "I am sorry, Anna."

Perplexed, Anna stared mutely at the back of Misha's red tunic.

"You *are* lovely," he said after a moment, turning around to face her again. "But too lovely for me to try to use you in such a way. Please forgive me."

"You have me completely confused, Misha," she replied with an attempt at a smile. "I do not know what you are sorry about, nor what to forgive you for."

"Maybe that is my problem," he replied in a frustrated voice, half-turning and beginning to walk farther.

Anna followed.

"I have never known what to do around women," he went on. "But that is no excuse. You are too pure and innocent to realize what I was trying to do—and that makes it all the worse!"

He paused, then let out a sigh of self-disgust. "I had intended to try to seduce you, Anna, and make you fall in love with me. But there is nothing lower than a man who would use an innocent girl to make another woman jealous. Or worse, to try to affirm his own manhood! But it appears that is the kind of man I am. I am sorry; I deserve nothing but disdain!"

"I am still confused, Misha," replied Anna. "But whatever you did of wrong intent, you have repented of it now."

"I do not deserve to be let off so easily."

"You asked for my forgiveness, did you not? So there—I forgive you."

"You *are* the most wonderful girl I have ever known—leagues better than that self-seeking Countess Dubjago! I do not know why I think she will ever notice me."

"Now I think I understand," said Anna gently.

"You must think me a cad *and* a fool, to waste my affections on a woman who treats me like dirt. Oh, but there is nothing worse than loving someone who does not return your love."

"Unless it is when they *do* return your love," said Anna without thinking.

He stopped and glanced down at her with a puzzled expression.

"I don't see how that could be. Why, it—"

He stopped all at once and looked at Anna intently, as if seeing her for the first time. Slowly a light seemed to dawn on his face.

"Anna, you speak of yourself when you say those words, do you not?"

Anna could say nothing. She had blurted out the careless words and could not undo them. Her cheeks began to flame.

"I have been so wrapped up in my own troubles, I hardly considered you," he went on, still gazing down at her. "Still, I don't see how such a thing could be, unless—"

He stopped himself short again, a look of dawning revelation gradually spreading over his face.

"Of course. Now it is all clear . . . your face lit up when I spoke of him. That could be none other than a look of love. It is Prince Sergei, isn't it, Anna?"

Denials were useless, and she knew it. She nodded mutely.

"He loves you, but of course it would ruin him to marry a mere servant."

Anna did not want to try to explain that their love had gone beyond the boundaries of class and position, and that her present heartache came from his mere absence. Still she did not speak.

"And you are an honorable girl," he went on, "and so remain silent. Poor, dear Anna! I've heard it said that 'love kills happiness and happiness kills love.' It must be true."

They walked on a few more paces.

"I would give anything to be finished with that woman," he exclaimed at length. "But when I see her I get crazy inside. I will never be happy with her, yet I cannot bear to be separated from her. Love is nothing but a fool's path!"

"In my English lessons I read an author named Thackeray who said, 'It is best to love wisely, no doubt; but to love foolishly is better than not to be able to love at all.' "

"He surely must not have been acquainted with Countess Dubjago!"

Anna smiled. "I would not trade the short time I was able to enjoy with my mistress's brother for anything. Not even to be free of the pain of loss I now feel."

"You are remarkable, Anna. I am glad to be able to count you a friend—I *may* count you as a friend?"

"Yes, Misha! I am honored that you consider me one," Anna replied. After a brief pause, she added, "I think it is no coincidence that we have encountered each other as we have. And I am glad you know my secret. I have longed for a friend to share it with."

"I wish I could do more to help you."

"Just listening can be a great help sometimes."

"When is Prince Sergei due to return to the city?"

Anna's downcast face gave Misha his answer well enough. "No one knows," she replied slowly. "Of course he cannot write to me personally, and what I gather from the family is scant enough. They hear only sporadically themselves. No one knows even where he is for certain. I know he must be struggling under dreadful burdens left over from the war. He said before he left that he hoped to finish his book—he is writing of his wartime experiences, did you know?"

"No, I had no idea."

"Yes, and he had high hopes for completing it soon. But no one in the family mentions a word of his writing. I fear perhaps there are more things on his mind, keeping him from his book . . . *and* keeping him away."

"I am sorry to hear this, Anna."

She smiled faintly at his kind words.

"It must be terribly hard for you, not knowing, and hearing nothing from him," Misha continued.

"Yes, but for one in my position I can expect nothing more. It is enough to be loved by so fine a man, much less a prince. It is more than I deserve, even if I never hear from him again."

"Do not say such words, Anna. He will come back. And if he is the same Sergei Viktorovich I knew on the battlefield, a man of honor, he will come back loving you just as strongly as ever."

Again she smiled. "I would like to think you are right, Misha."

"As for me," he sighed, "I ought to just forget the countess altogether. I don't know why I don't face reality. . . to preserve my sanity! But I suppose I am not as brave in matters of love as you, Anna."

"Or as foolishly hopeless?"

Misha chuckled lightly. "A good pair we make, you and I, Anna Yevnovna! Star-crossed lovers and all that. We must talk again and commiserate our woes together! But now I must return to my duties."

"And I shortly to my mistress."

They returned to the palace slowly, neither in a hurry and both feeling lighter and refreshed. Finding a friend to help carry a portion of the load, if only by lending a listening ear, brought great relief.

Anna would never have imagined the Cossack lieutenant as a confidant. Yet in a way it seemed fitting. Perhaps God had allowed Sergei to save Misha's life at least partially for her sake.

12

Even more of St. Petersburg's citizens planned to leave the city in the summer of 1879 than usual, not only to escape the stifling climate, but also because terrorist activity had risen to new levels. On principle, Viktor Fedorcenko decided to cancel his family's usual sojourn to the Crimea. He would not bow to fear from radicals.

His daughter, therefore, prepared herself to endure a rather boring summer, broken only by periodic visits from Dr. Anickin's son—visits that she more than welcomed. On one such occasion in early summer, Katrina and Basil had taken a steamer down the Neva to the St. Petersburg Summer Gardens.

It was a rather pedestrian way to travel, at least from Katrina's point of view. When she wanted to sail up or down the Neva, which in good weather was always the preferred mode of transport, she always had the family yacht at her convenience.

But she was learning that Basil Pyotrovich Anickin was, as Nicholas Osminkin had noted, a man with certain peculiarities. His attitude toward wealth, and especially toward the well-to-do who possessed it, was definite. He found the least hint of ostentation completely distasteful and squirmed with awkwardness when in the midst of any such show, refusing absolutely to participate in anything of the kind himself.

The day was a fine one, the air crisp and clean and fresh against Katrina's face. After they had embarked, they went inside the salon, where generally a better class of passengers who could afford a higher priced ticket congregated. She glanced out the window to the port deck, where Anna stood at the rail enjoying the brisk rush of wind and occasional spray of water shooting in a fine mist high over the bow. She took little notice of the people around her maid, the working-class men and women clothed in coarse garments. Katrina easily forgot that her Anna was part of that peasant class herself, and sometimes probably felt more comfortable with such people than she did mingling with the aristocracy of the Russian capital.

Katrina turned her attention back to Basil. Besides several visits to the Fedorcenko home, this was only the second time they had been out together, and the first time without either her mother or father.

She smiled when she caught him gazing at her. He seemed

forever studying her face, and she found it both delightful and disconcerting at the same time. He was certainly handsome, in a serious, studious sort of way—perhaps even as good-looking as Dmitri. But she could see why he did not have women hovering ever around him as Dmitri did. Basil Pyotrovich could be a bit too extreme in his serious, even fierce intensity. Katrina had rarely seen him laugh. He was not the sort of man you had a *good time* with, as you might with Dmitri. Yet at the same time, there remained a definite allure to his mysterious depth and hidden passion.

"This is really rather nice," she sighed, "even though a bit crowded."

"You are so sheltered, Katrina Viktorovna," said Basil. "You live in your gilded palace, drive about in your ebony carriage from one place to another upon the broad, fair streets. You know nothing of the true world, of the real *Russia*! You think that by taking the steamer you are mingling with the lower classes, although you sit in the clean, dry salon seeing them only through a pane of dusty glass. And at that, those you see are the fortunate ones who can afford a few kopecks for the luxury of a steamer ride."

"Are you saying I am a snob, Basil Pyotrovich?" Katrina asked with mock indignation.

His lips twitched upward into something like a smile, at least as much of a smile as she was likely to elicit from the brooding young man.

"Yes, you are, Katrina," he said softly, gently, with more regret than accusation. "These people you see here are not the *real* peasants. They are wealthy compared to many in the country, and even many in the lower quarters of St. Petersburg itself."

"Then why do you bother with me?"

"Why indeed. . . ?"

His voice trailed off wistfully, and he looked away, perhaps pondering the same question he had already pondered more than once before now.

"Because when I first saw you," he continued finally, turning back to rest his eyes upon her, "my heart stirred so within me that everything logical seemed to crumble. I could think of nothing but meeting you. I wanted to be near you. When you approached me that night . . . I ceased to care what anyone might think."

"Why should anyone *think* anything, Basil?" she asked, bewildered. "You are from a good family that is well respected. You would make a good match for any young woman of my position."

"Would I?" Something sharp and cold suddenly intruded into his tone.

"Oh, Basil, I didn't mean it like that. I only meant—"

"I know what you meant," he replied more mildly. "How can you possibly know any better? As I said, your experience is so limited, Katrina. Perhaps that is one of the reasons I am so fascinated with you. Oh, how I would like you to see things as I see them!"

"Tell me how you see them, Basil."

"Do you really want to know?" he asked, eyeing her intently.

"Yes. I would like to understand you better."

"Did you know my father is an ex-serf?"

"He has been my father's physician for years, as I understand it. But, no, I did not know that. No one has ever mentioned it."

"And no wonder!" Young Anickin's tone was noticeably bitter. "It is hardly the background to be proud of."

"How did he come to his present position?"

"He was orphaned at a young age, and a benevolent master, no doubt seeing promise in him, took him into the estate house where he was raised practically alongside the master's own children. He was given a university education, reading for medicine. He completed his studies with high honors."

"You must be proud of him," said Katrina.

"Proud? Bah! I despise everything he stands for!" returned Basil with shocking candor.

Katrina's mouth gaped open, and she stared mutely at the doctor's son. She didn't know whether she was jarred more by his words or by the way his demeanor had so suddenly changed from seeming sincerity to cutting disdain. Instinctively she recoiled.

"This is what you must understand," he continued, the chilling expression moderating somewhat, as if he were shutting a restless ghost into a closet with great effort. "My father rose from the lowest ranks to attain great position in society. Yet he has never felt the obligation to return some of the benefit of his good fortune to his own people at the bottom of the social ladder. He has at his disposal the means to relieve great suffering among the poor and helpless of our country. But instead he sells his abilities to the rich and pampered."

"The rich need doctors too, Basil."

"He had an obligation to fulfill. But he chose to sell it for material gain!"

"I think you are being too hard on him."

"Do you truly think his life's mission could be to relieve the downtrodden *aristocratic* masses? You are naive, Katrina, if you think that."

"If I listened to you, Basil, I could be insulted at the way you speak. *I* am an aristocrat, you know."

"I am not likely to forget it," replied Basil. "But I am talking about larger things than merely my father's relationship to your family."

"Is that why you defend peasants and revolutionaries?" Katrina asked.

"Do you think there is a better reason?"

Katrina shrugged.

"I want my life to *count* for some higher purpose than my father's."

"Are you . . . ," Katrina began, then swallowed, finding the next words difficult to voice. "Are you in sympathy with those you defend?"

"Katrina Viktorovna," Basil replied in a soothing tone, "when I am with you, is it not enough that I am a man—a man whose heart contracts at the mere *thought* of you? Is it not enough that you are here with me alone, and that I—"

He reached out a trembling hand and laid it over hers. "That is enough to make me forget all else. When I am with you, it is a haven for me—a refuge from reality. You have touched something within me . . . perhaps a chord of feeling that needed to be touched."

He was about to go on, but just then the steamer lurched slightly as it approached the landing. Katrina turned to watch out the window, and Basil said no more. In a few minutes they were docked at the Summer Gardens, with all the passengers stirring and jostling about. A moment later, Anna came in to see if she could help in the debarking.

Katrina found herself relieved by the interruption. She didn't understand half of what Basil said when he began talking about his ideas, but his passion stirred her in many different directions. Her heart beat wildly when he touched her. But her head began to throb also. She found herself confused, and she made sure Anna remained close by during the remainder of the afternoon.

13

That same evening was scheduled the long-awaited engagement party between Dmitri Remizov and Alice Nabatov. The celebration would be held at the home of Princess Marya Gudosnikov. Katrina had invited Basil to accompany her family to the festivities.

Her thoughts had been greatly occupied over the last few weeks with the person of Basil Pyotrovich Anickin. Yet even Katrina at her most superficial had to admit to herself that the infatuation was mostly a mental diversion. It provided her a way of ignoring, and thereby not coming to terms with, the heartbreaking fact of Dmitri's engagement. Under the positive influences of Anna, Katrina had become far less self-absorbed than in her younger years. But where Dmitri was concerned, it seemed she could not easily shake her old ways. Too much of her old selfish ego was wrapped up in Dmitri's rejection, and perhaps for this reason it was just too difficult to accept the reality of Alice becoming his wife.

She could easily have developed a raging headache by the time evening came, and thus avoided what was sure to be a painful experience. But she couldn't give it up so easily. Still a fighter at heart, she kept telling herself—if only on a subconscious level—that a person wasn't dead until he breathed his last. In her desperate analysis, Dmitri might still have a few more breaths left in his lungs.

She swept into Princess Gudosnikov's drawing room, her arm firmly hooked around Basil's, with a flash of triumph in her eye. She shrugged off her father's disapprovingly raised eyebrow and threw herself into the party. She danced and laughed and made over Basil with a syrupy show of affection. By ten in the evening she was exhausted and *did* have a headache, although she refused to give any outward indication of her discomfort.

When Basil and two or three men squared off at the refreshment table with talk of politics, Katrina took advantage of the moment to excuse herself. After a visit to an adjoining room set aside for the ladies, she thought that a few moments of fresh air would be all she needed to restore her vitality and ease the throbbing of her temples. She wandered alone outside onto the balcony that overlooked the garden. She stood, hands on the marble railing, looking out over the darkness dotted with lanterns here and there through the expansive garden. She breathed in deeply of the fresh night air, gradually beginning to feel somewhat rejuvenated. The stars shone brightly, the moon was full, and the breeze wafting through was both cool and subtle. It was indeed a perfect night.

"Katrina," said an unmistakable voice behind her, "I had hoped I might find you out here."

Her whole body suddenly contracted with an irrepressible

thrill of excitement. She turned. There stood Dmitri, only five feet from her!

Her first thought was of the kiss she had given him over two years ago at the New Year's ball. She had been kissed by others since. But none stirred her heart so much as that first kiss she had given the soldier she had loved so persistently.

Desire for him swept over her again as she saw him standing there, so close . . . and alone. It was no longer the fancy of a fifteen-year-old girl, but the longing of a near-grown woman. She knew she had to shake it away. She would not make a fool of herself again! But the smile he flashed upon her as she turned to face him nearly dissolved all her efforts at self-control.

"Dmitri," she faltered, "you . . . you were looking for me?"

He ignored her question, whether by design or not was difficult to tell. "Have the years seemed as long to you as they have to me?" he asked in an uncharacteristically philosophical tone. Katrina stood, facing him, trying to take in the sudden shock of seeing him, willing her fluttering heart to be still, attempting to figure out whether he was speaking words of love or just waxing vaguely eloquent. Was he *really* saying that he had missed her and had longed for her?

"I feel as if I have been away forever," he went on, not waiting for an answer. "It seems that the world has hurried past, and that I must race to catch up with it. I have never felt like this; I have always been the one that everyone *else* is trying to catch up with!"

He turned suddenly, threw his hands in the air, and laughed loudly. It was almost his old reckless laugh. Almost, but not quite. His whole character was so much like the former Dmitri, yet subtly altered.

"Do I sound bizarre, Katrina?" he said, still laughing. "I am going on like some intellectual rambler, like—"

He stopped himself short. When he spoke again his laughter had stopped, and he went on with greater solemnity. "Well, perhaps like Sergei," he said. "Only with him, it is all natural and right. The philosophical suits him somehow. With me . . ."

He looked intently at Katrina, then took to slowly ambling

about the balcony. "I don't know. It must be the residual effects of my exile," he sighed. "There is so little to do in Siberia. Nothing but think . . . think . . . think. That was the worst of it, I suppose. Worse even than the cold and isolation."

Katrina had by now gathered in her own emotions and was able to carry on the conversation without revealing her disappointment that he apparently had different intentions than she had hoped.

"It must have been terrible, Dmitri," she said. The sympathy in her voice was real and unaffected.

"No worse than the results, I suppose. Look at me—I've become a melancholy fool!"

He chuckled again, this time with more enthusiasm. "Maybe part of this ghastly turn in my character has to do with my future as well as my past. You know, the fearsome prospect of 'settling down.' "

"As I recall," Katrina said, turning her face away and pretending to gaze down upon the garden, "you once told me that a man's freedom was too precious to waste on marriage." She could not bear to face him when discussing so painful a subject as *his* marriage.

"Yes, I seem to recall something of the sort. Didn't I say something to the effect that I would never marry unless I found—"

He broke off. But since Katrina was standing with her back toward him she did not see the distress that flickered momentarily across his face.

Katrina reached back in her memory of that evening in the Winter Palace. It was not difficult to recall the words that he could not, or *would not*, finish. She had never forgotten them. He had said that he would never marry unless he found someone as special as she. Katrina had tried to take his words as a lighthearted jest, but they had remained permanently lodged in her brain. The tone in his voice did not ring with jesting now.

She turned sharply to face him. A hint of melancholy remained upon his face. What she ought to make of it she did not know. But before she could reply and finish the sentence for him, Dmitri started up in a new vein.

"The hardships of war and exile have a way of changing a young man's priorities, I suppose," he said. His voice sounded harder than usual. "*Life* has a way of intruding upon youthful fancies."

"Dmitri! You sound like an old man taking stock of a long and futile life!"

"I told you, this philosophical bent is contrary to my nature."

"Then, for heaven's sake, give it up! You act as if you had decided to stop living."

"Oh, I'm sure I'll be my old self again," he said lamely, "when these prenuptial jitters wear off."

"And when will that be?" Katrina's voice shook. "I mean . . . when are the marriage plans?"

"In a few months, after my enlistment ends."

"That long?" She could hardly contain the relief she felt. She had feared the wedding would be sooner. But Dmitri took her words wrong.

"So, Katrina, you'd like to get rid of me sooner?" He forced a grin and raised his eyebrows in question.

"No, that's not what I meant. I mean . . . there is time—time to get used to the idea of marriage. For *you* to get accustomed to it, I mean."

"I know what you mean," he replied, "and you are right. There is time. . . ."

He paused thoughtfully. Suddenly he took two large steps forward, grabbed Katrina's hand, and led her to a nearby bench. "Sit down with me for a minute, Katrina. I want to talk to you."

Her heart pounding in spite of herself, Katrina sank down onto the seat. When Dmitri took his place next to her, his arm touching her side, his nearness was almost more than she could stand. With desperation she tried to keep herself controlled, yet she feared her uneasiness was all too obvious.

"Katrina," he began after a moment in a tender, caring tone—not exactly patronizing, but more brotherly than she would have wished for. "A long time ago we pledged our friendship to each other. Do you remember?"

"I will never forget."

"Then please take what I am about to say in the spirit of that pledge, as an older brother speaking to a beloved younger sister. I only wish to protect you. With Sergei gone, I feel inclined to take his part for you. I know you never much appreciated being treated in such a manner. But it is important you understand I have nothing but your best welfare in mind."

"I am older myself now, Dmitri. What do you have to say?"

"Everyone in St. Petersburg is talking about your recent . . . friendship with Basil Anickin."

"Yes?"

"I know I don't have much room to talk. Heaven knows my own reputation has never been the most sterling. But perhaps for that very reason I might be most qualified to express my reservations about Basil Pyotrovich. It takes one to know one, and all that."

"I'm not sure I understand you exactly, Dmitri."

"I'll put it as simply as I can. The doctor's son is the kind of man you would be wise to avoid, Katrina. If he were merely a fool or a scoundrel, it might not be so bad. But I fear his problems go deeper than that."

Katrina was silent. Blood was beginning to rise into her cheeks, and this time it was not from Dmitri's proximity.

"Do you know why he left St. Petersburg?"

"Something to do with dismissal from the university," Katrina replied without enthusiasm.

"*Something*, indeed . . . something serious."

"I refuse to listen to gossip-mongers."

"This is not gossip, Katrina. This is fact. And it is not related to his years in the university. He managed to complete his studies in Moscow without incident, at least nothing to my knowledge. He has been practicing law there and, though there have been rumors—yes, and gossip—about his activities, I relate only what I have heard from an exemplary source. He was appearing in court for a client, a young man accused of printing seditious propaganda. While the prosecution was making its closing remarks, Basil flew into a rage—the man from whom I heard about it described it as a 'blind rage'—"

"I don't believe a word of it," interrupted Katrina.

"Basil attacked the prosecuting lawyer, Katrina, bodily attacked him! He did the man some fairly serious injury. It took three men to remove him. The lawyer he attacked was hospitalized with a fractured collar bone."

"He is a man of deep convictions," said Katrina. "Some might admire that in a man."

"Katrina, don't blind yourself. I saw him myself—several years ago while he was still a student at the university here. It was a friendly boxing match, but it soon turned into a blood bath. Basil pummeled the man senseless. And without the slightest provocation."

"He is so slender and soft-spoken—"

"He is a violent man, Katrina. I fear for you if you continue to pursue this friendship with him."

"I just cannot believe a word of this!"

"I tell you, it is true."

"He has been nothing but a complete gentleman toward me; kind and considerate. I admit he sometimes becomes passionate when speaking of his ideals. But I have seen the same trait in Sergei."

"The two cannot in any way be compared. Look deeply into Basil Pyotrovich's eyes, Katrina. Then try to compare him to your brother."

Again Katrina was silent. She *had* looked into Basil's eyes, but she did not want to be reminded of that now—especially by Dmitri.

Unless . . . was it possible that Dmitri had his own personal motives for speaking thus about Basil? It couldn't be. She had been disappointed so many times already. Still . . . he *had* come outside, apparently in search of her!

She lifted her head and turned to face Dmitri with renewed hope shining out of her own eyes.

"Dmitri," she said softly, "*why* do you want to protect me from Basil?"

"I told you, because I pledged my friendship, as a brother."

"Is that all?"

"I'm afraid I don't understand you. Isn't that enough?"

"I only thought that . . . well . . . you seem uneasy and uncertain about your engagement with Alice . . . and I thought that perhaps your words so long ago had caused you to reconsider—"

At last the truth began to dawn on Dmitri, and he saw that she had misunderstood him.

"Katrina, please," he said. "Don't make this more difficult than it is. There is *nothing* on my mind but trying to keep you from an unfortunate relationship that is doomed to bring you pain."

His emphasis on the word *nothing* made his meaning clear to Katrina in an instant.

"Well, you must have had some ulterior motive for attempting to defame Basil's character!" she shot back heatedly, trying to hide her chagrin at letting her feelings for him show once again.

Dmitri stood and turned on her, his eyes flashing.

"I have nothing in mind but concern for your best," he said in a measured but clearly intense tone. "I almost thought, Katrina, that you had outgrown your petty attitudes of the past. I came to you as a friend, and as a friend of your brother, and you repay me by accusing me of such low motive."

Katrina hesitated a moment. When she found her voice, her tone was caustic and sharp.

"Such friendship I don't need! Do you see me trying to spoil your happiness with Alice Nabatov?"

A confused expression crossed Dmitri's face. His simple words reflected it. "How could you?" he said.

The words hit Katrina like a blow. How indeed? Once again she suddenly realized she had been duped into all kinds of foolish and childish notions—thinking Dmitri was harboring doubts about his marriage, thinking that he had wanted her free of Basil and thus available for him.

How could she have been such a fool? Why had she done this to herself—again? Why couldn't she simply wash her hands of this man and forget he existed?

When she spoke again, she did not even make any attempt to conceal her bitterness.

"Spoil your happiness, Dmitri? That is the last thing I would want to do! I wish you every happiness in your marriage to Alice Nabatov—as I hope you wish me in mine to Basil!"

"You cannot intend to marry him, Katrina. You can't!"

"Who are *you* to tell me what I can't do? I will do what I please!"

"Katrina, please listen to reason."

"Reason? You are not my brother, nor my father, and I most certainly do not have to listen to you!" She jumped off the bench with a haughty flip of her silken black hair.

As she walked defiantly back toward the ballroom, he laid a restraining hand on her arm. She twisted and tried to turn away. "Sergei always said you were stubborn," he said, "but I never imagined just how bad it was. Katrina, do not ruin your life like this!"

"You have no part in my life, Dmitri Gregorovich!" she replied coldly. "Go to your fiancee—that's where you belong—and keep your advice and opinions to yourself!"

He took in a sharp breath, his emotion—whether it was anger or merely frustration—barely under control. "Have it your way, Katrina," he said, releasing his hand from her arm. "I have done my duty."

"Your *duty* . . . your duty!" she blustered, unable to utter anything further in the fury of her indignation. It took her several more moments to get out the next words, but when she did they were hardly ones to be misunderstood. "Leave me alone, Dmitri! I never want to see you again!"

Dmitri swallowed any further response, then turned on his heels to go back inside the house. He had not taken a full stride, however, when he unexpectedly found himself face-to-face with none other than the object of their altercation, Basil Anickin. Still Dmitri remained silent, then stepped aside and continued on, glaring at the doctor's son as he strode past him.

Basil rushed immediately to Katrina.

"What is wrong?" he asked. "Is there some problem with Count Remizov?"

"I never want to hear that name again!" she cried.

"Did he wrong you in some way?" The question was accompanied by a dark flash of his eyes. When Katrina did not reply, the look became darker still. "He shall pay." He turned and would have gone after Dmitri that instant had Katrina not clutched at his arm.

"No, wait . . . ," she said. In spite of herself, Katrina would have then believed Dmitri's slanderous words if she had allowed herself to. She shook the notion from her mind, yet still did not want to see Dmitri exposed to any danger.

"Forget about him, Basil," she added. "He's not worth the bother. Come, sit down beside me. I need company just now."

The muscles in his face and neck remained taut. Almost reluctantly, it seemed, he retreated to the bench and took a seat beside her. He glanced toward the French doors, where he could still see Dmitri on the other side of the glass shouldering his way back through the crowd of guests.

"Tell me what happened out here, Katrina," he said sharply. "What is Dmitri Remizov to you?"

If Katrina caught the note of jealousy in Basil's voice, she was more flattered by it than wary.

"Oh, he only thinks that with Sergei gone, he must take my brother's place. You know, bossing me around, giving me advice, telling me what to do . . . I hate it!"

"That is all?"

"Basil, you don't think. . . ?" she completed the unfinished sentence with a coy giggle instead of words. Having another man who loved her quickly restored the emotional balance of her girlish pride.

"What was he telling you?"

"Nothing. He just . . ."

He read more than was pleasant in her hesitation.

"Tell me, Katrina," he said, almost sternly.

"He was only repeating idiotic, vicious gossip. It's nothing really. I refuse to listen to it."

Basil reflected a moment.

"He was speaking of me, wasn't he?"

"Rumors . . . silly gossip. I tell you, I did not listen to a word of it."

"What did he say?"

"Honestly, Basil, it is not worth repeating."

"Did you believe him?"

"Well, I—"

He did not give her the chance to finish.

"They will say anything about a man," he broke in. "They will never give him peace. One man might err and they forget, but let another whom they have labeled with their malicious lies, and they continually throw it back in his face!"

"I did not listen to a word of it, Basil," she repeated, trying to calm him.

"I only want peace," he went on, still heatedly, "and the freedom to be myself and pursue my ideals. But they hound me until I become what they say I am. Is this fair? Is this right?"

As he spoke, his eyes were wide with a strange mingling of pleading and accusation. His voice trembled over the words.

"Katrina, I am a man of peace. Yet I must survive in a world that hates me, a world that would squash the very life from my soul if it could. It is important to me that you understand, Katrina. Do you?"

She only nodded, unable to form any appropriate response to his speech. In her heart of hearts she knew she *didn't* understand everything he was talking about . . . and wasn't sure she wanted to.

He turned toward her, laid his hands on her shoulders and drew her forcefully toward him. "Katrina, dear," he said. "There was a time when I believed that the love of a woman could never be for me. I thought I was called to a higher plane of existence, although there were times when I yearned for the touch of a woman, for a soft feminine voice to entreat me. But now everything has changed. When I looked at you the night of your birthday, I felt a deep yearning. And when you returned my gaze, I thought perhaps I could have both worlds after all."

He paused, still gazing intently into her eyes, though Katrina could not keep from looking slightly to one side. Sometimes his gaze was *too* powerful.

"I need you, Katrina!" he went on.

As he spoke, his hands gripped her shoulders harder and

harder until she felt as if a lead weight were pressing upon her. The very air from her lungs seemed forced from her, and she could hardly breathe. She felt as if she had to say something, that to remain silent might even be dangerous. Basil, however, continued to pour himself out.

"I love you as I never thought I could love another human being," he said. "Tell me you feel the same."

Katrina had never before felt the force of a man's passion. She had no inner measuring rod to help her discern the levels and types of passion. She had never experienced, for example, the kind of tender passion her brother felt for Anna. To Katrina's limited view, passion and force and love must all be somehow interrelated. She had *heard* one or two things that kept her from total ignorance in the matter of love. Her natural instincts cautioned restraint. She chose, however, to ignore them.

She ignored, too, the pain caused by the pressure of Basil's hands. She was being held by a man—held as Dmitri had never held her, as he had never touched her. Their only kiss was one *she* had stolen from him! His arms and kisses were only for Alice Nabatov now! So why shouldn't *she* have a man who felt for her as she had only foolishly dreamed Dmitri would feel? Basil was real. His love was real. His passion was real! Her feelings for Dmitri were nothing but a childish fantasy.

Her hesitation lasted only a second or two, then she turned and fixed her gaze directly on him and melted into his embrace. As she did so, the powerful grip of his hands eased.

"Oh, Basil," she murmured, "how I have longed to hear those words."

"Then you *do* love me!"

"I want you, Basil, that is all I know. I want you always."

14

As the fine summer evening deepened into night, a fog drifted in upon the city from the Neva. Wraithlike, it clung to the cobbled streets and sidewalks and wove through the alleys, so that a man venturing out at that late hour appeared like some grotesque caricature from a dream, his hands and feet shrouded in the mist.

Basil Anickin, leaving the Fedorcenko's family at their home after the party, had availed himself of the offer of their coach and had the driver take him to a tea shop on Nevsky Prospect. There he thanked the driver, entered the building, waited until the coach had driven from sight, and then exited again. He walked the remainder of the distance to his true destination.

He stood in the shadows across the street from the barracks of the Royal Guard. Ignoring the mist and the cold, he waited.

He should have felt ecstatic over Katrina's declaration. And to be sure, he did feel a certain euphoria that the beautiful daughter of the powerful Fedorcenko clan should want *him*.

The moment he had laid eyes on her he realized he wanted her more than his very soul. In fact, some of his acquaintances would accuse him of *selling* his soul for the sake of this aristocratic woman. And he could not help despising himself for it. But the passion, the love he felt could not be denied or ignored. He *would* have Katrina Fedorcenko, and he would *not* sacrifice his only other passion—the destruction of the hated Romanov regime and the government it fostered.

But whatever elation Basil Anickin might have felt at Katrina's avowal of love was dulled by the nagging interference of one man.

Scant though his experience may have been in matters of the heart, Basil was nobody's fool. He had seen Katrina's eyes stray to Count Remizov whenever he was present. The night of her coming out, he had noticed her eyes scanning the crowd, and he had seen the light in them when they fell on the count!

A more secure man might not have given such trivialities a second thought. Her attentiveness should have been satisfying enough.

But Basil was no such man. Katrina's hidden glances in the count's direction had disturbed and nagged at him. And the scene he had witnessed in the garden tonight added fuel to the fires of his passion. True, he had caught only the tail end of their conversation. But if it was not a lover's quarrel, it was something very close. When he had come upon Dmitri unexpectedly, he saw the unguarded look in the count's eyes—the look of pain that comes only from love. Basil had worn such a look himself a time or two.

Whether Katrina denied it or not, Count Remizov stood in the way of whatever Basil and Katrina might have together. And thus, Remizov must be dealt with.

Basil knew Dmitri by reputation only, for the count traveled in different circles and lived a different lifestyle than the intense young lawyer. In many ways Dmitri represented most of what Basil hated in life. His aristocracy, his social connections, his military commitment tying him to the crown . . . and that was just on a political level.

On a more personal level, Count Remizov's winning, charismatic personality was in every way the antithesis of Basil's. His reputation with women ignited Basil's ire. Although the prestige of his family name, along with the family fortune, had waned considerably since his father's death several years ago, Dmitri had been counted as one of the most eligible and sought-after bachelors in St. Petersburg—that is, until his recent engagement. Basil knew Dmitri's type; his amorous ways would not be restrained by marriage.

And it infuriated Basil that this man, who could have a

dozen other women, would toy with the affections of the *one* woman Basil loved. He had barely been able to contain his seething rage when he had seen the two of them together that evening. It did not matter that moments later Katrina had declared her love for him. It did not matter that soon enough Remizov would be safely married to another. What mattered was that Basil's place in Katrina's heart be ever secure. He could never be sure of it as long as a rival such as Dmitri Remizov remained in the way.

As Basil stood within sight of the barracks, he pondered what benefit would come of a confrontation with the count. He had no solid idea, and, moreover, he had no idea what *kind* of confrontation this would in fact turn out to be. Would he kill Remizov? The idea was not altogether repugnant. He had killed before. But those incidents had been crimes of honor, or principle. Could he kill for passion, for jealousy? Motive hardly mattered if he became ruled by that inner demon of rage that sometimes overwhelmed him. He had also killed under the influence of that unpredictable creature.

More than likely it would be enough simply to thrash the count about a bit—to batter those good looks, and let him know how unwise it would be for him to pursue Princess Katrina in the future.

He rubbed his hands together, blew in them once or twice, and waited.

Basil was fairly certain he had arrived here before the count, for the Fedorcenkos had been among the first guests to depart. As guest of honor, it was not likely that Remizov would leave until the party was over. But if for some reason he missed the count tonight, there would definitely come another time.

The time went by slowly. Basil let his thoughts trail back to the ride home with the Fedorcenkos. He was certain Katrina had said nothing to her parents about the seriousness of their love. After their mutual pledge of this evening, marriage was the next natural step. He and Katrina would have to choose the most opportune time to make such an announcement to the prince and princess. He doubted they would greet the news with joy. Prince Fedorcenko had been obviously perturbed with his daughter during the coach ride to their home. The look in his eye said more than his few words, which he had likely restrained in deference to Basil's presence. One reference only had he made about his daughter's "brassy behavior." And it was not exactly an idle observation, for Katrina had been more than demonstrative during the evening, laughing and dancing almost wildly, and clinging to Basil in a fashion that, had he not been the delighted object of her attention, would have raised even his own eyebrows.

Basil knew Prince Fedorcenko would not be quick to give willing blessing to a proposed marriage between his daughter and Basil Anickin, regardless of his own esteem for his father the doctor. The man was an ex-serf, and that alone was far more than sufficient cause to oppose the union.

Fedorcenko, however, may well cease to be a force to be reckoned with at all, thought Basil with a grim smile. He was too close to the crown for his own good. Sooner or later he might well fall prey to the uncontrollable political forces now flooding through St. Petersburg. With both Remizov and Fedorcenko out of the way, there would be no one to stand in opposition to his future with the princess.

Suddenly the noise of an approaching coach echoed with a heavy dullness through the still night air. Iron wheels clattered over the cobbles accompanied by the creaking of leather and harness, an intrusion into the eerie, fog-shrouded night. As the carriage pulled to a stop in front of the barracks, Basil's heart began to pound wildly. Perspiration beaded on his forehead, and his palms grew damp.

His quarry had arrived . . . it was Remizov!

Dmitri Gregorovich was a symbol of all that inspired Basil Anickin's deepest hatred and passion. This aristocratic scion of injustice, of lust for power, of all that brought misery to Russia—such a man deserved to die! They all deserved to die!

Slowly Basil's lips parted in a smile. The idea brought intense pleasure—perhaps even more pleasure than the thought of resting in Katrina Fedorcenko's arms.

With difficulty he remained in his hiding place until the coach rattled away. He could almost *feel* the fool's arrogant neck strangling and collapsing beneath the strength of his fingers. Basil was a strong man, although his physical power was well hidden under the scholarly facade he presented to society. He could kill a man with his bare hands, and he knew it!

His mouth gone dry with anticipation, Basil began to step forward. But just as he did so, the door of the barracks flew open. Four soldiers, laughing and swaggering, trooped down the wooden steps with heavy feet.

"Remizov!" bellowed one. "We thought you would never show up."

"And why were you malcontents not at my engagement party, I would like to know?" Dmitri shouted up to them with mock consternation.

"We cannot stand wakes!" laughed another.

"Why you no-good, fair-weather friends!"

"We'll make it up to you by allowing you to join us for an evening at Dauphin's."

"*Allowing* me!" repeated Dmitri. "Ha, ha! The question is only if I will *grant* you the pleasure of *my* company!"

They all laughed and went on with their inane banter. Basil grimaced, retreating back into the shadows. He was a strong man, yes, but not against five trained soldiers.

"Come along then," said one of the soldiers. "But you must promise that now that you are tied down to one woman you will not be a wet blanket."

"On my honor," replied Dmitri.

"We want no lethargic dullards in our company."

"Anyway, I am not married yet!"

"Well said! We knew we could count on you, Remizov."

The banter and laughter continued as the group ambled down the street in search of a cab. Basil spat on the ground. He had been foiled, and he hated them all for it!

They were a shallow, self-absorbed, self-seeking lot. But one day they would all be repaid for their lust and arrogance!

In the meantime, Basil's present intent thwarted, he fell back limply against the brick wall. His emotions were spent, although he had actually *done* nothing. He mopped his brow with a handkerchief. He was disappointed, but not disheartened. His moment would yet come.

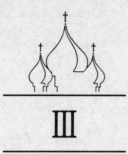

III

Our Rebel Brothers
(Summer 1879)

15

The meeting took place in Voronezh, a town four hundred fifty kilometers south of Moscow on a tributary of the Don. Here Peter the Great had first begun construction of his great navy almost two centuries earlier.

Paul Yevnovich Burenin marveled at his leader's ingenuity in getting them to Voronezh on limited funds. It had taken them nearly a week, traveling on fourth-class trains, on the back of farmers' carts, and finally on foot.

From the moment they arrived, however, Paul sensed that the effort was not in vain. He felt an energy in the air, an enthusiasm, a mounting force and fire. Those crowded into the dingy dockside apartment that served as a makeshift auditorium represented the core group of Russian revolutionaries. Kazan had hinted that this meeting would be momentous, that the most far-reaching decisions of their insurrectionist careers would be made here. And Paul could *feel* a vigor around him that confirmed the truth of those words.

He found himself surrounded by an odd assortment of characters. In actual fact, he was probably among the most peculiar himself, for there were few other peasants present beside himself. He had been introduced to a couple of working-class men, and a handful from the higher stratus of society and the nobility had come. But the group was comprised primarily of students and the *intelligentsia*, a term connoting not simply educated, thinking, progressive Russians, but extremists dedicated to the ideals of change—even, at the distant edges of the spectrum, to revolution.

Sophia Perovskaya, a pretty and petite young woman, was energetic and unswerving in her commitment to the purposes of the group. Her father had been a former Governor-General of St. Petersburg. Andrei Zhelyabov, a handsome, intelligent young man, had stumbled into the radical cause more by mischance than design. While pursuing his education, like so many it seemed these days, he ran afoul of Dmitri Tolstoy's administration by trying to help other students. Paul understood his motives particularly keenly, for he had wound up in this conclave of revolutionaries for precisely the same reason. And Alexander Mikhailov, rather a new face in the company, had already distinguished himself as an able leader, skilled in the conspiratorial aspects of underground activities.

One of the other prominent figures of this assembly Paul had not yet met. What Kazan had told him about this man gave Paul new understanding of the saying that politics make strange bedfellows. The tall, lanky fellow sat at the front with the others of the Executive Committee, his arms folded across his chest, his intense gaze turned strangely inward, as if decisions made here were a mere formality in a path that had been indelibly marked out for him long ago.

"There's Anickin," Kazan whispered to Paul. "The fellow I told you about . . . Basil Pyotrovich Anickin!"

This unlikely group formed one of the major forces advocating violent overthrow and change within Russia. They called their loose confederation Land and Liberty. And if numbers alone counted, they would not have amounted to much. The havoc thus far instigated throughout the land had been caused by a relative few, far less than many of the government officials imagined. They were much like David fighting against Goliath, but they had zeal, passion, and an almost frightening loyalty to their cause. These traits gave them utter confidence, even against a Goliath as ponderous as the great and mighty holy Russia.

In many ways Paul envied their single-minded devotion. He wondered if Perovskaya or Zhelyabov ever suffered from any of the same doubts and confusion he did. He did *not* wonder about Anickin, whose obsession was clearly written across his taut countenance.

Paul believed wholeheartedly in the concept of change, even radical change. But his loyalties became muddled in the question of how far to go in trying either to reform or to undo the Romanov regime. To some of those present, *any* means were justified in attaining the end goal. But Paul still felt that if the goal was a noble one, it must be realized only through noble means. From all Kazan had said, he had the feeling that today's meeting would be dominated by this very dilemma.

Kazan leaned toward Paul again, his eyes flashing eagerly at the prospect of what lay ahead. A steady buzz of several different conversations filled the room as the leaders awaited late arrivals.

"A confrontation is coming today, Pavushka, you can be sure of it," he said. "Look at Plekhanov and Axelrod. They are already gearing up for a fight. You can see the determination building on their faces. They refuse to condone the principle of terror. Propaganda and preaching to the peasants are a dead horse, yet they persist in beating it. Prepare yourself for several hours of debate."

"And what about you, Kazan?" asked Paul. "Are you still of the same mind as Zhelyabov and Perovskaya?"

Paul hardly needed to ask. He was fairly certain of the answer to his question. He and Kazan had discussed his mentor's advocacy of violence many, many times. Yet Paul still retained enough optimism to hope his older friend might one day come to moderate his views.

"You know where I stand," answered Kazan. "It is I who should be asking *you* that question."

"It is not easy to repudiate years of teaching."

"Progress means change, Pavushka."

"I have been taught that violence is wrong."

"In an ideal society, I would be the first to agree. But ours is far from ideal. And our oppressors force it upon themselves."

"Jesus himself taught us to turn the other cheek. My father taught me to respect authority." Paul sighed inwardly at the mention of his father, and the painful memories that even such a brief reference stirred. "I have long since given up that aspect of my childhood teaching," he went on, "but to go so much further as some of the things you would do . . ."

He merely shook his head to complete his unresolved di-lemma.

"If we all did what Jesus said, we'd still be laboring in serfdom, and worse! And where did it get Him? Nailed to a cross! I tell you, Pavushka, perhaps there is a cross out there for all of us if we don't strike back. Those mollycoddling teach-ings of the church have been almost as destructive as the tsar himself! They have bewitched the peasants and lulled them into apathy. Someone has to take *action!*"

"And that someone is us!" said someone seated nearby, and a couple of others within hearing applauded Kazan's impas-sioned words.

"You'd better save that for the meeting," someone laughed.

"Don't worry," returned Kazan jovially as he glanced over his shoulder, "there is more where that came from!"

Turning back to Paul, he added more quietly, "If my paltry words do not convince you, Paul, wait until you hear Mikhailov and Perovskaya. Their words will set the world on fire once they are heard, my friend. You will have a rare opportunity to hear rhetoric at its finest. I doubt you will leave here the same young man."

Paul sat back and prepared to listen. It was the least he could do.

Perhaps he would change. He had no way to predict what he would think in the future. He had changed so much already that the simple peasant lad he had once been was now a stran-ger to him. What would a little more change matter?

Only as the meeting progressed did he begin to discover the answer to that very significant question.

16

The meeting opened with colorless preliminaries. But before long, the organizers launched into the primary reason the conclave had been summoned: to debate the direction they should take in the immediate future.

"It is the duty of the Land and Liberty Party," began Zhelyabov in his stoic manner, "to do as much as it can. If it has sufficient strength to overthrow the despot by means of an insurrection, it must do so; if it has sufficient strength to punish him personally, it must do that; if its strength is not even sufficient for that, it must at least loudly protest. But our strength is unquestionably sufficient, and the more decidedly we act, the more it will grow."

"What does all that mean in simple terms?" asked a man who was identified with the more moderate camp among those present.

"It means," put in Sophia Perovskaya firmly, "that we intend to make the imminent disposal of the tsar our *immediate* and *sole* focus!"

An excited murmur rippled through the gathering.

"This must be put to a vote!" cried a voice from the audience.

"Down with the tsar!" shouted another.

"The monster must die!"

"Must we become monsters, too?"

Suddenly the shouts and accusations began shooting back and forth, filling the room. Zhelyabov stepped forward and finally was able to restore silence.

"There are many arguments on both sides," he said, "but they have all been voiced already. We have long known that what Sophia has outlined is the inevitable path we must follow. No lasting reform can come while the Romanovs remain in power. The people, in their ignorance, are too closely bound to him. We must act on behalf of the peasant masses."

"Think of it," said a fellow Paul knew only as Ivan. "Only we can give them what they need—a constitution and a National Assembly. Only *we* can provide what they lack the heart to get for themselves."

"When the tsar is dead, we will see to it that the blame is laid on the landowners!"

"Then the peasants will eagerly follow."

"Mass social uprising is the only way to topple St. Petersburg!"

"When the peasants see our power, our strength," added another, "and the willingness and ability to strike such a blow at the very pinnacle of the corrupt government, they will gladly accept our leadership."

"This is all madness!" cried Boris Filkin, one of the leading moderates. "The crime of tsaricide as *systematic, organized* terror is unheard of . . . unthinkable!"

Kazan stood up to answer him.

"We did not invent the idea, Filkin," he said. "The government came up with the solution of tsaricide long before any of us. Some of you may recall our beloved Herzen's response to the trial of Karakozov after his attempt on the tsar in 1866. He challenged the tsar's hangman, Muraviev, on this very subject when the scoundrel attempted to implicate, and thus condemn, the whole company of radicals."

Kazan paused, took up a pamphlet from a stack of papers he had laid out on the table, then glanced around the room to see if he held the attention of his listeners sufficiently to proceed. Judging from their looks that Herzen's words would be welcomed, he began to read.

" 'What is unheard of about tsaricide?' wrote Herzen. 'Only that the attempt on the tsar did not succeed. Is it possible that Muraviev's mouthpieces haven't heard of the murder of the

Tsarevich Dmitri in 1591? Or of the murder of Tsar Boris Go-
dunov and his son during the Time of Troubles in 1605? Or of
the murder of Peter III by the lovers of his wife, the esteemed
Catherine the Great? Or the murder of Ivan Antonovich by the
self-same fine lady? Or of the murder of Paul I, in 1801, by the
leading general with the participation of his "inconsolable"
son, Alexander I? And of the murder of the Tsarevich Aleksei
at the command of his most tender parent, Peter the Great?
Haven't Muraviev's defenders heard of the French saying about
an "autocracy limited by assassination"? That was our Magna
Carta. Poison, the knife, and the garrote—to this we must add
two more limitations upon power: bribes and filth.' "

"Hear, hear!" responded a chorus of enthusiastic voices.

"The government itself provides our example," added Kazan. "This is the only check and balance it gives us."

"Again I ask," countered Filkin, "do we become animals just
like our oppressors? Do we not stand for something nobler than
their barbarism?"

"By ridding the world of evil," answered Zhelyabov, "we are
not making ourselves into animals, but heroes! We defend right
and honor and freedom by eliminating the monsters."

"And where does it stop?" countered Filkin.

"When the end has been achieved."

"So you have finally espoused the philosophies of that de-
ceiver Nechaev?" Filkin spat out the name with disdain.

Paul had been only a child when Sergei Nechaev had
reached the heyday of his influence in militant circles. What
he knew about the man he had learned mostly from Kazan.
Nechaev epitomized the radical extremist. His charisma had
won—or deceived—many in the late 1860s and early 1870s. To
Nechaev, *everything* had to be subordinated to the revolutionary cause. And he believed any means was acceptable toward
that end. He stooped to recruiting followers by threatening to
expose them to the police, and thus "radicalizing" them by
coercion. He so beguiled the radical emigrant community in
Switzerland that he convinced the revered Bakunin to give him
a written statement supporting him as leader of the movement.
Even Herzen was nearly taken in, and much money from the

111

emigrant fund found its way into Nechaev's hands.

Finally, however, his philosophy led him to the inevitable consummation of violent men. He murdered a brother in the cause who had the effrontery to dispute his methods. Even such brutality was acceptable to Nechaev. He had declared, "The measure of friendship, devotion, and other duties with respect to such a comrade is defined solely by the degree of his usefulness in the cause of an all-destroying practical revolution." Here, however, the bulk of the movement parted ways with Nechaev, and he lost influence. In the end he was betrayed by a comrade and arrested.

"We have always repudiated Nechaev, and still do," rejoined Mikhailov. "His cold-blooded approach will always be abhorrent. To turn on a brother is beneath even the vilest crimes of our oppressors. But do we toss out the babushka with the bath? Nechaev was able to deceive because he so expertly blended truth and lies. We denounce the lies. But truth is truth, regardless of whose mouth utters it."

"And the truth is," added Sophia Perovskaya coolly, "that the tsar *must* die!"

More heated debate followed her cold, angry words.

After a lengthy discussion in which views on all sides continued to be freely exchanged, Plekhanov and Axelrod finally demanded a vote from the convocation.

"Nechaev preached unanimity and solidarity among revolutionaries," someone declared smugly. "Is that truth or lie?"

"You are not funny," Sophia shot back.

At this point in the proceedings Anickin seemed to rouse from his trance. His eyes became narrow with purpose and determination.

"You do not understand," he said, speaking for the first time. "All your arguments of moderation mean nothing. Vote or no vote, the primary agenda for Land and Liberty is the death of the tsar. We will not rest until that end is achieved!"

He glanced around at each of the faces of his adversaries as if challenging them. Paul shivered. It seemed that the ghost of Nechaev himself had come to Voronezh! As long as men like Anickin lived, no Romanov was safe. And perhaps neither were his brother rebels.

Axelrod jumped up. "You give us no choice. Continue on such a course, and we must inform!"

"Do you think even that will stop the hand of fate? Alexander II shall die. It is as much his destiny as it is ours to kill him."

Anickin's words took the wind out of the debate, but it did not halt it altogether. The rhetoric droned on for some time, although Paul sensed an air of futility entering into the arguments of the moderate opposition. Finally Axelrod and Plekhanov walked out of the meeting in protest. Several others followed. Someone called after them in derision, "Do what you must! We will serve the will of the people!"

"The people's will!" repeated several others. "We must serve the people's will!"

With the leading moderates gone, the final vote was anticlimactic. The few fence-riders left were fearful of countering the passionate insurrectionists, and the vote was unanimous.

The departure of the moderates dissolved the Land and Liberty Party. The remaining hard-liners, wanting an entirely fresh face for their new party, cast about for a name. They did not have to look far. Paul had thought the rallying cry shouted earlier had been a fine one—*The People's Will*. It caught the ear of others in the room as well, and thus the new organization, which would be dedicated solely to terrorism, dubbed itself The People's Will.

Yet Paul could not help wondering how accurate the name was. What "people" did it represent? Surely not the millions of Russian peasants who would have been both appalled and horrified at the mere thought of murdering their beloved "Little Father." Paul thought of his own father and mother. *They* would *never* consider themselves such "people."

But if the word *people* stood only for the handful of radicals left in that apartment in Voronezh, the phrase might be accurate. For their will in the end would be the only encouragement necessary to topple a centuries-old regime.

And where did Paul fit into this sinister organization? Did he stand with Kazan, who had become mentor and hero, friend and brother? He admired Boris Filkin, who was a kind and thoughtful man, a rational voice of reason in a sea of extremists. And he had to admit he envied at times the fire and vigor of some of the others.

Yet the final step in his mental evolution, his departure from all he had been taught to believe and respect—this final leap could come from nowhere but deep within his own soul.

The stakes of this dangerous enterprise required more of its members than a mere parroting of the philosophies of others. From within each individual heart must emerge the conviction that the agenda of The People's Will was indeed the only method to effect the change so desperately needed in their Motherland. Paul was closer than he ever thought he would be to such individuals. For as he had listened to the debates, the more he saw the lame reasoning and helpless futility of the moderates. What Zhelyabov and the others said made sense. The cherished goal was so high, so righteous, so imperative that it became necessary to reach it by *any* means possible.

As Paul mused quietly over these things, he happened to glance toward the solitary figure of Basil Anickin.

An involuntary chill shuddered through his frame. Was *this* the end of the violent road he was considering? Would they all become like this eerie man? Could Paul himself hope to maintain his essential self, regardless of the path he chose?

The answer would come soon enough. Events were careening along too quickly to allow a young man like Paul Burenin time for long meditation.

17

When he had accepted the appointment to the Imperial Advisory Conference at the outset of the violent wave of terrorism, Viktor Fedorcenko had hoped his moderate stance could have some positive influence on Alexander's increasingly conservative government. He hoped to rally many of the moderates like himself, and perhaps to sway some that were straddling the fence. He did not take into account the backlash of reaction that would soon sweep through the government.

It was nothing less than a panic.

The radicals wanted reform. And it was becoming clearer by the week that their violence would continue until they got it—or died in the effort. Instead of responding, the Imperial Conference only meted out more repression.

Viktor listened with growing concern to the present discussion among his colleagues at this morning's meeting. He was dismayed to find his moderate friend and ally Alex Baklanov suddenly emerging as one of the new standard-bearers for the reactionaries. He had his reasons, Viktor supposed. His brother, General Ivan Baklanov, a hero of the Crimean War, had been killed recently by an assassin. Nevertheless, the loss of Alex's support for the moderate cause was hard to take.

"First and foremost," Baklanov said, "we must recommend an increase of at least 300,000 rubles in order to hire more gendarmes. The higher the visibility of the police, the more those scoundrels will think twice before attacking any good Russian citizen."

"This ought to be extended to other major cities as well," said one of the other ministers.

"Three hundred thousand is more than triple the original allotment!" Viktor protested. Wherever did they think the money would come from? Imperial coffers were nearly bankrupt as it was. The war had depleted an already sick budget, and there had hardly been time since the armistice to replenish funds.

"We are in the midst of a crisis," declared Baklanov. "We'll get the money somehow."

"Prince Fedorcenko does have a point," said Reutern, Minister of Finance. "All of these proposals will take financial resources, which, as we all know, our government is in short supply of these days."

"Then we shall take it out of the hides of those bloody rebels!" exclaimed another member of the group.

Viktor grimaced at the applause the statement drew.

"If we are going to increase the police contingent," another voice urged, "then we must increase its power also. The men must be given the right to enter factories at will. It is apparent that this radical propaganda has been most widespread among workers, and many of them are starting to listen."

"It seems to me," said Viktor, "that further repression will only add fuel to the fire." Even as he spoke, he expected none of his colleagues to listen. Daily he became more like the squeaking shoe of the committee—an irritating sound that eventually comes to be ignored.

"In addition," added the Minister of Internal Affairs as if he had not heard Viktor's comment, "we must address the problem of the printing presses. I need more people if I expect to meet the tsar's expectations regarding increased searching and seizures."

"And we must also consider," added Vlasenko, the new head of the Secret Police, "tighter controls over newspapers and journals that have been too free lately in their criticism of the police."

Viktor looked over at Vlasenko with annoyance. His irritation was all the more keen in that his cousin seemed to be siding with the majority in opposition to him. But if Vlasenko was especially touchy on the subject, he might be forgiven on the grounds that he had been the target of an assassination attempt three months before, only a short time after arriving in the city for his new post from Akulin. But that was all Viktor would forgive him. The way Cyril had twisted his arm to get his post galled Viktor to the pit of his stomach. And now he practically had to work alongside the rural bumpkin.

"Yes," agreed the Minister of Internal Affairs, jotting a note on a sheet of paper in front of him.

"Now," said the committee chairman, "we need to consider recommendations on the disposition of political prisoners."

"We have to be just to them," sneered Baklanov. "I recommend that they be tried before they are hanged!"

Following a brief ripple of dry laughter, the subject of military tribunal was discussed. The definition of "state crime" was broadened to include *any* act of violence against a state official. And political prisoners were to be kept separate from other criminals and subjected to additional surveillance. Finally the conference approved a request by Vlasenko for the St. Petersburg secret police to be permitted to carry revolvers and to be given the right to use these weapons in self-defense.

Viktor had a throbbing headache after the morning of grueling discussion. When they broke up for food and drink, he was tempted to make some excuse and go home. But before he made good his escape, he found himself caught up in a conversation with Baklanov and Vlasenko.

"Every government committee needs its voice of moderation," said Baklanov almost apologetically. "The tsar appointed you especially for that purpose, Viktor."

"It is hardly gratification to be but a *token* moderate," replied Viktor, his bitterness still evident despite his efforts to control it.

"What would you have us do?" asked Vlasenko, enjoying his role of importance. "Capitulate to these terrorists, Viktor? Have you any idea what the consequences of that would be?"

"The government would crumble," put in Baklanov, as if the Third Section chief's question needed an answer. "Imperial power would become a joke, with anarchy as the end result."

"I have been clear in my opposition to recognizing terrorists," said Viktor coolly. "I have gone so far as refusing a protective escort. Terrorists are criminals who must be punished to the full extent of the law. I agree with you both. However, half the measures discussed today do not punish terrorists, but rather honest citizens."

"Our intent is to create an environment where terrorists will have difficulty flourishing," said Baklanov.

"And I contend that today's recommendations will not diminish terrorists but make *more* of them—perhaps turning honest dissenters into killers as well," Viktor responded. "I say our time would be better spent discussing reform, not larger allotments for the police."

"There have been more reforms during the reign of Alexander II than there have been since the days of Peter the Great," countered Baklanov. "And where has it gotten him? Three times the target of an assassin!"

"Maybe you'd sing a different tune if the attacks were closer to you personally, Viktor," added Vlasenko smugly.

"My loyalty to the crown, Cyril, is such that an attack on the person of the tsar *does* strike me personally, as you put it."

"When the bullet pierces a man's skin, Viktor, his perspective changes."

"You may be right," conceded Viktor, not wanting to argue with the man further. "But that still does not negate our desperate need to get on with the business of reforms in Russia. These changes must go beyond anything we have yet seen—not excluding the possibility of a Constitutional Monarchy."

"Ha, that will be the day!" said Baklanov. "No Romanov tsar would ever allow himself to be forced to *that* extreme."

"You may well be right," agreed Viktor. His voice maintained its businesslike quality, but his eyes were marked with a hint of despair. "It is a classic standoff. The rebels want nothing less than a constitution, but that is something the tsar will never give. Where will it all lead?"

"Where it must," said Vlasenko. "In the meantime, I need another glass of vodka."

18

When the chief of the Secret Police departed, Baklanov drew closer to Fedorcenko in a fashion that Viktor took for conciliatory.

"These are dreadful times, Viktor," Baklanov said.

Viktor nodded his concurrence.

"I frequently ask myself where it will lead," Baklanov went on. "But no matter what the end results, the only way left open to men like us is for Russia's noble classes to bind together. We are doomed otherwise."

"Alex," replied Viktor, "you and I both once believed that the only way Russia could survive was for the government to initiate drastic reform."

"You said it yourself," his friend replied. "These militants will settle for nothing short of a constitution. I believe it goes further than that. They want our destruction—a Russian Reign of Terror with a guillotine in every noble's future!"

"So then, our counter policy must be to 'get them before they get us'?"

"They have forced such a course upon us."

"I know how you have suffered because of Ivan's death, Alex. He was a good, fair-minded man. What happened to him was so senseless, so wanton. But do you think he would support this reaction that has set in?"

"My brother was a fighter," rejoined Baklanov. "We spoke of these violent attacks before he himself was struck down. He was adamantly opposed to any kind of appeasement for ter- rorists. This is a war, Viktor, nothing less. The insurgents must be treated not only as traitors to our country, but also as the enemy."

"That is a strong position."

"But the only realistic one. Besides, there is no reason for us to back down. They are relatively few in numbers."

"It is rather ironic when you think about it," said Viktor. "The Russian aristocracy is numerically small also. What would you say? A few thousand in each camp in this battle?"

"I still call it a war."

"I won't argue the point. The numbers *are* small, but we contend for the destiny of millions—millions who would probably be content and little affected, no matter what the outcome. Yet both the government and the malcontents believe that their way is best for the peasants."

"It sounds almost as if you are proposing the idea of a democracy for Russia."

Viktor chuckled lightly. "I have not gone *that* liberal, Alex. On the contrary, I think it would take decades, perhaps even centuries of intensive grooming before the Russian peasantry would be even close to ready for any form of self-government. In 1613, Russia stood at a historical crossroads. We were leaderless. At that point the option of self-government clearly rose before our predecessors."

"You do not think it was a *practical* option, even at that point?"

"It might have been. Democracy, from the little I know of it, always seems to emerge out of something else."

"Hmm," mused Baklanov. "Democracy in Russia in 1613—an interesting twist of historical interpretation."

"But the boyars and gentry chose Michael Romanov and an autocratic monarch instead. I believe they perceived something that these anarchists are quite blind about—the Russian character is far different than that which makes up the people of Western democracies. The Slavic temperament is as different from the Anglo-Saxon as the African is from us both. Self-rule is a very long way off in the future for us in Russia, if it *ever* comes at all."

"Then why are you so bent on conciliation to the radicals?"

"What I just said does not preclude the necessity for change, for reform, even within the governmental apparatus. I do *not* believe the Ivans and Peter can any longer be our models for leadership."

Baklanov said nothing.

"I believe the same principle applies today that the tsar used when he proposed emancipation of the serfs twenty-three years ago—that it is better for revolution to come from above than for the people to begin attempting to liberate themselves from below."

"Well spoken, Viktor. Though I do not know if the tsar would approve of the fine variation you have given his words."

Viktor tensed slightly. A man had to be careful what he said, especially when he was no longer sure of his friends. He answered defensively, "I believe I have kept to the *spirit* of his words, Alex."

Count Baklanov's mouth relaxed into a smile. "We have been friends a long time, Viktor," he said. "And though we have lately departed from one another politically, I hope a friendship I value greatly will not be sacrificed."

Viktor Fedorcenko was not a man given to shows of emotion. He did not embrace his friend at the kind words, though he felt like doing so. A relaxed grin melted his controlled features.

"Your words mean a great deal, Alex. Thank you for having the courage to speak them to me."

"It hardly takes courage to speak openly to a friend."

They shook hands, and Viktor, feeling more in the mood, suggested they sample the drinks and pastries that had been set out. But before they turned to join the rest of the contingent, Baklanov laid his hand on Viktor's arm to hold him back.

"Viktor, in the spirit of our friendship, I feel constrained to speak to you on a serious matter," he said, and his voice was grave.

Viktor stopped and turned toward him.

"I don't want you to take offense, but I hope our long years of association perhaps give me some right to candor."

"Go on, Alex," Viktor said apprehensively. What new calamity was about to befall him?

"I tell you this because the last thing I think you need or want right now is for your integrity at court to be compromised. You are a respected man in all the highest circles in St. Petersburg, and the tsar himself thinks highly of your counsel. Thus you must not have even one black mark that could be used against you. Especially in times like these, such a . . . such a mark, shall we say, could undermine your career."

"I am at a complete loss, Alex. A *black mark* . . . what are you trying to tell me?"

"I am referring to your daughter's recent association with Dr. Anickin's son."

"I still do not understand," faltered Viktor. Even if he did understand what his friend was driving at, he felt the need to refrain from drawing premature conclusions.

"Come now, Viktor, you cannot be unaware of young Anickin's associations. His trouble in Moscow is general knowledge."

"I know he holds some rather liberal viewpoints. I know he had some problem with deportment during a trial, and that he has from time to time taken it upon himself to defend radicals."

"And that does not disturb you?"

"In all honesty I suppose I would rather my daughter was seeing a man of better character. But he is the son of an old family friend, and thus I feel obliged to give him a certain courtesy," replied Viktor, hedging. He actually did not know what to make of Basil Anickin, nor of his daughter's recent infatuation with him. He had hoped, however, that by ignoring the situation it would dissolve itself. He simply could not believe that his daughter could ever be serious about a man like young Anickin. He also knew Katrina well enough to fear that undue attention might only force her deeper into the relationship. He said none of this, however, to his friend.

"I hope you have enough insight to realize that Anickin is more than a mere social curiosity," Baklanov went on. "There are many who invite him to social gatherings simply for the amusement he provides with his radical rhetoric. No one takes him seriously, choosing to think he is but a bag of jovial wind like his father. But he is more than that, mark my words."

"Honestly, Alex, I have not given it much thought. I wouldn't want my daughter to marry the man. But thus far I think she is just being hospitable to a young man who is rather new in town and needs a companion."

"I suggest that the next time he comes to your house, take a good look at him. He is a dangerous man."

"I can hardly believe that."

"You must draw your own conclusions, Viktor. Some consider him a buffoon, but there are others whose suspicions he has aroused. I have it on the best authority that the Third Section has had him under surveillance since his arrival in St. Petersburg. Out of respect for Dr. Anickin, that incident in Moscow has been played down, but the truth of the matter is that his son physically attacked the prosecuting counsel *in the courtroom.*"

"That is serious."

"Young Anickin was arrested, then he was sent to a mental hospital where he received a series of shock treatments before the police would agree to release him."

"Shock treatments! That is rather drastic, is it not?"

"Perhaps indicative of the extent of his derangement."

"Or of the overzealousness of the police."

"Do you then choose to defend Basil Anickin?"

"Out of deference for his father—"

"Unfortunately, Basil Anickin has been given too much latitude for that very reason already. I believe it is a mistake to underestimate him. And, Viktor, it is *especially* a mistake for you to do so."

"Do not misunderstand me, Alex. No one could possibly think that I am sympathetic in the least to his politics simply because I show him hospitality."

"Viktor, don't make the added mistake of underestimating court rivalries." Baklanov paused to give his words dramatic emphasis. "You are one of the moderates the tsar still listens to. And there are many, especially now, who think that is one voice too many. There are those who would silence you, Viktor."

"That is ridiculous!" They had been speaking quietly, but now Viktor's voice rose noticeably, drawing the attention of several at the other end of the room. He glanced around at the faces that had turned toward him and felt a chill. In that instant, every one suddenly seemed like a stranger.

After the conversation in the room gradually resumed to its previous level, Alex spoke again. "I only tell you this out of friendship, Viktor. Even the *implied* association with militants could ruin you, my friend. If you value your position at court and in the government, it would behoove you to cut any ties either you or your daughter has to Dr. Anickin's son. The doctor is greatly respected in this city, but believe me, it will not be long before even that will not save his son—or anyone who supports him."

By the end of the day Viktor's headache had not subsided. He went home, spoke to no one, and immediately closeted himself in his study.

What irked him most about his conversation with Baklanov was that, though he tried, he could not deny the validity of his friend's words. Even if Basil was nothing more than a harmless eccentric, it could still be damaging to Viktor if key officials deemed the young man dangerous. Men had been arrested and exiled on less evidence than that stacked against Dr. Anickin's son. Should such a thing occur, it would prove embarrassing, at best, to Viktor.

He did not like to capitulate to this wild reactionism that dominated the court lately. But he realized also that now, more than ever, his voice of reason was desperately needed in the Winter Palace. There must be a way to subtly distance himself from the Anickins for a time without insulting the good doctor.

Viktor usually traveled with his family to their estate on the Crimean Sea during the oppressive St. Petersburg summer. But he had already decided not to leave the city himself.

There was nothing to prevent him from sending Natalia and Katrina away. Natalia had become irritable when he told her they would not be going; she would readily leave, even without him. And Katrina's absence for a few months should take care of the Anickin problem—at least for the time being.

19

Days passed, then a week . . . then two. Viktor was too busy with pressing governmental matters to give attention either to his wife and daughter's trip to the south, or to his daughter's steadily deepening involvement with Basil Anickin. Tension over the situation mounted, though it remained hidden, building toward an explosive release.

One evening in late June the doctor's son paid a visit, as he now did most evenings. The day had been a difficult one for the prince, and coming home to find Basil once more on the premises irritated him. He remained rudely silent all evening, debating within himself how to get rid of the fellow for good without making Katrina so mad she would do something foolish. After a tense dinner, he excused himself and made his exit without a word to their guest. Basil was offended, but said nothing. Princess Natalia remained dutifully with the young people for the rest of the evening.

The two were alone only when Katrina walked Basil out to his coach. That brief interlude, however, and the words of love they exchanged proved sufficient to light the fuse for a volatile confrontation. When Katrina came up to her room for the night, she told Anna that she had consented to become Basil's wife, and planned to tell her parents in the morning.

If Katrina slept well in the contentment of her romantic bliss, Anna did not.

She had never believed her mistress would go so far with this infatuation; she had always thought Katrina strong and level-minded enough to bounce back from the disappointment of Dmitri's engagement. That Katrina truly might love Basil did not occur to Anna. She knew the princess better in some ways than Katrina knew herself. Anna did not understand Katrina's attraction to Basil any more than she understood her interest in Dmitri. But she had sensed from the beginning that the obsession with Count Remizov was deeper and more real than this sudden new fancy with Basil Anickin.

Anna's sleeplessness, however, came mostly from not knowing how to speak her mind to Katrina. They were friends, although the word was rarely used to describe the nature of their relationship. Stimulated at first by their studies, they had come to be able to freely explore their feelings and opinions on many subjects with each other. Katrina did most of the talking, simply by virtue of her nature, telling Anna things she had never revealed to another soul.

Anna returned this trust her mistress placed in her with sharing of her own, although her expressions were more guarded. She was still, first and foremost, a servant. And Katrina could as easily slip back into the role of mistress.

"It is a dangerous fence you walk, Anna," Nina Chomsky, Princess Natalia's maid, had commented to her more than once, "trying to be both friend and servant to someone so high-strung and flighty as Princess Katrina. It can only bring you grief in the end."

Anna puzzled all night over what to do, and whether she should say anything to her mistress. She recalled her father saying to her, "My dear Anna, do not forget that a friend who is not willing to risk his very friendship *for* a friend is perhaps not such a good friend as he thinks he is." Anna turned old Yevno's words over in her mind, and as the first rays of the bright June sun began to penetrate her bedroom window, she finally came to a resolution.

Her friendship and love for Katrina *must* take precedence over her position as a servant. If she was a true friend, as she was sure her father would have said, she must take the risk of sacrificing even the friendship itself for the sake of honesty, and the higher good of Katrina's future. Perhaps she had learned enough of the art of tact and subtlety to attempt speaking the truth without risk. But even if she could not, she must speak openly.

Anna dressed and completed several of her duties before Katrina awoke. She was in the sitting room mending petticoats when she heard a sleepy yawn from the princess's bedroom. Her heart immediately began to pound with anxiety. No matter what, she had to talk with Katrina before she approached her parents with the news of the engagement. The princess might not pay any attention to her words. But just in case she did, it would be better for her to change her mind *before* upsetting her parents.

Anna laid down the mending and went to the bedroom door and knocked softly. A sleepy "Come in" followed. Anna obeyed.

"Good morning, Anna," said Katrina, stretching lazily.

"Good morning, Princess. I hope you slept well."

"Like a baby!"

Anna could not help noting the redness of Katrina's eyes and a lethargy to her movements that belied her affirmation.

Anna walked from window to window pulling back the drapes. She wondered if Katrina's sleepless night had the same cause as her own. It gave her some hope as she mustered the courage to speak.

Katrina spoke first, however. "Isn't it a glorious morning! I think I shall wear a light, bright summer dress. It will be very warm by lunch time."

"As you wish, Princess."

"Get out my yellow cotton dress—the one with the white eyelet lace. My white linen shawl will go nicely with it, if by some chance the wind comes up and it becomes chilly."

"Yes, Princess."

Anna found the dress in the wardrobe, gathered up a petticoat and Katrina's other things and laid them neatly on the bench at the foot of the bed. She worked slowly, methodically, realizing she was stalling, and realizing also that it was no use. Finally she took a breath and turned toward Katrina, who had crawled out of bed and was bending over the basin splashing water on her face.

"Princess Katrina," said Anna, "may I speak to you about something?"

"Of course."

"Something personal?"

"Yes, Anna . . . what is it?"

But before Anna could answer Katrina added, "Oh, would you first fetch me a towel?"

Anna did so, then began again. Every word left her mouth hesitantly and she halted and stumbled along.

"I have given this a great deal of thought, Princess," she said, "so I hope you will not think me speaking just idle chatter."

"You never chatter, Anna. Now do go on with it. I'm rather in a hurry this morning because I want to speak with my parents as soon as possible."

"It is just that I want to talk to you about . . . ," Anna went on. "You see, I have been wondering—it may not be my place to say this, but I feel I must—I wonder if perhaps you ought to give these marriage plans more consideration."

"That is a rather presumptuous thing for you to say, is it not, Anna?" Katrina's tone was suddenly slightly cooler than before.

"It is only that I find myself remembering how not so very long ago you told me that you loved Count Remizov, and that your feelings went deeper than mere infatuation."

"You of all people should be glad I have given up on Dmitri," said Katrina. "I always had the idea you thought me something of a fool for my silly fixation on him."

Anna winced inwardly, but did not reply immediately.

"Well, Dmitri is a lost cause, and it is a sign of my real maturity that I can finally admit it," Katrina went on.

"Is it possible that you can fall in love with another so quickly after drawing such a conclusion?" Any other servant would have had her ears boxed for such a remark. Even Anna trembled a bit as she uttered the words. However, such was her valued and trusted place in Katrina's life that the princess only recoiled slightly at the pointed question.

"It only shows how shallow my feelings for Dmitri were in the first place. And from that experience, perhaps now I know something about love that I did not know before."

"Then you truly love Basil Anickin?" asked Anna.

"That is the silliest question I have ever heard! I'm going to marry him, aren't I?"

Anna did not miss the fact that Katrina did not give a direct answer to her question.

"I would have hoped, Anna," Katrina went on, the previous coolness in her tone heating up considerably, "that at least you would be happy for me instead of subjecting me to this inquisition."

The words stung Anna's heart. She wanted more than anything for Katrina to be happy. But she could not shake the nagging conviction that the princess would never be happy if she married Basil.

"I am sorry, Princess," said Anna in true distress. "I want this to be a happy time for you, but . . ." She began to lose her resolve.

"But what?" demanded Katrina caustically. "Go on, you may as well say it all out."

"I . . . I only—that is . . . it seems that Basil Anickin . . . that perhaps he is not perfectly suited to you."

"Not suited to me!" exploded the princess. "I suppose you listen to all those ugly rumors too!" she yelled. "What do you know, anyway? You are only an ignorant peasant! All you people still exist in the Dark Ages. You wouldn't know love . . . you wouldn't know a fine noble person if you bumped straight into him. Just because you don't have a man, you want to spoil my life for me. All I can say is . . . is . . ."

Katrina's anger and frustration overcame her. She could find no more words, and stamped her foot like an ill-tempered child.

"Oh . . . get out of my sight!" she blustered. "I am sick of you!"

Anna obeyed, fighting back tears.

She knew she had already gone well beyond the limits of her natural courage, and even further, beyond the propriety of her position. She hurried from the room, crying.

The hurt was not primarily a result of Katrina's harsh words. Her mistress had *said* angry words to her before. She knew Katrina did not mean half the things she said at such times.

What hurt Anna most of all was that she had failed. She had not been strong enough or convincing enough or even clever enough to persuade Katrina to listen, and thus shield her mistress from what was sure to be a disastrous path. She could not help but blame herself for her ineptitude.

And now she must stand by and watch Katrina make what she feared was a terrible mistake.

20

The rest of the day progressed no more pleasantly than it had begun. Anna remained studiously out of Katrina's way, and managed to go about her duties with only a few brief strained encounters with her mistress.

Under normal circumstances Anna would never have paid the least attention to any of the household gossip always circulating about among the servants. On this day, however, she not only found herself listening, but even venturing a question or two.

Some time after breakfast she heard about the confrontation between Katrina and Prince and Princess Fedorcenko. The parlor maid had overheard bits of the conversation from the corridor outside the upstairs parlor.

"There was lots of yelling," she told Anna.

"Who was yelling?" asked Anna.

"The prince was doing most of it. Although your mistress had a few loud words for him too—bless me, but that child has nerve! I am surprised Prince Fedorcenko didn't grab her and throw her over his knee right there!"

"What did he say?" asked Anna.

"I was not close enough to hear many words. I dusted that hallway until even Mrs. Remington could not have found a speck of dirt anywhere. But all I got for my labors was a phrase here and there, such as the prince saying, 'Over my dead body!' and Princess Katrina yelling back, 'You cannot stop me!' "

"Did Princess Katrina's mother say anything?"

"I did not hear Princess Natalia's voice until Princess Katrina had said, 'We don't need your blessing. We shall have a civil ceremony if necessary.' To that Princess Natalia exclaimed, 'Not get married in the church! Katrina, how can you do this to us?' "

"That was all?" asked Anna.

"Princess Fedorcenko mostly cried for the rest of the time."

"So the prince never gave his consent?"

"Not from the looks of Princess Katrina's face when she stormed out of the parlor a few minutes later. What do they have against the fellow anyway, Anna? Do you know?"

Anna did not answer. She knew nothing of Basil Anickin except for a vague sense of disquiet she always felt when around him.

"I've seen him once or twice," the maid went on. "He seems enough like a gentleman."

"There must be reasons," was all Anna replied.

Two other maids happened along and found ready excuse to join the conversation.

"I hear the man is the son of a former serf," one of them said, with knowing expression and raised eyebrows. "Imagine our princess wanting to marry such a man!"

"I have heard worse than that," said the other, lowering her voice. "I hear he is in league with the militant rebels."

"That may be," replied the other, "but I hear he's a loony one besides."

Later in the day the intended bridegroom himself paid a visit. By that time it was fortunate that the prince had left home on business. Princess Natalia begged Katrina not to see Basil, but to no avail.

Basil stayed only a short time, and when Katrina returned to her room afterwards, she appeared utterly spent. Thinking it might help, Anna went down to the kitchen to order a tray of tea for her mistress.

She brought it into the room about ten minutes later, where Katrina was lying on the bed. Anna set down the tray. The princess said nothing.

"I thought you would like some tea, Your Highness."

A lengthy silence followed. Why Anna lingered she did not know. At length she turned to leave. A moment later a small, strained voice from the bed spoke.

"Thank you" was all Katrina said. But it was enough for Anna just then.

Katrina remained in her room the rest of the day. She took her dinner there alone, though she hardly touched it.

Anna spent the early hours of the evening trying to read, but it was no use. Her mind was too full of Princess Katrina's troubles to be able to concentrate.

She could not escape the feeling, although she had nothing solid to base it on, that somehow in spite of Katrina's sharp words the princess was counting on Anna to help her in this horrible fix she had gotten herself into. What she could do to help, Anna had no idea, as everything she had tried to say already had been completely rebuffed by her mistress.

Yet Katrina seemed more miserable than anyone, and it did not seem to be merely as a result of her father's critical words about Basil. When she set her mind on something, the princess was not apt to be particularly sensitive about other people's opinions—even her father's.

Was the princess, in her own vague and unspoken way, actually hoping for Anna's help, waiting for her maid to come to her rescue in this mistaken commitment she had made?

Anna tried once more to focus her attention on her book. But it was no use.

What could be done? How could *she* possibly help?

Suddenly Anna snapped her book shut. There was only one

person left whom Katrina *might* listen to!

21

It was already mid-evening when Anna stole quietly out to the coach house.

It was a bold and daring plan. She had never done anything like it in her life. But for the sake of her mistress she was willing to risk it, including whatever repercussions might befall her.

Moskalev, even at that late hour, was still busily cleaning the leather seats on one of the carriages.

"I think I work harder at the end of the social season than during it," he told Anna. "With a half-dozen coaches, one or another is always in need of repair. And all of them constantly require cleaning." He gave a fanciful flourish with his cloth. "So, little Anna, what brings you out at this hour?"

"If it is not too much of an imposition, Moskalev," she said, "I would like a ride into the city."

"A ride . . . into the city? At this hour?"

"I must go to the Winter Palace."

"Ah, I see. You have an audience with the tsar, eh?" He gave a good-natured mocking laugh.

Anna could not prevent the tinge of pink that crept into her cheeks, but she answered earnestly. "Not quite that. But it *is* very important."

"Coming from you, I know it must be, Anna," replied Moskalev. "Let me hitch up a carriage."

His tone contained all the respect and affection he had come to feel for this little peasant girl. Since her first day in

St. Petersburg, he had always taken a special and personal responsibility for her.

He hitched the chestnut mare to the *vanka*—the smaller, plainer coach reserved for the use of the servants. When he finished, he helped Anna climb in, then hopped up onto the seat next to her. With a click of his tongue he urged the mare out of the coach house.

The day had been warm, but the nagging breeze of evening made Anna glad she had brought along her wool shawl, which she now drew close around her shoulders. Traffic on the streets was light. The St. Petersburg social season had ended some weeks ago, but even more significantly, the quiet streets reflected the recent trouble with rebels throughout the city. Those citizens who hadn't fled St. Petersburg were keeping indoors as much as possible.

"Shall I pull up at the front door, Anna?" jibed Moskalev as they rounded into the lane leading to the Winter Palace.

"Oh no!" replied Anna quickly, missing the humor in the coachman's tone.

Moskalev laughed. "So, where then? It is a huge place."

"Where are the soldiers' barracks," she asked, "where the Palace Guard lives?"

"Ah, so it is a soldier you want to see, then?" he said with a knowing tone.

Anna felt herself blush in the darkness. Moskalev must surely think this was some sort of romantic rendezvous. But as embarrassing as it was, it was better for him to think her in love than to know her true business.

Moskalev said nothing further. He merely nodded and drove to one of the back entrances. When he came to a stop, Anna prepared to step down. He laid a hand on her shoulder.

"Who is this soldier you must see, Anna? I will get him for you."

Anna sighed with relief. The prospect of approaching the soldiers' barracks alone had not been a pleasant one.

"His name is Lieutenant Grigorov," said Anna, "a Cossack guard."

"A Cossack?" returned Moskalev with a disapproving twitch

of his moustache. He climbed out of the carriage and headed for the barracks.

After waiting for ten minutes, Anna began to realize what an impossible task she might have set for herself and the coachman. If Misha was on duty, he could be anywhere in the huge palace. Even if he was off duty, what if he wasn't in the barracks? She had almost despaired of her whole impulsive plan when at last she heard movement and voices.

"Right out here, Lieutenant, sir."

Anna nearly laughed with joy. She jumped from the carriage and ran toward them. "Misha!" she called. "I was afraid we would not find you."

Grigorov reached Anna in two long strides. He gently took her hands in his.

"Anna, what is it?" he said. "What can be so wrong as to bring you here at night, and alone?" His voice was laced with concern.

Anna had already ceased worrying about what Moskalev might be thinking. "Oh, Misha, I need your help," she answered. But then she glanced at the coachman and hesitated, realizing that she could hardly speak openly of the princess in front of him.

Moskalev understood her meaning, although he still did not know what the whole affair was about. "I'll wait with the horse," he said. As he turned he shot a quick warning glance at Grigorov. "I won't be far," he added meaningfully.

Anna and Misha walked a few paces in the opposite direction. He kept her hand in his, and somehow she felt better already just being in his presence.

"There is trouble with Princess Katrina," she said at length. "She is determined to marry Doctor Anickin's son. I am convinced she does not love him, but she will not listen to reason. She will listen neither to her parents nor to me. There is only one person she might still listen to."

"Who are you thinking of?" asked Misha.

"Count Remizov. But even if I knew how to find him, I could not search for him by myself."

"You wish me to help you locate Count Remizov?" he asked,

his thick eyebrows drawn even closer together in perplexity.

"If you could, Misha."

"Who is this doctor's son? And how can you be sure she does not love him?" He paused. "Though perhaps you would prefer I do not know."

"If you are to help me, you deserve to know," replied Anna. "The situation is simple enough, I suppose. Princess Katrina has loved Count Remizov since she was a child. A few weeks ago the count announced his engagement, and the princess was devastated. Almost immediately she began to take up with Basil Anickin. And now she has agreed to marry him."

"And you do not like the man?"

"I would not like to think that is my only reason. He worries me. His reputation is widespread."

"What kind of reputation?"

"There are rumors among the servants that he is a militant, an agitator, that he defends those who are against the government."

"Defends them?"

"He is a lawyer."

"I see. And you believe these rumors?"

"I would give no weight to such things if I had not seen him on many occasions myself. Misha, there is something about him . . . something frightening, almost dangerous. He behaves as a perfect gentleman. But I have seen a smoldering fire in his eyes that makes me shudder."

"And the princess is aware of none of this?"

"She has given no indication of it. But I think she is so confused over the loss of Count Remizov that she has blinded herself to reality. I actually believe she would risk hurting herself, even condemning herself to a lifetime with a man she does not really love, if she could hurt the count in the process."

"It sounds to me as if Count Remizov would be the *last* person she would listen to should he attempt to dissuade her from marrying this Anickin. It might only deepen her resolve."

"You may be right," sighed Anna. "But with her brother gone . . ."

The momentary hesitation in Anna's voice caused Misha to

glance quickly into her face. But he made no comment over her reference to Sergei.

" . . . with Prince Sergei gone," Anna went on, "there is no one else."

"So you *do* believe there is a chance she will listen?"

"I do not know, Misha. But if there is *any* possibility, it seems it is a chance I have to take. From what the princess says, Count Remizov does feel at least a brotherly concern on her behalf."

Misha scratched his head, then rubbed his chin thoughtfully. "Why should Count Remizov want to intercede?" he asked at length. "What makes you think he will go along with any of this?"

"I know he has voiced his disapproval of Basil in the past."

"Well, Anna," he said after a long pause, "this all seems a rather confusing maze to me. But if you feel this marriage must be stopped, that is enough for me. Let us go immediately and find the count."

She smiled with relief. "Thank you, Misha!"

22

Anna felt uneasy about involving Moskalev further in such an affair that could cause his loyalties in the Fedorcenko home to come into question. But when she suggested he return to the estate without her, his refusal was firm and unwavering. Nothing short of an imperial edict would make him leave Anna alone with the Cossack!

Anna smiled inwardly at his protectiveness. If only he knew

what a gentle young man Lieutenant Grigorov was.

They covered a great deal of ground that night, the unlikely trio of Katrina's ministering angel and the angel's two protectors.

A stop at Count Remizov's barracks only told them that Dmitri was out for the evening. A disgruntled servant at the Remizov family home fairly burned their ears with rebuke at disturbing decent people at such an ungodly hour. A drive by Alice Nabatov's home proved equally futile. Seeing no sign of life or light in any of the windows, they moved on. Two or three other soldiers whom Misha knew throughout the city turned up not a speck of information either.

At last with a sigh, Misha said he knew nowhere else to look except the wine shops and gambling houses.

"Then we had best be on our way," said Anna.

He glanced at her sideways. "Anna," he said, "perhaps it would be best if I went the rest of the way alone." Moskalev was quick to nod his agreement.

"Will you have the same chance of convincing him to talk with the princess as I?" she asked.

"I don't even think Count Remizov likes me much," answered Misha with a half-smile.

"How well do you know him?"

"Not well. Our encounters during the war were brief enough, and I have only seen him a few times since, in a wine shop or two."

"Then why do you say he doesn't care for you?"

"There is no great love between Cossacks and soldiers of the regular Imperial Army. Sergei was the exception to the rule."

"Then it seems there is no other choice but for me to accompany you."

"Perhaps if we waited until tomorrow we could find him on duty," said Misha hopefully.

"I know I cannot fully explain it," said Anna, "but I sense a great urgency to this mission. Besides, I would rather speak to him at a time and place that will draw as little attention as possible."

"Hmm . . . I do see what you mean. Well then, Anna, I remain at your disposal." He bowed gallantly as he stood beside the carriage, then took her hand and helped her back into her seat.

They finally located Dmitri on the fourth stop. The gambling parlor was named Dauphin's, but from the sound of music and laughter escaping through the closed doors, it was apparent that considerably more than gambling was going on inside.

Misha went inside alone, as he had done at the previous stops. Anna and Moskalev sat in the carriage and waited.

During their long search, Anna's mind had turned over and over what she would say to the count should they locate him. By now she despaired of finding him at all. Fatigue had overcome her mind and body; she almost hoped she might not be called upon to make an awkward speech to a nobleman.

Within minutes, however, Misha reappeared with another man by his side.

23

A night of carousing had not left Dmitri Remizov at his best.

His uniform jacket hung open, revealing a white shirt stuffed carelessly into his trousers. Suspenders hung down at his sides. His bleary eyes were focused on Misha in an unfriendly manner.

"See here, Lieutenant," he sputtered, "this had better be important! I still have money on the table in there."

"I would not have insisted if it were not," replied Misha evenly.

When they reached the carriage, Dmitri looked up at Anna and the coachman. Whether he recognized either of them as belonging to the Fedorcenko household, especially in the darkness, was doubtful. Whatever he had been expecting, this was certainly not it.

"Well?" he said testily.

"This lady wishes to speak with you," said the Cossack.

"What? She looks like a servant!"

"Be that as it may, she has business with you."

"I never saw her before!"

"Look again, Count Remizov."

Dmitri squinted and thrust his face closer. "Why, you do look familiar," he mumbled. "Aren't you . . . yes, Katrina's servant, that's it."

"Yes, sir, I am," replied Anna quietly. In his present disheveled state, the count did not look as intimidating as usual.

Suddenly Dmitri jerked to attention, a look of distress briefly replacing his displeasure.

"Has something happened to Katrina?" he asked.

"She is well, Your Excellency, but . . . may I speak with you alone?"

"Of course."

He helped Anna from the carriage. As they started toward the building, Misha stepped forward and spoke. "Must you take her in there?"

"I will be fine, Misha," said Anna, with more confidence in her voice than she felt.

Moskalev jumped from his driver's seat as if to protest. But Misha laid a firm hand on his shoulder. "Don't worry, Moskalev; I will stay close to them."

His words only partially mollified the coachman, who still trusted Cossacks less than he did noblemen. However, throughout the evening he had denoted a few worthy qualities in this particular Cossack he had not expected. He was therefore able to stretch the limits of his personal views and trust him, this time, for Anna's sake.

Misha followed a few paces behind Anna and Dmitri. Just before entering the dark and rowdy place, he hurriedly caught up with them. "Look here, Remizov," he said, "you take care with this girl. She is not just *any* servant!"

Dmitri said nothing in reply, only casting Misha a sour look before ducking inside.

Never in her life had Anna been in such a place; she had never even set foot in Ivan Ivanovich's comparatively innocent little tavern in Katyk. This was no place for a girl like her, especially late at night, and she instinctively crossed herself as she entered.

In the dim, smoky light Anna could make out very few details at first, but only heard raucous sounds and saw vague shapes. She was thankful when they immediately turned away from the noisy, crowded, smoke-filled room. Dmitri led them instead down a poorly lit back corridor past several closed doors. Muted sounds of voices could be heard, and laughter.

They paused at the last door and Dmitri knocked softly.

A woman answered the door. She was dressed in a dark green evening gown, cut low at the neck, emphasizing a full, voluptuous figure. She was probably in her mid-forties, but her heavily painted face seemed intent on disguising her age. She spoke in perfect French.

"Ah, Dmitri, *mon ami*, what can I do for you?" The woman's eyes took in Dmitri's rather incongruous companions.

"Madame Dauphin, may we use your office for a few moments?"

"Certainly. But wouldn't one of my other rooms be more comfortable?" she offered, throwing a brief glance in Grigorov's direction, as if wondering what they were going to do with him.

Dmitri gave her an oddly amused look. "No," he replied, "I think this would be much more suitable."

"Then, please be my guests." She opened the door wide and motioned them to enter.

Misha did not follow, but he said pointedly, "I will be just outside the door, Anna." Then the door closed and he positioned himself in the corridor with no less attentiveness than if he were guarding the tsar himself.

Madame Dauphin gave him a coy wink. "Am I entertaining

a grand duchess in disguise, Lieutenant?" When Misha indicated that he did not understand French, she repeated herself in heavily accented Russian.

"You are entertaining far better than any grand duchess," Misha replied. His words carried deep conviction.

Inside Madame Dauphin's office, Dmitri had pulled together two chairs and insisted that a reluctant Anna be seated. Anna took only superficial stock of the spacious, well-appointed surroundings.

"So—" Dmitri said, but stopped almost as soon as he began. "I don't seem to recall your name."

"Anna Yevnovna, Your Excellency."

"Well, Anna Yevnovna, what is this matter of such urgency that you have deemed it necessary to seek me out in the middle of the night? You are certain Princess Katrina is all right?"

"Yes, she is fine. At least . . . physically."

"Then tell me, what has happened?" His voice again filled with distress. Anna thought it contained more than mere brotherly concern would account for.

He jumped to his feet. "Is it that Anickin fellow? What has he done to her?"

"Your Excellency, Princess Katrina has consented to marry Basil Anickin."

"By heaven, that can't be true!"

"I am sorry to say it is true. She plans to marry him . . . and against her parents' will."

"She loves him?" From his tone Anna could not tell if his comment was a question or an angry retort. "How can she?" he added softly, as if speaking to himself.

"I believe she is too confused to know her own mind about Basil Anickin, Your Excellency," said Anna.

"Why do you come to me about this?"

Anna looked down into her lap, embarrassed.

"It is hardly a servant's place to interfere in such a matter," Dmitri persisted.

How could Anna explain her unusual relationship with her mistress when she hardly understood it herself? How could she make this man understand—this nobleman and soldier who was accustomed to viewing servants as things rather than people? How could he comprehend her desperation at Princess Katrina's plight? How could she make him see that she was acting out of a deeply felt responsibility toward her mistress and her friend?

"Your Excellency," Anna began, fighting her natural timidity, "I have come to you because Princess Katrina has confided many things to me."

At last Anna glanced up. Her eyes met Dmitri's, which now pierced directly into her own. In that single look, he knew, without further explanation, that Anna *was* more than a servant. Suddenly it was clear why she had come, and that she possessed as much right to talk to him on Katrina's behalf as anyone.

"I know," Anna went on after a momentary hesitation, "that Princess Katrina has loved you, and that she was deeply stung by your engagement. I know you have behaved honorably toward her, yet still she was hurt because her own feelings went so deep. I believe she has agreed to marry Basil Anickin out of reaction to that hurt, perhaps in anger toward you."

"Then you do not believe she loves him—"

He stopped suddenly, glancing away in frustration, with a hand to his head. "It doesn't matter whether she does or not!" he exclaimed. "She cannot marry that man! He will ruin her life!"

"How well do you know him?"

"He is unstable at best—and I don't know what, at worst."

"I feared as much," sighed Anna.

"How could she ever consent to such an alliance?" said Dmitri, more to himself than Anna. "She always was a stubborn, headstrong thing."

"I believe she is determined to marry him."

"She must not!"

"I think you are the only one she may listen to, Your Excellency."

Anna's statement was met with a bitter laugh of irony. "I doubt that," he said. "When we last spoke, she was full of venom at me. I spoke to her then about Anickin and cautioned her against further involvement."

"But there is no one else."

"It is too bad Sergei is gone," sighed Dmitri. "He would be able to talk some sense into that hard head of hers."

Anna felt her cheeks warming, but forced herself not to dwell on thoughts of the young prince. "But you are still here, Your Excellency," she said.

"I tell you, she has already rejected my advice."

"I have nowhere else to turn," said Anna with a crestfallen tone.

Then suddenly, as if the thought had just occurred to him, Dmitri asked, "Does she still love me?"

"I can't—"

Anna hesitated. How could she make such a judgment? How could she say what she might feel, even if she did know the answer?

"Tell me the truth, Anna Yevnovna. I must know."

"She *says* she does not. But if she did not still harbor feelings of some kind, why would she have become so angry? In her confusion, it seems that perhaps she wants to hurt you as you . . . as she feels you have hurt her."

"But I have always been clear that there could never be anything between us," said Dmitri. "I was always so much older, and never said a word to lead her—"

He stopped himself. This was no time for denials or angry recriminations. Katrina was in trouble, and it appeared this servant girl was desperate to save her. Could he do any less? Perhaps it was time for him to look at his relationship with Katrina in a new light.

He turned his back on Anna and began pacing across Madame Dauphin's fine Persian carpet. Images flooded his mind— images of the past several years, of his best friend's little sister, so pretty and lively, so utterly bewitching even when he repeatedly told himself she was but a child who would always be too young for him.

The clearest image of all was the memory of a kiss. For one brief instant, he had realized she was no longer a child. Yet even in that moment, she was still Sergei's younger sister and, friendship aside, Sergei would think him no more a fit lover for his sister than Basil was.

His own words came back to him. *Had* he ever led Katrina on, even unknowingly—by a glance, a word, a flash of his eyes? Might he actually have played a part in driving her into a relationship with Anickin?

Dmitri Remizov was not a man accustomed to worrying excessively about responsibility for his actions. Usually a smooth word and a charming grin had been sufficient to ease him out of the stickiest of situations. The case of his sojourn in Siberia was a notable exception. But even that turned out to be far less unpleasant than it could have been.

Now, however, someone else was about to pay a price—a heavy one that could only result in terrible suffering in the end. Was his glib irresponsibility indeed a factor to be reckoned with here? A clever response or winning smile would not spare him this time . . . and would not spare Katrina a lifetime of hurt.

Dmitri faced Anna once more. "Why should she listen to me?" he said again, almost as though squirming one final time to shake loose any sense of accountability in the matter. "I told you, she as much as spit in my face. Perhaps I deserved it, but what more can I do?"

"Perhaps if you told Princess Katrina how you feel . . ."

"How I feel? I *have* told her how I feel. I think the man is practically a lunatic—"

"I did not mean that," said Anna with some trepidation, "but how do you feel about her—how you truly feel."

Her bold words brought Dmitri up short. He gazed with greater intensity than before into the eyes of this most unusual servant girl. Finally he could not restrain a smile.

"That is rather an audacious remark for the servant of a princess," he said, still smiling. "I don't recall such presumption when I first met you. I think some of Katrina's character must have rubbed off on you."

"That would not be so bad, would it?" She smiled.

"And perhaps the opposite has occurred in Katrina's case."

"I would not know, Your Excellency."

"I do not think that would be so harmful either."

He resumed his seat, and much of the tension between them dissolved. "The two of you are closer than just servant and mistress, are you not?" he said.

"I would do anything for the princess."

"That at least is obvious." He grinned again, this time with more of his accustomed ease. "You must feel very strongly that my intercession would help."

"I do."

"She will likely have me drawn and quartered for my efforts."

"And so you *will* do something . . . you will talk to the princess?" said Anna hopefully.

Dmitri sighed. "It may be too late. And I still doubt very much that she will listen to a word I say. But yes, Anna, I will at least make an effort to speak with her again." He paused, then added, "Perhaps it is time, as you insinuated, that I take a new look at just how I *do* feel about all this. In any event, I will see if there is anything I am able to do."

"Then I shall go, Count Remizov," said Anna, rising. "Thank you for talking with me."

Dmitri took Anna's hand, and bowed as if to an equal.

"Thank *you*, Anna. Your care for your mistress is unusual in this day. I know that if she could see your heart, she would appreciate what you have done."

He walked her to the door, then turned and faced her squarely. Dmitri's usually glinting, laughing, mocking eyes reflected an earnest sincerity; his voice, as he spoke, held firm conviction.

"Anna Yevnovna," he said, "I swear to you that if it is in my power, I will not hurt Katrina again as long as I live. At least I will not do so intentionally."

"I believe that, Your Excellency."

Again he tipped his head in a modest bowing gesture. "Thank you," he said.

"Thank you, Count Remizov," Anna responded. She did not exactly know why she had thanked him, except that she felt intuitively that his promise was directed as much to her as it was toward Katrina.

24

It was a long night for Dmitri Gregorovich Remizov—long not in span of hours, which were relatively few, but in anguish of mind. Always content to accept superficiality, he had never engaged in such unwelcome soul-searching in his entire life.

And this present quandary was unlike any he had ever encountered. As he tried unsuccessfully to sleep, he suddenly found his inner eyes riveted upon himself, and he did not like what he saw.

Dmitri had always enjoyed life, savoring it like a fine wine. Life was to be consumed for his pleasure, not scrutinized. He would simply pick it up and drink. More than once he had berated his best friend for his melancholy temperament. "You think too much, Sergei," he had said to him many times. "There's no future in it, man!"

He turned over restlessly in his bed. The tables had turned. Now *he* was the one lying sleepless, with his mind in turmoil! What would Sergei say to him now about the effect of morbid self-analysis on one's soul?

Everything that had seemed so clear in his mind less than twenty-four hours ago had all at once grown murky and uncertain. Suddenly the future seemed to press in upon him with a force he had never known, impelling him to look with new eyes at much he had taken for granted.

Had he made mistakes? Had he drifted along with life's

comfortable flow without considering the consequences?

The question itself brought pain, for he knew the answer was yes on both counts.

And . . . what now? What was he to do *now*!

If he had made mistakes; if he had failed to think beyond the present moment; if he had hurt others in the process, then the decisions that lay before him would have repercussions far into the future. Not only *his* future, but that of others besides.

Dmitri was enough of a man of honor and conscience to recoil at the idea that his self-absorption might have harmed others, especially ones he cared deeply about.

Unpleasant as the idea was to face, he was going to have to make some changes. He was a soldier, and he knew that the fastest way out of a quagmire was to retreat out of the bog rather than to stubbornly march forward more deeply into it.

He threw the blanket off and jumped to his feet in frustration. He wanted to curse the meddling servant girl for her impertinent remark! *How you feel about her . . . how you truly feel*. Why couldn't she have just left well enough alone?

Dmitri walked slowly to the window. He stared into the void a minute or two, calming himself, realizing that Katrina's Anna had put her finger directly on the source of his anxiety.

Slowly he turned, walked back to his unwelcome bed, and sat down.

To a deep, insightful thinker like Sergei, such dilemmas and questions were common. Sergei wrestled with the meaning of the universe all the time. But for Dmitri, his thoughts, and the decisions that might accompany them, were momentous. It was time he forced himself to examine his commitments on a level of personal integrity quite foreign to him.

With a groan, Dmitri let his body fall back onto the mattress. This was not going to be easy. But there was no one to turn to for help. If he wasn't made of strong enough fiber to get himself out of the quicksand he had carelessly walked into, then he didn't deserve to call himself a man.

With a weary sigh, he closed his eyes. He had to do it. There was no alternative. Manhood itself demanded it. The challenge before him held as much importance as his decisions on the field of battle, where life and death hung in the balance. He was about to face the supreme test of a man's character and worth—first admitting, then being willing to stand for the truth, whatever consequences might follow.

He turned onto his side and drifted into an uneasy sleep.

25

Katrina awoke late, as she usually did. Anna, however, had not yet made her appearance.

Katrina glanced around from her bed. It was not like Anna to sleep so late. Now she remembered—Anna had not been in her room when Katrina had retired the night before. That was strange too, not at all like her predictable maid.

Katrina promptly rolled over and went back to sleep.

When she awoke again an hour later, she heard Anna stirring. She rose, dressed herself, and went into Anna's room to question her about the night before. She did not mind Anna's having been out late, but when Anna gave only vague replies to her questions, Katrina was annoyed. She had a right to know where her maid had been. "With Moskalev," Anna had answered finally, only deepening the mystery from Katrina's point of view. What could her Anna have in common with the old coachman?

Before Katrina could press the inquiry further, however, she was interrupted by a parlor maid with the news that she had a visitor.

"A visitor . . . who?" said Katrina. "Is it Basil?"

"No, Your Highness," the maid replied. "It is Count Remizov."

"Dmitri?" said Katrina, flustered. "What could he possibly want?" Her tone carried a strange mingling of hope and annoyance.

The maid who had delivered the message detected the latter. "I left him in the parlor, Your Highness," she said. "I told him you would receive him there unless you were indisposed. Shall I tell him you are not yet dressed, Princess?"

Katrina had more than half a mind to be indisposed. Things were confusing and strained enough in her life right now. She did not need a visit from Dmitri to make it worse! And her irritation with Anna, coming on the heels of yesterday's falling out with her parents, combined to raise her temper quickly with respect to Dmitri.

"Yes," she answered, "tell him . . . tell him I cannot possibly see him."

What was he here for? To extend a personal invitation to his wedding? *The scoundrel*, thought Katrina. *I'll go to his wedding when he begs me on bended knee!*

Yet even as the angry thought formed, it suddenly dawned on Katrina Viktorovna, proud young princess of Russia, that the dashing count upon whom she had expended so many tearful emotions had come to her father's home asking for *her*.

"Stop!" she called after the maid, who was already retreating down the corridor. The maid turned. "Tell him I'll be down in ten minutes," said Katrina.

No matter how miserable she was, no matter how much she hated him, she knew she could never refuse Dmitri Remizov.

That is, I could never refuse to see him, she thought, her anger rising again as once more she pondered the probable reasons for his visit. She'd refuse him fast enough if he tried to browbeat her again about Basil!

Notwithstanding the words she spoke thus to herself, a strange warmth flooded her cheeks, a flush that anger alone could not account for. She hastened from her room a few minutes later without another word to Anna and walked down the hallway trying to calm herself.

Katrina flung open the parlor doors fully prepared for a

fight. But the moment she laid eyes on him, that peculiar flutter she always felt when he was near assailed her. She felt her knees weaken. Then she snapped herself back to attention. She would *not* make a fool of herself *again* by giving way to flighty passions from the past!

"Why, Dmitri Gregorovich," she said with mock civility in her tone. "*This* is an unexpected surprise."

"I hope you do not mind my coming like this, without warning or invitation."

"Of course not," she replied breezily. "Do sit down."

He did so. Roles were suddenly reversed for Dmitri. The little sister all at once became the intimidating matron of the estate, and he found himself inexplicably nervous as he obeyed her. He perched on the edge of the settee, unable to speak for the dryness in his mouth. His eyes were bloodshot from the fitful, sleepless night.

"Would you care for some tea?" Katrina asked, sensing his discomfort and relishing the superior position in which it placed her. What had come over him? Why was he behaving so strangely, almost like a boy?

"I, uh . . . do not wish my visit . . . to be an imposition," faltered Dmitri, despising the frivolous banter, yet unable to force himself to plunge right to the core of what was on his mind.

"Oh, not at all—really." Katrina pulled at the tapestry cord to call a servant. "My goodness," she said, glancing at the mantel clock. "It is nearly time for luncheon. Perhaps you would like to join us." Katrina didn't know what was on Dmitri's mind, but it was nice to see *him* squirming for a change.

"Thank you," he answered, "but . . . but . . ."

His distracted mind could not quickly come up with a polite refusal. He had about come to the end of his restraint. "Katrina, please—" he began with a determined voice.

Before he could continue, the parlor maid entered and Katrina asked her to bring a tray of tea for herself and her guest. When the maid left, a moment of awkward silence followed.

It was no easy thing for Dmitri to find his courage to begin again. And once he did, he knew he could expect at least one more interruption with the arrival of the tea. But it was too late now. His hands were cold and sweaty. What happened to the days when he had been so cool and confident, when he had been able to shrug Katrina off as a child?

He glanced over at her as she sat so primly in the brocaded chair opposite him.

Her kiss at fifteen had disturbed him. But he had still been able to delude himself about her youth back then. However, all that had become absurdly futile on the evening of her coming out. He had realized it sometime last night as he lay awake. He had been stunned when he first set eyes on her. It had not been what he had anticipated upon his return from Siberia! The impact was not so much mere beauty, although the elegance of her ripened features was enough to take any man's breath away. But with it, a mature charm, a gracefulness of movement, and even, if he could say it, a certain ruggedness of character in place of her previous tempestuousness—all this had combined with the splendor and radiance of her face itself to illuminate a very lovely young woman. One who could not help but grow more lovely as yet more time passed.

Last night he had wondered if that initial impression had not been merely induced by the separation of time and given heightened fervor in an imaginative brain by lack of sleep. But he saw all the same qualities now, even as he sat across from her. He saw too the impossibility of any longer hiding behind the little-sister-of-his-best-friend image.

"Katrina," he began again with firm resolve, "you would have had every right to turn me away today—"

"Whatever for?" she interrupted glibly. "You are an old friend of the family, and even I could never be so rude."

"I know I don't deserve your trust . . . ," he began once more, but again she cut him off.

"*Trust?* I do not see what occasion there is between us to talk of such matters," she said with stoic aloofness.

"Please, Katrina," he went on, "this is difficult enough for me. I would hope that the years of friendship between us might have earned me more than this cold indifference."

"You accuse *me* of indifference!" she suddenly flared.

"Granted, it was not a good choice of words," he said humbly. "I am not much accustomed to opening myself up honestly like this."

"No, you are not good at it. You would have done well to pay more attention to my brother."

"I do wish I could be more like him. I wish he were here now. He could tell me what to do, and explain to you what I am trying to say."

"What *are* you trying to say, Dmitri?"

"I am trying to tell you . . . that I am sorry."

"Sorry? For what? Is this an apology, Dmitri?" By the chilly tone of her voice it was apparent that she would be hard pressed to accept one.

"Call it what you will. I have come to see some things . . . in a new light. . . . I see that perhaps I was insensitive in the manner in which I rebuffed your feelings in the matter of my engage—"

"What do you know of my feelings!" she shot back.

"Please, Katrina . . . there is a great deal for me to make amends for . . . and you are making it no easier."

"Well, what has brought all this on?" she asked, cooling off but maintaining her distance.

"When I saw the disaster my callous behavior was leading to, I could not—"

"Just wait!" she broke in sharply. "If you are here to denounce Basil Anickin again, you can leave this instant!"

"Anickin is the furthest thing from my mind right now."

"I don't believe it," said Katrina suspiciously.

"Well, it is true that the fact that you are about to ruin your life by marrying him prompted me to think about many things."

"So, you *are* going to rail against him!"

"Forget Basil Anickin!" he shouted back at her, jumping up from his seat. "What I have to say has nothing to do with that lunatic—"

"There you go—"

"Stop it, Katrina! Listen to me for one moment. I may not have Sergei's sensitivity, or his way with words. But I do have feelings . . . I care about people. I can love!"

"As you love Alice Nicolayevna?"

"This has nothing to do with her, either."

"Nothing to do with Basil, nothing to do with Alice . . . who *does* it have to do with then?"

A strange look passed across Dmitri's face, but he did not answer. Instead he went on with what he had said previously, walking slowly about the room.

"I don't love Alice," he said. "I never have. I engaged myself to her solely for her money."

Katrina sat silent, without words for the first time during the entire interview.

"Do you hear what I am saying?" Dmitri continued. "Only a cad, a scoundrel would do such a thing. Half the things I have done in my life no doubt proceeded from such worthless motives."

"I . . . I do not understand why you are telling me all this," said Katrina at last, bewildered.

"A moment ago, I told you that your involvement with Basil Anickin caused me to think about some things I had not thought about before."

This time Katrina did not interrupt him, and he continued.

"But it did not stop with Basil and you. That only began the process. Before long I was thinking a great deal about myself, about Alice, about what I just told you—that I have never loved her—and I found myself thinking about . . ."

He paused. Several seconds of silence passed before he went on.

"I would be lying to you, Katrina," he said, "if I did not tell you that my initial reason for wanting to come to see you was to attempt one last time to dissuade you from becoming more involved with Basil Anickin. He is a dangerous man, Katrina—please, hear me out! And when I am through you can toss me out of this house and out of your life forever if you wish. All I ask is that you listen to me one time more."

Katrina nodded gravely and waved a hand for him to continue.

"As I reflected, I came to see that I was more involved in

your life than I thought at first. This caused me to look at myself, and before long my own involvement with Alice came under scrutiny. The long and the short of it, Katrina, was that I found myself thinking more about you than about either Basil *or* Alice."

Katrina looked down, keeping her eyes on her lap. This time the silence lasted longer, but still she did not speak.

"Do you remember when I went with your family to the Crimea that summer before Sergei and I entered the Cadet Academy?"

His voice took on a gentler quality as the pleasant memory returned to him, but he continued to pace about the room with agitation.

"You were twelve; I was almost seventeen. My father had died three months before, and your parents literally took me under their wing because my mother was quite out of sorts. For years I had been like a brother to Sergei anyway, so it seemed quite natural. They treated me like one of your own family, and I needed that just then.

"And then there was you, Katrina . . ."

At last she looked up and let her eyes rest upon him. He was standing still now, and she could only stare blankly at him as he paused for breath.

"You stirred something in me that summer that I had never felt before. You were such a child in so many ways, laughing, scampering playfully on the beach. Yet you were not altogether a child, and the woman you are today was emerging, even then. I recall catching momentary glimpses of it every now and then, and feeling sensations within me that . . . well, that seemed wrong. I remember one day you were playing with a favorite doll. You said to me that she needed a father, and you asked me to play the part. 'That means you'll have to be my husband, too, Dmitri,' you said. I did it, for your sake. But something didn't seem right about it. You were too young, and your family was like my own. You were too much like a sister. And so I found myself wondering what was wrong with me, denying those feelings that would flit through me. And I've been afraid to look at it ever since."

Desperately Katrina's mind tried to sort through all the implications of Dmitri's astonishing speech. She also recalled that summer on the Crimean Sea, when her childish admiration for her older brother's best friend had turned into the beginnings of love.

"In the years after," Dmitri went on, "many more barriers grew to separate us. I enjoyed my wild lifestyle, and I knew that your father would disapprove even more than your brother did. I simply never allowed myself to think about you . . . until now. I could *not* do anything that might displease your family. As the years went by I gradually squandered my inheritance. That is why I proposed to Alice—my mother delivered me an ultimatum: Marry someone with money quickly, or lose what little I had left."

He stopped, then turned his eyes toward her purposefully. "Do you know what I am trying to say, Katrina?" he asked.

"I . . . I'm not sure, Dmitri," she replied, suddenly feeling like a tentative, fearful young girl again.

Dmitri sighed deeply. "I'm asking you not to rush into anything with Basil," he said, ". . . for my sake."

"For *your* sake?"

"I need . . . some more time, Katrina. There are still so many things I must try to figure out. Please . . . I'm asking you—stop seeing Basil."

"And Alice?" The words were out of Katrina's mouth even before she realized it.

Dmitri's face showed a sign of his customary humor for the first time that morning.

"My one salvation is that her parents were none too overjoyed at the match," he said. "They consented mainly for the sake of the title I would bring to their family." His lips curved in a wry smile. "I am no prize, Katrina. My purse is as empty as my unsavory reputation is full."

"I . . . I don't understand."

"I stopped at the Nabatov home on my way here," Dmitri replied. "My engagement with Alice has been broken off."

Her eyes sought his once more, this time deeply. In them she read more than he allowed his words to say. But it was enough, and her heart was quiet.

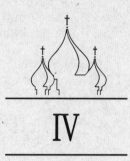

IV

THE WILL OF THE PEOPLE
(Fall 1879)

26

The imperial train, marked by the brilliant golden crest of the double-headed eagle stamped on its sides, journeyed along through the upper Dnieper Plain. The half dozen luxurious cars behind the steam locomotive could have gone faster than the leisurely pace of twenty kilometers an hour, but Alexander II, Tsar of Russia, found himself in no particular hurry.

He had just concluded several weeks of relaxing bliss at Livadia, his imperial residence in Yalta on the northern coast of the Black Sea, with his love Catherine Dolgoruky and their illegitimate family. Now he returned to resume the unrelenting stress and hardship of rule. And he was not looking forward to it.

He sighed as he gazed out upon the final stretches of the flat Ukrainian steppes. If only Catherine could have come with him now. But she and the children were so happy in the Crimea. The pleasant seashore and comforting breezes and sunshine kept them far removed from the intrigue of the capital— and the court gossip that was always cruelly directed at Catherine. Besides, Yalta lay only three days from St. Petersburg by swift train if he needed to call her.

He would restrain himself as long as possible, however— for many reasons. St. Petersburg was not the most desirable place to be just now. The dangerous activity of the militants was bad enough. Besides this, the empress was seriously ill, perhaps in the final stages of the consumption she had battled for years. Alexander did not want to expose his dear Catherine to the biting gossip of those who resented the displacement of the empress from the tsar's heart.

But it would not be long before they would have no choice but to accept Catherine as his wife, perhaps even as empress. True, she was a native Russian, a fact that would further prejudice the people and the Senate against her. Long-standing tradition held that all Russian monarchs must marry into the royal families of Europe to the west. But he had defied his father to marry Marie. And he would no less defy the Senate to have his Catherine.

A smile flickered over his lips. Compared to standing up to Nicholas I, challenging the Senate would be as easy as eating a sweet piece of kulich Easter cake.

He *had* done the one . . . and he *would* do the other. He was the tsar, and he would have the woman he wanted.

Alexander silently rebuked himself for even thinking of his wife's death that way. He did not really *wish* her dead. He still cared for her, after a fashion—at least in the sense that he had once loved her. And she had borne him six sons, after all. Although he doubted he would feel more than a perfunctory grief upon her death, he did not wish her dead. But if she must die, it might just as well be sooner as . . .

He shook the evil thought from his mind.

He also shook aside the notion that perhaps all his present troubles were somehow God's retribution for his adultery. Many at court whispered the idea among themselves. But except for his own annoying son, no one dared voice it within his hearing unless they had a special fondness for extremely cold climates. Before God Alexander believed himself guiltless. There was a different standard for a monarch with the weight of a nation pressing upon his shoulders. Tsars could not be judged like other men.

No, Russia's present woes were not his fault, at least not *morally*. Politically, he had made mistakes. But what did anyone expect? He was only human. And as far as he was able, he had given his best for Russia, always doing what he felt was right—for the nation, for its leadership, and for its people.

A man could do no more. That he chanced to be ruler of this passel of wild, unmanageable, unpredictable peoples called "Russians" was not his fault. He had not asked for the assignment; it had been thrust upon him. How he sometimes envied his Germanic forebears their rule over the practical, efficient, disciplined German states!

The awful sense of rejection he felt from his subjects had made Alexander all the more prone to depression after the war. But there would be no self-abnegation. He did not deserve their bombs, their bullets, or their hatred.

He glanced out the window again.

Dusk was beginning to color the horizon. By morning they would be in Moscow. And then on to St. Petersburg.

27

The work had taken all night under the light of a full moon, whose illumination was a mixed blessing at best.

Secrecy had been imperative, for there had already been too many foul-ups. Lanterns would have been cumbersome, and keeping them burning was time-consuming. Zhelyabov had thus accepted the moonlight with practical graciousness; he could not do anything about it, anyway. And as preparations turned out well, he cared not to complain.

He stood back and surveyed his work with satisfied pleasure.

It had been a job, to be sure. Climbing up the steep grade where the track passed along the edge of the rocky ravine, then maintaining precarious footing while digging into the stubborn ground had been no easy task. The surface dirt was dry and crumbly and fell away before a hole sufficiently deep could be carved out.

Once the crevice was large enough to hold the charges of dynamite, the next challenge was to string out the wires leading to the detonator, and cover everything so it could not be detected. There had already been one discouraging failure resulting from lack of such care. The attempt to bomb the imperial yacht would have proved a masterful coup if only the water hadn't washed away the adhesive holding the wires in place, thus exposing them to the view of a prying police guard.

That would not happen this time. In the darkness of a lonely stretch of mountainous train track, Zhelyabov could lay the wires above the ground and they would never be seen! But he decided to take every precaution nevertheless, and he carefully smoothed the dirt over the last length of wire. Everything was covered, from the sticks of explosive buried in the embankment underneath, all the way to the detonator.

Zhelyabov prided himself in his work. He had a fascination for this modern blasting technology, and had become rather adept with electrical tinkering. Several months ago he had convinced other leaders in The People's Will to give up the outmoded and inefficient use of handguns and hand-tossed bombs. Electricity represented the wave of the future. And if they were striving for the future of Russia, they might as well do so with the help of every modern convenience available.

He surveyed the slope over which the imperial train would soon travel. An eagle would never have been able to spot his work—not even a *double-headed* eagle!

He wondered how Sophia was doing at her demolition site.

The imperial train from the Crimea could take two possible routes along separate lines of track. The Third Section did not like to make it easy for people like Zhelyabov by announcing which pass the tsar's entourage would take. They took every precaution, often running identical trains simultaneously along each track to further confuse enterprising insurrectionists.

Zhelyabov was determined to outwit the Romanov oppressor, however. He had conceived the plan to mine *both* routes. And they would set still a third charge, for good measure, at the juncture of the two lines near Moscow. He had himself taken the main railway route, which his instincts told him the tsar's train would probably use. Sophia Perovskaya was in charge of planting the mines at the other two locations, for they were relatively close together and more accessible. The fact that they lay closer to Moscow presented additional risks. But Sophia was a capable girl.

He smiled as he thought of the pretty little firebrand.

Ah yes, she would manage just fine. And tonight they would celebrate—oh, how they would celebrate! Just the two of them, alone, with a bottle of wine and their passion for each other . . . and the sweet, sweet savor of vengeance.

"It looks good, Andrei," said a voice behind him, interrupting his thoughts.

"Yes," said Zhelyabov to his assistant. "This time I believe we've got him. Nothing can go wrong!"

From their secluded hiding place in the thick brush about a hundred meters from the mined section of track, Zhelyabov and his assistant sat back to wait. Their suspense did not last long. About twenty minutes later they heard the first distant sounds of the locomotive, then at last the long-awaited puffs of white smoke became visible in the pale moonlight.

They crouched down and watched the approach of the imperial train. The mighty engine chugged up the grade, followed by the rattling of the cars behind it. With every pulse of steam from the powerful iron wheels, the young seditionary's feverish anticipation mounted. He saw the Cossack guards standing watch at the fore and aft entrances of the third car.

That would be the tsar's imperial coach! He would blow the train at the precise moment to blast that car and everything in it to the moon itself!

The Cossacks were alert and vigilant, their probing eyes scanning the countryside. If Zhelyabov believed some Being from above listened to the entreaties of humankind below, which he didn't, he might have uttered a prayer that his work of concealment would stand the test.

But as he expected, no prayers were needed. His own skill and talent proved to be all that was necessary. The Cossack guards saw nothing.

Still Zhelyabov waited.

The passing seconds as the train came over the mined track seemed like several long Siberian winters. His mouth went dry as he moved his hands to the detonator. He glanced at his assistant, who was looking instead at the train, which was only moments from annihilation.

The locomotive passed, then the first car. The imperial coach drew closer. In his mind Zhelyabov began a silent countdown. Five . . . four . . . three . . .

The anticipation was almost more tantalizing than being with Sophia. In moments Russia would be leaderless! Yes, there was the tsarevich. But he would count for little when the masses saw the power of The People's Will and rallied behind them. The man who tried to become Alexander III would have a very short life.

Two . . . one!

Zhelyabov threw his body weight on the detonator, covering his ears with his hands against the deafening explosion.

The only sound to be heard was that of the engine still laboring up the grade, the cars still clacking rhythmically behind it.

Zhelyabov scrambled back onto his knees. He glanced toward his assistant, who had thrown himself onto the ground for safety. They looked in disbelief toward the track. At the site of the charge they saw only a thin, ineffectual stream of smoke rising from the grass and brush they had placed over the hole as camouflage. The effect was so small that the passing Cossacks did not even notice it as they clattered by.

The train should have been tumbling in flames down the embankment, but it chugged placidly on. The tsar should have been bloodied and dismembered, fallen at last in the violent death justified by his evil disregard for the downtrodden, oppressed masses—yet he lived! He sat in the plush velvet and mahogany coach, probably sipping his brandy before retiring, as oblivious to his peril as he had always been to the misery around him.

Zhelyabov stood and kicked at the ground, then sent the detonator flying with his booted toe, cursing bitterly.

When the train sped out of sight, he walked over to the detonator, stooped down and picked it up, then began to gather the rest of the equipment. The stuff was too precious to be left behind. Besides, there would be further use of it later . . . unless his compatriots met with more success than he.

28

Sophia Perovskaya and her assistants crouched under the dense cover of a clump of trees and brush.

Their view of the track from that vantage point was less than perfect. But they had purloined at a good price, from a sympathetic railroad worker, the expected time when the imperial train would pass this way. There was always uncertainty; the Third Section's attempts at trickery grew more and more canny every month. But she had a gut feeling that their information was sound and that this would be the day of her— the day of *their*, she should say—ultimate success. She would proceed on that instinct, and not be confused by governmental chicanery.

The moment she heard the roaring of the engine faintly coming into earshot in the distance, she sent one of her associates twenty or thirty meters away, higher up the hillside where he could see the approach of the train. He would give her the cue at the exact moment.

She sat down on the dry dirt and then placed her quivering fingers around the handle of the detonator, breathing deeply in an attempt to calm herself. The waiting seemed interminable. With agonizing lethargy the train inched closer. She fought against the urge to run up the hill to see it with her own eyes.

Still she sat. She *had* to await the signal. She could not be away from this most important post for even a second. Her fingers stiffened in readiness around the handle.

At last the night air was rent with the high-pitched shrill whistle she had been waiting for!

Sophia instantly plunged her hand downward with a force equal to the pent-up pounding of her impassioned heart. The blast that followed fairly rumbled the earth beneath her.

As she rose to her feet, her assistant ran back down the hill, jubilant. They had done it!

But she hardly needed his verification. Bits of debris and fiery sparks from the exploding train sailed through the sky overhead. As the echo from the thunderous blast died away, it was replaced by the crashing din of half a train, splintered and torn apart, tumbling down the hill from the track, ruptured asunder and engulfed in flames. In the midst of the holocaust, the screams of the dying could be heard.

The faction of The People's Will wasted no more time. They hurriedly gathered up their packs of equipment and raced through the woods to safety.

29

When the Moscow contingent of The People's Will learned that they had blown up the wrong train, Sophia Perovskaya truly began to wonder—although she despised the old super-stitious beliefs still so prevalent in Russia—if the tsar was lead-

ing a charmed life after all. Somehow it did not occur to her
to feel remorse over the fact that her error had cost the lives of
many innocent passengers on that ill-fated train.

In St. Petersburg, two days after yet another close escape
from death, Alexander Romanov was still noticeably shaken.
He took the news of this latest bombing very hard. In fact,
when Viktor Fedorcenko called on him soon after his return,
the tsar had never looked so poorly. He looked like a man walking about under a sentence of death—vacant, nervous, distracted, afraid.

Viktor's heart ached for his monarch. He could not begin
to imagine what it must be like to live each day not knowing
if it might be his last on the face of the earth, never knowing
if at some unexpected moment a violent, dreadful, bloody end
awaited him.

And yet it was more than fear for his own mortality that
ate away at the mental and emotional stability of the tsar.

He glanced around at Viktor and the two or three other
ministers whom he had called together. "What have I done that
has been so wrong?" he asked miserably. His eyes held the
bewilderment of a child. "Am I a wild beast that they must
hunt me down and kill me?"

"They are the beasts," said Viktor with clear conviction.

"They are lunatics!" declared Orlov. "And we will hunt them
down, to be sure, Your Majesty. Vlasenko has already made
some conspicuous arrests."

"So quickly?" asked Viktor. He was not exactly free to voice
his distrust for Cyril any more than his dislike for him. Yet
even as an impartial politician, in view of the circumstances
he feared that the new Third Section chief might well forsake
clear evidence in his zeal to exact retribution. Failures on the
part of the Third Section and the police must sooner or later
be called to account by the tsar. Knowing Vlasenko's propen-
sity for over-reaction and his desire to make a name for himself
in the capital city, Viktor would not put it past him to tell his
officials to haul in anyone they could, just to improve what had
till then been a miserable record.

"And why not?" asked Orlov. "These rebels are not only

fools, they are incredibly stupid."

"I want those arrested to go to trial immediately," said the tsar, seeming suddenly to come to himself. "These malefactors, these blackguard assassins must receive *no* mercy. They are unquestionably murderers, even if they did fail with me. How many others died in that explosion? That they missed their chief target does not lessen their crime!"

"At least this incident has curbed public sympathy toward these radicals," offered Viktor. "The press's sympathy is decidedly leaning in your direction, Your Majesty."

"There remain pockets of disloyalty," said Orlov. "Only yesterday I read an article in Danilcik's paper criticizing His Majesty."

"Danilcik. . . ?" mused the tsar. "Strange, I don't remember ever having done him a favor. Why then should he hate me?" He shifted moodily in his chair. "That is what I have learned in the bitter school of experience. . . . All I have to do to make an enemy is to do someone a favor." He stopped, then reached for a glass of water with a trembling hand.

Viktor recalled Alexander in his youth—kind, sensitive, idealistic. After twenty-three years of rule, that same sensitivity had degenerated into weakness, and the idealism had deteriorated into cynicism. When Russia most needed strong leadership, the Motherland was left with a wreck of a man at the helm. Even if the assassins continued unsuccessful, how much longer could Alexander hold up under this intense pressure?

"I wish you all to leave now," said the tsar at length with a weary wave of his hand. "We can continue this discussion tomorrow."

The small group bid their sovereign a good afternoon, then backed from the room. No one would dream of turning his back on His Majesty.

As the door opened and they began to file out, Alexander said to no one in particular, "Send in Totiev."

The secretary, who was close at hand, heard the command and entered the private chamber immediately. Before the door closed, Viktor caught the first few words spoken by the tsar in an agitated voice.

"Telegraph Livadia immediately. I must see Princess Dol-goruky!"

30

The Winter Palace rose silent and dark against the gray horizon of approaching dawn. Fall was in the air, crisp and damp. The sun would take away the chill before noon, but in another two months the unrelenting cold would pierce to the very marrow.

A furtive figure, thin, slightly bearded, and wrapped in a long oversized coat, darted from behind a building two blocks away. His gait was awkward; he held his right elbow tightly against his side, while his left arm stretched across the front of his chest, clutching at the loose-fitting coat. To all indications he might have been a peasant with a withered arm, using his one good hand to prevent his shriveled one from flying about uncontrollably.

In truth, the fellow was no peasant. And in spite of the frosty morning, the coat had not been donned an hour earlier for the purpose of warmth. Rather, it concealed the stock of the young man's trade, which his arms and hands tried to keep from excessive jostling about. It did, however, make his running a bit clumsy.

He ran along the side of the wide boulevard approaching the palace, and then into a deserted alley. He quickly stooped down in the shadows to catch his breath and to get himself again out of sight. It was early, and the streets were still deserted. But he must take no chances. The Cossack guards stationed around the palace did not sleep.

The alley gave him a last respite before the final leg of his odyssey. If he were going to have second thoughts, this was his only remaining opportunity. If he executed the final element of his reckless plan, when he stepped out of this alley into the sunlight of the morning, he would be stepping into whatever final fate destiny had chosen for him.

Whether that destiny would be immortality in the cause of freedom for Russian people everywhere, or the ignominy of his own senseless demise, only the next two hours would tell.

For his part, he was willing to pay the price of the latter in order to achieve the former. He was still enough of a dreamer to believe in his ability to strike quickly, and then get away in the pandemonium of the aftermath.

Carefully he opened the coat and laid his burden on the ground. He would have the final assembly ready within minutes. His eyes glowed with the fire of a passion known only to a select few; his fingers, trembling in anticipation and feeling not a bit of the cold, began fiddling with the various components of death.

———

Alexander II, Tsar of all the Russias, had slept very little that night; he was up before the roosters, dressed, and already pacing about. The overnight train from Moscow was scheduled to arrive at nine, but he was ready for his drive to the station by six.

His advisors counseled him against going himself. The Princess Dolgoruky could be summoned back to the Winter Palace with equal speed by his coachmen and private guards. But he had not seen Catherine in a week and a half, and he was determined to meet her coach in person.

"It is too dangerous, Your Majesty," they had insisted.

"Nonsense. The hour is too early for trouble."

"The streets are filled with radicals at every hour, Excellency."

"Then double the guard. Bring some of my Cossacks from inside the palace."

"Security has been lax, sir. Somehow these people seem to know of your every move outside these walls. It is with the most urgent recommendation—"

But the tsar's interruption ended the debate with summary finality. "I do *not* intend to be dissuaded from going to the station!"

The tsar's royal coach and best team of four was summoned to be made ready for His Majesty by half past seven.

———

Lieutenant Misha Grigorov likewise found a summons waiting for him early that morning, in the form of a rude knock on his door hours before he was scheduled to appear at his usual post.

"The tsar is going out this morning," he was told by the aide to the Captain of the Royal Guard. "You must be on duty at the street adjacent to the coach house in half an hour."

Groggily Misha pulled himself out of bed. He walked to the sideboard, splashed a few handfuls of water out of the basin onto his face, toweled it off, then began to dress in the bright colors of his uniform. Breakfast, it seemed, would have to wait.

Twenty minutes later Misha stepped into the cool morning air. No wonder the water in his basin had been especially cold, he thought. The Arctic had blown in overnight! He shivered and looked about, then greeted several of his companions who had similarly been roused early so that the tsar might fetch his mistress home in safety. "Well, if nothing else," he said to one, "the cold will keep our eyes open and alert."

Misha took up a position down the boulevard, some fifty meters from the iron gate through which the tsar, horses, carriage, driver, and accompanying guards would pass. A few persons were out, here and there a carriage clattering along the cobbled street. As usual, a growing handful of spectators clustered about in hopes of seeing their tsar. All in all, the street was far from crowded.

He could not tell whether it was the long coat or the peculiarly placed hands that first drew his attention to the man across the street.

The fellow was just standing there, seemingly innocent enough, leaning against the stones of the building at the mouth of the opposite alley. It was enough that Misha noted his presence, though his eyes continued to scan the rest of those present on the street at that early hour. But when his eyes returned to the same spot a minute or two later, the man had begun to inch along the building in what Misha could only think was a very odd series of movements. Something about the hands and the coat drew his eye again.

The man was moving very slowly, yet not randomly. Misha could not see his eyes, but he sensed purposefulness in the whole posture, an intent not seen in casual street-walkers or those hanging about in hopes of laying eyes upon their leader. *Too much purpose*, thought Misha, *for one so obviously trying to remain inconspicuous.*

Without further debate, Misha stepped forward into the street and began to walk across. If the man was a mere vagrant and up to nothing, he should not mind a morning's greeting from one of the tsar's guards.

Even as he reached the middle of the wide Palace Square, Misha heard the commotion of horses and the iron wheels of the tsar's coach making their exit onto the street. Still his eyes remained on the figure before him. The fellow had left the side of the building and was walking more rapidly now. Misha knew the man had detected him out of the corner of his eye, yet the fellow's gaze bore straight ahead toward the horses and carriage.

Misha quickened his pace. Something was wrong about the whole thing! He didn't like the way—

The man glanced around. He turned his eyes momentarily on the approaching Cossack guard. Still twenty meters from him, Misha saw the fire glowing out of his eyes. It was not the fire of love for his leader!

Misha broke into a run. "Halt," he said in a voice still low enough not to attract undue attention back toward the gate.

Ignoring him, the man started to run in a labored gait, without using his arms. "Halt, I say!" cried Misha, louder this time. "Halt!"

The shout of his voice and the echoing footsteps drew the attention of Misha's fellow guards. Some of them sprang into action and headed into the street.

"Turn the carriage around!" cried Misha in the direction of the gate.

He was running at full speed now and gaining rapidly on the figure in the flapping coat. "Stop!" he yelled again. "Stop now, and no harm will come to you!"

"Harm has already come!" screamed the man. His voice instantly betrayed his purpose. "Harm and destruction have been wreaked upon the land by the Romanov oppressor!"

Still he ran toward the tsar's carriage, shrieking as he went. His hands fumbled inside his coat. "Death must come, that life and freedom be born!"

Misha flew toward him.

"Death is the only justice for—"

Misha leaped into the air, crashing against the subversive. Both men tumbled to the rocky pavement with bruising thuds and scrapes. Even as Misha grabbed for the man's wrists to disable him, with a final desperate lunge the man tossed a small, crudely made bomb away and toward the carriage.

It rolled a short distance from them. The crowd that had been approaching suddenly scattered with screams and shouts. The driver, who had been attempting to turn the four horses, now lost control as they reared and whinnied, panicking at the sudden movement and loud noises.

Perceiving the mortal peril, Misha jumped to his feet and ran the few paces to where the lethal device had come to rest. Picking it up, he turned back toward the center of the street, then with one mighty motion heaved it from him, away from all the people and down the deserted opposite end of the cobbled square.

Misha did not wait to see the result. He lunged back toward the would-be assassin, who had already risen to his knees to make good his getaway.

Even as the explosion sounded behind him from the middle of the cobbled boulevard, the force of Misha's body slammed on top of the near-murderer for the second time in less than a minute. This time when the Cossack rose, he had the arms of the prisoner pinned behind his back in a viselike grip.

31

Paul told the authorities he was Kazan's brother.

If nothing else, he had learned over the last months to lie with a proficiency that would have shocked his father and mother. With an additional request by the lawyer of the accused, he was granted a brief visit with the prisoner.

Two days in the Peter and Paul Fortress had not diminished the enthusiasm of Paul's buoyant mentor and friend. He was, in fact, in remarkably good spirits considering the seriousness of his present trouble.

"It is no less than an honor to be interred here," he said to Paul. "Think of the great men—heroes of Russia—in whose steps I am permitted to follow!"

"Anickin says you will be executed if you are found guilty."

"That is the punishment for trying to kill the tsar."

"But you are innocent!" Paul was certain that his friend had not been involved in the affair of the dynamited train, for they had both been in St. Petersburg during the attempt. Kazan had kept young Paul Yevnovich ignorant of the gravity of the recent incident near the Palace. "There were no deaths, no killings. You are no murderer!"

Kazan sighed, thinking that such sentiments would hardly be enough to convince a court of law. "Yes, perhaps by your standard I am no murderer . . . this time. But not for lack of desire. I would surely have done so had it not been for that interfering guard."

"But why you? Why do Zhelyabov and Perovskaya still walk about free?"

Kazan smiled. "The police did not have the evidence of proof to arrest them. And because of the palace affair I offered a convenient scapegoat for them to hang the train bombing on as well. I'm sure they will make a full spectacle of me. Vlasenko has been after me for months. Now he can claim to have solved the train bombing along with my palace attempt on the tsar and claim full credit."

"But it's not fair," objected Paul. "You had nothing to do with the trains."

"I would surely have gone with them had I been asked," he said.

"But you *didn't* go! A man cannot be hanged for what he *wishes* to do."

"You forget, this is Russia, and Vlasenko wants my blood. And he has me dead to rights for what I *did* do."

"We cannot let them convict you. We must fight fire with fire. We must do anything we can to weigh the case in your favor."

"*You* are saying these things, my friend," said Kazan, shaking his head sadly.

"What is wrong, Kazan? I am finally seeing things your way. Is that not what you have wished for?"

"I know, and I am glad for that." He did not sound glad. "I only wish the circumstances could have been different." He paused. For the first time he began to regret his rash impulsivity that had landed him in such a hopeless place.

"Let me testify for you, Kazan," said Paul with fervor. "Let me testify that you were with me on the day of the explosion at Moscow."

"If only it were that simple, Pavushka," sighed Kazan. "If they are thwarted with the murder charge, they will convict me of my attempt on the tsar."

"I am willing to take the chance."

"Never, Paul! They would tear your story apart in minutes."

"But to prevent your conviction as a murderer perhaps would lessen the sentence."

"The answer is no. I will not have you publicly align yourself with me. It is too dangerous. A slip, a wrong look, a hesitant answer to one of the prosecution's questions, and you could yourself be charged with complicity in either of the crimes."

"But I would do it for you," Paul pleaded.

"I won't hear of it! It is bad enough that you have come to see me, and I would throttle Anickin's neck for allowing it if I dared. Unfortunately, he is probably my only chance, slim though it may be."

"Do you truly believe I am in danger?"

"For the moment we will hope you are viewed as nothing but an innocent younger brother. But should you take the stand, that would all change the moment the prosecutors began to grill you and present witnesses to testify that you are not who you claim to be and that you have been seen in company with other rebels and militants. No, Paul, you must leave here and forget me. Lose yourself, lay low, change your name, and keep miles away from any hint of trouble."

He paused a moment, then added, "And do not show your face around here again. Forget all this foolishness about testifying. I will not have it!"

Paul looked away in dejected misery.

"You know, Pavushka," said Kazan in a gentler tone, "you are very much like a little brother to me. I would not forgive myself if anything were to happen to you on my account."

A wide grin formed on his lips. "Anyway, perhaps they will not get rid of old Kazan so easily," he said optimistically, trying to boost Paul's spirits. "Just you wait—it will be Vera Zasulich all over again! It will be the government on trial, not me. This could well be the turning point, the great moment when the people finally rally around our cause. I look forward to this trial, Pavushka!"

32

Paul watched the execution.

It was the last thing he *wanted* to do, but he would not desert his friend now. He had not attended the trial, in faithfulness to Kazan's wish, yet he could not help feeling guilty for staying away. Perhaps some of that same guilt now impelled him to come out of hiding on this blackest of all days in his young life. He only hoped that his presence in the crowd of spectators would somehow give Kazan added strength in this awful, dark moment.

Paul wondered if he could even be seen among the hundred onlookers. If not, surely Kazan would *know* he was there, that he'd always remain loyal. Always!

Next to him stood Kazan's defeated lawyer, Basil Anickin. He seldom missed these public executions and, in large part, his presence aroused little suspicion, for many of the doomed radicals had been his clients. Beneath such professional interest, however, something greater drove him to these public displays, every one of which added more fuel to his silently seething hatred.

Glancing at him out of the corner of his eye, Paul noted the taut, hard lines etched indelibly on his face. His eyes focused ahead, smoldering with a deep fire that rarely burst into flame, yet burned all the hotter inside. With unrelenting malice he stared at the scaffold, not letting his gaze waver to the right or the left. Whatever thoughts simmered in the depths of the lawyer's mind, Paul could not guess. But he knew they had to revolve around the imperative for justice, for recompense . . .

for revenge. Only the spilling of blood could assuage the look he saw in those eyes.

As Paul stood there, had he been asked point blank, he could not have truthfully denied such thoughts himself. For the first time in his life, he found himself thinking—*really* thinking— about killing. He supposed he had wanted to kill the schoolmaster in Pskov, but he hadn't really given his actions any predetermined thought. It had all just happened. Now, however, he found himself considering what it would be like to kill, and reflecting on the idea with practical realism.

Unexpectedly, the thought did not cause him to shudder in revulsion. In fact, a certain morbid sense of pleasure surged through him. The thought of wrapping his hands around the throat of that brutal thug who had so humiliated both him and his father, who had so cruelly treated the peasants of the country around his home and was now carrying out the savagery of his lofty new position in St. Petersburg . . . just the thought of sending Cyril Vlasenko to another world gave him a thrill of satisfaction.

Had Paul been able to witness the changes taking place at that moment on his own face as he considered the demise of the Third Section chief, he might have been surprised, even shocked. For his youthful face suddenly bore an uncanny resemblance to that of Anickin, who stood at his side.

As Kazan mounted the scaffold steps, all Paul's hatred was swallowed, for the moment at least, by the anguished grief of what was taking place before his eyes.

He remembered the enthusiastic young idealist when he had first made an appearance in the towns and villages around Katyk. He had been full of hope then, and so convinced that Herzen's dream of rousing the fervor and support of the peasants would be fulfilled. The discouraging failure of his mission in the region disheartened and defeated many, who then turned away completely from the cause. But it had only strengthened Kazan's zeal. Some might argue that it drove Kazan toward cynicism and violence, but Paul believed he had held on to his hope of a better society right up to the end. His final words to Paul proved it: *"This could be the turning point, the great mo-*

ment when the people finally rally around our cause."

But there had been no great popular uprising. In many ways Paul did not understand this man, his best friend. He hadn't understood that Kazan's final words were spoken in futility, hadn't grasped the foolhardy inanity of his final desperate act, hadn't seen that the death sentence was insured the moment the cell door had clanked shut behind him.

At least Pugachov in the time of Catherine the Great had gone to his scaffold with the comforting knowledge that he had made some lasting mark, that his name would endure as one of the forerunners of freedom. Thousands had followed the Cossack who claimed to be Peter III, sweeping like wildfire through the Ural region and Volga Valley, capturing forts, killing whatever military officers, priests, and landowners happened to be in his path. Everywhere peasants flocked to join his makeshift army. Only merciless, sadistic governmental reprisals against his recruits depleted his forces enough to defeat him and bring his short-lived rebellion to naught. Yet he had died with the memory of scorched earth and aristocratic slaughter to comfort him, and with the knowledge that for one brief and glorious moment, he had struck fear into the tsaritsa and the hated nobles of her regime.

Poor Kazan had no such comfort. He was an unknown rabble-rouser who had come to the capital city thinking to make a triumphant mark in the birth of a new societal order. Instead, he had never reached the lofty pinnacle of his noble goals, had lost his perspective, and in a madcap and ill-fated rush for glory, had succeeded only in blowing a modest-sized hole in one of St. Petersburg's streets and getting himself arrested . . . for good. Even his trial had been an ignominious affair, attracting little publicity, sparsely attended, and providing no forum for the dissemination of radical ideals as Kazan might have hoped.

And now just barely a hundred people gathered to see Kazan breathe his last. Probably three quarters of them didn't even know his name.

Before he realized it, tears began to spill down Paul's face. The loss of his friend was a bitter sorrow, compounded by the fact that his death seemed such an utter waste. And the sentence was unjust. Radical leaders guilty of far greater crimes still walked the streets freely.

Paul wanted to be strong. He tried to stop the tears, squeezing his hands into hard, clenched fists at his sides. Yet nothing could help. He might have begun to blubber like a child had it not been for the sound of Basil Anickin's cold, tight voice in his ear.

"What are you crying for, you fool?" said the lawyer. "We do not need little babushkas—and our enemies do not merit your tears!"

Paul tried with difficulty to suck in two or three calming breaths of the chilly morning air.

"Forget your weeping," Anickin went on. "It will do neither your friend nor our cause any good. Give them your hate, do you hear?" He grasped Paul's chin in his slim fingers and jerked Paul's head up straight. "Look!" he commanded. "Do not stare down at the ground like a coward. Dry away those tears so you can *see* your friend die. Watch! And let it burn like a fire into your soul!"

Paul obeyed. Under the compelling force of Basil's grip he could hardly do otherwise.

Yet later, he realized that more than the lawyer's fearsome presence and imperious words had compelled him to breathe deeply and courageously, to make himself experience the full impact of the awful moment. Deep within him he realized that he wanted this moment to be marked forever on his brain and heart. He did not *ever* want to forget. It would have been impossible to forget, in any event. But he wanted to remember what he *felt* at this moment. He wanted to keep the present fires within him alive.

He *wanted* to hate! He wanted to carry on within him the passion Kazan had taught him to feel against the oppressors. And like Basil Anickin, he wanted to keep alive forever the fuel to continually ignite that hatred!

He watched as Kazan refused the priest's offer of unction.

Had Paul's heart not been so heavy, he might have smiled, for he thought he detected one last twinkle in Kazan's eyes in that final act of defiance.

Then the executioner slipped the noose around the thin neck, cinching it tight against the protruding Adam's apple.

With eyes transfixed upon the awful proceeding, Paul beheld the unfolding drama of death in silence. He fixed his eyes upon his friend's. And although he knew that it was impossible for Kazan to see him, Paul felt that with the last remaining spark of life he possessed, Kazan was focusing down upon the youth he had affectionately called Pavushka.

Courageously Paul did not turn away. With great force of will, he managed to hold his gaze steady as the trap door sprung open. He winced with a shudder as the rope, with an awful jerk, snapped the bones in Kazan's neck. As he dangled lifelessly at the rope's end, the last gasp of air squeezed out of Kazan's lungs, the hideous aspiration of death.

Paul watched . . . and he would never forget.

33

For several hours after the hanging, Paul walked the streets of St. Petersburg, having lost all sense of time.

Sometime after noon he wandered across Isaac's Bridge to Vassily Island. His progress was aimless, but all along he knew he would end up at Kazan's flat on Maly Prospect. The porter let him in without question, for he was a frequent visitor. He had, in fact, lived in the place until after the Voronezh meeting. As Kazan's activities intensified, however, Kazan had considered it unwise for them to be too closely associated. Paul located a flat with six or seven impoverished students two blocks away, where he had lived ever since.

Paul glanced sadly around the shabby room. It was a pitiful representation of a man's life. Whatever material wealth or possessions Kazan might have had from his father, who was by no means a wealthy man in the first place, he had given up when he answered Herzen's call to "go to the people." His remaining years, few though they were, he spent in poverty.

"I'm poor as a dirt-scratching peasant!" he would laugh. "And I am proud of it!"

But now it seemed only a miserable shame. Paul did not count Kazan's worth by his material possessions. Yet in view of the purposeless death he had just died, the condition of his living quarters made his life seem all the more futile.

The police had ransacked the place after Kazan's arrest. Paul bent over and picked up a chair that had been left lying on its side on the floor. One by one he set the rest of the furnishings in place. He gathered up some broken pieces of crockery and cookware and a few books scattered on the floor. Paul stacked the books neatly on a table—he supposed he would take them himself, for it seemed a shame to leave them for the illiterate porter who would no doubt soon be clearing out the place for a new tenant. They would be for Paul a small remembrance of his friend, something untarnished by blood and hate. God only knew how he needed something, something tangible, at this moment of uncertainty and despair.

Yet Kazan's books could not displace the hatred simmering within him. The ghastly memory of Kazan's death had been imprinted upon his brain and heart forever.

The events of that black day in his life had not yet directed Paul toward any certain course. But as he wandered around the dingy room, certain perspectives gradually began to come into focus. Each pitiful possession, each worn book, each broken chair began to speak silently to him, telling him what he must do. There was only one path for him to take now. In the midst of all this plundered emptiness, Paul must find a way to give meaning to his friend's life. He must elevate Kazan's memory out of this wretched poverty, to give him the legacy of honor he deserved.

In that moment, Paul knew that *he* must carry on the mission for which Kazan had been martyred.

Naive or idealistic notions about what that meant had disappeared.

Paul still believed fervently, now more than ever, that the mission was a just and noble one. But for the first time he saw that Kazan's chosen path—the path of violence and bloodshed—was the only one, the right one. A noble goal must be obtained by any means possible. No crime could be too evil, no method too distasteful.

He recalled something from one of Kazan's pamphlets, a quote from the writing of Sergei Nechaev. Paul had balked at the very idea when he first read it. But now he understood. Now he found himself on the same side of the fence with a man he had once looked upon as a depraved murderer.

Morality, Nechaev had written, *is everything which contributes to the triumph of the revolution. Immoral and criminal is everything that stands in the way.*

Perhaps he would not go as far as Nechaev had gone. But Paul was determined to go further than he had ever gone before. He was at last ready to make the ultimate sacrifice for the cause. He was prepared to give his very soul to the cause of liberation, even to the point of death, if his destiny followed that of Kazan.

He left the apartment with a great sense of purpose. Now he could hold his head high among any of Kazan's colleagues, even the leaders Zhelyabov, Perovskaya, and Anickin. He felt the zeal and single-minded determination that drove them, that had driven Kazan. At last, though it had taken his mentor's death to achieve it, he was one of them!

It was natural, then, that Paul's footsteps now turned toward these new comrades.

34

It was not easy to locate Andrei Zhelyabov. He kept his footsteps well concealed, and did not remain many weeks in the same place.

Paul, however, knew enough of the right people, and was sufficiently recognized as the protege of the now-ennobled Kazan, that with an afternoon's searching and questioning and walking about from contact to contact, he was able to find his way to the inner sanctum of rebellion.

The tall, lean, handsome revolutionary greeted him with a cool formality. He kept his true feelings under close guard deep within himself, and did not easily let his tone or facial gestures reflect what he might be thinking on another level. Paul found the leader of The People's Will to be of a kind and gentle disposition.

"It is a terrible shame about Kazan," said Zhelyabov with sincerity as he motioned Paul to a chair. "He will be sorely missed among us." The leader did not reflect on the fact that Kazan had been executed for his and Sophia's attempt on the tsar's train, nor that his comrade's death would take the heat off his own head. Kazan's death, in fact, would probably make things easier for him for quite some time.

The flat, on the fifth line on Vassily Island, was in a neighborhood populated largely by low-ranking government employees. It reflected that large St. Petersburg class with its threadbare, semi-poverty existence. It was several steps up in quality from Kazan's lodgings, but it was still poorer than many carriage houses attached to mansions throughout the city. Zhelyabov explained that the occupant was a friend who had permitted him to stay there temporarily.

"I must necessarily move about constantly," he said. "Freedom of movement is becoming increasingly difficult. The number of people who are willing to keep me are fewer and fewer. The particular friend here is nervous about my presence, and I am in the process of relocating once more. It is no small feat that you found me at all."

"Then I am even more grateful that I did," said Paul, feeling awed in the presence of this great leader. "And I appreciate that you consented to see me."

"I remember seeing you often with Kazan. I know he put great store in his friendship with you. Am I correct in assuming that his untimely death has brought you to me?"

"Kazan was a brother to me," replied Paul. "He gave me so much, cared for me when I was alone and lost in this big city, fed me from his meager supply, and opened his home to me. He helped me to be strong when I was a frightened boy in prison. Sometimes I do not know what I will do without him."

"You will do well, I am sure."

"I suppose I have no choice but to go on."

"Unfortunately, I am in no position to offer you succor."

"That is not why I have come."

"I thought not. I see some deeper purpose in your eyes. I hope I can help you."

"It is my hope that I can help *you*," said Paul.

"How so?"

"I feel I owe it to Kazan to carry on his mission."

"And you think you are capable of doing so?"

"For a long time I wavered," Paul said, "believing in the cause and yet still hesitant to make the kind of wholehearted commitment I saw in Kazan and I see in you and the others. Until today, I tried to hold on to a hope that there must be some middle ground."

"You say 'until now.' Has something changed?"

"Now I see that there is no such hope except that which you offer. There is no other way to fight an evil and unjust enemy except with their own methods."

"It is the same conclusion we have all reached, each of us in our own way and in our own time."

"And so," Paul said, "I want to offer myself to The People's Will for you to use however you see fit."

Zhelyabov thought for a moment, then spoke. "I must tell you, Paul, that although part of me applauds your decision, another part of me is compelled to be honest with you."

He paused and thoughtfully tapped his slim fingers against his chin. "You have been through a terrible ordeal in losing your friend in this way," he went on. "I fear it would strain and confuse a mature man. But for one so young—how old are you, Paul? Seventeen . . . eighteen? Certainly too young to fully comprehend all the complexities of life. You must understand that grief and a sense of indebtedness are simply not powerful enough as motivators to carry you along the path you wish now to take—not by themselves. Something deeper is required."

Paul was silent, staring down at the floor.

"Do you understand what I mean, young Paul Yevnovich?" the older man asked with something like tenderness.

This time he waited for Paul to speak.

"You are right, Zhelyabov," Paul said finally. "I do understand that such motivations are not strong enough to be *vehicles* for commitment. They are mere catalysts. They have only set me upon the path that I inevitably would choose. I understand what you have said, but I also know myself. I will continue to be dedicated to the purposes of The People's Will long after my grief fades." Paul spoke with a kind of self-assurance he had never before felt.

"I see Kazan did not choose his protege lightly," said Zhelyabov with the hint of a smile on his solemn countenance.

"Thank you, sir."

"And how exactly do you think you could best be of service to us?" Zhelyabov asked, turning suddenly serious and businesslike.

"I would like to kill Vlasenko."

"That is no small ambition. We have tried before and failed."

"That is no reason to stop trying, is it?"

"Assuredly not, but the man is slippery . . . and dangerous."

"Perhaps I might succeed."

"Why Vlasenko?" asked Zhelyabov with curiosity.

"Let's just say I have an old score to settle. He is from the same region of the country as I am, and his evil ways have been known to my family and the peasants of the area for years."

The smile on Zhelyabov's face grew wider. "You are a young man with vision, I'll say that for you! And how, precisely, do you propose to accomplish this feat?"

"I have no idea," replied Paul. "I have never done anything like this before."

"Never killed?"

"Never."

"Any experience with weapons?"

"No. I know nothing about guns or explosives."

"Ah, a novice . . . I should have guessed. Well, I will take you on as *my* protege then, at least in the matter of Vlasenko. I would hate to see you killed or arrested on your first assignment."

"You would truly do such a thing?" said Paul hopefully.

"I see in you what The People's Will needs more of, young Burenin. But I must tell you that I have higher priorities than the death of a mere Third Section chief at this time."

"I realize that."

"But the experience would do you good; and who can tell, it might lead you to bigger things. And there might be another advantage to targeting Vlasenko at this time. . . ."

He rubbed his chin, obviously in thought. "Come here."

Paul followed him as he led the way into a back bedroom, where Zhelyabov pulled a small crate from a wardrobe. "My host would have heart failure if he knew I had stashed these here. I just recently received them, and I will have to find a more secure hiding place for them before he returns home. But have a look—perhaps these will be your new stock-in-trade!"

He hefted the crate onto the bed, and Paul peered inside. Zhelyabov picked up one item after the other, turned them over in his fingers, and handed them to Paul, identifying the many types of fuses, connectors, detonators, blasting caps, friction matches, and explosives. Many of the names and technical terms he applied to the equipment were words Paul had never heard in his life. But he comprehended clearly the purpose behind each of the items.

"You can forget all about guns," said Zhelyabov. "They are a weapon of the past. They are too limited in their effect. Besides that, most of our people are such rotten aims that handguns are worse than useless. Vera Zasulich became quite a heroine for her deed against Trepov. But in truth, the incident bordered on the ridiculous."

"How so?" asked Paul.

"She emptied her revolver and only managed to *wound* the man—and at point-blank range. No one could be such a bad shot!"

Paul laughed, but Zhelyabov did not think the matter humorous.

"It was the same with Soloviev's attempt on the tsar," he went on. "Alexander was alone on that bridge and passed Soloviev at arm's length. He went to all that trouble to position himself perfectly, yet still he missed!"

He sighed. "I suppose I've had my share of misses too," he said. "But at least these more sophisticated methods give a fighting chance of escape for my people. You only have to be able to hit the broad side of a barn to blast someone to smithereens!"

Excitedly he took some fuses from the box. "These are brand new," he said, showing them to Paul. "And very effective, from all I have been told, though we still have to experiment with them. They are a *timed* fuse as opposed to a straight electrical charge, and are supposed to be much more reliable and efficient than old timed fuses. I have always preferred the electrical, but if these are as good as they say, there could be many incidents where a timed fuse could be the difference between success or failure. I plan to use these on my next major attempt on the tsar. You seem like a bright enough young fellow, Paul. I do not think it would take long to train you in the use of explosives. What do you say?"

"When do we begin?"

"Well, we can start by getting all of these things out of this apartment. I think between the two of us we can adequately conceal it all beneath our clothing in just a couple of trips."

35

"Anna, what *am* I going to do about Basil when he returns from Moscow?"

Katrina stood on top of a stool while Anna pinned up the hem of her dress.

"You are much better at talking to people than I am, Princess," said Anna around a mouthful of straight pins.

"*Talking* perhaps, but not tactfully."

"I'm sure you will find the best way."

"Oh, but I *must* think of just the right thing to say. I don't want to make him angry by telling him I mustn't see him anymore for a while. But . . . I can't help being fearful."

Anna put in the last pin. "You may climb down," she said.

Katrina did so, and Anna unfastened the dress. She helped her mistress into a pale blue muslin sundress, then gathered up the one she had been working on and prepared to leave.

"You are not going now?" Katrina asked.

"I'm sorry. I thought you wanted this dress finished for to-night."

"I do, but can't you sew on it here? We're not finished talking. I still don't know what I will say to Basil, and you must help me." She drew the dressing table stool on which she had been standing toward the bed and motioned Anna to it, while she herself plopped down on the bed. "Maybe I ought to write him a letter," she said enthusiastically.

Anna said nothing.

"I know you are thinking something, Anna," said the princess. "I can tell. What is it?"

Anna smiled. Try as she might, it was difficult for her to hide her feelings sometimes.

"Well, Princess," she said slowly. "I do not think Basil Anickin will accept a letter. If you do not confront him personally, he will confront you."

"Hmm . . . you are probably right."

"But perhaps your fears will prove unfounded. At least, I do not think you need to fear."

"Would you not be afraid if you were in my place, Anna?"

"Yes, I am sure I would be. I suppose what I meant to say is that you need not carry your fears alone."

"I know you will always be a friend beside me," said Katrina tenderly.

"I hope that I am, Your Highness. Yet things beyond our control may come between you and me someday."

Anna forgot her sewing momentarily and glanced up at her mistress. "But, Princess, I believe there is only One who will certainly *always* be there for you, to help with your burdens, and to carry your fears on *His* shoulders."

"Whoever do you mean?" asked Katrina.

"God, of course—our Lord Jesus Christ. He is the only one who can truly see us through our troubles."

"Well, I can use His help now!"

"He surely wants to give it—if everything my own father taught me and everything I feel in my heart is true."

"But, Anna, as much as I have admired your faith, I cannot feel the kind of closeness to God you seem to have. I go to mass, and this last Lent I was almost completely obedient. But, I don't know . . . I suppose I am not a deep enough thinker to understand all about God, and whenever I try to pray, my mind seems to wander."

"We all have to wrestle with such things, Princess," said Anna with a smile.

"Oh, but it comes easier to people like you, Anna. You like to think about spiritual things. I try sometimes, but I just can't keep my mind on them."

"Do you think that is a good excuse for not drawing as close to God as possible?" Anna asked. She did not quake at such a bold questioning of her mistress. They had grown a great deal together, and by studying side by side, they had learned to face difficult questions. "I have watched," Anna went on, "how many times you have struggled to master one of Fingal's mathematical or scientific principles. When something is before you that you want with all your heart, you will spare *no* effort to achieve it. And yet here is the highest of all life's goals—understanding and knowing about life with God. It hardly seems right to give up on it so easily."

Katrina sighed. "I know you are right," she said, without much conviction.

"There is a story in the Bible, Princess, that comes to my mind. Would you like to hear it?"

"I don't suppose it could hurt."

"It is about two women—sisters, actually," Anna began. "Mary, the younger, could sit all day and be content to meditate on the words of her friend Jesus. You see, these two women and their brother knew Jesus very well, and were among His closest friends. His words were precious to Mary, and she spent much time pondering things He had told them. Her older sister Martha loved to work about the house and entertain guests, cooking and tending the needs of people like Jesus and His disciples when they came to visit. She was always busy at some task about the house. And though she loved such work, at times it annoyed her that her sister spent all her time at the Lord's feet and did not help her."

"So what happened?" asked Katrina. "Did they have a fight?"

"One day Martha complained to Jesus about her sister not helping. Do you know what He said?"

Katrina shook her head.

"He told her that Mary had chosen the most important way, and that He would not keep it from her."

"But the cooking and cleaning and all that needed doing," objected Katrina. "*Someone* had to do it."

"The Lord did not think the less of Martha for her hard work. He loved her as much as He loved Mary. But He did not want Martha's busyness to make her lose sight of what was truly important—loving God."

"And not to use it as an excuse, is that what you are saying?" Anna smiled.

"But do you think it is possible for people like Martha who are busy, and people like me who don't think about God as much as people like you—can we still be close to God like that? Can I?"

"It doesn't seem to me that Jesus would have rebuked Martha unless it were possible, and unless He did want her to spend a little more time considering spiritual things. Everybody is different, Princess, just like Mary and Martha . . . and just like you and me. But I can't help but believe God wants us all to love Him a little as Mary did Jesus, and think about and treasure His words."

"Oh, Anna, how can you be so wise about all this?" exclaimed Katrina.

Again Anna smiled. "I don't think I am, Princess," she replied. "But I have spent time thinking about what I read in the Bible, especially the things Jesus says."

"How much easier it would be if I were more like you!"

"Everyone cannot be the same. God made us different for a reason. But He wants to be a friend to us all, and He can use many types of people. My papa used to say that even a mule can pull a plow if necessary—"

She stopped short and blushed at the implication of her words.

Katrina laughed. "More than once my own father has told me I can be terribly mulish!"

"Everyone is stubborn at times."

"Not *everyone* . . . not you, Anna!"

"I have a will of my own too, Princess," laughed Anna. "Perhaps I just keep it hidden."

"Well, I won't give up trying then, Anna. But I am still no

closer to knowing what to say to Basil than I was before."
Katrina sighed.

"At least you know who can help you."

"Yes . . . yes, I do." Katrina jumped suddenly from the bed.
"Anna, it is still early," she said excitedly. "Let's go to church.
I should like to pray."

"Why don't you pray right here?"

"Here? Oh no . . . I would feel too foolish!"

Anna recalled all the times she had heard her papa praying
in the fields or in the old barn full of cobwebs as he tended
their few animals. And how often she'd seen her *matushka* mur-
muring a prayer while washing the family's clothes. From
them she had learned to talk to God as she went about her
daily tasks. She did it without a second thought. Yet she knew
that many gave no more consideration to prayer than they
would to selling everything they had to join a convent or a
monastery. Prayers were for the priest to intone during mass.
But the older Anna grew, the more she realized what an unusual gift she had received in her parents' example without even
knowing it.

At the same time, she did not want to press it upon her
mistress. They could pray just as well in the church as in the
house, and she was happy that Katrina wanted to go. They had
not been to mass together since Easter Eve. So it was with a
particularly light heart that Anna set out that afternoon to St.
Andrew's church on Vassily Island in the Fedorcenko carriage
with her mistress.

36

Anna bought two candles. One she lighted for Sergei, glad that Katrina was too caught up in her own prayers to ask who the candles were for. The other she burned for her family.

When they exited the homely old church, both girls breathed in deeply of the warm afternoon air, feeling peaceful and refreshed. Anna saw on the face of her mistress a new look of confidence and strength, and she silently rejoiced for her.

The sunshine seemed bright after the dimly lit interior of the church, and they instinctively paused on the steps of the building while their eyes adjusted.

"Has the sun become brighter in the last half hour?" said Katrina.

"Perhaps you feel better *inside*," smiled Anna. "That can make all of life seem brighter."

"You may be right. Thank you, Anna—and thanks to God too, of course."

As they began to make their way to the carriage, Anna suddenly stopped dead in her tracks. Katrina turned toward her with a questioning look. Anna's face was pale, and all light had drained out of her eyes.

"Anna! Whatever is the matter?" she exclaimed, seeing her maid's distress.

"I . . . I just thought—but no . . . it can't be . . ."

"Thought what, Anna?"

"I must have made a mistake, Princess," said Anna, trying to shake off the cloud that had come over her. Yet even as she said the words, she continued to glance across the street nervously.

"Anna, you must tell me," insisted Katrina. "I can see that you are still disturbed."

"I . . . I thought I saw . . . someone I know," replied Anna at last.

"A ghost, from the look of you."

Anna did not reply. Katrina stared at her. She had never seen her maid so agitated.

"If I may have your leave, Princess," said Anna after a moment, "may I find my own way home?"

"So you *don't* think you were mistaken after all?"

"I must know, Princess. If I am wrong, I will find out soon enough. But if not, I would like to speak to the person I mentioned."

"I will wait, Anna."

"Thank you, Princess. But this is something I think I must do by myself."

"Of course, Anna. But are you sure you want to be alone in this district?"

"I will be fine."

"It is terribly seedy."

"I come to St. Andrew's often, remember?"

"If you are certain . . ."

"I am . . . thank you," said Anna.

Katrina gave her a few coins for a *droshky*, then stepped into her carriage.

Anna did not even wait for Moskalev to pull away before she hurried across the street toward the crowded and noisy market. Her heart beat violently inside her chest, and her face was still white despite the exertion.

The figure she had seen was no longer visible. She ran in among the wagons and booths and vendors with their carts, heedless of the shouts and commotion and marketplace haggling filling the air around her. Frantically she ran about, glancing up and down the rows, trying to focus her eyes upon the one face she now sought.

Suddenly she saw the familiar back and head. But he

seemed to be hurrying away from her!

She snatched up the hem of her dress and ran as fast as she could go with new energy. This time she would not take her eyes off him for a second!

She called out, praying he would be able to hear her above the din.

He seemed to hesitate, then went on. She shouted again, still rushing toward him.

He stopped and turned fully around to face her. As if with physical impact, their eyes met. He stared with shocked surprise, even pain. Anna slowed her pace and walked toward him, smiling. Why was there no joy in his face?

Suddenly he jerked around and rushed off again in the opposite direction.

"Paul!" she cried once more, anguish filling her voice. She knew he had seen her and recognized her . . . yet he had run away!

Again she tried to run, but the throng of shoppers and the haphazard arrangement of stalls and dogcarts and clusters of people impeded her progress. Still she managed to keep her brother in sight.

Then just as suddenly as before, Paul stopped again. The two uniformed gendarmes entering the market on the other side apparently caused him to think twice about the direction of his flight. In another moment or two, Anna caught up with him.

"Paul!" she exclaimed breathlessly. "You . . . I didn't know . . . What are you doing in St. Petersburg?"

"Hello, Anna," he said curtly, not even attempting to answer her questions.

"But what *are* you doing here . . . and why did you run from me?"

"It's a long story, Anna." His voice was husky. He was having difficulty masking his surprise at this meeting . . . nor could he conceal his dismay. Anna felt it and was grieved. Something must be dreadfully wrong!

"Paul, what *is* it?" said Anna. As overjoyed as she was to see her brother, the years had matured him, and she could not fail to see the hardness that had come over his countenance.

"So many things, Anna," he replied wistfully, then shot a nervous glance over his shoulder at the two policemen.

Anna gazed at his face a moment, trying to discover some remnant there of the innocent younger brother she had last seen in Katyk.

"There's a tea shop around the corner," she said finally. "Won't you join me?" Without giving him a chance to answer, she linked her arm in his and they walked away from the market. They went some distance in silence.

"Anna," Paul said finally, in an almost desperate-sounding outburst, "I am sorry."

"Dear Paul, that hardly seems the way to start a reunion. I want to hear about you, what you are doing." She tried to sound eager, although she knew from his voice that more serious matters were on his mind than mere visiting.

"I am afraid it is the only way to begin this one," he replied. "I am sorry for running when I saw you. But I am sorrier that we met in the first place."

"Paul, how can you say that? What has happened?" Anna could no longer restrain her emotion. Tears welled up in her eyes. There was much more to all this than his running from her. Paul had changed!

"It would be best for both of us if we parted right now," he said, "and forgot that we ever saw each other."

"You are my brother, Pavushka." He winced at the sound of the diminutive form of his name, *Little Paul*, and it made Anna's heart ache. From Kazan's lips he had felt it endearing; from Anna it made him feel like a child. "I cannot leave you," she went on, "until I know what troubles you, and how I might help."

"You can't help, Anna."

"Oh, but won't you let me try?"

"I would never allow you to be drawn into the troubles that may soon come upon me."

"Oh, Paul, I don't understand any of this!"

"That is why I left home, why I must be as one dead to you all. It is for your own protection."

"But don't you see, I *want* to help you—whatever is the matter."

"I am beyond your help, and I do not want or need it."

"Why did you leave home, Paul?"

"I was forced to leave—"

"Not Papa!"

"No. He would never do such a thing. He would live with my shame before sending me away."

"Of course. Whatever your trouble, he would love you through it."

"I couldn't do that to him. I could not bring shame upon him. So I left Pskov as soon as they released me from jail."

"Jail? What are you talking about, Paul?"

"It is a long story, Anna. Long and unpleasant. I don't want you to hear such ugly things—not about your own brother."

"Paul, despite what you have always thought, I am not a hothouse flower that must be protected and pampered. I will love you no less."

"You do not know the truth about me, Anna."

"I am strong enough to hear what you have to say—perhaps not within myself, but with the strength God gives me."

"I see you still believe in fairy tales."

"Oh, Paul, how can you say that?" She started to cross herself as she uttered a quick silent prayer for her brother, but he quickly grabbed her hand.

"Not for me, Anna. I want no prayers on my behalf."

She managed a smile through her pain. "It is too late, dear Pavushka," she said.

He slowly dropped his hand from hers. "All right, Anna, you want to hear about my troubles . . . I will tell you." His voice was filled with defiance and bitterness.

They walked past the tea shop. Neither was in the mood for tea, and the things Paul had to say were best not told in close proximity to eavesdroppers.

37

Up and down the streets of Vassily Island walked brother and sister—the one rebelling against what he saw as injustice in the world, the other full of a heart of love that could not understand his defiance.

Paul talked of his experiences with scornful relish, perhaps subconsciously wanting to hurt his gentle sister as he had been hurt. Yet after the worst of his pent-up anger had vented itself, he began to talk in the manner Anna was accustomed to, pouring out his heart. He reminded her, once in a while, of the youthful Paul she had known back in Katyk. He tried to maintain the tough exterior, but found it impossible with a sympathetic and loving listener like Anna.

But the moment his talk came around to Kazan's death, the hardness quickly returned. "It only proved that everything I have always said is true, Anna," he said. "The tsar and Vlasenko and all the rest are out to spill the blood of the radicals, whether crimes are committed, whether proof of guilt exists, or not."

"But you said yourself, Paul, that Kazan was one of them, one of the leaders . . . that he condoned the methods of violence. Isn't it possible—"

"I think you have lived among the nobility too long, Anna!" he snapped.

"I'm sorry, Paul. I didn't even know Kazan. I don't know whether he deserved to die, but—"

"He was my friend," interrupted Paul again, in mingled anger and fresh pain at the thought of the hanging.

"Oh, Paul, but don't you remember what Mama always used to tell you about getting into trouble just by being with that group of *strangers,* as she called them. Kazan was part of it all, even if nobody died in the incident he was arrested for. Isn't that being an accessory? And he *did* threaten the tsar's life; you said as much."

"So when I was arrested in Katyk along with Kazan and the others," he replied, ignoring her second comment, "you would have believed *me* guilty for the same reason?"

"Guilty of breaking the *existing* laws," she answered slowly, tentatively. She did not enjoy this kind of debate. "So . . . weren't the police only doing their duty to arrest you?"

"And if the laws themselves are wrong?"

"Then they must be changed, not broken."

"There is no other way to change the laws, my dear simpleminded sister. The people of Russia have been trying for three hundred years. But the government of this land spends very little time listening to its people!"

Anna shook her head. For the first time she was glad for all Fingal had tried to teach her and the princess about the roots of the strife presently dividing the Motherland. "Civil protest, even civil disobedience may be justifiable in some cases—perhaps in this case, Paul. But murder is another thing entirely. That goes far beyond the breaking of some minor law as you did in Katyk. To kill is to defy the most serious of *God's* laws, Paul. How can you possibly argue against a truth you have been taught and know to be true?"

Her brother was silent a long time before he answered.

"Anna, you have only to step out of your little fairy world of pampered princesses and gilded corridors for one minute to truly see what the real world is like." As he spoke he gave her a hard, penetrating glare, almost a challenge. He waited a moment, then went on.

"Nothing is *normal* in Russia; *nothing* works as it should; *nothing* operates according to the pat maxims we learned as children at our father's feet. You admit there is injustice, yet you have no concept of its true scope. Perhaps you might if you saw your friends rotting in prison for crimes no worse than reading unacceptable literature, or meeting together to exchange ideas the government finds offensive. . . ." He paused, then took a breath and continued. "Houses of the innocent are searched and their lives turned upside-down for a *rumor* of so-called 'anti-government' sympathy. I have seen men and women exiled for no more than carrying a banned pamphlet in their pocket. I might even have suffered such a fate in Pskov had I not been so young. Even at that I was . . ."

He faltered momentarily as the memory of his imprisonment came painfully back to him.

"But how does our ruler, our benevolent 'Little Father' respond to our cries for justice? He answers by making more arrests, by greater censorship and repression of the press, by calling for more hangings, and by giving a wider range of power to animals like Vlasenko. You know him, Anna. You know what cruelty he showed to Papa's friends. And he is worse now with such power in his hands! Tell me, Anna—what recourse is there?"

He did not wait for her to reply. "The monsters in power leave us no other path. They have signed their own death warrants by their blinded eyes and injustice!"

"Paul . . ."

Anna was too stunned to say more. She shuddered at his use of the collective *us*. She refused to think he condoned all this violence, much less that he might be *part* of it! How could her sweet, sensitive, innocent Pavushka possibly be involved in . . . in killing? Yet she feared his own words condemned him.

"I suppose it is too much for me to ask you to understand," Paul said. "How much do your princes and princesses see of all this anguish?" he went on bitterly. "What do they know, what do *you* know all hidden away behind the wealth of the aristocracy?"

He was right. How *could* she understand? Could she ever accept that her own brother was in league with cold-blooded murderers? But even if everything he said was right, there *had* to be some other way!

"I am sorry, Paul," she said with anguish. "But no, I cannot understand. People are being killed by these attacks on the tsar and other officials—innocent people! There is no possible justification for that. There *can't* be any."

"It is unfortunate," Paul replied distantly. "But in a just cause, sacrifices must be made."

"Paul!" she cried, her voice drawing the stares of passers-by as they walked along.

"I am willing to sacrifice my own life, Anna," he said intractably.

"Oh, my dear brother . . ."

She was weeping now, and took a handkerchief from her pocket to wipe away the tears.

"How shall I tell Mama and Papa?" she asked, at last voicing the greatest agony in her wrenching heart. "How can you do this . . . to them?"

"They are dead to me, Anna, as I should be to them," he replied coolly.

"Paul! How can you say such a horrid thing?"

"My only family now are my comrades in this cause."

"And me . . . am I no longer your sister? Do I no longer love you?"

He did not answer. Anna glanced away, her heart torn in two, struggling to fight against breaking down completely.

"I cannot prevent you from telling them all you have learned about me," Paul said in another moment. "I don't care for my sake. It would be best for all if they buried me in their minds. But for *their* sake, Anna, take care what you say to them."

She looked up hopefully. "Then you *do* still care about them?"

"Of course. But it is now only in the way a man grieves for a lost loved one who has gone away never to return—"

For just a moment, even amid her pain, Anna was reminded of Sergei, and her brother's words stung all the more.

"It's the only way it can be, Anna," he went on. "I am dead, Anna."

"I can never accept that, Paul."

"You *must* accept it! You don't even have to tell them you saw me."

"I doubt I could hide that, even in a letter."

"Ah, my transparent sister!"

He smiled lightly and touched her cheek in one last sign of tenderness. For a moment he was the same dear Paul, still an earnest, idealistic young country lad. But the moment was all too brief. The next instant the dark, heavy shroud fell again over his youthful countenance.

"There is nothing more I can say then, Paul?"

"Not if you think you can try to talk me out of the principles I have come to hold. Nothing can do that, Anna—not even you."

A long silence fell between them.

When again they began to talk, they walked on for ten more minutes, each making pathetic attempts at trivial conversation. Yet each one's lifestyle and beliefs were so offensive in the other's eyes that there remained very little left to say that did not add salt to their already wounded hearts. Finally, they neared the approach to Nicholas Bridge. There was nothing to say except goodbye.

"Will I see you again, Paul?" asked Anna softly.

"Not by intention," he said. "And if you should see me as you did today, Anna, it would be best, for both our sakes, for you to turn in the other direction and pretend you do not know me."

"That would be *so* hard, Paul. How could you expect it of me?"

"Life is hard, Anna."

Anna could no longer think about discretion, or even about what Paul himself might think. She turned and wrapped her arms lovingly around her younger brother. He stood woodenly for a moment, refusing to give in to the affection he still felt for his sister. But her tears finally overcame him. It was much easier to think of his family as dead to him when they were miles away.

Slowly he raised his arms and returned Anna's embrace, tentatively at first, then with an almost desperate fervor. When they parted, his cheeks were also streaked with tears.

"Goodbye, Anna," said Paul.

"Paul . . . I love you," said Anna. "And I always will—no matter what."

"Thank you."

"Goodbye, Paul," she said softly, reluctantly. Then he turned and was gone.

Anna stood at the entrance of the bridge and watched as Paul threaded his way down the crowded street. Would she ever see him again? He had not even told her where he lived. His life and cause had swallowed him up completely.

Yet as she turned and began her way across the bridge, she could not keep herself from clinging to the small glimpses of an earlier Paul, not completely dead but struggling for life beneath the tough skin of the embittered rebel youth. If only she could have said something to coax that Paul out of hiding. Yet her intuition told her that words would probably not have helped.

She must commit her brother the rebel into the hands of God, who loved Paul more than she or even their own papa did. Only that love could now keep him—if he would only accept it—from a life that was sure to end in destruction.

38

The minute Anna returned, Princess Katrina noticed something was wrong.

"Are you ill, Anna?" she asked with genuine concern. "I have never seen you so pale."

"I suppose I am not feeling my best," replied Anna. The sickness in her heart had, in fact, begun to make its way to her stomach. All she had said to Katrina only hours ago about God sharing burdens and delivering from fear was still true, but oh, how she hurt inside!

"Why don't you lie down, Anna?"

"I must iron your dress for the ballet this evening."

"Oh, pooh! Someone else can do it. This isn't a labor camp, Anna. You don't have to work on your deathbed, you know!"

Anna managed a smile. "I suppose I imagine myself more indispensable than I am."

"But you are, Anna! When I caught you in the garden that day I would never have imagined that you would become such an important part of my life. I do need you. You have become as necessary to me as Nina is to Mother. But I think I can manage for a few hours without you—as long as you are well and fit by the time Basil returns from Moscow."

Anna went to her little room and lay on her bed with a book in hand, thinking that reading might distract her mind. She could not remember the last time she had fallen asleep in the middle of the day, yet before long she was fast asleep, dreaming vaguely of lying beneath her old willow tree at home, a book in her lap, with the fragrant breezes of summer blowing gently past her face.

She awoke two hours later with a start. The shadows slanting through her bed chamber windows had lengthened and darkened. She could not tell how late it might be. Could the princess already have left for the ballet without her assistance?

For the first moments after waking, Anna's mind was filled with thoughts of Katrina and her responsibilities to her mistress. Then suddenly she remembered why she had taken to her bed in the first place.

Her little brother was a rebel, a subversive, a comrade of assassins and murderers! He had turned his back on his family, perhaps even on God himself. Every memory of Paul's words flooded back to her, as painfully sharp as the moment she had first heard them.

She crept out of bed, still fully clothed, and opened the door. Peeking out into Katrina's sitting room, she saw a lamp burning. Perhaps it was not as late as she feared. Her gaze moved across the room to the mantel clock. It was nearly seven.

Anna knocked softly on Katrina's bed chamber door, but there was no answer. Just then the outer door to the sitting room opened and Nina entered, bearing a heavy-laden tray in her hands.

"Ah, there you are," she said in a brusque, but not unkind tone. "Up at last, and feeling better, I hope?"

"Yes, I am. Thank you."

"Well, you still look pale. Princess Katrina thought that if you were up, you might benefit from some tea."

"That was kind of her. And also of you, Nina. You didn't have to bring it to me here."

"Of course, I have never felt it a good idea for servants in our position, Anna, to make a habit of waiting on other servants. But in your case, I don't mind so much."

The hint of a slightly embarrassed smile played upon her lips. "Now, sit down and drink this tea before it gets cold."

"Thank you, Nina . . . for everything."

"Are you well enough to receive a visitor?"

"A visitor?" repeated Anna. "I don't understand . . . for me?"

"Yes, for you," replied Nina. "It was the only way the princess would have consented to my disturbing you."

"But who could it possibly be?"

"I have no idea, Anna."

"No one would call on me," said Anna, the possibilities already tumbling through her mind. "Everyone I know lives right here in the house." Could it be Misha, Anna wondered? He *had* visited once or twice, but never without letting her know ahead of time. It could not possibly be Sergei, although the very idea of seeing him again, fanciful though it was, nearly sent her mind reeling. And the only other possibility was nearly as wonderful, but she had not told him where she lived. Could it be possible that Paul had had a change of heart and had come seeking her out? "Nina," she added, the color returning to her cheeks, "is it a young man, about seventeen, with dark hair?"

"Not that I make it a habit of assessing other servants' visitors . . . but he is old, thirty or forty if he is a day. And his hair is brownish, as is his bushy beard."

"Oh. . . ." Anna's color drained once more.

"Anna, don't tell me you have a lover!"

"Nothing like that, Nina. I thought it might be my brother. I just recently discovered that he is in St. Petersburg."

"I doubt this man could be your brother. But you'll never find out unless you have some tea first—that is the princess's order."

39

Ten minutes later, Anna descended to the small anteroom where Nina told her the man was waiting.

"Vassili Ivanovich!" she said in bewildered surprise.

"Anna Yevnovna," he replied, greeting her in the same voice Anna remembered, "you look well."

"Thank you."

"They said you were ill, and I am glad to see you looking better."

"It is good to see a familiar face from the village, but . . . but whatever brings *you* to St. Petersburg?"

Vassili Ivanovich, whose father Ivan owned the tavern in Katyk, was one of the last persons Anna would have expected to see so far from home. She did not know him well, but in a village the size of Katyk there were no strangers. She remembered him as a retiring, soft-spoken man who had never married and had always seemed content to sweep the tavern floors and perform other menial tasks for his aging, overbearing father.

"I came seeking work in a cotton mill," Ivanovich said in answer to Anna's question. "My papa is selling the tavern, and there is no place there for me anymore."

"Why do you not keep it?"

"Papa does not think I am able," he said. "I am sure he is right."

"I am sorry to hear that. But I am sure it will work out well for you."

"The city is a frightening place. I hope I will get used to it."

"I have learned my way around a bit," offered Anna, feeling sorry for this country man with such a woebegone expression, "so I shall be glad to help you any way I can until you are settled."

"That is kind of you, Anna, but that is not why I have come to see you."

A puzzled expression crossed Anna's face.

"When your mama heard I was coming here," Vassili explained, "she came to me in the village. And she said, 'I don't care what Yevno says, I want you to bring a message to Anna.' "

He spoke slowly and deliberately, as if each word required deep thought. Anxious as she was to hear any news of her parents, Anna sat patiently on the edge of her chair, waiting for him to get the words out.

"You see, Anna Yevnovna," Vassili continued, "your papa did not think it necessary to worry you—"

"*Worry* me?" interrupted Anna, unable to restrain herself any longer. "Whatever about?"

"He told my papa one night at the tavern that you had big responsibilities with your important position in the city, and that you did not need to be bothered by our little problems in dusty old Katyk. And I see that you are very important here— why, even the princess herself intercedes on your behalf! Your mama thought you should know, but she did not want to upset your papa—not in his delicate condition. So she came to me in private—"

"His *delicate condition*? Please—tell me what is wrong with my papa!"

"I am so sorry, Anna. I am no good at getting anything right. My papa always said I was simple-minded. How am I ever going to find a job in the big city? But they tell me you don't have to be too smart to work in the mills—"

"Please, Vassili Ivanovich, tell me about my father!"

"Do you see what I mean? A simple message and I have botched it up already." He shook his head slowly, as he did everything.

"Vassili. . . !"

"Your papa has not been well, Anna," he sputtered out at last. "He took ill about a month ago. They think it is an ailing heart, and the doctor—"

"He has seen a doctor!" Anna exclaimed in horror. She knew that for her father this was the extremist of measures.

"A doctor from Akulin happened to be in the tavern. My papa fetched your mama right away to speak with him."

"What did he do?"

"He looked at your papa, and then said all poor Yevno needs is to rest, to cut down on his work. But you know your papa. He has worked all his life. So he goes out and works in the fields and then he tires himself and must stop. But he will not stop in time, and once he fainted right in the field!"

"And he would never tell me this," said Anna softly, more to herself than to Ivanovich.

"That is what your papa himself said, that he would never tell you. He did not want to worry you. But your mama would have none of it—and so here I am, the bearer of bad tidings, you might say."

"I must get word to them," said Anna thoughtfully.

"I am not returning to Katyk, so I cannot take a message back for you I am afraid."

"No . . . of course not. But a message alone would never do," mused Anna. She rose and walked slowly about the room as if unaware of Vassili's presence. All at once the years in St. Petersburg—the life she had grown so accustomed to in this mansion, her duties as mistress to a princess, even the very room she was now standing in—suddenly seemed to fade away, and images of her past life rose before her. When she spoke again, she was once more Anna Burenin, peasant daughter of Yevno and Sophia of Katyk.

"I must return to the village myself," was all she said.

40

No one hesitated in giving Anna permission to return home—not Natalia, not Katrina, not Mrs. Remington, not even Nina. Katrina accompanied her to the Nicholas Station two mornings after Vassili Ivanovich's visit, offering Anna enough money for a second-class round trip fare.

"The only thing I ask, Anna," Katrina said as they sat in the carriage waiting for the train, "is that you return to me. For I shall be lost without you."

"Oh, Princess, I will return as soon as I am able."

"Take as much time as you need. Think only of your father, and not of me. I only pray he gets well very soon."

"Do you mean that? Will you pray for him?" asked Anna, looking deeply into Katrina's eyes.

"Yes, Anna. I *will* pray. I am learning many things, remember?"

"Thank you, Princess," said Anna. "You cannot know how much that means to me." Anna paused. "I am only sorry to have to leave you during this difficult time. We both seem to have uncertainties."

"Oh, Basil?" Katrina gave a careless wave of her hand. "Don't give him another thought. I'm sure all will go well."

"I too will pray for *you*," said Anna sincerely.

"Oh, but I do hope you will return before *too* long—by Christmas, or the New Year. I think I will be able to endure being without you for a month or two, perhaps even three. But more than that will be torture for me."

Anna laughed, but a sadness filled her own heart. In all her trouble about her father, she had not until now realized how much she was going to miss the princess, too.

"I shall do my best, Princess."

"Wonderful! I shall not miss you half so much then." Katrina smiled and squeezed Anna's hand. "I just know everything will work out splendidly and your father will be well in no time."

Anna instantly responded with a halfhearted smile. Katrina saw through it. "What is it, Anna? Are you dreadfully worried about your father?"

Anna sighed and glanced away. "It is my brother, Princess," she said after a moment, looking again at Katrina. "He was the one I saw at the market the other day. He is here in St. Petersburg. I only learned of it that day, and my parents do not even know. If I had seen Vassili Ivanovich even a few hours earlier, I would have been able to inform my brother of our father's illness. He might have had a change of heart had he known. But now I have no way to inform him."

"Where is he living? I will take him the message myself."

"I don't know, Princess."

"Didn't you find out when you spoke with him?"

"He would not tell me."

"Why ever not, for heaven's sake?"

"He has been very confused and troubled lately. He thinks it best if the family forgets about him entirely."

"Anna, I am so sorry." Katrina paused. "But I suppose I can understand what you must feel. It is similar to what Sergei has done to us."

Anna was silent. It seemed all the people she loved most were drifting away from her, and now she and the princess had to part ways as well.

"Can't they see how their attitudes only hurt us whom they think they are helping by going away?" Katrina said.

Anna scarcely heard her. She looked down into her lap for a moment, longing to be able to tell the princess of *her* own pain at Sergei's absence as well. She realized she could not, however, and remained silent.

"I wish I could help you in some way about your brother,

Anna," Katrina added after another moment.

"He must find out himself what is the root of the turmoil in his mind," said Anna sadly.

"We each have our brothers, both rebels in their own ways."

"I suppose there is nothing to do but pray for them," said Anna.

"I *will* do that, for your brother as well as your father, then, Anna," said the princess genuinely.

"Thank you again, Princess, for all you have done for me," said Anna.

Katrina embraced her. Anna returned the hug and they held each other for a moment. When they relaxed, both had tears in their eyes.

A train whistle in the background drew their attention. Anna took Moskalev's sturdy hand and stepped down out of the carriage.

"Just come home soon, Anna," said Katrina, her voice soft and tentative.

Again there was a slight hesitation. Suddenly Katrina jumped down from the carriage and threw her arms around Anna again and kissed her on the cheek. She sniffed, then stepped back and added in a husky voice, "Now be off with you before I change my mind about letting you go."

Moskalev grabbed up Anna's bag and escorted her to the train bound for the south. She shook his hand warmly and said goodbye to the first friend she had ever known in St. Petersburg. Anna found her way inside, took a seat by a window, and waved to the burly coachman, who then turned and made his way back to the carriage.

Just come home soon. . . !

Katrina's final words rang over and over in her ears. It should have sounded strange for the mansion of a prince and princess to be called *her* home! Yet Katrina's use of the term warmed Anna's heart. Katrina considered this Anna's *home!* She had become part of this family.

Anna remembered her first frightening arrival in St. Petersburg. She could never have imagined that the day would come when she would leave this place reluctantly, with tears in her eyes for all the friends she was leaving behind: Katrina, Polya, Sergei—wherever he was, Misha, and Paul. Even old Moskalev and Nina, in her own way, had become part of her life.

Anna had promised Katrina she would return, that she would come *home*. Yet at the same time in the south away from the city, another *home* called to her, where her mama and papa and little brothers and sisters waited. Joy and melancholy mingled in Anna's heart—the bittersweet pain of loving and letting go. Perhaps it would always be that way for her, love and loyalties ever divided.

V

HOME TO THE COUNTRY
(Early Fall 1879)

41

Anna awoke in the predawn hours and crept quietly from the warmth of the family bed.

She had slept alone for so many months that it took a few seconds after awaking to recall the lifelong necessity of not disturbing others. The little ones still slept soundly. But when Anna glanced to the other side, she saw that the place usually occupied by her mama and papa was already empty.

Sophia bent over the cook fire stirring the pot of kasha, the embers of the fire casting a warm glow onto her round face. As Anna dressed in the corner, she watched in silence, taking in the familiar scene with a quiet joy. Until she arrived back home two days ago, she had not fully realized how much she had missed her dear family, and all the homey details of the life she had left behind—right down to her mother's morning rituals over the fire. She slipped her feet into a pair of *lapti* her mother had made and then approached the fire.

"Ah, good morning, my dear little Anna," said Sophia, as if she too had been thinking how much she had missed her daughter.

"Good morning, Mama," replied Anna. She walked on to the "beautiful corner," where she crossed herself before the icon of St. Nicholas, then knelt for a brief prayer.

When she rose, her mother was gazing at her with a pleased smile on her face. "It gives my heart joy," she said, "to know the ways of the city have not corrupted your faith."

"You and Papa have taught me too well for that," said Anna.

"It is not so for all those who go to the city, daughter. The

217

stranger's ways have turned many a well-bred Russian peasant from the beliefs of his parents."

Anna wondered if her mother was thinking of Paul as she spoke. She had told them she had seen Paul in St. Petersburg and that he was well. But she had heeded his advice and given them no details. In her very vagueness they no doubt read much of the truth. Yet by remaining silent, she left a thread of hope to cling to. Anna refused to believe it was a false hope by which she deceived her parents, for she still prayed that Paul would see the error of the road he was traveling. God would not give up on him, she knew that. And thus, she somehow felt that by keeping alive her parents' hope, she was at the same time honoring God. At any rate, Yevno and Sophia did not question Anna too closely. They wanted to retain their hope for Paul as much as Anna wanted it for them.

"Where is Papa?" asked Anna.

"Taking care of the animals."

"Should he be doing such things, Mama?"

"I am his wife, Anna, not his jailer. I can ask him to do this or that, but he does not *have* to listen." Sophia laid down the wooden spoon with a heavy sigh. "He hoped his son would take care of the land and the animals in his old age."

"Oh, Mama . . ."

"We take the lot God has given us. That is all we can do."

"I am here now, Mama."

"And it is a comfort to us, daughter."

"I will help."

"But your papa is a proud man."

"How have you managed these last months?"

Sophia took a loaf of bread from a cupboard and began to slice it. "Anna, will you fill the *samovar*?" she said. "Your papa will want his tea when he comes in."

Anna obeyed. In the silence that followed, she began to think that her mother was going to ignore her question. But after a few moments Sophia spoke.

"God provides for us, Anna. He has used you to do so more often than you may realize."

"It has not been much."

"For us, it is a great deal. I do not know what we would have done without the money you sent."

"Papa would say that God could have found another way," put in Anna as she poured water from a pail into the samovar.

"No doubt, no doubt. But you know how the saying goes, 'We do not eat the bread, but the bread eats us.' Maybe that is how God wants it sometimes. People starve—not because God doesn't care, but because that is just what happens."

"Is it that bad, Mama?" asked Anna in alarm.

"No. Thanks be to God we have not come to such a pass!" Relief spread over Anna's face.

"I will tell you, though," her mother went on, "it is no thanks to our landlord. The moment the rent was due, after word got out that your father was ill, his factor Korff was at the door bright and early to collect. They are waiting impatiently for us to fall behind so they can snap up our land. I know he would love nothing more than to make us their servants again. And a stranger was here one day asking about Paul. I did not know what it meant, Anna, but I did not have the heart to tell your papa when he returned home."

The two women fell silent, busy with the tasks before them. At length Sophia spoke.

"Anna," she said softly, but with firm resolve, "you are not to worry about us. You have your own life in the city now. Your Papa and I both feel that is where you belong—"

Anna opened her mouth to protest, but Sophia shook her head vigorously.

"When you first arrived home, I saw that the time in St. Petersburg has been good for you. You have matured and grown into a lovely, genteel young woman. There are many changes in you, dear daughter, and they are all good. You are not a peasant girl any longer. You are being made into something greater. I feel it just being near you. You must return to your life there and let God finish this work He has begun."

"But, Mama, now that I am home, it feels so right to be here again," said Anna, voicing the dilemma she had not expected to face so soon. "How can I know if He wants me to go back? Perhaps I belong here with you."

"You will know, child," said her mother. She dried her hands on her apron and went to Anna, placing a loving arm around her shoulders. "We will all know. He will give us peace in our hearts when the time is right."

"I hope so," said Anna. "But it doesn't have to be soon. Surely it is right for me to stay long enough to help you and Papa until he is better."

"You are more than any father and mother could hope for in a daughter," said Sophia.

She smiled and dabbed the corner of her apron at Anna's eyes, which had begun to fill with tears. "Now, run along and find your papa," she added, "and tell him his breakfast is nearly ready."

42

Anna had missed many things about her home while in St. Petersburg. But as she entered the little barn attached to the back of the *izba*, she knew this certainly had to be foremost among them.

The great city had its gardens and parks. Anna and Polya often went to the Summer Gardens when they had free time together, where Anna enjoyed a taste of the outdoors she loved so much. There were no gardens within miles of Katyk to match the grandeur of the Fedorcenko estate's modest private Promenade Garden, much less the public gardens of Peter the Great's magnificent city.

But in all of St. Petersburg, Anna had found nothing to compare with her father's earthy, warm byre. The pungent fragrance of dirt and straw and hay, combined with animal flesh and manure, brought a smile to her face. She drew in a long breath and filled her lungs with the homey aroma. The pleasant sounds of the doves cooing in the rafters, the old cow's gentle moo, and Lukiv's soft whinny floated through the air in response to Yevno's quiet chatter.

Here lay the heart and soul of the Motherland—not in its army or its emperor or its resplendent capital that mirrored the great cities of the West, not even in its noisy radicals filling the times with their shouts for change. Russia was *here*, in ten thousand such barns and byres and peasant dwellings, many of them far poorer than Yevno's. A foreigner traveling to this huge land where East met West would never really *feel* the pulse of this continent of a nation until he had stood inside the windblown, creaking, weathered barn of some rural peasant *izba*.

On her first day home, relishing anew the sights and smells of this place, Anna had recalled Paul saying that his new-thinking friends wanted nothing but to liberate the peasant masses. Their motives seemed to have changed in a short time. She herself hoped that one day the heavy burden of poverty, such as her own mother and father now faced, could be lifted from the backs of the vast Russian peasantry. But at the same time, she prayed that these humble, earthy roots of a people strengthened by labor and love for the land would never be lost. For if they were, the price of "liberty" would be too high.

"Good morning, Papa," said Anna, walking up to her father where he stood rubbing Lukiv's graying nose.

"Ah, you are awake early today, my Anna."

"It has been light out for some time now, Papa."

"Has it? I suppose I have been out here longer than I thought. Poor Lukiv has been restive lately, and I was trying to calm her."

Anna drew nearer and laid a hand on the horse's speckled flank. "She is a faithful old work horse."

"The best I've ever seen."

"She is getting old, do you think, Papa?"

"Like all good animals, her time must one day come." Yevno

sighed. "The same can be said of a poor old *moujik*."

"Oh, Papa—"

Yevno held up his hand. "There, Anna . . . not to fret about me."

"I can't help it for love of you, Papa," said Anna softly.

"Everyone's time comes—with men and with horses. God calls for His people and His beasts to come back to Him sooner or later."

"But, Papa, that does not mean we should give ourselves up to fate with resignation."

Yevno let out a chuckle, as if humoring the idealism of youth.

"We mustn't cease taking care of the temple God has given us," Anna added.

"And that is what you think your papa has been doing?"

"So I have heard, Papa," Anna answered quietly, not wanting to appear disrespectful.

"I have worked all my life," Yevno sighed.

"Perhaps it is time to work a little less strenuously."

"It is an old habit, and hard to break."

"But Papa, Ilya and Tanya and Vera need you to be with them a good while longer. So do I, Papa, and even Paul."

The mention of his son brought another sigh. Yevno shook his head wearily.

"But even if not for us," Anna went on, "the little ones are still young, and they need you especially—not only to put food on the table for them, but for your love and wisdom as well. Don't take that away from them—from us, Papa. I am not ready to say goodbye to you."

"I am happy to hear that, because I am not leaving Katyk anytime soon!" Yevno smiled. "Now, if you are finished scolding your poor papa . . ."

"There is one more thing," said Anna tentatively.

"My, but I have been a naughty papa to deserve such a tongue-lashing from my own shy little Anna!"

In spite of her attempts to remain earnest, Anna laughed at her father's good-humored teasing.

"So, what else have you to say, my daughter?"

"Now that I am here, Papa, you must let me take on more of the work."

"My little girl has become a hard worker in the city, eh?"

"I have always helped you and Mama. I can feed the animals in the morning, and you can have more time to rest. I can care for them and quiet them down in the evening, too."

"Ah, but being in here does rest and soothe me," said Yevno.

"I can work in the fields, too."

Yevno turned serious. "The time for harvest is nearly here. The weather is already changing."

"You know the harvesting is hardest on you."

"It must be done. I am already too far behind. If the rains come—"

"Then let me help."

"Just you, my little one? I fear you would be slower than your tired old papa."

"I will find help."

"And you expect me to sit on a cushion, like a *boyar*, while others do my work?"

"Yes, Papa, you must."

Yevno rubbed his beard thoughtfully.

"Hmm . . . ," he mused, with a hint of a smile about his lips and a crease still across his brow. "The city has changed you, Anna."

"I am sorry, Papa."

"I do not say it as something for you to be sorry about, dear Annushka."

Anna tried to smile.

"They are not bad changes I see," Yevno went on. "You have learned to stand and speak out. I believe that is good. But—" He chuckled again. "It will take me some time to accustom myself to it."

"Then today you will let me go to the village," said Anna with more confidence, "and find helpers? Some of the men are already finished in their own fields. I am sure there must be one or two who can be spared to help in ours."

"I suppose it will do no harm to allow you to ask about." He paused. "I suppose also that now your papa will have to do a little changing too, eh? Just like his daughter."

"What do you mean, Papa?"

"This stubborn pride of mine was never my best quality."

"It won't be missed, Papa," Anna said with a laugh. "Not much, at least."

"It has been with me a long time. I do not know if I can let go of it so easily."

He scooped another handful of hay into Lukiv's trough. "What do you think, Lukiv, eh? Will you mind putting up with a new Yevno Pavlovich, one who watches while others do his work?"

The horse whinnied, obviously unconcerned with such portentous changes.

"Well, I promise to make sure you always have hay," added Yevno, giving the velvety old nose a loving rub, "no matter what."

Arm in arm he walked with Anna out of the byre and around to the front of the house. Inside they could hear the sounds of the children scurrying about getting ready for the morning meal. Their young voices made Anna all the more grateful that she had summoned the courage to speak to her father. He must not work himself into his grave, not yet. His passing would be a grievous loss, but it would be hardest of all on the little ones. She did not want to think of such things, yet her father's illness had forced many new and hard considerations upon her.

But he had taken her words to heart just now. For that she inwardly rejoiced. She was more determined than ever to take the pressing needs of the harvest off her father's shoulders and not allow him to intervene.

43

As the fall of 1879 approached, the harvest—known as *strad-nya pora*—lived up to the deeper significance of its name: the period of suffering.

Beginning with the severe winter, the entire growing season had been plagued by fickle weather. Reb Plotnik had predicted that the growing season would produce crops only for the most fortunate, and as the year progressed his words bore the ring of truth. Ground-freezing frosts had lasted too long, well into April and even early May. And then unseasonably heavy rains turned many of the newly plowed fields into bogs, delaying planting until much later than was safe. Throughout the months of summer the men of Katyk and Akulin and Pskov anxiously watched and fretted over the rising green shoots and developing heads of grain, hoping and praying that they would reach fruition before the colds of autumn returned upon them out of the north. But the summer seemed shorter than any previous summer they could recall. Crops that should have been put to the sickle and stored away in barns by the end of August were still struggling to ripen on their slender stalks in mid-September.

It was much too late; dangerously late. The stalks had long since browned, but the heads rubbed between the coarse hands of a peasant farmer revealed tiny grains with hints of green around their edges.

Anxiously they had watched the skies, walking to and from their fields many times daily, as if somehow one more test of the grain between their hard fingers could miraculously speed up nature's process. But every day the sun's rays grew less powerful, and still the grain contained too much moisture.

The harvest began prematurely, but in earnest, one evening when old Reb Plotnik made a second pronouncement.

"Rain is coming." He rubbed his shoulder meaningfully.

"How many days, Reb?" asked someone.

Plotnik was silent several long moments, still rubbing his shoulder. "Days . . . weeks, who can tell?" he said finally. "All I can say is it's in the air, and moving toward us."

The old Jew was usually right in his weather predictions. He dictated the plantings and harvests of the surrounding region with a single voice, although it was not openly confessed by the independent farmers. Moreover, most of the Gentile citizens of Katyk were reluctant to give any Jew his due credit, even a lifelong neighbor like Plotnik. Skepticism and debate always followed any of Reb's pronouncements.

Notwithstanding, later that night the sharpening stones were put to the sickles and scythes, and the stalks began to fall the very next day. This was no time to take chances with the crop nearing its peak of readiness. Another week, maybe two, would ripen the rye and wheat to golden perfection. But a rainstorm would ruin the crop, and a partial harvest was better than none at all.

A few farmers delayed, repeating the ritual of checking the grain in their hands and biting into the kernels, while their neighbors took their families to the fields with wholehearted resolve.

Yevno's condition had been steadily declining throughout the summer, and although he had begun in his own fields with the first of his countrymen, he was only about a third of the way through. Most of the others were still at work themselves, and despite Anna's optimism, she could find little help from her neighbors.

"As soon as my own grain is in, I will be there the next morning," several men promised.

But that did not help immediately; people sniffed the air and looked northward with foreboding, anticipating the early fall storm that Reb had predicted.

Yevno refused to listen to his wife and daughter's pleas to let them shoulder the brunt of the labor. Let the rain come when it would, they said; they would get in as much of the rye and wheat as they could and let the birds and the ground have the rest. But Yevno argued, and with good reason, that *he* must go to the fields too.

"My family will starve if the crop is lost," he insisted.

"We will make do," Sophia implored him. "We can eat less for a few months."

"Months of snow and starvation?" said Yevno. "No, wife, *stradnya pora* is no time to rest." He tugged on his coat and frayed work gloves. "I will have the entire long winter to rest once the harvest is in."

He took up his scythe, sharpened the night before to a razor's edge, and marched out to the nearest field, followed by Anna and Vera, who would gather the sheaves as their father cut them. Sophia carried a smaller sickle to assist him as she could between caring for Tanya and Ilya back at the *izba*. As they marched into the field of standing grain, all eyes looked up at the grayish-blue sky, hoping that the rumor of rain would be forestalled in its fulfillment.

Yevno attacked the tall, golden stalks of rye with a will, raising the blade over his head and swinging it down powerfully. He cut out a large semicircular swath from the very point he had left the day before. The girls trailed behind, gathering, binding, and stacking the sheaves. But Yevno's huge scythe toppled the stalks much faster than they were able to gather them, and by midday both Anna and Vera were ready to drop with exhaustion. With their mother's help, when time came for the noon meal, they had managed to bind and stack most of the morning's harvest.

Appetites were scant from the exhausting labor, although a great deal of water was consumed before the small band of laborers took to the field once more. It had not taken even half a day for Anna to realize the absurdity of her plan to see to the harvest without her father. Throughout the afternoon, even as she prodded her ten-year-old sister not to fall behind, it was all Anna could do to keep up herself. After three years waiting on a pampered princess, she had forgotten the rigors of this kind of labor.

But the exertion told most visibly upon Yevno. The burst of energy with which he had begun the day waned as the day wore on. The scythe barely came waist high with each swing by mid-afternoon, and the swaths of its course became narrow and sloppy. His steps became more plodding and his breathing labored, coming in short, panting gasps. After every two or three swings he paused, looking back to see where the girls were, and then started forward again. With every stop it seemed more and more difficult for him to gather strength to move forward and raise the scythe once again into the air.

The afternoon proceeded slowly. As she watched him, her own arms hanging nearly limp from her shoulders, Anna recalled how tireless and strong her father had always been. When the men competed with one another, displaying their skills, Yevno had been able to outstrip many a younger man with the great swings of his scythe. Now he could barely complete a day's labor. Could three years have taken so much life from his powerful frame? With a trembling heart, Anna realized that the drama being played out fifty meters away had little to do with old age. Her papa was ill!

Gradually the sun completed its arc behind the persistent clouds. Steadily the two girls gained ground on their exhausted father and closed the gap between his work and theirs.

At last Yevno turned to see the two dirt-smeared faces a mere ten or fifteen meters behind him. He rested the large blade on the ground and leaned against the long wooden handle.

"Ah, daughters," he sighed wearily, "you have overtaken your old father."

"Papa," said Anna, "it is nearly dusk. Do you not think we have done enough for the day?"

"Enough? It will never be enough until the crop is in," he replied, although his tone did not sound as eager as his words. He turned and lifted the scythe high as if to emphasize his determination, but after a single swing paused again. "If you girls are too tired to go on, you go back to the house. I will help you gather tomorrow."

"Please, Papa," said Anna helplessly, knowing he would not listen, "it is time for you to rest also."

"Nonsense! You go, but I must continue as long as there is daylight."

"I will go on with you, Papa," said Anna, as determined as he.

Yevno smiled through his exhaustion.

"I see you are as stubborn as your father," he said. "Then, Vera, you go. Your mother will be out soon anyway to bring supper."

Vera did not need to be told twice, but scampered off quickly. Yevno forced himself back into motion without further words, as Anna watched with burdened heart. For the rest of the evening, even without Vera and as tired as she was, she had no difficulty keeping up with her father's declining progress across the field. She even found herself slowing intentionally so as not to make it too obvious that he was scarcely moving at a tenth of his morning's pace.

Anna prayed that the rain would not come, or that help would soon arrive. She wondered if God was too busy answering the hundreds of other similar prayers to hear her concerns for her father. Whatever His intent, Anna's words seemed lost in the humid gusts of wind stirring over the still-standing grain. *God, take care of my father!* she prayed. And still she followed him along, gathering into bundles the grain falling beneath the swishing and cutting motion of his scythe.

No more was said between them, although both expressed relief when Sophia brought bread, water, and apples out to them. In the half hour's pause, as they sat on the stubbly field, Yevno's breathing continued labored. The moon rose as the light of day faded, adding to the paleness of his skin.

Sophia and Anna exchanged concerned looks. In the moonlight, Yevno's complexion looked as dusky as the cloudy sky. He handed his cup to his wife, then struggled to his feet and took up the scythe.

"Husband," said Sophia, able to keep quiet no longer, "your life is worth more than any amount of rye and wheat. Come back to the house and rest."

"Without the grain, there is no life," insisted Yevno. "What would you have me do—let the little ones starve?"

"Yevno Pavlovich, we will not starve!" implored Sophia, the alarm clearly evident in her voice. "Please, husband, do not do this to yourself."

Yevno plodded back to work, ignoring her words. He raised the scythe again and began to swing it once more in rhythm. But his movements had lost all their vigor, and the blade scarcely came above his knees before he sent it downward again. The very weight of the instrument was too much for him and the steel blade plowed errantly into the soil. Anna and her mother followed, as much to be near their struggling father and husband as to gather the feebly falling grain behind him. In a gigantic effort Yevno summoned the strength to raise the huge, cumbersome tool one last time. Even as it reached its zenith, something gave way within him. With the forward movement, his hands could not keep hold their grasp. The scythe crashed unceremoniously to the earth, and Yevno collapsed to the ground at its side.

"Papa!" screamed Anna, rushing forward and falling to her knees.

Sophia was beside her the next instant, throwing herself across his chest, speaking feverishly to her unconscious husband.

"Anna," she said, once she realized she was unable to rouse him, "run to the house. Send Vera for the priest. Come back with Tanya and Ilya."

Anna was already on her feet.

"Bring the cart," added Sophia.

"Yes, Mama."

"Hurry, Anna . . . *hurry!*"

44

It took all the strength Sophia, Anna, Tanya, and little Ilya could muster to get the worn-out body of poor old Yevno Pavlovich Burenin onto their rickety cart and back across the field to the *izba*. The priest was already hastening along the road to the cottage by the time the family arrived with their fallen papa.

With the priest's help, they managed to get Yevno onto the bed where the priest immediately began the ceremony of the last rites. Sophia quickly put together a makeshift straw pallet on the earthen floor at the "beautiful corner" of the cottage. As soon as she had it ready, according to custom, they transferred her husband to it, with his head pointing in the direction of the icon of St. Nicholas above. As the priest continued with the rites, Sophia prayed softly, sprinkling Yevno with kernels of grain and salt.

Yevno's labored breathing gradually began to grow more relaxed. The priest had finished with Yevno and was praying in front of the icon when at last Yevno opened his eyes.

"What . . . where am I?" he sighed softly.

"You are safe in the cottage," replied Sophia, who knelt at his side with tears in her eyes. "Go back to sleep, Yevno. All is well."

The old man's eyes widened and he began to take in his situation. "Why am I not in my bed . . . what is the father doing here?"

"We did not know, Yevno . . . we thought it best—"

"What?" interrupted Yevno, trying to rise. "He has not been praying me into the next life?"

The priest knelt down and tried to soothe him.

"Ah, now I remember. The scythe fell from my hand . . . I must have fallen as well. . . ."

"You collapsed, Yevno," said Sophia. "We were frightened. We dragged you here in the cart and sent for the father."

"That accounts for the bed. You are a good wife—you did not want me to die too hard, eh?"

Sophia's tears of joy at seeing her man smile again were her only reply.

"But you have not cut open the wall yet?" asked Yevno suddenly in alarm. "Winter is too close for that!"

"No, husband, we have not had the chance yet."

"Don't touch the wall or the roof. I am not about to die yet! And even if I do, my soul can get out of the *izba* well enough without you cutting any openings."

"Yes, husband. I will do nothing to the *konek*."

"Then get me back into the bed. I am not so close to death that I need to be here. I can see the good saint well enough from the other side of the room."

Seeing her father finally resting contentedly, Anna quietly stole from the cottage with the intent of working on in the moonlight. She found the great scythe where it had dropped, but the effort of lifting it and then trying to swing it with any effect showed her what a strong man her father was, even at his weakest. She laid it down and returned to the barn for the hand sickle, then attacked the standing grain with a hopeful, if weary swing. She was only able to work another two hours, and she felled stalks equivalent to what her father could have sliced through in twenty or thirty minutes. Yet with a feeling of satisfaction she dragged her tired body back to the cottage about midnight and dropped into bed next to her sister.

How she found the strength to rise at dawn was a mystery. All the others except Sophia still slept. Anna could not recall a time her father had slept later than she. But there he was, his breathing labored and noisy, his skin still pale.

Anna dressed, then picked up her coat from the floor where she had dropped it the night before. She joined her mother in front of the fire, took a chunk of brown bread, and headed for the door.

"Where are you going?" asked Sophia.

"There is work to do, Mama."

"The animals need tending, that is true."

"In the fields, Mama. The younger ones can take care of the animals."

"Anna, your face was nearly as gray as your father's last night."

"But I am younger, and strong. The work will not hurt me."

"You cannot cut all the wheat. If the rain comes, it comes."

"Even if I cut only a little at a time, it is something."

The mother looked over her daughter from head to foot. "I think in your own quiet way," she said with a smile, "you are nearly as stubborn as your papa."

Anna took the words as high praise, as her mother had meant them. Sophia wrapped her arms around her daughter and gave her a kiss on the cheek.

"I will help today," she said. "I will leave all the children here to make sure your papa stays in bed."

"That may be hard on him, Mama, to know that two women are doing his work."

"He has himself said more times than I can count how pride goes before a fall. Now he has fallen, and I think only a reminder will be necessary to keep him in the cottage."

"The butcher's son, Peter, came by yesterday while we were in the field and said that their crop is small and he expected to be through in a day or two."

"And. . . ?"

"He said he would help, Mama."

"Bless him—if only the rains hold off."

"And now you are taking Papa's part and worrying about the rain, Mama," smiled Anna.

"The land has been my life as long as it has been your papa's. It is too much a part of my soul not to think about."

Anna nodded. She was of peasant stock too, and understood.

"Now get along, child," said Sophia, "and God be with you."

Despite her aching arms and shoulders, Anna walked into the field with high hopes, attributing the previous night's exhaustion to the full day she had already put in. She picked up the scythe where it still lay, and to her joy found it felt lighter than it had seemed in last night's moonlight. She lifted it and began swinging as she had seen her father do. But by the time she was able to wield the clumsy instrument, her shoulders had already begun to tire, and within an hour her arms felt as though they had been wrenched out of their shoulder sockets. She set the monstrous scythe down and found she could barely lift her hand to tuck back several loose strands of hair.

It was no use. She was simply too small and weak. She would rest a while and then gather and bind what she had cut. After that she would have to be content for the rest of the day with the smaller sickle, and would just have to do the best she could.

The day wore on. Sophia made better use of the scythe than Anna had been able to. Vera gathered, and Anna alternated cutting with the sickle and binding and stacking. Near noon, her mother and sister returned to the house to check on Yevno and prepare their meager lunch.

The rain had still not come, but the air was heavy with its scent and the clouds in the north appeared darker than they had yesterday.

With increasing difficulty Anna tried to remember all the words of faith and hope she had so often spoken to Katrina. But the exhaustion of her body brought despair to her mind. Her right arm hung limp at her side; the tiny sickle had grown as heavy as the giant scythe. "Dear God!" she moaned, collapsing onto the ground, crying in hopeless frustration. She lay on the dry earth a few moments and wept, sweat dripping into her eyes and mingling with her tears.

Her dejection lasted only four or five minutes. She pulled herself up and glanced once more toward the north, in the direction of the ominous clouds. She swung her gaze around toward the west. From the village, she spied a man in the distance walking toward her.

With a pang of renewed hope, she thought immediately of Peter. He was coming to help earlier than he'd said!

But . . . the figure was taller and broader than the fourteen-year-old son of Katyk's butcher. He was dressed in a peasant tunic, belted at the waist with an embroidered belt, his baggy trousers tucked into high black boots. And there *was* something familiar about him. . . . Perhaps one of the neighbors had sent one of their field hands to help. Still . . . she thought she recognized the gait. This man did not walk like a field hand. He walked like—

Suddenly Anna jerked to her feet.

It could not be! It was impossible!

The sickle, which had still been clutched in her hand, fell to the ground with a dull thud. Suddenly Anna was unaware of dirt or stubble or grain, of sickles or scythes or rain or her ailing papa!

She took several tentative steps toward the edge of the field, her eyes fixed on the approaching figure. Her fatigue left her in an ecstatic rush of joyous anticipation, and she broke into a run.

He had not seen her where she knelt, and was looking in the other direction as she rose and began running toward him. By the time Anna emerged from the tall stalks of grain onto the pathway to the village, she was certain her eyes had not deceived her.

Against all hope and reason . . . it *was* him, as though he had stepped from her very dreams into reality itself!

He saw her coming, and his face lit into a huge smile. His great military boots thudded heavily across the hard-packed earth toward her.

45

"Sergei. . . !"

Anna could say no more, for the tears flowed freely, choking out her voice.

"Anna . . . is it really you?" he said with equal emotion, opening his arms and drawing her close.

All the questions of how and why Anna could not even voice. She stood panting, feeling his arms around her shoulders, fearing that this was all a mirage, some phantom of her exhausted brain brought on by the fatigue and lack of sleep. And yet . . . there were his strong arms about her trembling body! This could be no mirage, no phantom. It was a miracle as if from God himself.

The noble prince and the peasant girl stood in each other's arms for only a few moments, yet it seemed like hours. At last they fell apart, slowly. Sergei took hold of Anna's shoulders and looked deeply into her sweaty, dirty, tear-streaked face. He smiled broadly.

"I . . . I cannot believe . . . ," faltered Anna. "How can you actually be here? How did you find me?"

"They said you had returned."

"You've been home, then?"

"Oh yes," he replied, "I've been *home*—though briefly." For the first time a shadow crossed his face. He released Anna, looked away momentarily, then sighed and added, "And quite a homecoming it was." A hint of bitter sarcasm filled his tone in spite of his present joy.

"You don't sound happy about it," said Anna. She and Sergei turned and slowly began to make their way back along the road in the direction from which she had just come.

"I have been away a long time . . . much has changed."

Anna smiled. "You must mean with Princess Katrina."

"I must admit, it was no small surprise. I love Dmitri like a brother, but . . . a brother-*in-law*?"

"You do not approve?"

"I don't know—I just think the idea will take getting used to. But worse than that was finding you *not* there."

Anna glanced down at the dirt path.

"It has been a year of such turmoil, Anna," Sergei went on. "I have tried to think through many things that I cannot say I even yet understand. So much about this country of ours, its government, its ways . . . the war . . . my purpose as a soldier . . ."

His voice trailed off, and it was clear that many of the same questions that had driven him away in the first place still plagued him.

"Have you . . . ," began Anna, not quite sure how to phrase the question that was on her heart. "Have you reached any . . . conclusions about it all?" She glanced up and saw in his face the same look of bewilderment and pain as on the day she had last seen him in the garden.

A long pause followed, during which Sergei could not return Anna's gaze. His eyes were fixed in the distance, and Anna knew he was seeing and thinking things too deep for anyone to feel with him. She could tell his personal search for meaning was not over yet.

At length he sighed. "I wrote a great deal," he said. "It helps when I can tell my thoughts to someone, even if I am only telling them to myself on a sheet of paper. And I talked to many people . . . and saw many things."

Again his gaze grew distant.

"But conclusions, Anna," he said after a moment, "have been scarce. In fact, I would say the time away has brought me only one."

At last he glanced down to her. She met his eyes with a questioning look.

"And that is that I still love you," he said softly.

Anna looked away, her heart pounding for joy at his words. She felt his arm go around her shoulder and pull her toward him. She could not imagine a greater ecstacy as long as she lived.

"I had to come back to see you," he added. "I could not wait another day."

He gave her a tight squeeze, and they walked on slowly and in silence for some minutes.

"Now do you see why I am here?" Sergei asked at length, "why I have come to Katyk?"

Anna gave a gentle laugh. "I think so," she said.

"I was at home only a day and a half, and then I took the first train south."

"Did you tell . . . do they know where you are?" asked Anna, suddenly thinking of the implications of Sergei's visit.

"No, I masqueraded my intent."

"But how did you find out where my home was?"

"Where do you think Katrina learned her clever ways?" said Sergei with a sly smile. "I extracted the information from her without her suspecting the slightest interest on my part."

Anna smiled at the thought of someone else beating Katrina at her own game.

"And your father?" asked Anna.

"He was none too pleased, either with my arrival *or* my hasty departure," replied Sergei sarcastically. "At first he *refused* to see me at all. Then when he heard I was leaving again so suddenly he *demanded* to see me." He sighed and looked away for a moment. When his face turned again toward her, Anna saw an even deeper pain in his eyes. "It was not a pleasant exchange," he added.

"I'm sorry, Sergei," said Anna sincerely.

Again silence fell between them. It was broken abruptly by Sergei, who now seemed to see Anna's condition for the first time.

"But just look at *you!*" he said.

Anna's face reddened and she grimaced. She realized she was covered with dirt from head to foot.

"I must be an awful sight," she said.

He stopped and turned her to face him, then slowly ran his thumb across her cheek. He held it out where they could both see the smear of dirt across it and looked at her with a tender smile.

"Do you have any idea what this dirt on my hands means to me?" he asked.

"That the hand of a prince has been soiled by a filthy peasant girl?"

"How could you say such a thing?" rejoined Sergei.

He stepped back a couple of paces and surveyed her. "You are more beautiful than I have ever seen you, Anna," he said. "I have never seen such beauty in all the ballrooms and drawing rooms of St. Petersburg!"

"Sergei," said Anna, smiling and flustered, "the year away has taught you to lie!"

"Never have I spoken so truthfully," he said seriously. "There is nothing so wonderful as a woman with the grime of good, clean, honest toil on her brow. It is something I have seen all too infrequently, and now to see it on you fills me with even more love for you!"

He took one of her hands in his and saw it covered with blisters and scrapes and small cuts.

"Why, Anna," he exclaimed in dismay, "you have been working *hard* . . . too hard!" He brought the hand to his lips and kissed it. "Dear, Anna, what have these poor hands been doing?"

"My father is ill—surely the princess told you that," Anna replied.

"Yes, but that cannot account for rough, bleeding hands on the woman I love."

"He was struggling to harvest the rye and wheat before the storm comes," said Anna, "but he could not do it. He collapsed in the field last evening."

"Oh, Anna, I am sorry. Is he. . . ?"

"He is in bed now, but very ill. And the grain still must be brought in. My family must have it or starve."

"Surely you exaggerate the severity."

"We are peasants, Sergei. The winter is long and bitter. Without food, peasants like us *do* starve. Every winter many go hungry, and many die."

Sergei sighed and looked away, sharply aware of his aristocratic ignorrance.

"And as long as there is strength in this body of mine," Anna went on, "I must do all I can to make sure my own father and mother and brother and sisters are not among them."

"So you have been out trying to harvest the grain by yourself?" Sergei said in astonished admiration.

"You mustn't forget—I am a peasant of strong stock, if I indeed have my mother and father's blood in my veins. And I am a Russian besides! We are a strong people, we Russians for whom Mother Earth is our life."

"You are amazing, Anna. It makes me proud of you!"

Anna's face fell with an embarrassed sigh. "To tell you the truth, in spite of my brave words, I'm afraid I have been a hopeless failure."

"I doubt if I believe that!"

"It is true. My papa, weak as he is, was able to cut ten times more grain than I could. I am afraid all my blisters and aching muscles will not prevent most of the crop from being lost."

Sergei glanced over his shoulder at the sky, then turned thoughtful for a moment.

"Are you the only one?" he asked, glancing around him.

"My mother and one of my sisters have been working with me, but they are back at the cottage just now."

"Well, then, Anna," he said, marching off quickly down the path. She stood watching him in astonishment.

Sergei stopped and glanced back. "Come, Anna," he said, "where is this grain that must be cut?"

"But . . . I don't understand . . . do you mean—"

"I mean that if there are only two of us, and if those clouds are moving this way as I think they are, then every minute counts."

"But, Sergei, I could never ask you—"

"Because I am a pampered, city-bred prince, does that mean I am too proud to swing a sickle?"

240

"Oh, Sergei!" Anna laughed. "But I fear we will not do much against the uncut grain with only a sickle. Do you think you could manage the scythe?"

"How much different can it be than swinging a sword? And I have done that to good effect."

"I know I am hardly able to lift it, let alone swing it accurately through the dried stalks."

"You can show me what to do?"

"I think so."

"Then I will learn to wield it, if it takes me the rest of the day! Come, Anna . . . we can talk more later. There is work to be done!"

46

When Sophia returned to the field with a jar of water and a plate of brown bread, she was shocked by the incredible progress that had been made. Even more surprising was the fact that a complete stranger was swinging the huge scythe through her husband's field like an expert reaper.

Anna had shown Sergei how to balance the scythe in his hands, how to bring it upward and high to the right, and then swing it down and through the stalks just above the ground. His first attempt landed the blade in the dirt, and his second slashed through the heads of grain themselves nearly a meter off the ground, an effort which doubled Anna over with laughter.

But the young prince stumbled back to his balance, attempting the difficult swing a third, then a fourth time. Gradually he discovered the weight and balance of the strange tool, and attacked the standing grain with the same courage he had demonstrated when wielding his sword on the battlefield of Plevna. It was a great relief to Anna's hands and muscles not to be swinging the sickle, but before long she found herself lagging behind in gathering and binding the stalks as they fell faster and faster beneath Sergei's blade. As she followed his swishing circular pattern across the field, her heart sang with a quiet song of joy. Never had a Ruth felt such a devotion of love to her helper and protector. And on Sergei's part, never had a Boaz so sacredly given himself with all the strength he possessed to care for this kinswoman whom he loved. Their roles were reversed from the Biblical model—the stranger Boaz felled the grain for the father of his Ruth, in whose field he had come from a distant land to labor. But the love in the hearts of this man and this woman was no less full than that of their ancient Hebrew counterparts.

As her mother approached, Anna left her place and walked toward her. Sophia could not possibly have guessed the reason for the smile her daughter wore.

Anna called to Sergei, who willingly laid down the scythe and came toward the two women. The introduction of the stranger did little to alleviate the mother's perplexity. But there was no time to question the unlikely fact that a St. Petersburg prince was standing in the middle of their field, sweat pouring down his face, dust covering his trousers and tunic, swinging *her* husband's scythe! They took only a brief pause for the water and bread Sophia had brought, and then began the work again. Sergei had to urge himself to a faster pace, for behind him came both Ruth *and* Naomi, gathering, binding, and stacking the sheaves!

"How is Papa?" asked Anna as she and Sophia scooped the neatly fallen stalks in their expert hands.

"He is awake and breathing easier," replied her mother. "But it was all I could do to keep him in bed."

"Perhaps we should go tell him that he has nothing more to be anxious about."

"I will return shortly," said Sophia. "But there are only four or five more hours of daylight. And with the prince mowing so well, we must gather all we can."

About thirty minutes later, Anna heard an exclamation from the lips of her mother. She looked up to see her father heading toward them, leading Lukiv across the stubble of the field from the cottage, pulling the old wooden cart that had borne him unconscious the night before.

Dropping the grain she had just gathered in her arms, Anna ran toward him.

"Papa!" she cried.

"What is this?" he said, staring at Sergei, who had not yet seen the older man's arrival and continued to swing the scythe in large swaths.

"We are not alone, as you can see, Papa," said Anna. "You must rest and let us finish the work."

"God be praised!" said Yevno. "Help has come!" His face was pale, and beads of perspiration stood out on his forehead merely from the exertion of the walk.

"Yes, Papa—help has come."

"Yevno Pavlovich," scolded Sophia in the same tone she used with her errant offspring, "you promised to stay inside with the children."

"And I have only broken one tiny part of the promise, wife!" He nodded his head back in the direction of the cart, a sheepish grin spreading across his lips. The three children now stood where they had been crouched inside the cart, each with happy smiles on their faces. "I am well enough at least to load the grain and carry it inside."

"*We* will load it, Papa," said Anna. "It will be enough if you and Lukiv haul it back to the barn."

"Ah, you make a tired old man feel useless," he sighed. "But who is this stranger who has come from heaven in answer to our prayers?"

Anna ran off in Sergei's direction. He was so absorbed in his labor she had to shout as she approached to keep her legs from being cut off from beneath her. He stopped and smiled wearily, wiping a sleeve across his sweating brow. He laid down the scythe, and at Anna's side strode toward the little gathering, breathing heavily.

"Papa," said Anna, with pride in her voice, "this is the brother of my mistress, Prince Sergei Viktorovich Fedorcenko."

Yevno opened his mouth, as if to make some ordinary expression of greeting. Then he stopped abruptly as the import of Anna's words struck him like a thunderbolt.

"*Prince. . . ?*" was all he could utter in astonishment.

"Yes, sir," replied Sergei. "I am the son of your daughter's employer." He made a deep bow. "I am honored to meet you at last, Yevno Pavlovich." His tone before the humble peasant was as respectful as though he had been addressing the tsar.

"The honor is entirely mine, to be sure, Your Excellency!" said Yevno, partially recovering his tongue. He bowed also, bending so low that his hands nearly touched the ground. But as he attempted to rise, light-headedness suddenly overcame him. He staggered slightly, nearly toppling to the ground. Sergei jumped forward, caught his arm to steady him, then pulled him upright once more.

"I am more in debt than merely for your help with my grain, Your Excellency," gasped Yevno, catching his breath.

"Please, sir," said Sergei, "I neither expect nor deserve such deference. I am merely a friend of your daughter's. And as such, I hope you will do me the honor of considering me yours as well."

"You do me a great honor. I do not have words to reply, Your Excellency," said Yevno again. "You call me 'sir' and work in my fields—you are surely the most unusual prince of Russia I have ever heard of! How shall I ever be able to repay you?"

"There will be no talk of repayment," said Sergei. "Please say only that I am welcome in your home—as a friend."

"My humble cottage is yours, and all that is in it," said Yevno, having no idea how deeply his words went into both the prince's and his daughter's heart.

Sergei smiled at the humble peasant man he hoped might one day be his father-in-law. But if the man's heart were as weak as his pale complexion indicated, now was not the time to add to his shock with such a request.

After another few minutes, Sergei reminded them again of

the impending change in weather. They all glanced toward the northern skies, and then with one accord took to the fields again.

No one tried to dissuade Yevno from doing his part. They all sensed that for him to lie in bed while a prince brought in his grain would probably have killed him as surely as the exertion of leading Lukiv slowly back and forth between byre and field.

Sophia did manage to get him back to bed shortly after sunset. Anna and Sergei remained in the fields under the light of the moon until after midnight.

One more day the weather held. One more day the young prince and the young peasant maid labored on behalf of the ailing father, from the rising of the sun until only the moon shone pale over Katyk.

On the morning of the second day after Sergei's arrival, several hours before dawn, the rains came at last from out of the north.

47

Katrina's melancholy over Anna's absence struck deeper than she had anticipated, deeper than she should feel over a mere *maid*.

Even the usually oblivious Princess Natalia noted how dispirited her daughter appeared.

"Would you like to come to the opera with your father and me this evening, dear?" her mother asked Katrina on the morning of the third day following Anna's departure.

"I don't really feel like it, Mother. I think I shall read a while and retire early."

Sergei's sudden appearance provided the tonic to bring Katrina out of her doldrums. But no one anticipated his equally sudden departure. The atmosphere on the estate grew tempestuous and emotional as a result, but at least his brief visit had injected his sister with something of her old vitality.

Sergei's appearance also ushered in thoughts of a less pleasant nature. She had been so distracted for several days that she had hardly even remembered the dilemma she was certain to face sooner or later. Suddenly her thoughts turned to Basil, and a sickening sense of foreboding began to come over her.

Had he returned from Moscow? His inevitable visit would come soon. What should she tell him? She had still not come up with a comfortable way to inform him of her change of heart toward him. A number of stories and excuses had come to mind, ranging from the unlikely tale that she had decided to join a convent, to the more morbid concoction that her mother was ill and she must give up thoughts of marriage in order to care for her.

But Basil was no fool. Whatever else Katrina did not know about him, of that much she was certain. There would be no pulling the wool over his eyes. Probably only one thing would do in the end, and that was the truth—a somewhat watered-down version of it, at any rate.

She was worrying about nothing, Katrina tried to tell herself. He would accept the news in a gentlemanly fashion. She still only half-believed all the gossip she had heard about him, anyway.

Her attempts to put her mind at ease met with only partial success, and when the doctor's son was unexpectedly announced the following afternoon, Katrina found herself in a sudden dither. She could escape it no longer. The unpleasant task must be done.

As she walked down to the parlor where he was waiting, she was struck with the brilliant idea that her news might go down better in the tranquil surroundings of the garden, with the peaceful serenity of the autumn afternoon to soften the blow. Basil agreed with her suggestion and followed her outside.

Katrina continued deep into the garden. When she finally stopped, Basil immediately approached and took her in his arms. She squirmed free, then retreated several paces.

"Please, Basil," she said, "I have something to say first."

"Something other than how much you missed me?" he rejoined, with as close to a smile as Basil Anickin's lips ever revealed. He still had not apprehended his impending doom.

"Yes, Basil. I'm afraid I'm not going to be able to marry you after all," Katrina blurted out. The words were past her lips before she had a chance even to consider how to say what she knew she had to.

The color drained from Anickin's cheeks as he stood staring at her in mute disbelief.

"I can't believe I heard what I think you said," he said finally.

"You heard it, Basil. That's exactly what I said—I can't marry you."

"What? But I don't . . . *why*, Katrina? What has come over you?"

"I have my reasons, Basil."

Again he stared at her in dumb silence.

When he spoke again, his voice had a cold, strangled quality. "You can't do this to me, Katrina," he said.

She turned away and walked a few paces along the path, then spun back to face him, doing her best to act cheery and nonchalant about the whole thing. Basil had not moved a muscle, and still stood like a statue.

"Oh, Basil," said Katrina lightly, "I don't want to hurt you. And you have every right to hate me for my stupid behavior. But really, it would hurt you far more if I did marry you while loving another man. You would not want that, now would you?"

"Another man?" he repeated numbly.

"You would not want me to try to keep it secret, would you? I'm only trying to do what is best for you."

Something began to change in the man standing before

Katrina. She hardly took notice at first, but gradually what had initially been wounded shock took on a hard, steely edge. And as he spoke, his voice sounded like a tightened coil ready to spring.

"The best for me?" he said with icy sarcasm. "You toy with a man, and then delude yourself into thinking you can spit in his face and call it 'for *his* best'? Don't tell me about hurt and pain, Katrina. You are just like all the rest. What do you care? I am only an ant to crush beneath your aristocratic heel! Chattel for your noble whims!"

"It isn't that way at all. Oh, Basil, don't make it harder than it needs to be! I didn't intend for it to happen this way."

"Well, don't think you will get away with it so easily." With a sudden motion, he stepped forward, grabbed her arms in his hands, and jerked her toward him.

"Basil . . . please! You're hurting me!"

"I will not give you up, Katrina," he said, gripping her arms all the more tightly. "Do you hear?"

"You . . . you can't *force* me to marry you," she said, shuddering as if for the first time aware of her peril.

"Can't I?" he seethed. "We shall see, Princess . . . we shall see!"

Katrina winced in pain, but bit down the scream that tried to rise to her lips.

"Basil, please . . . let me go," she said, whimpering.

"I can make you do whatever I will. I can . . . and I shall!" As proof of his words, he forced her backward against the trunk of a large tree, then pressed his body close to hers, covering her face and neck with unsought kisses. His touch was taut and cold, as only burning hatred can be.

For one rare moment in her young life, Katrina knew what powerlessness felt like. The sheer force of Basil's dominating physical strength overwhelmed her.

"Basil . . . please!" she heard herself saying in a strange voice of desperation. "My father is in the house," she lied. "If I scream, you will regret—"

But her threat was immediately cut off by a muscular hand clamped over her mouth.

"I shall have you, Katrina—one way or another!" he said with a quiet, savage resolve. "And if this secret lover of yours, whoever he is, does marry you in the end, he will be getting nothing but the harlot you are!"

He pressed closer, his breath pouring over her in searing hot bursts as she squirmed and struggled against his strength.

Oh, God! she cried silently, *maybe I deserve this for the way I have behaved. But please, God . . . please help me!*

Suddenly footsteps thudded behind them. A shout rang out—the last voice Katrina had expected . . . but the one she most wanted to hear!

48

Dmitri took in the whole ugly scene in an instant.

"What in the—!" he exclaimed as he rushed forward. The words barely left his lips as he closed the gap between himself and the interloper, seized him by the shoulders, and threw him off Katrina, who stood paralyzed in terror against the tree.

Basil recovered with uncanny resiliency and leaped upon his unwelcome assailant with the fury of a wild beast. He threw himself against Dmitri, knocking him to the ground on his back.

Basil pursued the assault, and before Dmitri could struggle back to his knees he found himself stung by a rapid series of punishing kicks to his legs and midsection. His hands and forearms flew over his head to ward off blows from Anickin's boots that might otherwise have left him unconscious or crushed in his face.

Seeing Dmitri helplessly writhing on the ground trying to protect himself brought Katrina back to her senses. How could she have been so blind to Basil's insanity all this time? Suddenly a maniac was before her, a man she didn't even know, kicking Dmitri with deliberate cruelty.

She screamed in terror and flew forward, hurling herself against Basil. In vain she tried to grab at his arms and pull him away. But the man's strength was given added potency by the vehemence of his hatred; Katrina might as well have been an ant trying to stop the attack of an enraged she-bear. But the distraction of a second or two was enough to allow Dmitri to recover himself and spring to his feet.

Basil gave a wicked thrust to get her off him, and Katrina toppled sideways to the ground, screaming. Dmitri's clenched fist smashed into Basil's mouth and nose. The blood began immediately to flow. A quick side step by Basil sent Dmitri's second blow wide into the air, and suddenly the two men squared off facing one another.

"You will pay dearly for this," said Basil spitefully from between clenched teeth. "You do not realize what you have done!"

"I realize all too clearly what *you* have done, Anickin," rejoined Dmitri, moving slowly to one side, keeping his eyes warily fixed on his opponent. "You are no gentleman to treat a lady so shamefully. You are nothing but a—"

If he thought to help matters with such words, Dmitri could not have been more mistaken. Whatever word was about to leave his lips was lost as Basil lunged forward. And despite all his words of warning to Katrina about the man, even Dmitri was not prepared for the ferocity of Basil's attack. Before he knew it, he found himself stumbling backward, his head ringing and his vision blurred from a lightning-quick fist to his cheekbone. Before he could gather his wits, another blow landed on his neck, followed by still another to his chin. The taste of blood trickling from the corner of his mouth finally cleared his reeling brain. He jumped aside and raised his hands in front of his face, warding off Basil's next two punches.

Katrina was back on her feet, screaming wildly now for

them to stop. She rushed at Basil again. This time he raised his arm against her, and sent the back of his hand against her head, knocking her down again, the side of her upper cheek red and her eyes filling with tears of pain.

"How dare you strike a woman?" cried Dmitri, filled with renewed passion.

He rushed forward, perhaps unwisely, yet two or three of his furious punches found their mark, one squarely across Basil's left eye. Despite the fact that he was a seasoned war veteran, the young count was no match for the lawyer's hand-to-hand experience. Incensed all the more by the pain inflicted by Dmitri's blows, Basil attacked with half a dozen rapid jabs into Dmitri's ribs and stomach. He was used to having his own way in a fight; the taste of his own blood oozing from his nose and the stars that swam in front of his eyes were new sensations that sent the merciless rebel's rage to new levels of madness. Even in the midst of her own pain, Katrina saw the murder in his eyes. She struggled to her feet, terrified for Dmitri's life, and ran from the garden.

As Dmitri doubled over, gasping for breath, Basil came after him in a paroxysm of frenzied hatred, clubbing him viciously on the head. With one last punch Basil sent Dmitri staggering backward and toppling to the ground.

The next instant Basil leaped on top of him. Dmitri, virtually defenseless, struggled to get his hands in front of his face and eyes. He kicked about to try to throw the lawyer from him, but to no avail.

Dmitri swung wildly with his own fists, but none found their mark. His swollen eyes could make out only blurry forms, his ears unable to distinguish between distant cries and yells and Basil's venomous curses raining down upon him along with the punishing blows. All was a confusion of dust and yells, stinging pain, and the warm taste of blood.

Then Dmitri felt the viselike grip of Basil's sinewy fingers on his throat. He reached up, groping in vain to free himself from the stranglehold. But the fingers of mad passion steadily tightened, choking off his air. Dmitri gasped frantically, unaware of the sound of voices approaching through the garden.

To Katrina's horrified cries were now added men's voices.

"You there!" shouted Peter, the head footman, rushing up along with Moskalev and three or four others. Dmitri felt the fingers being torn from his throat. Loud curses from Basil's voice filled the air. He felt himself being pulled to his feet by Moskalev's huge hand. One eye was swollen shut; with the other he saw Anickin a few feet away, restrained by three of the Fedorcenko servants but trembling with murderous wrath.

"Do not think you have been spared, *Count Remizov!*" he spat with venom. "A man who must be rescued by women and servants is no man at all!"

"It is *you* who have been spared," Dmitri answered. "There is no coward so low as he who would strike a defenseless woman."

"You dare to call *me* a coward," Basil jeered, "after the thrashing I just gave you?"

"You could take my life, Anickin, and you would still be the lowest form of coward alive. Yes, I say it to your face—you are a despicable coward!"

"You are a spineless swine! You have courage to speak so to me when I am restrained in this manner. But tell these men to let me go, and then see if you are so brave as to repeat those words to my face!"

"You could whip me lifeless, and it would change nothing in your coward's heart. I know what manner of man you are, and it is no man at all!"

"You have said it, Remizov," said Basil, now with sudden icy calm that belied his previous passion. "Let your own words condemn you. The time will come when I *will* take your life."

"Take him away," Dmitri said to the servants, ignoring the threat.

"Shall we call a gendarme, Your Excellency?" asked Peter.

"Do you hear him, Anickin?" said Dmitri. "I could have you arrested. And considering your past record, it would not go well with you. This young lady's father is a man of importance in this city. More than that, she happens to be the lady I love. Show your face around here again, and I will do exactly what Peter suggests."

"And you think I am frightened by your paltry threats?"

"I frankly do not care. I merely feel it is my duty to inform you what I will do if you bother this young lady with your presence again. She is mine now, and I will protect her, especially against the likes of you."

"I will kill you, Remizov. Do you hear me?"

Dmitri gave Peter a wave of his hand, then turned toward Katrina, offering the lawyer no further reply.

Peter and the footmen led Anickin away, while Dmitri went to Katrina. Weak from shock, exhaustion, and pain from the blows she had taken, she sat on a nearby bench, weeping.

Before he could speak, she was on her feet rushing toward him.

"Oh, Dmitri, your face is scraped and bleeding!" she cried. "And one eye is so puffy I can hardly see it!"

"I will recover," said Dmitri, trying to smile lightheartedly.

"But he has hurt you so!"

"I am a soldier. Pain is my profession, remember?"

"Oh, Dmitri!" She reached out and touched his bruised face with a tender hand.

One of the house maids had come to the garden on the heels of the footmen. Dmitri saw her at the same time that he noted Katrina's deathly pale complexion.

"Take her to her room," he said to the maid, who stood in silent bewilderment over the events she had just witnessed.

Dmitri walked toward her, Katrina's hand in his. He handed her over to the maid. "See to it that she rests for an hour, and has some hot tea," he added to the girl. Then he bent over and kissed Katrina's forehead. "Now be off with you both. I will call again in the morning."

49

Peter and his fellows deposited Basil outside the gates. The man slunk ingloriously away from the Fedorcenko estate. Remorse and regret, however, were the two emotions furthest from his agitated thoughts.

A meeting of The People's Will was scheduled for later that afternoon. After changing clothes and attending to his blood-splotched face, he went directly there. When he arrived they were already in the midst of a rousing discussion of a planned attempt on the Third Section chief's life. Zhelyabov's young protege, whom Basil had seen a time or two but did not know personally, was describing the usual route Vlasenko took for his morning constitutional.

"He never varies?" asked one of the listeners.

"Hardly ever. I've watched closely for several days."

"Doesn't he realize his danger? How can he be so confident as to go about his business as if no one cares?"

"Vlasenko's a fool!"

"And it shall be the death of him," added Zhelyabov. "Go on, Paul. What do you have in mind?"

Basil had entered quietly, unnoticed by all but the guard at the door, and had listened for a time in silence. At length he stepped forward. As a respected leader in the movement, all eyes turned toward him, and Paul hesitated. Noting Basil looked more sinister than usual with his bruised and puffy face, Paul wondered what trouble the lawyer had been in.

"Why are you wasting energies on Vlasenko?" Basil said. "The tsar will probably get rid of him long before we do. He is little more than an incompetent fool."

"Well, Anickin, we wondered if you were going to show," said Zhelyabov. "I was afraid the *incompetent* police had finally gotten to you, and it looks like perhaps they have tried."

"I haven't the time for banalities," rejoined Basil sharply. "And we as an organization haven't time or resources to spare for a small, inconsequential cog in the governmental apparatus."

"The Secret Police chief is hardly an insignificant cog, as you put it."

"There are bigger fish."

"A few months ago you applauded the attempt on his life."

"That was then. Priorities have altered."

"Don't worry, the tsar remains our prime target, but I have some materials I want to test beforehand. I intend on full success the next time our ruler encounters one of my explosives."

"Fine," said Basil. "But the chief of Secret Police is still a distraction to our larger purposes."

"In killing him, we deliver the clear message that brutes such as he will not be tolerated," broke in Paul, surprising even himself with his boldness in disagreeing with Basil Anickin. "The tsar will think twice about whom he appoints to replace him."

"Don't be naive. If past experience serves, he will appoint an even more savage animal."

"And I suppose you have a more worthy victim in mind, Basil?" asked Zhelyabov, with more curiosity than rebuke.

"I propose we strike someone whose death will make a broader, more profound statement," answered Basil. "I submit that our cause will be furthered by a subtle shift in our tactic. Instead of the message, 'Don't put bad men in office or we will kill them,' I suggest we say, '*All* who support the evil dictatorship of the Romanov tsar will be subject, as accessories, to the same death sentence as the tsar himself.'"

He paused to allow his words to sink in.

"We all know the government has gone far beyond the point where fair appointees, or even fairer laws, will heal the breach," he went on. "The entire Romanov dynasty and every mechanism by which it rules must go. Everything! Nothing else will suffice to take our message to the people."

"High words, Anickin," said Zhelyabov.

"It is a high cause we are about."

"So then, whom do you propose we mark for death?"

"Prince Viktor Fedorcenko," said Basil flatly. He would have liked to have included the name of Count Dmitri Remizov as well, but he would take care of him personally. The Fedorcenkos would not be so easy; he would need the assistance of his comrades for them.

Paul concealed his shock at hearing the familiar name. His mind spun with the implications.

"Andrei," said Sophia Perovskaya, "there is a certain poetic justice to Basil's proposal."

"How so?"

"Fedorcenko is close to the tsar, not only politically, but socially as well. This would strike a 'double-headed' blow to His Majesty."

She grinned mordantly at her clever wit.

As Paul sat listening, his only immediate conclusion was that these people must never know of his association, however distant, to the clan whose elimination they were now plotting. He would kill for this cause, even die for it. But he was not ready to sacrifice his dear sister for it. So he remained silent, glad he had revealed the name of his sister's employer only to Kazan.

"I don't know," Zhelyabov was saying. "I assured Paul that we would—"

"And since when are we in this for the purpose of fulfilling our *personal* goals?" asked Basil quickly.

His words were poorly chosen. His social activities with the daughter of the prince in question were not entirely unknown to his comrades.

"I might ask the same of you, Basil?"

"If personal pleasure happens to coincide with political expedience, it is no fault of mine."

"Then it is a question of expedience?" challenged the revolutionary leader.

"As I see it," answered Basil.

"I still think it would serve us best to keep the police in a state of turmoil," Zhelyabov said. "A 'poetic statement' such as you propose will probably pass right over the head of our dull-witted tsar."

"Let's put it to a vote," suggested Basil. He was confident. He knew Sophia Perovskaya was on his side, and she carried almost as much weight in the group as Zhelyabov. And Zhelyabov's arguments were lame at best, clearly aimed as much *against* Basil, with whom he had never been on the best of terms, as they were *for* any particular principle or objective of the group.

The vote was taken, and the target for their next attack was changed from Vlasenko to Fedorcenko. The outcome of the vote only partially made up for Basil's humiliation. Only the thought of revenge against Katrina and Remizov could soothe the aching mortification of being rejected by the one and bloodied by the other. And then to be manhandled and tossed off the estate by the prince's lackeys completed the bitterness of the abasement. Even as Basil walked out into the night after the meeting, a plan had begun to take root in his mind in which a strategically placed bomb would destroy the whole family at once.

50

When Dmitri had left the Fedorcenko estate, in spite of the pain all over his body, his first thoughts were for Katrina's safety. He trusted Basil Anickin no more than he would a bloodthirsty Turk.

To insure that the madman was not lurking somewhere in the shadows about the estate, he embarked upon a lengthy and, in his condition, rigorous walk about the entire outer perimeter of the grounds. He made his way to the point where the river bordered the property. Not even Basil would have the fortitude to brave the chilly water to gain entry.

When he was at last satisfied, he returned to his barracks. There he changed out of his soiled uniform, washed his bruised body, soaked his swollen eye with a cold cloth, and lay down. But he found he could not rest. The quiet building was too deserted. He finally got back up, concluding he needed to find some friendly activity to unwind.

A light rain had begun to fall. Dmitri walked outside, looked up into the sky, quickly darkening in the descending dusk, and breathed in deeply. The cool mist felt good on his hot, puffy face. He walked to the mews and there proceeded to hitch up his small covered carriage to his horse. He drove to Lomonosov Prospect and pulled up in front of Dauphin's.

Inside, he made a valiant attempt to distract himself. But in the end the music and smoke and laughter and raucous conversation proved more oppressive than relaxing. He could not concentrate on the faro game, and ended up losing more than he could well afford. In the end, the losing streak and vodka and noise combined with his lingering concern over Katrina and the welts on his cheek, jaw, and eye to give him a raging headache.

He left Dauphin's in far worse shape, and even less prepared for sleep, than when he had entered. For a fleeting moment he considered returning to Katrina. But it was quite late, and her parents had likely returned home. Prince Fedorcenko was the last person he wanted to face just now.

He wondered what Basil was up to at that moment, and if it had been a mistake to let him go free. But even if the man was crazy, he surely was not stupid enough to commit murder. That would be one entanglement his father's respected reputation could not possibly help him out of. Yet try as he might, Dmitri could not shake from his mind the memory of the murderous look Basil had worn earlier that day.

"Ah, the vodka is making a woman of me," he said to himself. "Anickin is home licking his wounds and wishing he'd never returned to St. Petersburg!" Trying thus to reassure himself, he headed toward his carriage.

He lifted his foot to the board and climbed inside. But as soon as he had taken up the reins in his hands, he felt a sudden movement behind him. In less time than it took to gasp in surprise, a strong arm snaked around his throat, while the barrel of a revolver instantly pressed against his neck.

"You have not a care in the world, is that it, Count Remizov?" sneered the familiar voice. "You dispose of the doctor's worthless, crazy son, then go blithely to your favorite vodka hole, leaving the woman you supposedly love to her own fate—"

"If you have harmed Katrina—"

"Have no fear, Count," said Basil patronizingly. "First you must go. Then with you out of the way, she may yet have a change of heart."

"Now that she has seen what kind of beast you are? Ha!" exclaimed Dmitri, the vodka in his blood making him too brave for his own good.

"I would hate to kill the beautiful princess without first giving her the chance to do right by me," said Basil with cunning, evil humor.

"You *are* crazy if you think she would look twice at you now, Anickin!" Dmitri struggled to break free of Basil's grip.

"Be still, you cur!" hissed Anickin. "I would prefer not to kill you in such a public place, but I will if I have to."

"Give me a gun and let us fight this out like men of honor."

Anickin barked a low, humorless laugh. "You deserve no honor. None of you do!"

"And your kind, I suppose, do?"

"Shut up! When they find your rotting body in an alley, it will be chalked up to one more political killing. And they will be half correct."

"You are insane!"

"Your death will give me particular pleasure, as vengeance for ruining everything with Katrina. But at the same time it will make me a hero with the masses!"

"You will never get away with it."

"Who's to stop me? Now silence—and drive!"

Dmitri recalled the grip of Basil's fingers around his throat, and the memory sobered him. He was not dealing with a man who would have the least compunction about using a pistol. He probably had done so already many times.

Without another word, Dmitri flicked the reins and urged his horse slowly forward into the night.

Leaving the meeting earlier, Basil had felt a certain slight gratification, but he was not entirely satisfied. Assassinating the Fedorcenkos would take time. It would be pleasing when it finally took place, but such delayed pleasure did nothing to satiate the hunger for revenge burning in his guts *now*. He had been rejected, dishonored, assaulted, and treated as less than dirt. And that must be atoned for immediately! Blood had to be spilled!

Basil still held a small hope that he might yet win Katrina. In his deranged mind, none of his behavior was sufficient to repulse her. He was only a victim whose actions were justified by circumstances.

But winning Katrina was secondary to drawing *blood*. Remizov must die whether any real hope for Katrina existed or not.

The carriage rattled along the cobbled street, now slick and glistening in the moonlight. The farther they went, the less Dmitri doubted the validity of Basil's threat. That he had come back to hunt him down so soon after the afternoon's incident was proof enough that the man was not to be taken lightly. He was not only dangerous, but unpredictable as well. It was a lethal combination. And if Basil had his way, Dmitri knew he would be a dead man within the hour. He was gambler enough, however, to consider his odds and wager, with no less than his life at stake, on his surest option for escape. His only hope lay with the unexpected, to take the very risk Basil had cautioned him against. And he must do it soon, while they were still on a public street where help might be summoned. To let Basil lead him to some lonely section of the city or deserted dock by the river would be nothing short of suicide.

Fifty meters ahead the street veered to the left. Gradually Dmitri relaxed his grip on the reins. His well-trained horse increased his pace. As they approached the corner, with his left hand he suddenly yanked the rein. The horse pulled quickly left, the carriage lurched sideways, and with a quick movement Dmitri thrust his right shoulder brutally into Basil.

Only quickness and strength kept him from getting his head blown off. Basil's disorientation lasted only long enough to make his aim, when he finally managed to discharge the pistol, off its mark. Instead of hitting Dmitri's head, the wild slug only grazed his shoulder. Pain seared through him, but he had to ignore it if he was to follow up on his daring move.

Without even thinking about it, he lashed the reins with his uninjured left arm, yelling his horse into a gallop. On even footing he had already discovered all too clearly that he would have no chance against Basil's superior strength. His only hope was to keep him off balance. In a careening carriage, he might somehow be able to keep the madman off him.

Again he lashed the reins, turning at the same time and kicking futilely at his foe, who was attempting to take aim to fire again. But the jostling on the rough cobbles and the horse's panicked movements delayed him. Dmitri's third jab with his foot found its mark just as Basil's fingers completed their work. The gun exploded through the quiet night as Dmitri's boot crashed against the murderous hand. The bullet ripped through the leather roof of the carriage, and the pistol clattered to the floorboards. Loud cursing from Basil followed.

The sharp report of gunfire was enough to attract the attention of two or three policemen some distance away, who came running in the direction of the sound. At the same time, the frightened horse reared, then lunged forward with frenzied fear in his eyes. The two men tussling inside were thrown about by the swaying carriage. In vain Basil tried to land several blows, but Dmitri's feet proved better weapons than his fists had earlier in the day, and for a minute or two as they sped recklessly along the street, Basil had the worst of it.

At length, sensible animal that he was, the horse began to

slow. Basil took advantage of the steadying carriage to right himself, and the next moment sent a punishing smash of his fist directly into the side of Dmitri's already painfully throbbing head.

An involuntary cry escaped Dmitri's lips. But the reflex action brought on by the intensity of the blow sent his booted foot into Basil's midsection with a force neither man had anticipated. Slightly off balance from the punch he had just thrown, and still wobbling from the movement of the carriage, Basil lurched onto the wet cobblestones, and Dmitri found himself alone again in his carriage.

Instinctively he tugged at the reins to stop his horse. Knowing the danger of prolonging the fight, he yet had to keep track of his adversary. Leaning across the seat and peering out the other side, he saw Basil lying flat on his back a few meters away.

Dmitri jumped out and ran back. Basil lay motionless, a gash on the side of his head above the right ear where his head had struck the cobbles. Dmitri scarcely had time to focus his own blurred vision or take stock of the pain that suddenly shot through his wounded shoulder before two uniformed policemen approached, swinging clubs in their hands and shouting.

Dmitri had no thought of resisting when one of the men roughly grabbed at his arm and yanked him away from Basil's prostrate form. Still he was unable to speak when they began to interrogate him. Apparently they believed a murder had taken place right before their eyes.

Only Basil's moaning as he began to come to consciousness succeeded in shifting some of the attention away from their hasty accusations.

Once on his feet, Basil silently surveyed the scene, and was not long in concluding that for once his best position would be to keep his mouth shut. While the police were distracted with Dmitri, he began to wander off down the street. Suddenly Dmitri found his tongue again.

"Don't let that man go!" he cried.

Basil immediately quickened his pace, but not before one of the men went after him. Basil would have quickly outstripped him and found safety in the darkness had it not been for a sudden wave of dizziness from his wound. He had risen too quickly to his feet, and now stumbled and staggered for two or three steps. In a moment he felt his arm restrained. He fought to resist but had none of his usual strength. A minute later he was hauled back to the scene.

"Now, what's this all about?" said one of the gendarmes to both men at once.

"That man took me at gunpoint and tried to kill me," Dmitri began.

"Can you prove it?"

"You'll find his gun on the floor of my carriage over there," said Dmitri, cocking his head in the direction where his horse stood. "And if you'll examine my shoulder, I think you'll discover I have been wounded by his gunfire."

"And what have you to say to that?" the gendarme asked, turning toward Basil.

Anickin spit in his face.

"Do you see what I mean?" said Dmitri. "The man's an animal. And if you check your records, you'll find he's a known insurgent. Earlier today he tried to attack a young woman. I advise you to arrest him immediately."

The gendarme glanced back and forth between the two men. "I half believe you, Lieutenant," he said at last, eyeing Basil again suspiciously. "But I'll have to take you both in until we can sort this all out."

At the words, Basil began to twist and writhe in his captor's grip.

"You miserable swine!" he snarled. "Let me go! I am the only justice left in this city!"

The policeman who had spoken to Dmitri now turned savagely on Basil, swinging his club toward his head.

"Hold your tongue, man, or I'll give you a gash on the other side of the head to match the one you've already got!"

He turned toward Dmitri. "Bring your horse along, Lieutenant. All right," he added to the others, "let's go. And hold on to that one!" he said, indicating Basil, who continued to shout out vile imprecations as he was led off down the street.

51

Hours later, as dawn streaked the sky over the Gulf of Finland between layers of black clouds, and as the previous night's rain descended in torrents into the heart of the Motherland, the St. Petersburg police had sorted out the violent incident.

They were more than pleased to have a solid charge by a distinguished soldier and citizen against young Anickin, whom they had been watching since his return to the capital. Dmitri was satisfied for Katrina's sake, although part of him could not help wishing he had killed the lunatic in fair battle. He swore he would do his best to see that Basil's father would not use his influence to get him off this time, and the policeman in charge of the affair hinted that a long stay in prison was in order for the young troublemaker, lawyer or not.

Without the least knowledge of any of these events, Paul Burenin had spent the night wrestling with his conscience, torn, as seemed his eternal lot, between his ideals and his inbred sense of duty. Had his sister not been involved, he probably would not have given the outcome of last night's meeting more than a passing thought, for the Fedorcenko name meant nothing to him. He might have even offered to carry out the job himself. As much as he wanted to kill Vlasenko, he could see the ingenuity of Basil's rather warped reasoning.

But he could not ignore Anna. He could not accept the possibility of her becoming an innocent victim in Basil's vendetta against the aristocratic family that employed her. And Paul knew that the greatest hazard with the use of explosives was the inescapable fact of their unpredictability. The innocent were often brought down with the guilty. It was an unfortunate fact he had already debated within himself and eventually decided to live with. *No sacrifice is too great for the cause*, as The People's Will put it.

No sacrifice . . . except for Anna!

Suddenly everything had changed. Could he knowingly place *her* life in jeopardy? His own sister? Had he sunk that low?

In order to insure her safety, the only path that lay open before him was to betray his comrades. Could he do that? What if they found out? Where would that place him in The People's Will, except in the most despicable position of all—that of a traitor!

Thus he debated back and forth with himself most of the sleepless night in great agony of mind. In the end he knew what course he must take.

He waited until morning had come to full light so that his presence in the exclusive South Side district would not be suspect. Dressed in his shabby working garb, a belted red tunic over baggy brown wool trousers, he might have been taken for a housebreaker in the middle of the night. But in the gray, drizzly morning he looked the part of a poor errand boy.

The guard at the gate of the Fedorcenko estate scrutinized him closely, then, accepting his story that he bore a message from Dr. Anickin, admitted him. It was all Paul could dream up, but it seemed good enough. After inquiring of a gardener, he found his way to the kitchen entrance, where the servants were already preparing for the day's meals.

"I have a message for one of the servants," he said to a tall, slender woman passing by with a tray of late-ripened fruits.

"Who do you want?" she asked, pausing.

"It's for Anna Burenin."

"Give it to me," said Polya. "I'll see that she gets it."

"It is a verbal message. I must deliver it to her personally."

"That will be impossible. She is not here."

"When will she return?"

"I don't know."

Frustrated, Paul asked anxiously, "Surely she does not

come and go without some word to someone?"

"She no longer works in the kitchen."

"But you seem to have some knowledge of her where-abouts."

Polya surveyed the young man carefully. "And you think I am under some obligation to give out her private information to every stranger that comes along?" she asked finally. There was still caution in her voice, but it was weakening. Perhaps something in the young man's eyes hinted to her of the truth even before Paul's next words.

"I am not a stranger," he said.

Polya's eyes narrowed imperceptibly.

"I must know where she is," Paul went on. "This message is extremely important."

Polya hesitated, looking him over one last time. She then seemed to arrive at a decision.

"She has gone to her home in Katyk," she said.

"Home!" exclaimed Paul. "But why . . . when will she return?"

"I do not know. It is for an undetermined length of time. Her father is ill."

Paul gaped at the unexpected news. His mind began spinning in several directions at once as a myriad of conflicting emotions surged through him.

He could *not* think of his father just now! It made everything too confusing. His father was dead to him. *He had no father!*

All he must think of was Anna. She was safe. That was all that mattered. His purpose had been accomplished. There was no more for him to do.

He said nothing else to the scullery maid. Polya saw the glazed look come over the young man's face. If she did guess his identity, she did not betray her suspicion but merely watched as he slowly turned around and shambled down the walkway and back outside.

In a daze, Paul stumbled back the way he had come. The thought of giving any warning to the Fedorcenkos or anyone of the household did not occur to him. Even if it had, he would have dismissed the absurd notion out of hand. He would be arrested just for delivering such a message.

Anna was home . . . Anna was safe. He could not let himself dwell on anything else.

Papa is ill, his distraught mind tried to scream at him. *Papa is ill.*

But he shook the thought away. He made his way back along Nevsky Prospect, utterly oblivious to the rain falling upon him. As the drenching downpour soaked his head and hair and clothes, chilling him to the bone, he forced his footsteps along by repeating, *It does not matter . . . he is dead to me . . . I am dead to him.*

He had a *new* family now and to *them* his heart and soul were committed!

Even as he forced himself to say the words, he ignored the tears streaming out of his eyes and down his hot cheeks. There were no tears, only rain! The People's Will . . . *they* were his brothers and sisters and father and mother! He would kill for them . . . he would die for them!

Faster he walked as the rain beat upon him. Faster came the tears that were not tears! The cause was everything, and it made no room for those whose hearts were weak with weeping!

But even as he made his way across to Vassily Island, he could not keep back the terrible longing he suddenly felt deep in his soul for the shabby little *izba* in Katyk where he had been born.

52

Yevno knew the rains had begun even though he could hear nothing of the drops on the soft thatch of his roof.

He *felt* the change rather than heard it, and it had awakened him. He had been a man of the earth too many years, and the very marrow of his being quietly resonated with the changes of the seasons and weather and atmosphere. And now as he lay awake in the dark stillness of the early morning hours, listening only to the breathing of his family, he knew that for this year, *stradnya pora* had come to an end.

As quietly as he could, he slipped out of the large bed. Sophia moved slightly, but then resumed her peaceful slumber. By the light of the embers of the fire, he drew on his coarse trousers and heavy woolen tunic, then crept across the hard dirt floor and out of the cottage.

It was equally dark out in the byre, but the shifting movements of the animals gave evidence that dawn was not far away. As silently as he was able, so as not to disturb the prince asleep on a makeshift straw bed on the other side near Lukiv, Yevno opened the great barn door and stood staring outside. A faint glow from the moon shining somewhere above the clouds combined with a hint of gray in the east to cast an eerie luminescence over the fields of Katyk. He could hear the rain, thudding softly into the earth below, rustling the uncut ears of grain in the distance. It was a gentle rain at first, but the gusty wind indicated fiercer weather was probably on the way.

Yevno breathed in deeply. His senses took pleasure in the aroma of newly moistened soil, the heavy, wet air, and the scent of cut grain lingering over the fields from the previous day's activity. Most wonderful of all, however, was the warm, pungent smell from inside the barn, where enough grain was stored to keep his family from starvation. He smiled, lifting his hands in thankfulness to the Maker of children and grain and rain alike. The work had been strenuous. He had himself brought cartload after cartload back from the field yesterday; the children had helped him unload it in the great stacks that were now piled almost to the roof. Anna and the prince had labored in the fields for as long into the night as their arms would allow. They had probably only been asleep three or four hours before he had himself arisen.

Yevno rejoiced, in his own quiet way. More than two thirds of his crop had been saved—no small feat, considering his condition and progress until two days ago.

He sighed and sat down on his favorite wooden crate, staring out the open door of his barn. And so he sat, keeping silent communion with his own thoughts, and watched both dawn and storm arrive in earnest. By the time he rose an hour and a half later, the rain was falling in drenching sheets that mercilessly pounded down the remaining stalks of uncut grain. Yet still, in his deepest heart, old Yevno was thankful.

His was not the only household in the village in the mood for rejoicing. Most of the village grain had been spared, or, as in Yevno's case, enough to get a family through the winter with sufficient provision. And thus, by common consent, all of Katyk declared a holiday of sorts. There would be the traditional harvest celebrations to come, as there were every year. But on this particular day, the men and women who had labored day and night to gather in their grain ahead of the storm spontaneously came together for a well-deserved afternoon and evening of gaiety.

By mid-afternoon, the local peasantry began to crowd into the large common room of Ivan Ivanovich's former tavern. By evening nearly the whole village had arrived.

The new owner of the place, son of a merchant from Pskov, had not yet arrived in Katyk, and thus Ivan was more liberal than he might otherwise have been about opening his remaining inventory of vodka and kvass to the merrymakers. The free-flowing drink was accompanied by spirited music. For as poor as the people of Katyk might be, they were yet able to produce a violin, a *balalaika*, and two tambourine-like *bubens*. Nicolai Petrovich brought his fine goatskin *volynka* bagpipe safely through the rain as well. Known as the best piper in the whole countryside, he made splendid and lively music with the others, rousing workworn souls and stirring the most somber of Russian hearts.

But no one was somber this evening. Their spirits rose even higher when they learned that a prince from St. Petersburg was among them—a prince whose blistered hands and aching muscles were proof of a well-deserved respect. He had bent his back over the grain and swung the scythe as heartily and skillfully as any of them.

Dancing followed. Several young women, Anna among them, demonstrated the traditional harvest dance of thanksgiving, the *Makovitza*.

How lovely and vibrant it all looks, thought Sergei as he stood watching. Many of the peasants were decked out in their best festive costumes. Full skirts and long-sleeved blouses of richly embroidered linen whirled wildly with every intricate step. The high velvet headdresses, trimmed in colorful braids, made each girl seem as regal as a grand duchess. At least Sergei, with all his experience, declared he had seen no women lovelier, keeping to himself his surprise at seeing such finery in a poor peasant community.

When the *Makovitza* finished to the raucous shouts and cheers and clapping of the men and women watching, Petrovich slowed the tempo of the music to a well-recognized minor tune. Immediately ten or twelve of the village men stepped forward, linked arms, and performed their own local version of the Cossack *Hopak*, in which the lively "bear step" was expertly featured by Peter Popovich. The *volynka* was joined by violin, *balalaika*, and *buben*, as with slow, somber movements the men squatted and kicked out first one leg, then the other, gradually quickening as the tempo slowly gathered momentum until the pace became too rapid for any but the most skilled to continue.

Laughter and clapping and shouts encouraged the men onward in their attempts, until the music slowed once more. The dancers rose and spread out among the observers to enlist new participants to add to their ensemble.

"Let us see how the nobility of St. Petersburg does the *Hopak*!" someone shouted.

"Not well, I assure you!" replied Sergei, laughing.

But it was too late. The guest of honor already had three or four of the dancers crowding about and leading him to the center of the floor, amid happy shouts of encouragement.

He could not refuse their entreaties, and thus joined in with gusto. And he further proved himself worthy of the village's respect, for the young Prince Fedorcenko was no stranger to the vigorous dance. When it was over, laughing gaily amid the cheers and offering his own shouts of hurrah for his companions, he sat down, exhausted, next to Anna.

While the dancers and musicians took a rest from their boisterous activity, *kvass* was passed around to the men, and tea to the women and children. The entire company indulged in the sweet honey cakes the women had spent the afternoon baking.

Sergei looked at Anna and smiled. He reached over and took her hand in his. She glanced down shyly at first, wishing she could prevent the pink from rising to her cheeks, and glad the table in front of them hid his gesture from view of the others. But she did not pull away at his touch. She did not ever want him to leave her side.

"This must surely be the most wonderful two days of my life," he said quietly. "You are used to this country life, Anna. But it is all new to me—the work, the people, the spirit of community that exists between your father and all his friends. I have never known this side of life."

"And what do you think of it," asked Anna, "now that you have seen it?"

"What do I think? What can I think but that it is more full of *life* than anything people from a background such as mine can ever know! I don't know . . . I almost feel as though I have finally found where I really belong."

Anna hesitated in making a response. All the practicalities she had been trying so hard to forget since Sergei's arrival began to flood unwelcomed into her mind. While she was in St. Petersburg, she had wondered if she could ever belong in *his* world. Now he was speaking of belonging in *hers*! Should she rejoice, or be afraid? Her inexperienced emotions could hardly distinguish between the two. Much to her relief, she was spared having to say anything.

The young women were beckoned to dance once more, and Anna eagerly rose to join them in spite of her fatigue.

The musicians struck up the lively chords of the romantic Russian tune "In the Garden." The girls formed a circle, placing their left hands on their hips while their right hands, each grasping a handkerchief, curved high over their heads. They danced through the lively progression three or four times, then scattered out among the onlookers to choose partners for the *Lezghinka* by holding out their handkerchiefs to likely village youths.

When Anna presented her handkerchief to Sergei, it seemed so very natural. How she wished he *was* one of the village sons, a simple young man of peasant origin whom she could love freely and without embarrassment.

But these were not his roots. And the fact that the handkerchief he accepted had once belonged to his princess sister drove the reality all the more painfully home to Anna even as they took their places side by side for the dance.

53

The evening went merrily on.

Gradually the women began to set out, taking themselves and their sleepy children home. The men, no doubt even more fatigued after their long hours of recent toil, still continued with their drinking and laughter long into the night. None would have readily admitted being so tired that he was willing to be the first to take to his bed, and thus the vodka continued to flow from the hand of Ivan Ivanovich.

Even Yevno, not a man normally driven by false pride, stubbornly remained with the others. It was hardly to be wondered at that he was having great difficulty adjusting to his weakened condition. A Russian man was nothing if he was not the virile, stalwart provider and autocrat over his personal world. This was the ingrained code by which the men of the Motherland measured themselves—a standard Yevno must somehow deal with if he hoped to survive this crisis of his own frailty.

Under any other circumstances, Sergei would have left with Anna. But when he saw the concern over her father in her eyes, he decided to remain behind with Yevno. Besides, it would have represented a serious snubbing of Katyk's hospitality for the officially declared guest of honor to leave the celebration prematurely.

Sergei had never possessed much of an inclination toward drink, although once or twice he had succumbed when in the company of Dmitri and their military comrades. During this evening, although he had been a lively participant in the joviality, he drank only what deference to his hosts demanded.

He exited the tavern clearheaded and with the assurance that he would awake in the morning with no ugly reminders of the night before.

The only other one of the company at Ivan's who seemed to share his moderation in drink was Anna's own father. Sergei wondered if Yevno's weakness had something to do with this uncharacteristic behavior for a peasant man. Yevno was clearly tired and had to struggle to keep up with the conversation, sometimes breathing a bit heavily. Sergei could not help being concerned. Yet for most men, illness and hardship drove them *to* drink, not away from it.

As they walked together away from the tavern along the muddy road that led from the village to Yevno's cottage, Sergei questioned him about it.

"I have never been to such a celebration, Yevno Pavlovich," he said. "I won't soon forget it."

He nodded toward one of the villagers not far away where their paths had just diverged. The man had stumbled to the ground and was being helped, with comical ineptitude, by another.

"Some of them, I fear, are so drunk they will forget everything about the evening!"

The young prince and old peasant laughed together.

"Ah, yes," said Yevno, "their heads will be swelled tomorrow."

"Is such drunkenness common?"

"I fear so, though not an everyday occurrence."

"It hardly seems good for men who must work so hard to survive."

"Perhaps not, Your Excellency," replied Yevno. "But you must understand, it is the very severity of life that drives some men to it, and they must be forgiven a lapse every now and then."

"I did not mean to sound disparaging of them," said Sergei apologetically. "Yet I find myself curious about one thing."

"What is that, Your Excellency?"

"Your life is no less hard, Yevno Pavlovich. Yet you leave the tavern quite sober."

"I have found another way to live with my hardships."

"Anna has told me of your deep faith in God."

"I do not find that vodka and *kvass* quench a man's thirst deep enough to satisfy me."

"And you have discovered something that does . . . in your faith?"

"Jesus said that if we drink of mere water we will thirst again. But if we drink of the water that He gives, He said we will never be thirsty again."

"What is that water He gives?"

"His water, the water of eternal life."

"You speak in riddles, Yevno Pavlovich."

Yevno laughed. "Sometimes I find the things of God are riddles to me, too. Yet within my soul I feel the reality of His life, even though my simple brain may not be able to understand it."

"Explain what you mean. I confess, I do not understand you."

They walked on awhile in silence as Yevno thought how best to answer.

"I do not know if I can make you understand," Yevno said at length. "But I will try." He drew in a breath, then went on. "Do you know what I was doing this morning, just before dawn, while you slept on the straw?"

"I don't know," replied Sergei. "I presumed you also were asleep."

"No. The coming of the rain awakened me while it was yet dark. I came out to the barn, opened the door, and just sat looking out upon the rain, and upon my field—some harvested, some ruined. Do you know what I was thinking as I sat there?"

"Wishing the rain had delayed a few more days . . . sorrow that so much of your grain was lost?"

Yevno chuckled. "Most of the men of Katyk managed to get in their entire crops, though one or two did not finish. I heard some of them tonight, cursing the heavens for the rain—bitter, angry. None of them lost as much grain as I did, and yet my thoughts were not bitter as I sat there this morning."

"I am curious, then," said Sergei. "What were you thinking?"

"I was filled with a heart of gratitude and thankfulness—for the grain we did get in, for my family, to have my daughter back with us again, for many things."

"And that is the *water* you speak of, what you call the water of life—thankfulness?"

"That is part of it, but not all. Do you not see—God's life inside me makes me able to be thankful when other men around me are bitter and angry. They drown themselves in vodka. I have no such need, for I am content with the life I have been given. Perhaps that is what I mean by having something inside which keeps my soul from being thirsty, which keeps me content. Jesus said that the life He gives will become like a spring of living water that cannot be quenched. Sometimes that is how I feel—as though God were continually putting new life within me to bubble up to the surface. I did not awaken this morning with thoughts of being thankful for the rain. I simply rose and walked out to look at it. And then from inside came a contentment and gratefulness to my Father in heaven for watching over old Yevno with such kindness."

"You are a remarkable man, Yevno Pavlovich."

"Not so remarkable, Your Excellency," laughed Yevno. "Lately my very beliefs have been tested to their limits. I speak about the living water, but I must tell you, there are times I forget my Father's provision."

"After all you've just told me, I have difficulty believing that."

Yevno shook his head sadly. "Only days ago I was fretting anxiously about the grain, forgetful of the very things I have been saying to you. I am ashamed to admit it. I was even wondering the other day if God had deserted me altogether."

"That does not sound like the man I see."

"Your kind words shame me all the more, Your Excellency. Yet even though I was praying without faith, God answered me!"

"How so?"

"With you. You came to Katyk in answer to my prayers."

"Me?" exclaimed Sergei.

"It is true."

"Many in this country would question whether a nobleman could be an answer to anything, much less a man's prayers."

"God is not choosy whom He uses as His instruments. But I think in your case, Your Excellency, He made one of His *best* choices. You are a good man, I can tell—and not only because you harvested my grain. Anna makes wise choices in her friendships."

"Sir, about Anna . . ."

"Your Excellency need make no explanations. I know you are a man of honor."

"I am. And therefore I feel I *must* explain."

"It is not necessary," insisted Yevno earnestly. "To be truthful, it may be better to keep silent."

"You must realize that Anna cares for me?"

"I have eyes, Your Excellency."

"And you think, perhaps with good reason, that a man of my position, who also happens to be a man of honor, would be seeking some means to keep the poor peasant girl from being hurt. Is that what you are thinking?"

"Such things happen, Your Excellency. It is not to your discredit."

"But does it not concern you that your daughter may be hurt?"

"Of course. But I blame no one. She is young and impressionable, away from home in the city, perhaps lonely. You are a soldier and a prince, and a very handsome one at that—"

"Then you should be furious with me for toying with your daughter's affections."

"I do not believe you have done so. As I said, you are a man of honor."

"I had come to believe, Yevno Pavlovich, that you were not a man to be so servile to any man, even a prince."

"I am not such a man, especially where it concerns my family. This is no empty subservience I show you—you are not worthy of that."

"Then what is it?"

"I merely speak my mind. Whether I am with prince or beggar, my yes is yes and my no is no. If I thought you deserved my anger because my daughter's heart has been pricked by you, or if I thought my anger would protect her, you would see it fully aroused. But she would only be hurt the more. And I would do nothing to turn her against either of us, and thus perhaps force her toward being deceived into any false hopes."

"Why do you say *false* hopes?"

"That is obvious, Your Excellency." Yevno paused and scratched his head. "Your question perplexes me. You are a prince; my daughter is a peasant, a mere—"

"A mere servant?" cut in Sergei more sharply than he intended. For a moment he forgot that he was speaking to a country man, not the usual aristocrat he was accustomed to. He hardly needed to justify his liberal views on the class system to *this* man! But Yevno's peasant mentality was more ingrained than he realized.

"Is that not enough to show the gulf between her and yourself?" Yevno asked.

"Sir, I am disappointed that you would think me above her, and that you do not realize that she is noble enough to be considered my equal."

It took Yevno some moments to digest these strange words. "Do you mean. . . ?" he began, then let his words trail off.

"I mean that your daughter need feel no shame in being a servant or of peasant stock, any more than I can take pride in being a nobleman."

Yevno shook his head. "I have said before, Prince Sergei Viktorovich, that you are the most unusual prince I have ever known. My daughter's judgment is better than I had ever dreamed. You and she are indeed very much alike."

"There are *no* differences between us," said Sergei, "not where it matters, no separations of the kind you spoke of, no gulfs."

"I am honored that you speak so of my daughter," said Yevno humbly.

"The honor is all on *my* side," rejoined Sergei. "I am honored, humbled, that a woman of Anna's high character and purity and devotion would care for me. I have no intention of either toying with her or of finding some painless means to turn her eyes off me. I would die before hurting her."

"I am afraid I am too dull-witted, Your Excellency," said Yevno. "I do not understand you."

"Yevno Pavlovich," said Sergei earnestly, "it is my hope and intention, with your permission, to marry your Anna."

Yevno's shock at the incredible words was registered by a falter in his step rather than with his voice. He turned and looked through the darkness, trying to see if he could find anything in the face of his young companion that would shed further light on the astonishing words he had just heard. But it was too dark, and no additional light came, either from the heavens or from Sergei's eyes. The words hung echoing in the air just as the prince had spoken them.

Their conversation had brought them to the cottage, and Yevno was able to avoid an immediate response to the shocking revelation by busying himself with more practical matters.

"I hope the straw is dry and soft, Your Excellency," he said, leading his guest around the back of the *izba* to the attached barn. "I know it is not what you are accustomed to, but it is all we have."

"I have rarely slept so well as the last two nights," replied Sergei.

"My son used to sleep out here when he grew older."

"The luxury is not in soft blankets but in warm company."

Sergei's comment seemed to hint toward the previous conversation. Yevno turned toward him. "Perhaps we will talk more when we are both rested," he said.

Sergei nodded. "I meant what I said. There is no vodka in my brain causing words I will later repent of. I have wanted to say this to you, Anna's father, for a long time."

Yevno turned and started for the cottage, then paused and looked back. "If I may keep you from your sleep a moment longer, Your Excellency, I have one question more."

"Of course . . . what is it?"

"Your own father and mother—what do they think of what you have just told me?"

Sergei looked away with chagrin. "They know nothing of my feelings for Anna."

Yevno nodded in understanding. "Then she may yet need the protection of those who care for her."

"I was in earnest when I said that I would not allow her to be hurt."

"Ah, if only we were powerful enough to keep away all hurt . . . ," Yevno sighed. "We will talk again, Your Excellency. God be with you this night."

Yevno shuffled with heavy step back to the cottage, his shoulders slumped forward, his head bowed slightly. Sergei wondered if it had been wise to burden the man like this. But everything had come out without his planning it. He had thought to let a few more days pass, perhaps go back to Pskov and take an inn, hire a carriage and horse, and then return. Now suddenly here he was, sleeping in the man's byre, after just announcing his intention to become his son-in-law!

His thoughts strayed toward his own sister and best friend. Two more poorly suited than Katrina and Dmitri he could hardly imagine. Yet because they were of the same class, their marriage would receive the sanction and blessing of society. Yet he and Anna . . .

He could not even complete the thought. Would they have to skulk about through life in dark corners, hidden from view, for no more reason than accident of birth?

As he lay down on the bed of straw and pulled the worn wool blanket about his shoulders, the thought struck him of stealing into the cottage in the middle of the night and carrying Anna off with him.

He smiled at the foolhardy notion. No, there had to be a better way. At least Anna was blessed with a wise and prudent father who didn't seem to take offense with having a nobleman as suitor to his daughter. Yevno had spoken of protecting Anna from hurt, as he himself had. Yet what greater hurt could there be than to endure long years of separation?

Hurting others was no solution; neither was running away. But what was he to do?

At last the fatiguing hours and lack of sleep overtook him.

Even as his heart cried out in despair, his eyelids drooped and finally closed in exhaustion.

54

Sergei's days as a guest in the humble Katyk cottage of Yevno and Sophia Burenin slipped by as quickly as autumn passed into winter. He and Anna made the most of every fleeting moment, not knowing when such a time might come again.

The cloak of secrecy that had hung over their brief stolen moments together in St. Petersburg was lifted in Katyk. It did not matter who might see them together. And the wide, vast countryside was scantly populated anyway. Now that the sheaves had been gathered into the barns, most of the men were inside threshing and winnowing the grain into bags and storage bins, where it would be used throughout the winter months.

But the greatest joy of all for the young soldier and peasant girl was that here in the environs of Katyk they were no longer prince and servant, but simply man and woman, friends, companions. No shadows hung over them except their own uncertainty about their future together.

The chores to be done did not stop because an honored guest was among them, and Sergei was up at daylight, thoroughly relishing being part of every aspect of country life. By the time Sophia reached the barn in the morning, her chickens had been fed, the few eggs gathered, and their roost cleaned out and supplied with fresh straw. Astonished, she saw the happy, whistling prince up to his ankles in manure, wearing an old pair of her husband's boots, mucking out stalls.

"Good morning, Madame!" he called to Anna's mother, whose only response was a gaping jaw and disbelieving eyes.

As he went on with his work, Sophia heard an amused chuckle behind her. She turned to see Yevno sitting on his crate watching the prince, but even more watching the reaction of his wife.

"So, wife," he said in a humorous tone, "what do you think of our prince from St. Petersburg?"

"Every day I believe less and less that he *is* a prince," replied Sophia, only half in jest. "I think perhaps he is a homeless peasant that Anna felt sorry for."

Sergei laughed. "Sometimes I almost wish your words *were* true!" he said. Had he been capable of it in that moment, he would have traded his entire St. Petersburg heritage to be one of these country people.

"Well, perhaps you are a prince," added Sophia. "But one from a fairy tale, who will suddenly vanish before our eyes, never to be heard from again."

The joviality of their words had not kept Yevno from serious thought concerning their guest, although he and Sergei had not resumed their conversation from the night of the celebration. He had watched the young prince carefully, listened to his words, observed his treatment of his daughter, his eagerness for hard work, the humility that found no task distasteful, the deference he showed Yevno as Anna's father and head of the home. He had taught Sergei to milk their cow. The young man had probably kept his wife and children from starving, or at least from extreme hunger during the winter to come. And as Yevno had sat watching him, he was unable to escape the conclusion that he could not hope for better for his daughter than this young man. Even if he was a prince and she a peasant, why shouldn't such a fairy-tale marriage come to his home?

How could he possibly withhold his paternal blessing from such a union, unlikely though it was? He could not . . . and he would not. And he would tell the young prince at the first opportunity. In the meantime, he would enjoy teaching him the ways of the Russian farmer and peasant, so that when Sergei did take his daughter as his wife, he would know as much about her life as she had learned of his.

Once the morning chores were completed, as breaks in the inclement weather permitted, Anna took Sergei over hill, through wet fields, across meadows, and into the nearby forest, joyfully introducing him to all her favorite places on the land that had nurtured her for fifteen years. For a day or two, Yevno lay in bed most of the afternoon, at his wife's insistence, to regain some of the strength the harvest had cost him. Sergei milked the cow both evenings. And after the humble fare of Sophia's supper table—which Sergei declared the best food he had ever eaten anywhere, including the Winter Palace itself—Anna resumed her tradition of reading to the family. It did not take long for Sergei to begin assisting her, the two sharing the book and reading different stories, or taking the parts of different characters. Everyone loved to hear the mixture of their voices, and Sergei took the dramatization to new heights by changing the inflection and emphasis with great result, adding many sound effects besides. Tanya and Vera and Ilya were so delighted after the first such night that they gave him no rest thereafter, begging him for stories, not merely every evening but all day long whenever he walked through the door. He took it all with smiles and laughter, scooping one or the other of them up into his arms, tossing them into the air, and repeating a phrase from one of the stories he had read with particularly comical voices. Never had such giggling and laughter been heard in the Burenin cottage!

Still insisting this man could be no real prince, but was in fact only a prince in one of the fairy tales he himself was reading to them, even Sophia began to laugh at his playful antics. And when he kissed her cheek one night as the stories came to a close, the rising blush in her face gave evidence that he had at last won the heart of mother as well as daughter.

Feeling gradually more rested physically, and increasingly relaxed in the presence of one society considered infinitely his superior, Yevno too entered into the festive spirit of the time. With the pressure of harvest over, he began to recover. His color and breathing improved, and much of his old vigor returned.

After two days, he announced himself fit enough to begin separating the grain.

"What is your hurry, Yevno Pavlovich?" objected Sophia. "You can take all winter if you like."

"I will go slow, wife," he replied. "A small pile of grain each day is all. But I cannot stay in bed any longer or I will wither up and die!"

The prince was at his side the moment Yevno headed for the byre, followed by all the children, and Anna last of all.

After clearing a space on the floor of the barn, Yevno took one of the bundles from the top of the stack, untied it and tossed it down. He then took up a wooden pole with a flat board attached to its end with leather. "This is the flail," he said to the prince. "Stand back, children!" he added.

With that, he lifted the odd-looking instrument over his shoulders and brought it down with a great blow onto the heads of grain. After a few more such blows, he threw down a second bundle, continuing to beat the sheaves. The wheat flew, and the chaff fluttered into the air; the stalks of straw flattened and broke and spread out all around. At length, Yevno stood back, breathing deeply, beholding the small pile of threshed grain on the floor. He took a broom, lightly swept back the accumulated straw, then swept the greater portion of the wheat onto a wide, flat, woven mat. Without a word, Sophia stepped forward, taking one side of it with her two hands, while Yevno grabbed the other. They took it a step or two outside, then began tossing the grain into the air. The breeze gently carried off the lighter chaff. In two or three minutes, all that remained in the center of the mat was a pile of golden grain.

He and Sophia brought it back inside and proudly deposited it into a large wooden bin built into one of the barn's walls.

"So, Your Excellency," said Yevno, "that is what we must do now—first thresh with the flail, then winnow away the chaff to make what you cut in the fields fit to yield bread."

Already the flail was in Sergei's hands. Anna grabbed a sheaf, unbound it, tossed it to the floor, did the same with another, then stood back. Sergei raised the awkward thing high, but his first swing only managed to bring the flopping board at the end of the pole against his back.

"Ow . . . aah!" he cried in pain. Anna winced. Yevno could not help chuckling.

"It is perhaps even more difficult than the scythe," said Yevno. "Try it slowly, so that the free-swinging swiple on top does not hit you in the head but comes down on the heads of grain."

Again Sergei made the attempt, this time with more success. Within five minutes the flail was threshing with as much accuracy and impact as Yevno himself would have been able to muster.

For the rest of the day, Sergei threw himself into the threshing with a zealous joy, heightened by Anna's presence beside him. Yevno and Sophia continued to winnow the grain and chaff throughout the morning, until Yevno began to show signs of once again being taxed beyond what was good for him.

During the afternoon, therefore, Anna and Sergei alternated between threshing and winnowing, and by day's end a sizable pile of wheat had begun to rise at the base of the storage bin.

55

Too quickly the pleasurable days came to an end. It was time for the prince who had become part of a peasant family to return to his former and future life.

The day before his departure, Anna wrapped a small loaf

of bread, a hunk of goat's cheese, and a few turnips in a cloth, and they walked to the stream that flowed by the great old willow to partake of one last simple meal together. The rains had passed and the day was bright and clear, although the crisp breeze that wafted over them carried with it the bite of the coming winter.

Sergei lay back on the grass, closed his eyes, and drank in the exquisite sounds of the meadow—the splashing of water in the stream as it tumbled across the rocks, the sweet call of a lark, and the gentle rustle of the lacy fingers of the willow.

"So, this is the place you love most of all, Anna?" he said dreamily, a smile of contentment spread over his face.

"It always used to be," she replied. "And now that I am here again, I think I would say so still."

"What makes it so special?"

"No matter what the season or the time of day, I find myself enchanted here."

"Enchanted? How do you mean?"

"Mostly I came here to read and think. I suppose you could say this was where I first left Katyk—in my mind. Under these spreading branches I have taken many a long journey to far and exotic lands. And this tough old bark has heard more than its share of a young girl's secrets."

"And what kind of secrets do you tell an old willow, Anna?"

"Oh, nothing that would amount to much in the larger scheme of the world, I suppose. But if my ramblings went up to heaven as the prayers I meant them for, then I am sure they meant something to God."

"If I spoke to the willow," said Sergei lightly, yet with a definite earnestness in his tone, "do you think God would hear and answer me?"

"Why not speak directly to God?"

"And put some poor priest out of his job?"

"You know better than that, Sergei."

"Because of you, Anna, I suppose I do know what you mean." He paused and closed his eyes again as if he had re-sumed listening to the sounds of nature about them. "If I did

pray right now, I would ask God to make this day go on for
ever and ever."

Anna sighed. "And I would join you in it."

"But it would be a foolish prayer, would it not?" he added.
"Good things don't last forever; otherwise how would we know
the difference between sadness and happiness?"

When Anna did not reply, Sergei changed the subject. "I
have never yet told you much about my year away."

"I hoped you would before you left."

"You want to hear about it, then?"

"Oh yes . . . of course!"

Sergei remained quiet for a few moments, collecting his
thoughts. Hints of the mental turmoil that had sent him away
in the first place seemed to settle over his countenance, even
though when he spoke again, his voice remained cheery for
Anna's sake.

"Yasnaya Polyana, the 'bright glade,' is a remarkable
place," he began. "It is a world all its own, and I doubt it has
changed one iota in the past hundred years. Tolstoy attributes
his love for the Motherland to be a direct result of his life in
the glade."

"Didn't you tell me he wrote while there?"

"Yes, both *War and Peace* and *Anna Karenina*. I suppose I
harbored a secret hope it would inspire me as greatly."

"And. . . ?"

"I'll get to that in a minute." He lazily plucked a blade of
grass and began to examine it as if it held the secrets of life he
had been searching for in his travels.

"Count Tolstoy is a tremendous man," he went on after a
moment. "But he can be rather intense. Nevertheless, he taught
me a great deal and was extremely tolerant of my occasional
'frivolous lapses,' as he called them."

"He called *you* frivolous?" smiled Anna. "He must be unusual as well as talented."

"I'll always be grateful to him. But after a while I knew it
was time I moved on, for both our sakes. I did not want to wear
out either my welcome or his patience."

"Where did you go then?"

287

"I had hoped to find my own Yasnaya Polyana," answered Sergei. "Some place where I could capture the same creative spirit that he found there. I traveled east as far as the Urals, then south to the Caucasus. I visited the provinces and the Russian peasantry, as I've always wanted to do. But I only *saw*. I was a spectator and always a stranger."

He paused again reflectively. Anna said nothing, but waited for him to continue.

"Do you know where I finally ended up? On my family's estate by the Black Sea. It was an ingenious place to hide, don't you think? The last place anyone would think to look for me. There were only the caretaker and his wife, and I swore them to absolute secrecy. I stayed there through the winter and finally finished my book."

"Did you really? Oh, I'm happy for you, Sergei!" exclaimed Anna.

"When I return to the capital I hope to deliver it to a publisher. Count Tolstoy says for me to expect the censors to tear it to ribbons—"

"It won't get you into trouble, will it, Sergei?"

"Trouble is routine for writers these days, unless you are a Tolstoy or a Turgenev, to whom the censors are more generous. Otherwise, they are as nit-picking as a gaggle of old women. It's part of what you have to expect. A few years back they went so far as imagining that the notes in musical compositions might contain subversive codes."

"What will you do if they censor what you have written?"

"There are ways to get around all that, in the most natural of Russian traditions—greasing the proper palms. But my book is not seditious, Anna. It is honest, and unfortunately in this country that often amounts to the same thing."

"Tell me what it is like . . . can you?"

"It is simply a young man's war experiences. I would have brought the manuscript for you to read, but as I was getting ready to come, I found myself reticent about showing it to you."

"Whatever for?" asked Anna, incredulous.

"I can't imagine now. Simple embarrassment, I suppose. Now I regret that decision. I would value your opinion."

"I know it must be wonderful!"

"Your *objective* opinion, please."

"I'm sure I shall *objectively* think it the most wonderful book I have ever read," she said with a grin.

He smiled, and looked deeply into her eyes. "Tell me, Anna," he said, "after this time together, do you believe we might have a chance for happiness together?"

"I never had a doubt of that," she answered. "But what of the realities of . . . the differences between us?"

"They mean nothing to me—surely you can see that."

"I meant *your* family, Sergei. Your father would never give his blessing if he knew where you were right now."

"My father . . . should I care what he thinks?"

"Sergei, you know you love and respect him. You know how you desire his approval."

"I grudgingly admit to that weakness in my character. But for over twenty years I have been struggling to gain that approval—without success. Does it not seem time that I give it up altogether?"

"Do you really think so?"

"I told you how cool he was when I was at home. Anna, we sat at the dinner table together *twice*, and he did not so much as look in my direction! Is it any wonder that I repacked my bags immediately to come to you?"

"Going away as you did a year ago hurt your family deeply, Sergei. They just don't understand what you've been going through. Perhaps if you tried to talk to your father—"

"Oh, but I have—so many times! Anna, don't you see—he is just not interested in what I think about, nor does he care in the least to *try* to understand me. I see nothing for it but to quit trying and not worry about him anymore. I have to live my own life."

"Do you really mean that?"

"Yes . . . yes, I do."

Sergei paused and took two or three deep breaths to calm himself.

"Anna," he said, "I am sorry you have been thrust into all this. But the difficulties with my father really have nothing to do with you at all. He knows nothing about us. My father and I have been at each other's throats for years, and I know in advance what he is liable to say if I try to seek his approval—to marry you or for anything else, for that matter. That is why it is best that I keep him out of my considerations altogether. The only way we manage to get along is to keep miles apart. Why my departure from St. Petersburg last year should have upset him, I cannot imagine. But I do not intend to subject you to his stinging criticism, any more than I intend to be talked *out* of marrying you because of him. *You* cannot even talk me out of it, Anna!"

Anna smiled. "I wasn't trying to dissuade you," she said quietly. "I was only trying to be practical about the differences in station that *are* there. I do disagree with you about one thing, Sergei, and that is that we mustn't ignore them."

"I'm sure my father will make that impossible," Sergei said.

"Princess Katrina tells me he is under a great deal of pressure these days," said Anna, trying to be conciliatory. "Both from the terrorism and the awful uncertainty of never knowing where the next explosion may go off, and from all the dissention within the government itself."

"How you manage to stay so well informed, Anna Yevnovna, is always a surprise to me. Such an amazing young peasant girl you are!"

"Sergei, please—this is no time for all that. Be serious. It is important that you think of your father's position. It is not easy to be so close to the tsar, to act as a voice of moderation in such a volatile political climate."

"There you go again, the political expert," chided Sergei with a smile.

"Katrina says your father has made dangerous enemies on both sides," Anna went on, not to be diverted.

"Maybe you are right," sighed Sergei. "Perhaps I am being insensitive to his position." He rubbed his chin thoughtfully. "A man in a battle zone, which St. Petersburg has certainly become, who walks such a perilous line between life and death—I suppose he would take a more serious view of family ties. My father must wonder what kind of heir will follow him.

That no doubt intensifies his disappointment in me all the more."

"How can he be disappointed in you?"

"Aren't fathers always disappointed in their sons never measuring up to their expectations?"

"He must know how brave you were in the war, and how you risked your own life to save Lieutenant Grigorov."

"How did *you* know about all that?"

"Lieutenant Grigorov told me."

"I didn't realize you knew him."

"We have run into each other several times in the Winter Palace when I have accompanied the princess."

"And are the two of you friends?"

Anna thought about the question momentarily. "I suppose you could say so," she replied, "as much as a servant girl and a Cossack guard could ever be."

"That *is* an interesting connection," he said. "I have not even thought of the fellow since the war, and now he turns up crossing paths with you and Katrina. But as to my father," Sergei went on with a shake of his head, "sometimes I think that the only way I can please him would have been for me to die in battle instead of being only wounded. Then he could have been proud of me forever. As it is, my wound healed, and we are back where we started."

"If he knew you better, Sergei, he would be proud of you. He couldn't help it—I just know it. If only you could—"

Anna stopped.

"If only I gave him the chance, is that what you meant to say? If only I would stop running away from him?"

Anna shrugged. "Now that you say the words, I don't see how I would ever have the right to think that," she said. "I'm sure you have done all you could."

"Maybe not all I could, but certainly all I know to do. And how can my presence help matters when he will hardly speak to me? It is a classic dilemma of misunderstanding between father and son."

"A dilemma that needs no further obstacles in the middle

of it," said Anna, bringing the conversation around to its previous thread.

From her tone, Sergei knew exactly what she meant.

"I will not choose between you and my father," he said defiantly. "If he does love me, as I suppose he does in his own way, he would not require that of me. And please, Anna, neither can you."

"I will not," replied Anna quietly. "But neither will I stop looking for a new tolerance on the part of your father toward you, and perhaps in time even toward me."

"As you wish, Anna. It will be difficult for me to hold out such hope. At least I can be sure that *your* family will give us their blessing."

"I suppose it is easier to move up socially than down."

"Don't ever speak of yourself as *down*, Anna. You are leagues worthier than I or any of my class could hope to be. Your father's acceptance of me simply transcends trivialities like social classes. Perhaps it is the natural result of his faith in God . . . I do not know. He has judged me by who I am, apart from name and title and money—things that aren't truly my own in the first place."

"Then I shall pray *your* father comes into such an acceptance of the two of us as well."

"I must admit, Anna, I cannot be confident in such a miracle occurring."

"Then I shall have enough confidence for both of us!"

56

Sergei left Katyk the following morning.

Anna watched as his figure retreated down the dirt road leading to the village, where he had arranged for a ride to Pskov to catch the train.

She tried to keep the sadness away with bright reminders that she would see him again soon, and of his promises that he would remain in St. Petersburg until she returned. But she could not prevent an awful sense of emptiness and loneliness from overwhelming her. It would have been simpler, she told herself, if he had never come back into her life. Yet she would not have traded the last week for anything; the time together had confirmed the bond between them. No matter what fate, or God in His infinite wisdom, meted out to them, she would never be able to commit her heart as deeply to another.

As the dreary day wore on, Anna wandered about listlessly, detached from everything about her. Before supper she found herself entering the barn. Her steps were mostly aimless, but she knew she would find her father inside tending the animals.

He had drawn a stool up to the cow and had just begun milking.

"Let me do that, Papa," Anna intervened.

"Ah, it is a sorry pass when a man cannot even milk a poor cow!"

"But it is my job, Papa. We agreed. And just because Sergei is gone and cannot do it for me any longer doesn't mean you should."

"I thought perhaps today, you would not . . . feel up to it."

"That is kind of you, Papa," Anna said smiling.

"It is good to see you smile again. Your heart is heavy this afternoon, I know."

"You always know me better than I do myself."

"Parents are blessed with a certain kind of wisdom hidden from the young."

"Thank you just the same, Papa," said Anna, forcing Yevno to yield the stool to his daughter. "But I think a diversion will be good for me."

"I will feed Lukiv, then."

Anna shook her head helplessly. "I think you would just wither up and die if you could not work, Papa."

Yevno shuffled to the narrow stall where the gray mare patiently waited for her supper. He continued to speak to Anna as he filled the wooden trough, while the stream of milk squirted out and rattled in the bottom of the pail.

"Soon you will return to the city, my daughter," he said. "I will not be so sad as I was before, because now I know you will be happy there."

"I have found a home there," admitted Anna. "But this will always be my *real* home. You know that, don't you, Papa?"

"Yes, but young people must grow and sometimes find new places to call home," said Yevno sagely.

Anna did not reply.

"Your young *moujik* is a good man," Yevno said after a moment. "He will take care of you."

"He is a good man, Papa," agreed Anna.

"Then what is troubling you, daughter?"

The sound of the milking stopped and Yevno knew Anna was thinking.

"Is it wrong for me to be concerned about what his family will think?" she said at length. "To worry that they will not accept me?"

"But they have accepted you, have they not? You write to us about all you do with the princess, and about how kind they have all been to you."

"They have been kind—more kind than I deserve."

"But you do not think they accept you?"

294

"They accept me, Papa—as a maid . . . not as the wife of their son, a prince."

"Ah, I see what you mean."

"I love his sister too, Papa, and it would hurt me deeply if I became a source of strife or contention within the family. Oh, Papa, there just seem to be too many obstacles in the way!"

There was silence for several minutes. The milking resumed, while Yevno busied himself with Lukiv's oats and hay.

"Did you know the young prince spoke to me?" asked Yevno at length.

"What do you mean, Papa . . . what about?"

"About you, of course. He told me he wanted to marry you, if I would give my consent."

As familiar as she and her father were, Anna could not help her embarrassment at discussing such a matter.

"And . . . what did you say, Papa?" she asked timidly.

"At first I said nothing," replied Yevno. "I wanted to know him better. But when he came to me last night to ask again, I took his hand in mine and told him he had earned my admiration and respect, and that I was honored to give my consent."

"It makes me happy to hear you say those words," said Anna, "but I cannot help being afraid."

Yevno left Lukiv and walked slowly back to where Anna sat, halfheartedly trying to coax more milk out of the cow.

"Only God is able to conquer the problems and hardships you and your prince may face, Anna," he said, his voice full of tender love for his eldest daughter. "I can only say to you, my Annushka, that you cannot do better than to leave it in His hands."

"I know, Papa," she replied, feeling her throat tighten as tears began to rise in her eyes. "But I am so afraid we might be destined to remain apart. What if *that* is God's will?"

A sob broke through her trembling lips. She rose from the stool, and by the time the single sob had become an unexpected torrent of tears, Anna was in her father's warm embrace. She laid her cheek gratefully against his coarse, work-soiled tunic, weeping like a child.

Yevno ran his hand over her soft curls.

"Be certain of this, Anna," he said. "Whatever our Father above has planned for you, it is a destiny of His choosing. How can it be anything but for your best? And whatever obstacles and difficulties are part of it, He will give you the strength and courage to face them."

Anna nodded, but said no more. She was content for the moment to be a little girl again, and feel the safety of Yevno's gentle arms.

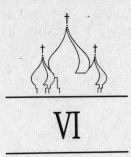

VI

A HOUSE DIVIDED
(February 1880)

57

Intermittent bursts of warm breath hung suspended in the icy air, then slowly dispersed into the frigid night.

This was as cold as it would get in St. Petersburg. February was no month to be standing idly about on the street corners of the city. Paul Burenin fidgeted nervously; he and Andrei Zhelyabov would attract attention if they did not do something soon. They were milling about Senate Square trying to appear interested in the statue of Peter the Great and the grandeur of St. Isaac's Cathedral. But the two young men hardly looked the part of tourists, especially given the hour and the temperature.

Zhelyabov dug a gloved hand beneath the layers of his winter clothing and withdrew a pocket watch. He flipped the lid open, shook his head, and clicked his tongue. He snapped the watch closed, then buried it once more in its warm hiding place.

"We've time," he said, a steamy vapor rising on his words. "I'm afraid in my eagerness I got us here early. It is only 6:15."

"How early are we?"

"Dinner will not be served, according to our sources, until 6:30."

"Perhaps we should walk about," suggested Paul, hoping his words did not betray his growing faintheartedness. In the last few months he had been involved in an increasing number of incidents, but they had all been minor and inconsequential compared with tonight's mission.

"Good idea." Zhelyabov turned and they continued talking

299

as they struck out across the Square, heading toward Marskaya Prospect, passing St. Isaac's on their right. "Have courage, Paul," the leader said. "In another fifteen minutes all your fears and anxieties and months of faithfulness will be well rewarded. You shall even be able to forgive me for depriving you of Vlasenko. Why, even Anickin might find it in his heart—if he has one!—to render absolution for his loss of vengeance."

"I doubt such things trouble him now from his prison cell."

"On the contrary, Paul. If I know anything about the workings of Basil Anickin's mind—and who could claim to understand such a twisted brain as his?—I have the feeling it will eat away at him still. I pity his enemies if he is ever released. A man like Anickin never forgets, and stops at nothing for the sake of revenge."

"How long will he be in?"

"Technically speaking, he is no longer in the Fortress."

"They released him?"

"Hardly. From what I heard he suffered a complete breakdown in prison and was taken to a mental ward. I'll warrant he's still in chains, but some of our comrades have been talking about aiding an escape."

"Do you think it's possible?"

"To tell you the truth, I have been dragging my feet in giving it my sanction. I don't know what to think of Anickin. He will never submit to anyone but himself. To have someone like that running loose can only hinder our cause, especially now that his own thirst for revenge is driving him to the edge of lunacy."

Paul made no response. He agreed completely with his mentor, though for his own personal reasons. As long as Anickin was locked up, the Fedorcenkos would be safe. And if they were safe, Anna was safe. And fortunately, without the force of Anickin's presence, the planned attack on the Fedorcenkos had been stalled.

They continued walking in silence, and Paul turned his thoughts to matters closer at hand. It still seemed incredible to him, but in less than fifteen minutes, The People's Will would make its most audacious strike yet against the hated Romanov dynasty. A bomb was about to be detonated in the very lair of Russia's emperor—in the Winter Palace itself.

A few weeks ago, some repairs had been commissioned inside the palace. One of their number, a man named Khalturin, who as yet had no official reputation or record to hide, had been hired on as a carpenter. He also received permission to sleep in the basement with a handful of the others while the work was in progress.

Over the last several weeks, Zhelyabov supplied explosives for Khalturin to smuggle into the Winter Palace. After accumulating over fifty kilograms of TNT, he laid a mine in the basement directly under the imperial dining room, using enough dynamite to blast the room to splinters—and most importantly, to end once and for all the life of Tsar Alexander II, last Tsar of Russia.

Yes, thought Paul, it was worth laying aside his desired vengeance against the Third Section chief to see the hopes of their movement at last fulfilled.

Slowly they made their way back to the rendezvous point. Zhelyabov carried a small bag containing coat, cap, and forged identity papers for their comrade—just in case anything went wrong with his escape from the Palace.

They both scanned the darkness for any sign of movement. He should appear at any minute.

58

At quarter past six, Lieutenant Grigorov, Cossack guard attached to the tsar's personal wing of the Winter Palace, took up his post at the imperial study door, he on one side, another Cossack in identical dress on the other, both standing at rigid attention. Within moments the remainder of the retinue, of which these two had been the vanguard, appeared.

The emperor, Alexander Romanov, walked next to his nephew and namesake, Prince Alexander of Battenberg, newly elected Prince of Bulgaria. The tsar's distinguished dinner guest had been expected some time ago, but due to a delayed train had only just arrived. The tsar, however, appeared unconcerned that dinner had to be postponed. The fact that the chef was near the point of heart failure over the expected ruination of his beef cordon bleu was of little import to the ruler of all the Russias. Dry and tasteless meat, cold potatoes, warm champagne—those were the servants' problems, and mattered little as long as everything came out perfect in the end.

The emperor approached his study, chatting quietly with his nephew, giving no thought to the servants who had to stand in the dining room an extra half-hour or forty-five minutes. His only apparent concern was that his guest not be rushed to dinner before he even had a chance to wash the dust of travel from his hands with warm wash towels and from his throat with a slightly chilled before-dinner sherry. Dinner was delayed anyway, and His Imperial Highness thought the sherry would help calm his nephew's travel-frazzled nerves and aid his digestion. Besides, he was in the habit of taking sherry before dinner himself, and court protocol must be observed, the unreliable Russian railway system notwithstanding.

Misha did not care much for diplomatic decorum, although he knew and observed every jot and tittle in his court position. He knew it was an honor to be selected as a member of the Imperial Cossack Guard. Yet every once in a while his heart yearned for the outdoors, to feel a powerful horse beneath him, to fulfill the purposes of his Cossack heritage.

Every time he heard fresh reports of the glorious adventures of the White General Skobelev in Central Asia, Misha found himself tempted to give up the great "honor" of standing guard at dinner parties and teas. Unfortunately, such a request on his part, especially during these tumultuous times, might be mistaken by his superiors. To be labeled a sympathizer toward the rebel cause did not concern him as much as being thought a coward for deserting his monarch when the need seemed greatest. And since the incident last summer when he had saved the tsar from the madman's bomb out in the street, he had been a little more successful in convincing himself that his assignment was more vital than it appeared on the surface.

At least the tedious duty kept him near Countess Dubjago, for whatever *that* was worth. He was a fool, and he knew it. Yet he seemed powerless to change the course of his heart, which always returned to the countess as surely as the compass needle pointed northward.

He often pondered his ironic fate. He was a man whose breeding was, if anything, wild and free-spirited. A Cossack did not *ask* for a woman—he *took* her! Yet here he was, a slave not only to his duty, but also to a woman—and a pale, aristocratic one at that.

Sometimes Misha Grigorov felt far removed from his heritage, his true beginnings of blood and soul. In his deepest heart, however, he knew that he could never fulfill the Cossack reputation for untamed savagery. If he was not at peace standing here at attention, neither would he have been at peace carrying out many of the bloodthirsty exploits upon which the Cossacks of history had built their fame. He was, in fact, a gentle Cossack, willing to fight on the battlefield for a just cause and for the emperor, but unwilling to plunder and destroy for the sheer pleasure of ferocity.

Perhaps if he returned to his little village, he could find the balance of manhood he longed for. He'd find himself a hearty Cossack girl who knew how to treat a man better than the countess ever would, even if some day she *did* happen to notice him!

Misha was surprised to find Anna Yevnovna suddenly enter his thoughts. No, not even she could satisfy him, even if she were not already spoken for. He doubted he could take to the agrarian life of a peasant farmer. For him it must be either battlefield or steppe.

Yet here he was in the gilded corridors of the Winter Palace. And he would not even have *this* honor much longer if he did not attend more rigidly to his present duty! The emperor of

Russia was in his care. It was not a responsibility to be taken lightly, especially considering those forces in the nation out to do him harm. A handful of Cossacks might be all that stood between the throne and revolution.

The tsar gave not so much as a nod at the two guards as he strode past them into his study. For ceremonies they were fine, but half the time, even with all the current troubles, he insisted on going about the city without his Cossack detachment. And if he did take them, he brought along only a few, which made their ability to guard him almost ineffectual. But Misha understood the man's aversion to this ever-present reminder of constant danger.

From inside the study Misha heard a clock chime half past the hour. He wondered how long the delay before dinner would be. Not that it mattered one way or the other to him—his own dinner would have to wait for several hours yet.

59

Khalturin joined his co-conspirators shortly before 6:30.

He was breathless and, even in the icy temperature, perspiring freely. Quickly he threw on the coat Zhelyabov handed him, took the cap, and pulled it far down on his forehead. He glanced nervously around to make sure he had not been followed.

"You are safe, my friend," said Zhelyabov. "We have been all the way up and down the street. No one is out. You have not been seen."

"We must be off then," said Khalturin hastily. "I had to push my way past one of the Cossacks at the outer gate. I made up a lie about a medical emergency, but they are sure to look into it the moment the bomb goes off. The man was suspicious, and he saw my face clearly. Come, let us go!"

"Not yet," insisted Zhelyabov. "You are safe awhile longer. We must watch for the results of your work. How much longer?"

"Any second," replied Khalturin. "In setting the timed fuse on the bomb, I only allowed myself the barest minimum of time to get out of the palace before detonation. That's why I couldn't let that guard stop and question me."

He glanced back over his shoulder. "It should have gone off by now. I tell you, I made the fuses short. I didn't want to take any risk of discovery."

"That is good," said Zhelyabov. "We have had too many failures in the past, and we have taken too many risks with this attempt. It will not fail. Be patient."

The three stood in Senate Square, having great difficulty masking their anticipation and keeping their eyes casually averted from their target. Remaining behind was foolish, and Khalturin kept imploring the others to go. But Zhelyabov was not willing, even for safety's sake, to leave before the assurance of success.

He removed his pocket watch again. "Six-thirty, you say?" he asked Khalturin.

The carpenter nodded. "Don't worry. Nothing can go—"

Considering past performance, the words he was about to utter were a bold pronouncement. But the statement, only half spoken, was suddenly confirmed as a deafening blast shattered the night air.

The explosion was of such magnitude that it shook the ground beneath their feet two hundred meters away. They looked toward the palace but saw only billowing smoke and shattering windows. As soon as the echo from the terrific blast began to die away, screams and yells and shouts could be heard from inside the palace.

Khalturin, who had become intimately familiar with that particular section of the palace in recent days, vividly pictured the collapsing walls and the caving in of the floor, sending the elegantly laid dining table, the tsar and the imperial family into the basement. Falling bricks and boards, collapsing structural beams, further explosions of dynamite, fires, crashing chandeliers, toppling bookcases—splintered glass and flying plaster and roaring flame would consume them all!

Unconsciously, Paul glanced toward his comrades. He tried to make himself feel the same joyful exuberance as he saw in their eyes. This was the victorious culmination of all their hopes and dreams and plans. *Everything* had come down to this one delicious moment! Yet as he stood there, he could not keep other ugly images from crowding unbidden into some sensitive place in his mind where his heart still ruled—images of the injured, of innocent servants and guests. He saw blood. He heard the cries of agonized pain. Hadn't Anna written that *she* had been in the Winter Palace a time or two? Hadn't she even been close enough to the tsar to touch him? What if she—

No. She wasn't here now! He had to push such thoughts away!

He shook himself awake in the cold night air. This was no time to drift off into such worries. *No sacrifice is too great for the cause.* Over and over he forced himself to say the words, trying to make himself believe them again.

No sacrifice is too great . . .

It did not take long for the entire area to come alive with activity in the immediate aftermath of the explosions, and Paul was spared having to dwell long on his confused and conflicting thoughts.

Squads of gendarmes and guards rushed toward the palace. Medical and fire wagons, most stationed not far off, raced wildly down the street, bells pealing furiously to announce their arrival. Crowds of spectators began to form in spite of the cold. Survivors poured out of the palace, swelling their ranks. In the midst of the mayhem, shouts of confusion and question and panic only added to the uncertainty of what had happened. And still smoke poured from the palace, adding vivid reality to the flying rumors.

"The whole palace is in flames!" shouted some anonymous

messenger of doom running from inside as if in terror for her life.

"Hundreds killed!" cried another.

"Every minister dead!"

"The entire imperial family—gone!"

The three silent observers intuitively knew that less than half these reports could have any validity in fact. Clearly their plan had met with success, but who *exactly* had been killed— that was the critical question. Yet they could not stay around any longer to find out.

The place was crawling with the kind of people they made a habit of avoiding. And the initial confusion and throng of onlookers could provide cover for only so long. Soon the police would begin making summary arrests, as they always did, hauling in any spectator who appeared even vaguely suspicious or showed a little too much interest in the proceedings.

Still unsure of the specific nature of their success, the three separated and lost themselves in the growing crowd.

60

After the initial shock of the explosion, it took several minutes for the Cossack guards in the hallway to comprehend what had happened. The blast shook the floorboards so violently they were nearly thrown off their feet.

Still somewhat dazed and confused, Grigorov did not forget the object of his duty. He came to himself, then turned and grabbed the brass handle of the study door and flung it open wide.

The emperor sat in his armchair, his hands gripping the upholstered leather sides so tightly that his knuckles were as white as his stricken face. The prince was on the floor, struggling to get back to his feet. As Misha rushed to him, his boot crushed the shattered pieces of a sherry glass into the hard oak floor.

He took his arm and helped the prince back to his chair. After determining him to be unharmed, Grigorov turned his attention back to the emperor.

"Your Majesty, please forgive my unauthorized entry," Misha stammered. "Are you . . . does there seem to be any further injury?"

"I am fine, Lieutenant," said the tsar in a taut voice.

"You are not harmed or hurt?"

"No. Thank you for helping my nephew. What happened?"

"I don't know, Your Majesty. Some kind of explosion. I had feared it was here, in your study."

"Thank God, no."

At that moment several members of the palace staff burst into the room. "There has been a terrible explosion!" said the chief steward. "As far as can be determined, it was centered somewhere in the basement under the dining room—"

"The dining room!" broke in the emperor.

"Yes, Your Majesty."

"We were to have been there by this time!"

"The fact that you were not saved your life. A fire is raging even as we speak."

"But for a trivial fluke of the rails . . . ," said the emperor, turning still whiter. "What about casualties?"

"Many, Your Majesty," replied the steward, "though it is too soon to determine an exact count. Several scores of the Finnish Regiment are believed trapped under the rubble. And there were a number of servants in the dining room itself."

"Dear God!" A moment more the tsar sat in benumbed silence, then suddenly jumped from his chair. "The empress! Has she been harmed?"

"Untouched, Your Majesty. I am told she slept right through the blast."

"I must go to her." His wife was dying, and despite the dismal state of his marriage, he did not want her to learn of such an outrage except in his presence.

Telling his nephew he would return as soon as possible, the tsar dismissed the Cossacks to give what assistance they could to the relief efforts, then hurried from the room toward his wife's living quarters.

Even the horrors of the battlefield did not prepare Misha for what met his eyes as he approached the demolished section of the palace. All his thoughts about how tame this assignment seemed suddenly faded away. This present atrocity was all the more revolting because this *wasn't* a battlefield. The victims were innocent. These were no soldiers trained for war and prepared to bleed and die for their nation. Here were servants, women and cooks, whose only crime was service to their tsar.

How could this have happened, here in the heart of Russia's might and power? This palatial fortress was supposed to be impregnable! No one would believe that this disaster was a mere accident.

Once the fire had been contained, a preliminary investigation bore out the careful planning of the incident. Fragments of dynamite casings were found strewn throughout the rubble. The evidence proved the unthinkable: The terrorists had penetrated the very citadel of the emperor's domain.

For the next several hours, Misha worked alongside Cossacks, servants, workmen, and firemen, first extinguishing the fire before it spread to other sections of the palace, then digging through the rubble, pulling those still living to safety, and carting the bodies of the dead to the waiting wagons that had been summoned from the morgue. The carnage sickened him. What kind of animals would knowingly do such a thing?

When the final toll was taken, fifteen had been killed and dozens more injured.

Was the world perched on the brink of insanity? Those people were lunatics if they thought all their revolutionary prattle justified this! Misha wished he could drag a couple of them in here right now and force them to extract the bleeding, broken body of a simple house servant—a man they were supposedly fighting for—from his shallow grave in the debris. But they would never witness up close the results of their "noble" cause!

Misha wiped a grimy hand across his eyes. If ever he wished himself able to shed tears, this was the moment. But there were no tears. A Cossack did not know how to cry; his only weeping came from the heart.

But if ever he wished himself able to shed tears, this was the moment.

Though what would be the use? Weeping would do no good. Misha Grigorov was a Cossack, a man of action. All he wanted was a slim revolutionary neck to get his hands on!

But there was no satisfaction for Misha that day. The only deaths he witnessed were those of the innocent.

61

Cyril Vlasenko knew he was in trouble. Heinous criminals did not penetrate the very walls of the Winter Palace without seriously compromising the position of the head of the tsar's own Secret Police.

Vlasenko was walking on very thin ice. Heads turned in his direction, tongues wagged, and his enemies gloated. They all awaited his fall with anticipation, waiting for the iron fist of the tsar to come crashing down upon his head.

Vlasenko paced back and forth before the narrow window in his office, chewing on the cigar clenched between his teeth. His wide forehead actually oozed sweat, which dripped down the fleshy folds of his sallow cheeks. Then he remembered the handbill clutched in his sweaty fist.

The filthy swine! They should be ashamed to claim responsibility for the despicable act, for the innocent lives, and for the supreme failure of their attempt on the tsar. But as usual, the rebel scum had found a way to twist the truth to their own favor, and to make the government look bad in the process. And upon this occasion they had especially aimed their venom at the Third Section chief.

Vlasenko brought the crumpled paper to eye level, and again read the disgusting words:

To All Honest Citizens! Be it known that the struggle against evil is and must be the business of all loyal citizens of the Motherland! For three hundred years the noble people of Russia have lived beneath the weight of governmental terror: mass arrests, shipment to labor camps, crass brutality. Now is the time to loose the shackles of fear, of oppression, of bondage!

The very walls of the citadel of the tsar himself have been breached. At last a decisive blow has been struck against the forces of tyranny. That the blood of brave and virtuous Russians has been spilled in this noble cause is but one further impetus to continue the fight. Let not their blood be shed in vain! Arise now! Take up the cause of justice, of freedom.

Narodnaya Volya! The People's Will is triumphant.

Demand that the voice of the people be heard and heeded! Demand that His Imperial Highness bow to that righteous will, that his evil henchmen pay for the innumerable crimes they have committed long before any bomb was laid in the Palace. Begin with the brutal and heavy-handed director of that reprehensible organization, the Third Section. The blood spilled in the Imperial Palace is on his head. He must pay!

Citizens of St. Petersburg unite! The world is watching. The oppressed of the world look to you as the vanguard of freedom!

He must pay, indeed!

Vlasenko spat on the floor. He would show them who would pay! They wanted vengeance? Well, he was an expert at that game! And with his job, his very future at stake, they would experience such reprisals as even their most villainous members could not imagine!

And the first thing he was going to do was destroy the press that had printed the garbage he now held in his hand. Perhaps he hadn't yet been successful at apprehending the culprit who had laid the bomb in the palace. Perhaps that usurper, Loris-Melikov, *had* been lucky enough—and Vlasenko indeed attributed it to nothing more than luck—to purloin a few successes. But Cyril Vlasenko was not out of the capital's power halls yet. If he was doomed to go down, he would not do so without exacting his own retribution. He'd take every revolutionary he could lay his hands on with him!

62

The underground propaganda that went on in spite of governmental censorship galled the Secret Police. Their own statements minimized the activities of the terrorists, and especially the most recent outrage of the bombing at the Winter Palace. But still the Third Section fumed at its impotence in stopping the propagandist efforts.

Some of the members of The People's Will had argued against laying claim to the palace bombing. The deaths of innocents, they said, had incited public opinion against them, and now was a time to lay low. Others believed, and perhaps rightly, that they must grasp the offensive, declare their innocence, and shift blame where it properly belonged. Thus they had followed up the bombing with the fiery handbill that had quickly found its way into the hand of the Third Section chief.

Paul was manning the press hidden away in a corner of a tenement basement in the ignominious Tartar district of Russia's capital. This was by far the largest and most important underground press; they regularly printed the leaflet *Narodnaya Volya*. Paul himself had helped write the most recent installment claiming righteous responsibility for the palace bombing. The ingenious phrasing that elevated the innocent casualties to the status of heroes of the revolutionary cause had come from his own head. Zhelyabov told Paul that if he didn't have an adept hand with explosives, he would make Paul the official scribe of the movement.

And Paul had to admit, he did enjoy the clanking and rattling of the printing press, the smell of ink and paper. It all signified such vitality and motion, the very throbbing life of the movement to which he had dedicated his heart and soul, putting ideas and vision onto paper that would be distributed and carried far and wide. The dirty, dingy, noisy basement operation was in one way the very heart, the very life's pulse of everything they hoped to achieve!

Two smudge-faced little girls sat in a doorway next to the grimy, trash-strewn alley.

One of them held a filthy, ragged blanket near her face while sucking contentedly on her thumb. The other, a year or two older, was occupied with a doll that appeared even more destitute and pathetic than she.

"You be a good little babushka and go to sleep," purred the older child. She bent over and kissed the soiled wooden face. "Mama loves you."

The sound of hurried footsteps intruded into the quiet scene. All at once a young man dashed into the alley, panting hard, and rushed by the children without even pausing to notice them.

The girls glanced up, but paid no more attention than he had to them. This was Grafsky Lane, and even at their age they knew it was not healthy to take too much interest in the goings-on around them.

The young man flung open a nearby door, bolted inside, and leaped down the steps that led immediately from the entrance to a basement.

"We've been betrayed!" he shouted.

"What?" came Paul's shocked reply. His three companions joined in exclamations and questions of disbelief.

"No time for explanations! The gendarmes are only moments behind me. Flee for your lives!"

"But the press!" protested Paul. "We can't leave it to them!"

"There is no choice . . . hurry!"

"Who betrayed us?" said Paul, dropping the engraving plate in his hands. The others were already heading out the door.

"Later, Paul. No time now . . . come!"

Paul hastily shut off the clanking press, still hoping, though futilely, he might hide its presence from the police. He then rushed up the basement steps on the heels of his companions.

But the gendarmes had already reached the entrance of the close. One grabbed the older of the two girls and shook her violently.

"A man just ran through here," he demanded. "Where did he go?"

The child said nothing.

The gendarme shook her again, this time so hard she dropped her doll to the ground.

"Babushka!" cried the girl.

"Where did he go?" questioned the man again, moderating his tone slightly as a result of the girl's tears.

Another man, puffing into the alley directly behind the contingent of six gendarmes, interrupted the interrogation.

"Forget the brat!" yelled Vlasenko, panting from the exertion of chasing the elusive young man. He was unaccustomed to such exercise, and since it was not expected for the chief of the Third Section to go out on the streets with his henchmen, he could well have shirked this duty. But with the tenuous state of his position and reputation at the moment, it could only help his cause if he were seen to be zealous enough to confront the terrorists in person. If nothing else, his detractors would have to admire his courage in leading the dangerous raid in person. "Seal off this corridor," he added with authority. "We know he's in here somewhere."

A woman came into the alley and approached the door where the children had been playing. Seeing her daughter in the clutches of the police, she gasped.

"Please . . . don't hurt my child!" she pleaded.

"We are not in the business of harming youngsters," said Vlasenko. "But if you know what's good for you, you will tell us the whereabouts of the traitors and insurrectionists."

"I know nothing about them."

"We know they are in this building. It will go all the worse for you if you protect them."

The woman stood obdurately silent. She did indeed know of the young men who used the basement of the tenement. Her own brother was one of them.

"Please, my baby!" She clutched the younger of the two girls to her.

"You'll never see this child again unless you talk," said Vlasenko. "You will be arrested and your little girl here will be made a ward of the state."

"Please!" The woman wept, wrestling inwardly with the dilemma of whether to protect her brother or save herself. But the awful thought of her children at the mercy of the cruel and heartless government finally overcame her loyalty. She jerked her head toward the basement door. *God forgive me,* she silently prayed.

At Vlasenko's signal, the gendarme set the girl down none too gently. The contingent of secret police swept past the child, knocking her over and trampling her doll, which tore into four separate pieces, and stormed toward the basement door. The child cried, not for the bruise on her elbow, but for the death of her babushka. She picked up the several doll limbs and held them close to her chest.

Just as the police reached the door, it burst open in their faces. Five young rebels ran head-on into the storming faces of Vlasenko's men. Only the utter surprise of the encounter, and the fact that none of the gendarmes were armed, gave Paul and the others a chance to escape.

But if the police had no pistols, they did have nightsticks. They bashed several heads. One rebel fell unconscious; another was down, and an official continued the assault with well-aimed kicks at his head and back.

Paul and his two remaining allies fought back as successfully as they could, although Paul was bleeding profusely from his mouth where a blow had dislodged a tooth. They were trying to work their way toward the entrance of the alley. A few more steps and they could make a run for it. One of the three broke free, then hesitated before making a dash to safety.

"Go!" yelled Paul. "Warn the others!"

The young man was quickly followed by his comrade, and Paul too was about to make a break. In one last desperate burst of fury, Paul smashed his fist into the face of one of the gendarmes, and while the man still tottered from the blow, Paul spun around to escape.

But a hand shot out, seemingly from nowhere, and grabbed at his shirt. Desperately Paul wrenched around, frantically trying to pull loose. Swinging his head toward his captor, he was momentarily paralyzed with shock. The man was none other than the hated *promieshik*, Cyril Vlasenko!

"You!" growled Vlasenko, equally astonished to see who he had hold of. Even in the brief instant when their eyes met in recognition, Paul could not miss the triumphant glint in the man's evil eyes.

In one wild and supreme effort, Paul jerked his whole body. The violent energy of his final outburst came as much from hatred as from the determination not to have his career as a revolutionary end so quickly. He was not ready to hang or rot in Siberia yet!

With a force of strength that surprised even him, Paul wrenched himself free and raced out of the close. Vlasenko staggered backward with the force, struck his head on the corner of a brick wall, and fell, unconscious.

Paul's only concern at that moment was the hammering pursuit of four policemen on his heels. Swiping a hand across his bloody mouth, he frantically looked both ways down the street, but hardly paused to make a decision about the best way to go. He raced to his left toward the market, hoping to lose himself in the midday crowd, hoping that some conscientious citizen did not betray him along the way.

Dodging to and fro between kiosks and vendors' wares, knocking a tray of sausages to the ground here, a stack of baskets there, Paul widened the distance between himself and his pursuers. The police were soon joined by the angry vendors, who did not like to see their meager profits destroyed by either police or rebels.

Soon Paul reached the end of the market. Facing the prospect of the open street, he ducked into another alley. Such a move could mean his capture, but he knew he could not run forever. Already he was beginning to feel lightheaded and weak from the loss of blood and the pain of the blow to his mouth.

The alley was deserted except for a couple of mangy tomcats. It was a dead end!

In mad desperation, Paul began pounding on all the doors, not knowing, not caring, where they led, as long as it was out of sight and away from the police. He shook several latches, nearly yanking one from its rusty nails.

But all of his efforts were in vain. Panting and sweating, he stood in the dark alleyway like a caged animal. Out in the street he could hear the booted feet drawing nearer.

One more time, he struck his fists against the doors. Then, at last, he gave up, leaned up against one of the locked doors, and closed his eyes, helplessly awaiting his doom.

"Over here!" came a hoarse whisper, as if from Paul's distraught imagination.

He shook his head, thinking his mind was playing tricks on him.

"Here . . . hurry!" said the voice again.

Paul opened his eyes and wearily swung his head toward the sound.

A lad of about twelve or thirteen was standing in one of the doorways that had previously been shut against him. The boy motioned Paul to come.

Paul hesitated.

"Come," the boy said again. "You'll be safe here."

317

"And what of you?" replied Paul, finally finding his voice.

"Don't worry . . . just come."

Paul knew that he was finished if he did not follow the boy, yet he was reluctant to bring danger upon another. Thoughts of Kazan's hanging suddenly came into his mind. He was not ready to die, either!

He moved quickly and entered the open door where the boy beckoned him. As it clamped shut, he could hear the sounds of pursuit just entering the close.

63

Viktor Fedorcenko was not a man given to morose bouts of philosophy. Neither was he a man accustomed to rising early to stroll about aimlessly, contemplating the mysteries of the universe. Practicality had always been everything for him. He was a soldier, not a sage.

Nevertheless, he had awakened before sunrise and, unable to sleep, had gotten out of bed and dressed. Without realizing where his steps were taking him, he had walked outside and into the Promenade Garden just as day was beginning to dawn. It was a strange time of day to be out. No other sound accompanied his steps but the soft chirping of the birds preparing to herald the coming sunrise. On he walked, through this unfamiliar portion of his estate.

At last he stood at the very edge of his property, gazing out upon the swiftly flowing Neva as chunks of ice floated down the swollen March waters toward Finskij Zaliv. His feet were nearly frozen, yet he was unconscious of the cold. His gaze was fixed across the water upon the city in the distance. St. Petersburg, the tsar's city, built and named for the tsar of all tsars. *How would the mighty Peter have met the crisis that faced Alexander?* Viktor wondered. With his iron fist, would he have met the rebel forces head-on, crushing them beneath the very might of his domination? Or would he too find himself helpless, a victim of forces he could not control with brute autocratic power?

As Viktor stood gazing across the river, the words a friend had recently spoken to him rose up in his mind. Intimately acquainted with the great composer Tchaikovsky, the man had read to Viktor a passage from a letter he had received from the musician shortly after the Russo-Turkish war. The words had made such an impression upon Viktor that he asked his friend to read them a second time. Now they came back to him almost verbatim.

We are living through terrible times, Tchaikovsky had said, *and if one stops to think about the present, one is terrified. On one side a completely panic-stricken government . . . on the other side, ill-fated youths, thousands of them exiled without trial to lands where not even a crow flies; and between these two extremes the masses, indifferent to everything, waist-deep in the mire of their egotistic interests, watching everything without a sign of protest.*

The composer could not have more succinctly summed up the horrors of the times into which they had all been thrust. The worst of it all was that there were no simple, clear-cut answers. If you hoped to be a moral man, it was not even clear which side to take. Where did truth lie—with the tsar, or with the rebels?

Viktor was horrified, appalled, *outraged* over last month's bombing at the palace. Those responsible deserved the firing squad—nothing less. They had murdered fifteen innocents, and for that the guilty ones deserved to die.

Yet Viktor had to admit that he was nearly as incensed over the police raids and the cruel mass arrests that followed. What had Vlasenko done but provide additional fuel for the rebel cause with his ill-timed and heavy-handed tactics? But Viktor had by now learned better than to expect any middle ground in this country!

Russia had become a nation divided, warring within itself, countryman against countryman, brother against brother, father against son. He thought of his own conflict with Sergei, of Alexander's strife with the tsarevich. How much longer could either the House of Romanov *or* the house of Fedorcenko stand with such division eating at their very cores?

Yet perhaps there was hope, at least in the case of the former. When the long winter night seemed darkest, only last week an unexpected ray of light, a remarkable injection of sanity, began to penetrate events in the Winter Palace. Viktor had initially been delighted that at last the tsar seemed ready to listen to voices of moderation with something more than polite boredom. And although it took an outsider to finally impress upon the emperor of Russia what Viktor and a handful of others had been trying to tell him for a decade. Viktor was not too proud to welcome the ally, no matter where he came from.

The voice that finally rose above the din was that of General Michael Loris-Melikov, the Armenian Governor of Kharkov, who had distinguished himself in the past war in the Caucasus, and had even won the praise of Dmitri Milyutin. Melikov had been summoned to St. Petersburg only last week, when the initial principles of his plan were unveiled to Alexander's ministers and advisors. Viktor liked the man, in spite of the jealousy some of his colleagues felt at his sudden rise in imperial esteem. But Viktor tried not to be the petty sort—he was just glad the tsar was at last willing to heed a more moderate voice than that of the reactionaries who had been bending his ear for so long.

The most astounding precept of Melikov's program was a proposal to grant the people a constitution.

Instant objections had sounded from all corners of the room that day.

"Peasants will come to power and take control of everything!"

"Never in Russia! The masses are different here . . . they must be ruled with an iron will!"

"What would you have, Melikov? Would you turn Russia into another England, or even worse—into a replica of the United States!"

"Wait . . . wait, please!" pleaded the governor.

"Let him have his say," boomed Alexander's voice. "I for one want to hear the proposal out in its entirety."

"Just imagine," Melikov had continued once silence was restored. "What better way to stop the terrorists than to give the people the very thing these radicals say they are fighting for?"

It was easy to see that the tsar was listening to every word with great care. Viktor supposed the bombing had had one positive result. The emperor had grown desperate enough to take even the most outlandish ideas under serious advisement.

"By so doing, you undercut their very message. They have nothing else to be up in arms over. Don't you see—we meet their demand, *without* giving in! We destroy public sympathy for the terrorists by turning the support of the masses *toward* the crown."

The room fell silent. It was indeed an audacious proposal.

Yet it would take time to research the details involved in the implementation of a constitutional regime. And it was clear that something had to be done *now* to curb the terrorism.

What *was* being done concerned Viktor. As pleased as he was to see Alexander listening, he didn't quite know what impact these changes would have in the immediate future. His own internal debate had awakened him and sent him out on this morning's lonely trek.

Almost immediately after the decisive meeting, the tsar had formed the Supreme Executive Commission, headed by Melikov himself. In essence, with one sweep of Alexander's imperial hand, Melikov was given powers that made him a virtual dictator over all of Russia, superseding all but the tsar himself.

Viktor supposed that if Russia had to have a dictator in the interim period before a constitution could be implemented, the tsar could have done worse than Melikov. He was a liberal-minded man with a good head on his shoulders, and even something of an intellectual. He offered to Russian law enforcement something more than the dull-witted, brute force of Vlasenko. His plan was to root out the terrorists without resorting at the same time to mass *government* terror. He hoped to imprison the real criminals without breaking the hearts of those "ill-fated youths" spoken of by Tchaikovsky. And beyond this, he hoped to win back the hearts of the many who had been driven away from patriotism by the corruption and brutality they saw in the government. His was indeed an idealistic dream, and a gargantuan task. Viktor hoped Melikov could pull it off.

He proved his mettle when The People's Will made an unsuccessful attempt on his life. Within two days the guilty man was caught, quickly tried, and hanged, leaving the disgruntled Third Section chief looking foolish for his ineptitude during the past year.

Viktor knew it would not be long before Melikov abolished the Third Section altogether, removing Vlasenko and taking complete control of all police power himself.

Thus far, Melikov had proved himself able and astute. But it had been less than two weeks, and Viktor did not know if he was entirely comfortable with the idea of a man other than the tsar holding such immense power. Why should one autocrat be brought in to do the job of another? Yet if in the end some of the repression could be lifted, and the people could see themselves as less alienated from the forces that ruled them, perhaps the changes were acceptable. At this point, at least, Viktor was not going to make *his* the voice of protest.

Suddenly aware of the chill that had come over him, Viktor turned away from the river and strode stiffly back in the direction of the house.

64

Anna had been back in St. Petersburg only a couple of weeks before the terrible bombing at the Winter Palace. Like the rest of the city, she was still in shock over the incident, especially because the Fedorcenkos, and to a lesser extent she herself, were regular guests there.

Her thoughts had been so much occupied with Sergei, who had now rejoined his regiment in St. Petersburg, and with the resumption of her duties with the princess, that Anna had scarcely had time for anything else. She had only seen Polya once or twice, and even after a month back in the city they had not yet been out together. Anna often thought of Paul, but she had not had the chance to attempt locating him. The preparations for Katrina's wedding kept both girls so busy there was little else to be thought about. Anna had not given Lieutenant Grigorov so much as a thought.

Thus, her surprise was even greater one afternoon when one of the parlor maids came to the door to announce that he was downstairs, requesting to see Anna. She looked toward Princess Katrina, who gave her willing consent.

"May I take him to the garden, Princess?" asked Anna.

"But it's so cold out."

"I haven't been outside all day. It will feel good."

"As you wish, Anna. But don't be more than an hour. I don't want you to freeze, and we have to finish the lace on this sleeve."

"Thank you, Princess."

Anna descended the stairway and led her visitor out into the garden, which was covered with a thick blanket of March snow, stark bare trees replacing the thick summertime foliage. As long as she had a warm house to return to, Anna enjoyed the winter as much as any other season, for it held a quiet beauty that would stir any Russian heart. Especially in the knowledge that spring lay right around the corner, the cold seemed endurable.

"I needed to see a friend I could talk to," Misha began after they were some distance from the house.

"What happened?" asked Anna.

"Oh, I butted my own head against a brick wall like the fool I am," he replied.

Anna looked at him with a puzzled expression.

"I went to visit Countess Dubjago this morning," said Misha. "I hoped that *she* would be a sensitive ear to what happened last night. Ha! I should have known better! She just laughed in my face and called me a sap."

"Last night?"

"I had a nightmare about the bombing. Please, Anna, if *you* think me an idiot for admitting such a thing, don't tell me."

"Oh, Misha, I would never say such a thing! There's nothing to be ashamed of about a nightmare. It just shows you're more sensitive than most men about pain and suffering."

"I would like to think you are right. Unfortunately, that's not the way Countess Dubjago sees it! She thinks it a sign of weakness in a man."

"Forgive me for saying so, but I do not agree."

"And I've been trying to find the courage to propose marriage to the countess . . . and now this. Perhaps I am exactly the sap she takes me for! She would probably let me go down on one knee and pour out my heart to her, then throw her head back and laugh at my proposal!"

"Misha, don't say such a thing! I'm sure she would be honored."

Misha sighed and shook his head. "No," he said in a forlorn voice, "I'm afraid there never could have been anything between us. It has just taken me all this time to realize it." They walked on awhile in silence.

"Would you care to tell *me* about the nightmare?" Anna asked at length.

Misha continued to stare straight ahead, as if he too considered what he had experienced the night before a sign of weakness. Slowly he began to tell her of his dream, still averting his eyes.

"It is not the first time," he said when he was through. "There have been several since the bombing. I don't think they come from being afraid. Perhaps it is from the anger, from the horrible things I dream of doing to those animals who are causing such destruction in our country."

Anna said nothing to Misha about Paul. The Cossack's imperial loyalties were so strong that he would never be able to understand. How desperately she hoped Paul had not been involved in anything where people were hurt.

"Perhaps in time," she said, "the vividness of all that has happened will subside, and you will have peace. Prince Sergei has told me that he had many nightmares after the war, but they do not plague him as much now."

"The war never bothered me as much as this," mused Misha. "I don't know why. How can I explain the difference? On the battlefield, armies are trained and armed and ready to confront one another. Death is an expected element. Everyone is prepared to accept it. Perhaps the sight in the palace haunts me because it was so unnatural. A shattered vase of flowers caught between slabs of broken masonry. A polished dining table splintered into pieces with its china and crystal scattered in the midst of the rubble. The *reality* is a nightmare all its own!"

"I am sorry you had to be there in the middle of it, Misha."

Misha pondered Anna's words for a moment or two. "In a way, perhaps it was more than mere chance that placed me in the very center of events. You see, for some weeks I have been on the point of requesting a transfer. I had begun to feel like a thoroughbred prematurely put out to pasture. The walls were closing in on me, and more and more lately I have found myself thinking of my native land in the south, and the wide, beautiful, warm steppe. How much my frustrations with the countess may have contributed to this desire to escape St. Petersburg, I do not know. All I do know is that I have wanted to get away from the city."

"And now?"

"Suddenly the bombing has given me a renewed sense of purpose. Or at least it has shown me the true purpose of my position, that being stationed at the Palace *does* have purpose. The danger to our emperor is very real. They will stop at nothing to try to kill him. And I am one of those who must protect the tsar from those maniacs. I only hope I will be rewarded with the opportunity to cut down a few of them before it is all over."

"It makes me shudder to hear you talk so, Misha. You have always been so gentle and kind to me."

"You probably think me as much an animal as those who are bringing this terror to our land."

"I could not think that of such a good friend."

"I know how you feel inside, about the love of God . . . about forgiveness."

He turned a penetrating gaze toward her.

"Yes, I do believe in forgiveness," said Anna sincerely.

"I cannot forgive for what happened," he said bitterly.

"Give yourself time, Misha. Forgiveness sometimes comes by degrees."

"Why should I want to forgive at all?"

"Because that is what Jesus himself would do—and do we not all strive to be like Him?"

"Not I, Anna. I am a practical man, and it seems to me that it would be the height of impracticality to try to attain something that is clearly impossible."

"There is another reason you should forgive, then," she said, taking up his challenge. "Maybe even a better one."

"What is that?"

"Hate and unforgiveness eat away at a person's soul. If left rotting down inside you long enough, they would turn you into . . . into someone like Basil Anickin."

Even as she said the words, Anna thought of one other example. But she pushed aside all thoughts of her brother.

"Do you want to become a man who has sealed off all access to his heart, Misha?" she went on. "Princess Katrina tells me Basil has gone completely insane. Hate has destroyed not only his heart, but his mind as well—what used to be a brilliant mind. Please, don't let such a thing happen to you."

"Well, for you, Anna," he replied with a thoughtful smile, "I will remain open. But do not expect a miracle too soon."

She smiled. "I have faith in the greatness of your heart. And I have faith in the greatness of God also."

They walked on, trying to put thoughts of violence, bombings, and hatred out of their minds. The setting was too peaceful for all that.

"Ah, Anna, I have missed you these last months!" Misha exclaimed all at once. "I have missed having a friend to talk to. Sometimes I so badly need your sanity to help me see the world a little more clearly."

He paused as they came to a bench. "Shall we sit for a while?"

She nodded. He brushed aside a layer of powdery snow from the wooden surface and they sat down side by side. "We must forget about all these morbid topics for the rest of the day. Tell me about your family. Is your father well?"

"He nearly killed himself trying to get in the harvest." She went on to tell him of all the hard work they had done getting in the grain in advance of the storm.

"Rest is what he needs most," she concluded, "and he has had plenty of time for that through the winter. When spring planting comes the villagers will be able to help. And Prince Sergei has been so kind as to make arrangements for a hired hand to help out during the times of heaviest work. I believe he is feeling much better now; otherwise I would not have come back."

"But you wanted to return to the city?" he asked.

"Yes. Odd, isn't it?"

"Why do you say that?"

"When I first came here I felt so alone and adrift. But now I will always have ties to St. Petersburg. I know that Princess Katrina considers me part of her family and will take me with her after she and Count Remizov are married."

"And yet you continue to wonder if you will ever be part of her family in *another* way?" questioned Misha.

Anna could think of no immediate reply. Of course she wondered. Of course she hoped. But she didn't have to say any of that to Misha. She could tell he knew.

"You mentioned Prince Sergei before," said Misha after a pause. "I take it then that you have seen him?"

"He is back in St. Petersburg," replied Anna evasively.

"But what has he to do with your father's affairs?"

"He came to the village when I was home," answered Anna. The glow that accompanied her words was unmistakable.

"I am glad for you, Anna! You deserve to be happy."

"It is all very complicated," said Anna with a sigh.

"Surely it will not remain unresolved much longer, now that he is back."

"You are not trying to act the part of matchmaker, are you, Mikhail Igorovich?"

"You should be married, Anna. With lots of babies to love and take care of. And a little *izba* in your precious Katyk. Laundry every day, bread to bake, a garden to tend . . . a man to care for you."

"It does not sound like a nobleman's life."

"I can just as easily see you the mistress of an aristocratic mansion! Wherever you are, Anna, I know there will be love and happiness."

"It is a wonderful dream, Misha. Perhaps one day . . ."

"And until then. . . ?"

"I do not know. I have only seen the prince two or three times since my return. He was sent away on some military business two weeks ago."

"Ah, look!" said Misha, changing the subject. "It is starting to snow."

He flicked a small flake from his greatcoat, and several more immediately took its place. "I suppose it is time for me to go."

They rose and walked through the park until they came to the outer gates. Misha hailed a *droshky*. He haggled with the driver over the price, though it was a halfhearted effort so as not to insult the *vanka* who expected at least some questioning of the fare. Anna could tell there was more on her Cossack friend's mind, for he had grown quiet as they made their way to the gate.

"It was wonderful seeing you again, Anna," he said.

Anna waved as the *droshky* jerked into motion.

VII

A HOUSE UNITED
(April 1880)

65

The day of the Fedorcenko-Remizov wedding dawned with a bright sun and brilliant blue sky.

Katrina awoke and gave a long, languid stretch. Anna had not been in yet to pull back the drapes, but she could tell immediately that the day was going to be perfect.

And why shouldn't it be?

This was the day she had dreamed of for years. This was the day she had been anticipating, with something less than the patience of a saint, for over six months. She, of course, had wanted it to take place much sooner, but her father had insisted on a "period of adjustment." Who, Katrina wondered, needed to adjust? Perhaps her father wanted the time in order to get used to the idea himself! But at least he had given his consent, even though it had been with reservations, and for that she was grateful.

"I am not entirely convinced that Dmitri Gregorovich is completely reformed from his previous lifestyle," he had said.

But Dmitri's admirable behavior in the unfortunate incident with Basil had impressed Viktor sufficiently for him to capitulate. By then other difficulties prolonged the waiting, foremost among them Anna's absence, followed by the palace bombing. No one but Katrina was up for such a festive celebration after the stunning shock to the city.

After that, Princess Natalia had conceived the brilliant idea of scheduling the wedding on her daughter's birthday, which happened to fall on a Sunday and came shortly after the close of Lent. That was certainly longer than Katrina wanted to wait. What perturbed her most of all was Dmitri's seeming contentment with the plan.

The future bridegroom's only response was to reveal that wonderful smile that could always melt Katrina's heart, and say glibly, "It is perfect, my love! Now I shall forget neither your birthday *nor* our anniversary!"

And now the day had come at last—the first Sunday of April, accompanied by blue sky and a sunny glow. The chill in the air would make the day more crisp and clear. And best of all, the horrible trouble in the city seemed to have come to a standstill since the bombing. Prince Fedorcenko said the new governor-general had cracked down so hard on the dissidents that those who had not been arrested had fled the city. Moreover, after this most recent outrage, the people had turned against the radicals and no longer were willing to hide and protect them. The capital breathed easier; more to the point, everyone was in the mood for a celebration. And Princess Katrina Viktorovna Fedorcenko was more than willing to accommodate them!

Prince and Princess Fedorcenko planned a truly spectacular affair for their daughter, an event that would come near to rivaling an imperial wedding. The ceremony would take place at four o'clock in the afternoon at St. Isaac's, followed by a gala ball and a lavish banquet with French champagne and mounds of Black Sea caviar. Another dinner and ball would follow the next day, given by the tsar's aunt, the Grand Duchess Helen, during which the emperor himself would make an appearance. Alexander had expressed his regret that he could not host the evening himself for his old friend and faithful minister's daughter, but the tsaritsa's ill health and the recent disturbances made it impossible at the time. Even if he had not been the emperor, no one would have faulted him for that.

The third day, Dmitri's mother, Countess Eugenia Remizov, would host a reception for the newlyweds. And finally, four days after the wedding, the couple would be taken to Warsaw Station to embark on a four-week honeymoon excursion on the Mediterranean.

As Katrina let out a long, sleepy sigh, she decided it all

sounded like those Hans Christian Andersen fairy tales Anna was so fond of reading. Or, rather, it was more like the ending of a tale that concluded with the words "And they lived happily ever after . . ."

She jumped out of bed, suddenly wide awake. The fact that she was now nineteen years old escaped her altogether. All at once she felt like an excited little girl again! There was so much to do! She threw on a robe and skipped from the room.

"Anna!" she called, in a voice as impatient as her ecstasy would permit. "This is no time to be sleeping in!" She strode through the sitting room and, without so much as a knock, entered Anna's bedroom.

The maid's bed was not only vacant, but neatly made. "Well," said Katrina good-naturedly to herself, "I suppose I shall never catch that girl malingering about!"

She spun around, running nearly headlong right into Anna herself. "Oh, there you are," she said, startled. "I suppose you have been up for hours."

"No, Princess," laughed Anna, "just long enough to wash and dress and see to some of your laundry. But, Princess, you should have tried to sleep a bit longer. This is a big day."

"That is exactly why I couldn't sleep! My wedding day, Anna! Can you believe it?"

"And your birthday."

"Oh, my! I'd forgotten!"

A smile crept, almost unbidden, across Anna's lips as a past memory flitted into her mind.

"You *don't* believe it, do you, Anna?" said Katrina, half in fun, half in earnest circumspection. "You think I'm still a precocious adolescent?"

"Oh, no Princess! I just recalled the first moment I saw you—all sprawled out in the snow chasing after your mother's dog."

Katrina also smiled. "You were in no better condition," she said in jest. "An uninvited interloper, quaking at the expected retribution from your new employer."

Katrina paused in a rare moment of thoughtful introspection. "We have both changed a great deal since that day, haven't we, Anna?"

"I am sure we have, Princess. At least I have heard others say so."

"I was such an incorrigible brat."

"You are no longer, Princess. How wonderfully you have opened your heart, not only to me, but to everything about you. Yet you are still so lively and full of energy I cannot help admiring, even envying you for that."

"That is as much as to say that I can still be an ornery, stubborn little chit when I want to be," said Katrina laughing.

"I said nothing of the kind," insisted Anna. "I said I admired and envied you."

"Well, you have nothing to envy *me* about! I have always envied your calm and peace. Anyway, Anna, thank you for your kind words. But I have a long way to go before I'll be within sight of sainthood."

"We all do, Princess. It is a willing heart that God looks for rather than perfection. You *do* have that, Princess, and so, to answer your first question, I have no doubts about your readiness for marriage."

"That means a great deal to me, Anna."

Impulsively, Katrina threw her arms around her maid and kissed her on the cheek. "Thank you for everything!" she said.

"If I have done anything for you, Princess," she replied, "it has been for me an honor."

"You always know just what to say, Anna, and that is one thing I appreciate learning from you. I think that will be a quality I will need in the future more than ever."

"How is that, Princess?"

"You know when I am married you will come with me to live in Dmitri's family home?"

Anna nodded. They had discussed such plans, and though Anna did not relish the change, she'd rather move with Katrina than be relegated back to scullery service under Olga Stephanovna!

Katrina continued. "You haven't met Dmitri's mother yet, Anna," she said. "And I haven't said a great deal about her. But

I suppose you should know that she is . . . well . . . she is quite the opposite of my mother. I don't even know her that well. For as close as Dmitri has been to our family, she keeps very much to herself, spending most of her time on their estate near Moscow. Dmitri has warned me that she can be extremely demanding. To tell you the truth, I am a little nervous about her. I am glad we will be at the St. Petersburg house and she in Moscow. Anyway, whatever tact I possess, which I don't say is much, I have learned from you, Anna. And I hope it serves me well with her."

"You will have no trouble," said Anna sincerely. "She will not be able to keep from loving you as her very own daughter."

"I would like to think you are right, Anna."

Katrina paused a moment, as if considering further the prospects for the new life that lay before her. Then she shook away the thoughtful mood and sprang to life.

"We hardly have time to be standing about talking, Anna. We have to get ready for my wedding!"

66

By three o'clock in the afternoon, the bride was dressed and her hair styled to perfection.

Since there were plenty of bridesmaids and aunts and cousins, not to mention a very frazzled mother, to attend to the remaining needs of the bride, Katrina gave Anna permission to slip away so that she would have plenty of time to get to the church before the ceremony. Only an elite handful of servants would be in attendance, those who had been with the family

337

a long time or were in positions of particular authority. Anna accompanied Nina outside where a carriage waited for them. Mrs. Remington, Olga Stephanovna, and a few others were already inside.

Shortly after 3:15, a sudden flurry of activity in the Fedorcenko home threatened to interrupt the orderly movement of events toward the appointed hour. Several minor crises in the kitchen had Polya in a dither over what Olga would say upon her return. One of Katrina's bridesmaids turned an ankle and now sat immobile on a settee while some of the others fluttered anxiously about her. And finally, the day at last proving too much for her, Princess Natalia fainted from all the stress of being mother of the bride.

When the doctor arrived, he wrapped a cloth bandage around the bridesmaid's ankle and handed a small vial to one of the aunts hovering around poor Natalia's prostrate form. The distraught woman was no better under the circumstances than Natalia would have been, but she did manage to get the bottle of smelling salts close enough to Natalia's nose to begin to revive her. In a minute or two the doctor pronounced the young girl's ankle to be less severe than feared, then walked to the other side of the room to attend to Natalia, now groggily coming to her senses.

Katrina began to wonder if her optimism of the morning had been premature. She sat at the dressing table amid flounces of lace and satin, her elbow propped on the table and her chin resting, almost dejectedly, on her hand. She gazed in the mirror at the reflection of those ministering to her mother and cousin on the other side of the large upstairs sitting room. Here she was, the object and reason for all the hubbub, and yet everyone was fussing over ankles and smelling salts, and she sat observing it all with nothing to do.

Katrina smiled to herself. It really was rather humorous. She wished she hadn't sent Anna off yet. Right now she would give anything to be able to glance over at her maid with a wink and a smile. *Anna* would know just what she was thinking! Even though she had only been gone fifteen minutes, suddenly Katrina, on the very verge of the happiest moment of her life, missed Anna very much.

She supposed she ought to be thankful her mother had survived the ordeal this long without collapsing from exhaustion, or something worse. The elder princess had actually done very little in direct preparation for the wedding. Her chief contribution had been endless anxiety and weeks of fretting, which was certainly labor enough for one of Natalia's delicate sensibilities.

No one in her right mind could ever be angry with Natalia, no matter how useless she proved to be. Katrina loved her, and as ready and anxious as she was to marry Dmitri and begin her life with him, she felt a sudden wave of melancholy at the thought of leaving her mother. It was not a feeling she had expected on this day. All else aside, there would be one less person around to protect the elder princess from the hard realities of life.

I'll visit her often, Katrina resolved. And the thought helped a little.

When Natalia had revived and was sitting up again, a knock came at the door. One of the bridesmaids answered it, spoke a moment to the maid who was standing there, then turned and walked across the room to Katrina.

"Your father wishes to see you, Princess," she said, "if you are free."

"Of course!" Eagerly Katrina jumped up, forgetting the mounds of wedding dress behind her and nearly sprawling to the floor before she found her feet.

Her father sat waiting for her in his study. Katrina threw her arms around him and suddenly felt tears, the first of the very emotional day, rise to her eyes. He put an arm around her and led her to his leather divan. Because the fullness of Katrina's dress prevented him from sitting next to her, he drew up a chair as close as he could get and sat down across from her.

"I may not have another chance to talk with you today, Katrina," he began in his earnest, soldier-like tone.

"Papa, if you had not sent for me, I would have come to find you," burbled Katrina. "I want to thank you so much . . . for everything! You are the best papa a girl could ever have!"

"A man sees his daughter married only once," he said formally, "and I want this day to be a memorable one for you, my dear."

"Oh, it will be, Papa!"

"I had to admit, I had my doubts about your Dmitri."

A little smile parted Katrina's lips at her father's profound understatement.

"Although he has nearly been a member of our family for years," Viktor went on, "I could not but wonder what kind of husband he would make. You must remember, I have known him longer than you have, Katrina. And settling down will not come easily for a man like him. Thus your task as his wife may be all the more difficult."

He paused, grimacing at his difficulty in expressing to his daughter what was on his heart.

"I do not mean to dishearten you," he continued, "and I don't suppose I am going about this at all well. But what I mean to say, Katrina, is that a year ago I could never have given my consent to this marriage. Considering your own maturity, too, I would have had serious doubts that you could meet the challenge. Yet, since that time, I have seen what I think are hopeful signs in Dmitri, and I am tremendously impressed with the maturity you yourself have shown as well. I believe you are up to the responsibilities marriage entails, especially this marriage. I am proud of you, Katrina!"

"Oh, thank you, Papa!" Katrina's words were accompanied by a rush of tears. "Everything you say means *so* very much to me!"

Viktor pulled a handkerchief out from the pocket of his dress uniform and handed it to her. Katrina blotted her damp eyes and blew her nose.

"Dear me, I am going to be a sight!" she exclaimed.

"You look beautiful, my dear!" rejoined the proud father, relieved that he had discharged his duty so admirably, and succeeded in conveying more or less what was on his mind. "You are the loveliest bride I have ever seen!"

He rose, took her hand, and helped her to stand. "The carriages are standing by. Are the rest of the women ready?"

"I think so, Papa. I know *I* am."

"It is time we were leaving. Go tell your mother and the others."

Before they left the room, Katrina laid her hand on her father's arm. "Papa," she said, "I will always have a home here . . . won't I? Suddenly I am beginning to miss you all so terribly!"

"My dear Katrina," he said, placing a broad arm around her. "I could not let you go otherwise!"

They walked to the door of the study. Katrina started in the direction of the parlor where the women were gathered, and Viktor began the descent to the front of the mansion where a fleet of carriages and footmen were waiting. Katrina turned once again to her father, and thought she detected a glistening in his own eyes.

It was as close to tears as she had ever seen her father come.

67

When Anna and the others arrived in the carriage driven by Moskalev, many people were already crowded around Senate Square in front of the church. Mostly the crowd was made up of curious onlookers who had heard that the daughter of a high government official was to be married, and hoped to catch a glimpse of all the finery. Scores of carriages carrying the invited guests were streaming down the avenue.

Anna climbed down from the carriage, holding firmly on to Leo Moskalev's hand, feeling almost as alone and out of place as she had on that first day when she had arrived in St. Petersburg. She felt as if she should take her place among the throngs of spectators rather than entering the church along-side the prim and proper Mrs. Remington in the midst of all the grandly attired aristocrats.

As she had done on that first day, she cast a rather fain-thearted glance toward the old coachman as she followed the older Fedorcenko employees.

He grinned in understanding. "Be off with you, Anna," he said quietly, so that only she would hear. "You're as good or better than the lot of them!"

"I just hope I can keep from tripping over my own feet!" she replied, then hurried off between Nina and Mrs. Reming-ton.

They displayed their invitations to one of the uniformed men in attendance at the doors, then entered the church, which was quickly filling with guests. They made their way toward the back and side, where a small cluster of other servants and footmen were gathering. Nina and Mrs. Remington treated her more warmly than ever before, and even Olga Stephanovna, who persisted in thinking of Anna as her own personal "little protege," gave out with an occasional rugged smile.

They had been standing in their places only a few minutes when a robed ostiary walked up to Anna, tapped her arm, handed her a note, then went off about his business. Nina glanced downward with a skeptical wrinkle across her brow. But Anna tried to take no notice, and managed to read the words without divulging the contents of the message to her colleagues.

The note said simply: *Meet me at the west entrance . . . hurry!*

"I will be back in a few minutes," said Anna to Nina, then turned and walked off before any of them had the chance to question her.

Her heart beat wildly as she exited the church and hurried around the corner as the note had directed her. She knew the handwriting well enough, and could hardly keep herself from running!

Sergei stood at the door, striking in his dress uniform. The bright green coat with white braid and sash, accented by pol-ished gold buttons, set off his Teutonic features admirably. But it wasn't the uniform that put a glow in his eyes or gave the high color to his complexion. He had been filled with a new hope ever since his visit to Katyk, and Anna rejoiced to see him free of the despondency which had characterized his spirit after the war. She never presumed to think the color in his cheeks had anything to do with her.

"Come, Anna," he said with no other greeting, then led her inside the church and along the darkened inside wall. In a recess of the thick stone wall, behind one of the huge supporting columns, he stopped and turned toward her.

"We should have a minute or two of peace here," he said.

"I wondered if I would see you," Anna said. "There are so many people!"

"I only have two or three minutes before the rest of the family arrives and I will have to take my place with them. I got back into the city only two days ago and have been trying to find a way to see you ever since, but that sister of mine has been keeping you busy every second."

Anna laughed. "I have been working hard. But the day has finally come."

"You look beautiful, Anna," said Sergei. "And a new dress too, is it not?"

Anna nodded, blushing at his words.

Sergei took another moment to look at Anna in her pale blue linen dress, embroidered at the hem with a colorful garland of flowers. The bodice was also embroidered at the neckline, and under it she wore a blouse of white gauze with full, long sleeves. Ribbons were braided into her thick, pale hair, and her curls fell loosely down her back.

"You look like no servant I have ever seen in my life," he said at length. "I would take you for royalty if I did not know you!"

"Your sister bought it for me," said Anna, still embarrassed.

"Ah, how well my sister treats her maid. But you should be one of the honored guests at this wedding, rather than having to stand with the other servants."

"She *is* good to me, Sergei."

"You really ought to be one of her bridesmaids, Anna—her

343

maid of honor, if the truth were told. Instead, you have to stand at the back of the church, grateful for that."

"Let us not talk about that now," she said. "I *am* grateful for all she has done. That is enough."

"Agreed," he said reluctantly. "But it becomes harder all the time to see you treated like a maid, when I long to make you something better."

"The time will come, I am sure, Sergei," said Anna. "But we must be careful that we wait for just the right time. I am still concerned for you and your father."

"I know, and I love you all the more for your care for me. But you must forgive me if once in a while I display the reckless impatience of a Russian soldier."

"I would not love you if you were anything other than who you are," smiled Anna.

"I brought you a gift," said Sergei.

"What . . . why me?" said Anna. "This is the day your sister should be receiving gifts, not her maid."

"I don't know," smiled Sergei. "I suppose I thought her hardworking servant deserved something special, too."

From behind his back he drew out a parcel wrapped in brown paper. "I must confess," he said, "that in the way of selecting gifts for young ladies, I am not very imaginative. I am afraid it is another book."

Sheepishly he handed it to her.

Anna took it and carefully opened the paper. In her hands lay a brand new volume, bound in blue calf leather, with a brown leather spine and corners. She held it carefully, then slowly read the gold-embossed title: *A Soldier's Glory.* Beneath the title was embossed the most thrilling aspect of the gift, the author's name—Sergei Fedorcenko.

"Oh, Sergei!" exclaimed Anna. "This is wonderful! I am so happy for you!"

He stood beaming with pride as she opened the cover and gently, almost reverently, turned the first few pages, pausing here and there to allow her eyes to fall on a sentence, then reluctantly pulling herself away.

"I will hardly be able to concentrate on anything until I

can get alone in my room tonight to read it!"

"Don't show anyone," he said, with peculiar caution in his voice. "You are the first person in the whole city to receive a copy."

"That makes me feel so special. Oh, thank you, Sergei! Your parents will be so proud of you!"

"We will have to wait to see, I suppose."

"But why can't I show anyone?"

"I decided to wait until after Katrina is happily married and on her way to Greece before making it public. Just in case, you know. Besides, I don't want to diminish Katrina and Dmitri's special time."

Anna rewrapped the book and held it lovingly in her hands.

"Now, I must go," said Sergei. "It would hardly do for the best man to be late for the wedding. Dmitri will probably be wondering about me. When may I see you again?"

"You know where I shall be," replied Anna. "With nothing for me to do during the princess's honeymoon, I will have plenty of time for reading, and looking forward to visits from a certain soldier!"

"That will be difficult to manage without raising eyebrows. Though perhaps it is time to tell my parents of my intention to marry one of their servants at the same time I present them with the book. I might as well give them every shock imaginable all at once! But now I must go."

"Goodbye, Sergei. Thank you so much! You make me feel like the most special girl in all the world!"

"And that you are! I will get a message to you."

He took her hand, kissed it lightly, then was gone.

Anna left the recess and made her way back as she had come, out the west door of the church, around the corner, and back in as she had first entered. The carriages of the wedding party were starting to arrive—all gilded and shining in the cold sunlight, as befitted the daughter of one of the wealthiest and most influential men in all of Russia.

Anna clutched the rewrapped book close to her side, hoping it would not be noticed, and slipped through the door. She glided softly back to her obscure place at Nina's side. The next

345

time Nina glanced in her direction, Anna stood there as if she had been there all the time. Nina gave her a look of question, to which Anna merely smiled, then turned her gaze toward the front of the church. The music had begun.

Anna could not help wondering if the *son* of the great man all these people had come to honor would ever receive his due. Or would Sergei Fedorcenko, even possessing the dubious distinction of being a Russian author, be doomed to the same obscurity as the woman to whom he had given his heart?

Anna felt a little sad for him, desiring for him all the best, all the fame she thought he deserved. But she realized that Prince Sergei Fedorcenko thought nothing of the accouterments of wealth. Reputation meant nothing to him. His happiness was measured by the kind of moments he had just had with her—private, sincere, real, and full of life and love.

Sergei, author though perhaps he now was, had felt richer and more content when working in the field at her side, and when sharing a simple meal in a poor *izba* in Katyk, than ever in a lifetime of riding in splendor through the streets of St. Petersburg or striding through its corridors of power as the son of one of its great princes.

68

Anna's tears flowed freely as she watched her mistress enter the church on the arm of her father.

Katrina looked stunning in a white satin gown, its bodice and hem studded with a fortune in pearls and diamonds. Her dark hair shone rich as ebony under the jewel-encrusted headpiece of satin and lace. Although Anna had helped work on the gorgeous gown, she had never seen the whole effect once the jewels had been added.

It was rumored the dress cost in excess of ten thousand rubles, but Anna did not allow herself to think about how many starving peasant mouths that money could feed. She was too caught up in that moment with the beauty of the bride and the entire wedding party to think of anything but Katrina's happiness.

She was thankful, too, that God had protected the princess from marrying the wrong man. He had set her upon the right path, and in a few moments Katrina would be united with the man she had loved since childhood. The ironies of her own life did not invade Anna's thoughts just now. There was only room for pleasure at this sacred day of Katrina's fulfillment.

How beautiful and mature Katrina looked on this, her nineteenth birthday! Not even a hint of the usual premarital doubts or jitters showed on her glowing face. She radiated the calm assurance of a young lady who at this moment possessed everything she had ever wanted in life. When her father gave her hand to Dmitri, she gazed up at her husband-to-be with perfect love and contentment. And he returned the look with still-deepening awe—he, who until so recently had viewed this radiant jewel as little more than an inconsequential child. If Dmitri knew anything at all, he at last realized what a prize he possessed in Princess Katrina Viktorovna Fedorcenko. He had been drawn by her strength and vitality long before he had been able to admit it. But in womanhood, these qualities had finally caused the blossoming of the love that now filled his heart.

Dmitri did not view himself as a religious man. And even if he had admitted to some passing acquaintance with deeper realms of thought, his spiritual sensitivities were far from keen. Yet he was aware of a new depth in Katrina, some spiritual change which he suspected had something to do with her association with Anna. She could still prove headstrong, but she was far less self-absorbed. He saw this quality not only in the devoted way in which she loved him, but in how she loved

Anna, and in how she treated the other servants. She was a woman now. But more than that, she was a woman of substance and character.

The bride and groom knelt side by side at the altar while the choir chanted the *Te Deum*. The priest went on with the mass and readings, blessing the couple and sprinkling holy water over their foreheads. Then they rose to pledge themselves to each other.

"I, Dmitri Gregorovich, give to you my hand, my possessions, my home, my future, and my love. To you I promise to be a faithful husband who cares for you, watches over you, provides for you, and protects you, all the days of my life."

When he had completed his pledge, Katrina turned her gaze upon her groom, full of love and wonder. "I, Katrina Viktorovna, give to you my hand, my life, my future, and my love. I promise to be a faithful wife and companion and mother to your children, all the days of my life."

As Katrina's voice died away, two candlelighters approached from either side and lit the candles the bride and groom held. The priest chanted a solemn litany, then pronounced them husband and wife.

Anna's tears were flowing in earnest. Nina reached over and took her hand, giving it a warm, affectionate squeeze. Tears stood in the eyes of Princess Natalia's maid too.

Against her strong determination, Anna's eyes strayed from the groom to the best man standing next to him. A quick hand wiped away her tears so that she could see him clearly. Even though the distance was too great for their eyes to meet, somehow she knew that Sergei was looking her way, and that he too was thinking, *Will this day ever come for us? Will we stand here before the priest to receive this sacred sacrament of the church? Or will we perhaps make our vows before a country priest in Akulin?*

As she witnessed the splendor of the ceremony and beheld the full weight of the wealth and nobility of the Fedorcenko family, such questions seemed to Anna all the more presumptuous and fanciful. Was the thought that one day she would be the bride of Sergei Viktorovich Fedorcenko, Prince of Russia, nothing more than a dream, an unreachable fantasy?

She forced her eyes away, glancing down at the floor as the heat raced up her neck to her face. Unconsciously she clutched Sergei's book tighter to her side.

When Anna glanced up again, she forced herself to keep her gaze focused on the bride and groom. Before long the crowd was pouring out of St. Isaac's behind the wedding processional. Hand in hand, Dmitri and Katrina turned to face the hundreds of family and relatives, friends and spectators.

They were married now—married at last!

Anna struggled through the press of men and women to get closer, losing all contact with Nina and Mrs. Remington and the others. Katrina and Dmitri were attempting to move toward the waiting carriage that would take them first back to Katrina's home, and then propel them along the seemingly endless stream of parties and receptions that lay ahead over the next few days.

Anna wanted to get close enough to wave one final greeting to her mistress. She struggled forward through the happy, shouting crowd.

Dmitri was helping Katrina up to her seat now, then he climbed up next to her in the open carriage. Katrina turned toward the throng one last time, smiling broadly and giving a wave of her hand.

Anna struggled to the front of the throng, unaware of the green soldier's uniform next to her. The driver of the elegant marriage coach gave a small flick of his rein, and the carriage jerked into motion.

Anna fixed her eyes upon the happy couple. Suddenly Dmitri seemed to look straight at her as the carriage clattered off. But his words were not addressed to her at all. "Thanks for everything, Sergei, my old friend!" she heard him cry out.

Just as Katrina was about to turn around and settle back into her seat, suddenly she spotted Anna waving to her. Her face lit up in a huge smile. Anna saw the movement of her lips saying, "Oh, Anna . . . I love you!" But the sound was lost in the din.

The next moment the carriage turned into the street, and

Katrina was lost to Anna's view. She turned timidly to face the soldier standing next to her. He still had not seen her.

She gave his elbow a tug.

"Excuse me, Your Excellency," she said with a half-bashful smile, "but you seem to have forgotten to sign your book."

Books by Judith Pella

Blind Faith

Lone Star Legacy
Frontier Lady
Stoner's Crossing
Warrior's Song

Ribbons of Steel‡
Distant Dreams
A Hope Beyond

The Russians
The Crown and the Crucible*
A House Divided*
Travail and Triumph*
Heirs of the Motherland
Dawning of Deliverance
White Nights, Red Morning

The Stonewycke Trilogy*
The Heather Hills of Stonewycke
Flight from Stonewycke
Lady of Stonewycke

The Stonewycke Legacy*
Stranger at Stonewycke
Shadows over Stonewycke
Treasure of Stonewycke

The Highland Collection*
Jamie MacLeod: Highland Lass
Robbie Taggart: Highland Sailor

The Journals of Corrie Belle Hollister
My Father's World*
Daughter of Grace*
On the Trail of the Truth†
A Place in the Sun†
Sea to Shining Sea†
Into the Long Dark Night†
Land of the Brave and the Free†

*with Michael Phillips   †by Michael Phillips   ‡with Tracie Peterson

Books by Michael Phillips

Best Friends for Life (with Judy Phillips)
George MacDonald: Scotland's Beloved Storyteller
A God to Call Father†

THE HIGHLAND COLLECTION*
Jamie MacLeod: Highland Lass   *Robbie Taggart: Highland Sailor*

THE JOURNALS OF CORRIE BELLE HOLLISTER
*My Father's World**   *Sea to Shining Sea*
*Daughter of Grace**   *Into the Long Dark Night*
On the Trail of the Truth   *Land of the Brave and the Free*
A Place in the Sun   *A Home for the Heart*

Grayfox (Zack's story)

THE JOURNALS OF CORRIE & CHRISTOPHER
The Braxtons of Miracle Springs *A New Beginning*

MERCY AND EAGLEFLIGHT†
Mercy and Eagleflight   *Goodness and Mercy*
A Dangerous Love

THE RUSSIANS*
The Crown and the Crucible   *Travail and Triumph*
A House Divided

THE SECRET OF THE ROSE†
The Eleventh Hour   *Escape to Freedom*
A Rose Remembered   *Dawn of Liberty*

THE SECRETS OF HEATHERSLEIGH HALL
Wild Grows the Heather in Devon

THE STONEWYCKE TRILOGY*
The Heather Hills of Stonewycke *Lady of Stonewycke*
Flight From Stonewycke

THE STONEWYCKE LEGACY*
Stranger at Stonewycke   *Treasure of Stonewycke*
Shadows Over Stonewycke

*with Judith Pella   †Tyndale House